Praise for Quintin Jardine's novels:

'Jardine's plot is very cleverly constructed, every incident and every character has a justified place in the labyrinth of motives, and the final series of revelations follows logically from a surreptitious but well-placed series of clues' Gerald Kaufman, *Scotsman*

'Remarkably assured . . . a *tour de force*' *New York Times*

'Perfect plotting and convincing characterisation . . . Jardine manages to combine the picturesque with the thrilling and the dream-like with the coldly rational' *The Times*

'Deplorably readable' *Guardian*

'If Ian Rankin is the Robert Carlyle of Scottish crime writers, then Jardine is surely its Sean Connery' *Glasgow Herald*

'It moves at a cracking pace, and with a crisp dialogue that is vastly superior to that of many of his jargon-loving rivals . . . It encompasses a wonderfully neat structural twist, a few taut, well-weighted action sequences and emotionally charged exchanges that steer well clear of melodrama' *Sunday Herald*

'Engrossing, believable characters . . . captures Edinburgh beautifully . . . It all adds up to a very good read' *Edinburgh Evening News*

'Robustly entertaining' *Irish Times*

Wearing Purple

Quintin Jardine

headline

First published in 1998
by HEADLINE BOOK PUBLISHING

First published in paperback in 1999
by HEADLINE BOOK PUBLISHING

10 9 8 7 6 5

ISBN 0 7472 5666 7

Typeset in Plantin by Avon DataSet Ltd,
Bidford-on-Avon, Warwickshire

Printed and bound in Great Britain by
Mackays of Chatham plc, Chatham, Kent

Headline's policy is to use papers that are natural, renewable and
recyclable products and made from wood grown in sustainable
forests. The logging and manufacturing processes are expected to
conform to the environmental regulations of the country of origin.

HEADLINE BOOK PUBLISHING
A division of Hodder Headline
338 Euston Road
London NW1 3BH

www.headline.co.uk
www.hodderheadline.com

This book is for my two 'honorary' sisters, Meg and Fiona.
The honour is mine, ladies.

Prologue

It took us by surprise, when we sat down and talked about it. Sure, we loved each other dearly, sure we had enjoyed a few delicious, exhilarating, dangerous months together. On top of that, we really liked each other. But when I climbed back up from my nocturnal walk along the beach, when she and I sat on the starlit terrace, we both knew that the time had come to face the truth.

She didn't want to grow old with me, nor I with her.

How we did it, I'll never know for sure, although maybe sincerity and honesty helped. There was no blame, there were no recriminations; I won't pretend that there weren't any tears, but they were the friendly sort, rather than bitter. The finest achievement of our relationship, I remember telling myself as I drove across the border, may have been the fact that we were able to end it with smiles on our faces.

So I headed north in the Ozmobile, going back to the girl I should never have left, going back to fall at her feet, to make her mine, to become hers, to live happily ever after . . . But then I always was a naive lad.

1

He loomed in the doorway. The verb really doesn't do justice to the experience, but it's the best I have in my vocabulary. Maybe if I add another couple of 'o's, you might get the picture.

Apart from a patch of carpet, all I could see as I opened the door was him. He filled the entire frame, a great dark shape in what had to be a tailor-made suit, with crinkly, close-cropped hair and designer glasses.

'Mr Blackstone?' he asked,

'That's me. But call me Oz. You'll be Mr Davis.'

He extended an enormous hand, on the end of an arm like a medium-sized tree-trunk. 'Yeah, I'm Everett Davis. I wasn't sure I got the right apartment. The floors are confusing in this building.' His voice rumbled up as if from the foot of a very deep well. It was as dark as he was, but soft too, like treacle.

'Come in,' I said, standing aside as I opened the door wider. I had been transcribing a statement for a client, but it was nothing that couldn't wait. Anyway, he had called to ask if he could come to see me. 'It's the glass door to the left, at the end of the hall.' He had to duck under the lintel, and step in sideways. Inside the flat he looked even bigger. I guessed that he was at least seven feet tall: and as for his weight . . . I felt a cold shiver run down my back as I thought of our new furniture.

Fortunately we had gone for heavy, wooden-framed leather sofas rather than armchairs. Still, I watched nervously as my visitor lowered himself onto the two seater . . . at least that's what it is for most people . . . but its joints were up to the challenge.

'Can I get you a coffee?' I asked, wondering if we had a mug big enough for him to hold comfortably.

'No thanks, man. I don't touch that stuff. Mineral water would be okay though.'

All we had in the fridge was an unopened 1.5 litre bottle of AquaPura. I rattled some ice into a tall glass, filled it to the top and took it through to him, together with what was left. 'Just help yourself as you like.' He smiled and nodded his thanks.

'So, Mr Davis, what can I do for you?'

The black giant looked at me. 'You really don't know who I am, do you?' I imagined that I detected an edge of hurt in his voice. I hoped that the water tasted fresh.

'I've been abroad for a while,' I offered, lamely. 'My wife and I have only just settled down in Glasgow.'

'Don't apologise, man,' he said, easily. 'I kinda like it when someone treats me like an ordinary Joe. Most times, people make me feel like a freak.

'I'm involved in the sports entertainment industry. I have a professional identity, a kinda alter ego. They call me Daze.'

I gulped in air and looked at him. A wrestler, for God's sake, the guy was a bloody wrestler! And then I looked at him again.

It must have been the suit that had thrown me: that and the gold-framed glasses. The last time I had seen Mr Everett Davis he had been wearing a flaming red cat-suit and had been dropping an almost equally enormous white man on his head. It was on Boxing Day, in Anstruther, part of some live grapplefest that Jonathan and Colin, my nephews, had been watching on satellite television. My dad and I would have ignored it ourselves, you understand, but it was on, so we sat down with them.

There had been all shapes and sizes in action that day, fat men and musclemen, bruisers and athletes, heroes and villains, predictable winners and professional losers. My dad and I, being men of the world, knew of course that it was all rehearsed, but that didn't keep us off the edge of our seats from time to time.

As I gazed at the giant on my sofa, I remembered the boys' excitement as his entry music had begun to play, and as the huge figure had sauntered down the ramp towards the ring, a flamboyant red cape over his ring costume. He had been wearing a big gold championship belt around his waist, and he had been accompanied by his 'manager', a scrawny white guy wearing glasses and the loudest jacket I'd ever seen on anyone, other than a professional footballer. What a show he and his opponent, the Mastodon, or some such name, had put on; they had seemed to knock seven different colours of shit out of each other for almost half an hour. Finally the giant had decked the other fellow with a flying drop-kick from the top rope, had picked him off the floor bodily and had despatched him with the aforementioned dropping-on-head move before pinning his shoulders for the three-count.

And then my sister Ellie had come in. 'What have I told you boys about watching that rubbish! And you two,' she had yelled at us, 'encouraging them. You should be ashamed of yourselves.'

Reproved, my dad and I had slunk off to the pub. I hadn't thought of Daze again until the moment he made my sofa look inadequate.

'So how can I help you, Mr Davis?' I asked him lamely. 'You weren't really specific when you phoned. Other than saying that you had a problem.'

'Call me Everett, please,' he replied. 'A guy I know said I should talk to you. His name's Greg McPhillips: he's my lawyer.'

I nodded. I'd known the boy Greg for quite a few years, and done a lot of work for his firm. Now I was back in business, a lot more was rolling in from that direction; but normally I went to see his clients, to take formal statements from them. It was unusual for him to send them to see me, and I wasn't sure that I appreciated it.

'What's the problem? Matrimonial?'

He laughed, but in an odd way that I couldn't fathom. 'Hell no!' Then the smile disappeared: he looked at me with a curious helplessness written on his huge face.

'My problem, Oz, is that someone's out to get me. And I'm scared.'

All I could think of, as I stared back at him, was what Jonathan and Colin would have thought if they had heard him. I could see their childish illusions shattered by those few simple words. For a few seconds I was sorry for him, until common sense took over; that and a feeling I knew from the past, the kind that comes over you when you know that you're in danger of stepping in way over your head.

'Everett,' I said, very sincerely, 'anyone who scares you is going to bloody well terrify me. What do you expect me to do?'

'I'd like you to find out who it is.'

I smiled at the mountain on our sofa . . . apologetically, I hoped. 'Look,' I tried to explain, 'I don't really do that sort of work. I'm a Private Enquiry Agent, not a Private Eye. I work mostly for lawyers, taking statements from people, and stuff like that. I'm a bore, really.'

'That's not what Greg told me,' the wrestler rumbled. 'He said he'd recommended you once to a stockbroker buddy of his and that you'd handled a pretty delicate job for him. Yeah, and he said too that you were into that line of work over in Spain. He said that once you fasten your teeth into something you never let it go 'til it's all chewed up.'

I'll fasten my pearly white teeth into Greg, I thought. But he had probably reckoned that he was doing me a favour; also this colossus was a client of his, after all. I decided to talk Daze out of my life, politely, of course.

'Well,' I bullshat, 'the Spanish operation was more business-focused, I'll grant you, but that really had more to do with my former partner. One of the reasons I came back to Scotland was to get back to basics; to get away from all the excitement and do the things I do best.

'Quite frankly, I can think of a few thousand people who are better equipped than me to handle your problem.'

'Oh yeah? Like who?'

'Like the police for a start.'

Everett Davis sat forward on the sofa, which for the first time creaked quietly in protest. He jabbed our inlaid coffee table with a thick, baton-like finger; I'll swear it bent a little. 'Absolutely not,' he rumbled. 'This is not for the cops.'

'Okay, then there are real detective agencies.'

'All of which are staffed by ex-cops. I need discretion, Oz, and that's why Greg sent me to you. He said you might not be no secret agent, but you're very private.'

Now I didn't know whether or not to feel slighted by my friend, as well as mad at him for putting me on the spot with this humongous geezer. Then I thought about all the day-to-day business he had given me over the years, and about the rest that would come in the future.

I decided to bend a little. 'Fair enough, Everett,' I said. 'Tell me about it . . . after you've promised me that you don't expect me to do or cover up anything illegal.'

The big man smiled. 'You got my word on that, man.' He

poured himself some more mineral water, then leaned back again on the sofa: more gently this time.

'Let me give you some background on our industry, just for openers. Pro wrestling has been around in the US for decades—'

'Here too,' I interrupted. 'When I was a very small kid, I remember this huge guy on television called Big Daddy . . .'

Everett nodded. 'Yeah, his real name was Shirley Crabtree. He *was* wrestling in the UK. When he started to get old, your television stations just lost interest in the whole business. The sport was never such a one-man band in the States though. Back in the fifties and sixties, we had guys like Lou Thesz, Gorgeous George Zaharias, Fred Blassie, Antonino Rocca, Killer Kowalski, Gorilla Monsoon . . .' A look of reverence came into his eyes. For a second I thought the designer specs were going to mist over.

'They were big stars, heroes, all of them. They could sell out Madison Square Garden, and they had a television following too. But they're all legends now, and when they started to fade, so for a while did people's interest. The game kept going though, and gradually new guys appeared, like Dory Funk Junior, Pat Patterson, Roddy Piper, Ric Flair, Bret Hart, Hogan . . .' He paused, as the awe returned. '. . . and of course, André the Giant.'

I nodded. Even I'd heard of André the Giant.

'The way it worked out, these guys carried things through its tough period, right up to the time when television began to expand, and cable took over in the States. Pro wrestling went with it, only it sort of repackaged itself, and called itself "sports entertainment". Some of the promoters were afraid of that, since it was a tacit admission that not everything is spontaneous. But it works.

'Now we build in story-lines, we have feuds between performers, factions even, we hype the whole thing up for the audiences and they love it. We ain't just wrestlers any more; they call us . . . hell, we call ourselves . . . superstars.'

The big man had my full attention now. 'How did you get into the business?' I asked him.

'I wrestled at college; on the mat, for real. I was National Inter-Collegiate Champion two years running. At the start I boxed too. Might have made the Olympic team in Korea, but they found a weakness in my left eye. It meant I'd never have got a pro licence, anywhere, so I quit, and concentrated on the mat instead.' He grinned. 'Pity. I'd have made it as a fighter, and the money's bigger.'

He poured himself some more water, emptying the bottle in the process. 'Not that the dough's bad in rasslin', though. I went pro with what was then the second of the big organisations in the States, Wrestling World Wide. I was Triple W's big new star, the start of their attack on the top dog in the business, Championship Wrestling Incorporated. I signed a three year contract for one and a half million dollars. Man, was I an innocent!'

'Why?' I asked him. 'Could you have got more?'

He shook his head. 'Not then. College wrestlers weren't the only guys they were signing. Some ex-footballers used, and still use, sports entertainment as a way of extending their careers. No, that's not what I meant. I was naive because I had no idea how the industry worked. I didn't wrestle for four months after they signed me. They began by christening me Diamond. Then they had me play the part of a bodyguard to one of the established guys, watching his back when he was in the ring, beating up his opponents while he distracted the referee.

'All that time I was in the gym, building my muscles and learning pro moves, the kind that just don't feature in college wrestling.' He made a huge, lightning fast sweeping move with his right arm. It made me wince. 'The Lariat, like that. Then there was the fisherman's suplex, DDT, bodyslam, piledriver; all that stuff. I was also learning how to control my hits and how to absorb: those are the core skills of sports entertainment.'

'Why's that?'

He looked at me as if he thought I was daft. I suppose I was. 'Oz, I weigh three sixty-five pounds. I hit you properly, you dead. Jerry Gradi, the Behemoth, he weighs three eighty; he hits me and I don't handle him properly, I'm out of it. Sports entertainment is all about knock down, drag out brawls. If we didn't master those core skills, our matches would be over in a couple of minutes, and a lot of people would be crippled; some killed, maybe.' He finished the water and glanced at me hopefully.

'Milk?' I ventured. He grinned. I went off to the kitchen and came back with a pint glass and a full two-litre container.

'Anyhow,' he continued eventually, an empty glass in his hand and a very thin milky moustache on his top lip, 'eventually I got to take off the bodyguard suit and wrestle. That was when my boss told me that Diamond was a heel.'

'A what?'

Everett laughed. 'A heel; a bad guy. Trade terminology. There's two sorts of pro wrestler; the heels are the villains, and the faces are the good guys. It's so the marks . . . they're the fans . . . know who to cheer for, and who to boo.'

'And the good guys always win?'

'Hell no! More often than not they get the shit kicked out of them. When Diamond came into the ring, he . . . I . . . carved my way through all the good guys. For a while, I was undefeated, and after six months they put me in a title match with the top man in the organisation, at one of the big feature events.' He caught yet another puzzled look and explained.

'That's the way the industry works. They build up the feuds between performers, tag-teams and factions, then every so often, half a dozen times each year there's a feature event where they all come to a head. In the States, they're mostly pay-per-view, on cable, at thirty-five bucks per head . . . that's where the real dough is made these days.' He switched back to his story.

'So there I am, Diamond, this big menacing guy who's cleaned up everything in his path, ready to take the title. Man, I really took it personally when they told me I'd have to job.'

'Job?' The guy's terminology was as clear to me as Gaelic.

'Lose, man,' he said patiently. 'There are the rasslers like I am today, who hardly ever get beat, other than by disqualification, then there are the rest, the majority, the journeymen, who do. In the business, they're called jobbers. In practice a lot of them have all the skills, but they don't have the personality, the looks or the articulacy you need to really hype up a feud.

'As a newcomer, in my first really big match, I had to job. It was in my contract. I beat up the champ, he beat me up, I beat him up again, until finally he got me in his figure-four leg lock, and I tapped out.' He beat me to the question. 'Submitted man; I quit.'

Everett whistled, a soft sound for him. 'I'll never forget that moment, when they rang the bell. I'd never lost in my life before, anywhere, yet here I was tapping out to a forty-one-year-old guy I could have thrown from mid-ring into the third row. That's when I learned what makes pro wrestling great.'

'And what's that?' I asked him, fascinated.

'Tradition, Oz. Our game is a form of performance art, a form of dance, if you like. That old champ and I rehearsed our match until we were move-perfect, and together we put on a great show. I lay there on that mat, my leg not so much as aching from the finishing hold, and I realised that although they didn't know it, the marks were cheering for us both. It might not look it, but pro wrestlers are team players. We rely on each other for our physical safety and for our creative performance, and our overriding tradition is that no one is as big as the organisation of which he's a part . . . or should attempt to be, ever. When it's your turn to lose, you do it with class, and skill.

'Six months later, the old champ and I had a rematch, and I won the belt. A year later, he took it back, when he hit me with a chair while his manager argued with the referee. Finally, in the last year of my contract, I beat him twice in succession.'

The one-time Diamond chuckled. 'I was still a heel, though. Until contract renewal came up, that is. By the time it did, Championship Wrestling Incorporated had made me an offer. They were showing me big dough. No way I'd ever have gone there, for reasons of my own, but it did waken me up to how much I was worth.

'So, five years ago, I said to Michael Fanucci, the President of Triple W, "Look, you guys gave me my break, so I owe you some loyalty. But that cuts both ways. I'll stay with you for one and a half million a year, plus I want reasonable creative control." That meant having a say in the style and outcome of my matches. "And I want to be a face, with copyright ownership of my new persona and a share of marketing income."

'I wasn't being greedy, just realistic. Michael said yes to all three, in as many seconds. I took a six-month sabbatical, to rest up and to learn some new moves. When I came back, I was Daze, and man, I was great. For the next three years, I was the main man . . . not always the champ, because we had to keep the story-lines attractive . . . but always Numero Uno with the fans.'

All of a sudden a question begged to be asked. I plucked up my courage and spoke it out. 'In that case, Daze, what exactly are you doing in Glasgow?'

Darth Vader never laughed in *Star Wars*, but if he had, he would have sounded just like Everett. 'Advancing the frontiers, man,' he rumbled.

'When my second contract was up, two years ago, I could have signed another for double the money, but both Michael and I could smell staleness a year down the road. Instead, I took a chance. I had done a few European tours in my six years in the business, and I reckoned I had spotted an opportunity.

'I'm not as dumb as I look. Remember, Oz, I went to college. I did a law degree, then an MBA. I decided that I would set up my own Sports Entertainment company. Michael saw to it that Triple W took ten per cent of the equity in redeemable shares, and he loaned me some working capital. With his backing, I did deals with most of the European satellite broadcasters to supply them with shows, shot live in front of European audiences.'

He smiled at me. 'Why am I in Glasgow? I based the operation here, on the motorway system and not far from the airport, because it was the best location package I was offered anywhere in Europe.

'I had competition for the deal; there was talk of an orchestra from Italy putting in a rival bid for the package. I won though; I guess your Government took a look at the sort of revenue my business can generate as opposed to a symphony orchestra, which runs break-even at best for most of the time.

'All that was two years ago. We ain't looked back since. I've repaid the loan capital already.'

'Great. Now, to come back to the point. What's your problem?'

He frowned, carving great lines in his brown forehead. 'Like I said, man, someone's out to get me. Every cent I've ever made is tied up in this company, and someone is trying to bring it down. Before I explain, I'd like you to come visit me; get a feel for our organisation.' He paused, and leaned forward, looming at me again.

'Well, are you going to help me?'

As he finished I heard a key turn in the Yale lock. No way did I want him to have to go over the whole thing again. 'Okay,' I agreed. 'I'll come to see you at ten tomorrow.'

To my surprise, he looked almost childishly grateful as he handed me his business card. I glanced at the multi coloured logo 'GWA', and at the gold lettering, 'Everett Davis, President'.

'That's good, man,' he said.

I don't know why, but I asked him if he'd like to stay for dinner.

'Thanks Oz,' he boomed, as my astonished wife appeared in the doorway. 'No offence, but I don't reckon you'd have enough food.'

2

Jan and I had always liked high places.

When we were kids, one of our treats was to take the pleasure boat from the harbour to the May Island, climb up to the top of a grassy rise and sit there, on the edge of the cliffs, gazing back across the Forth to Fife. The long rugged island was in the background of our wedding photos, when they were taken in the front garden of my dad's big house overlooking the sea.

I'll never forget the look on either of their faces when the two of us walked into the kitchen, together, and told them . . . my Honorary Auntie Mary and Mac the Dentist, on the point of marriage themselves . . . that they were going to be step-mother and step-father respectively. They didn't know whether to laugh, cry, or hide under the table. After my mum's death, and later, after Jan's dad's departure with his new lady, they had stayed put in Anstruther, getting on with their lives, and gradually getting closer together. Janet and I had done the opposite; we had left the East Neuk and had grown gradually away from each other, until finally, each of us with new partners, we had been brought in different ways to recognise that we really were inseparable.

Yes, we had loved . . . the other ones . . . But we were us; we were something else. When we thought about it, as we explained to our respective parents, we had never really been apart, and we couldn't bear to be, either.

My dad has always had an eye for a bargain. So, once he had got over the shock, there was nothing for it but we had to have a double wedding. 'Look what we'll save on the receptions, son.' I wasn't so sure, but Jan surprised me by being all for it; so, decision made, they rearranged their nuptials to coincide with ours. We put the whole thing together very quickly. Three weeks later, the local minister married us in the Craw's Nest Hotel. It was only a short distance from the house. But Auntie Mary, Jan, and my sister Ellie, their joint Matron of Honour, put their feet down when my dad suggested that we all just walk there in procession, to save on the cars.

We were the talk of the village, of course. There was an outbreak of gossip, the rumour mill deciding that Jan was up the duff, although a splinter group put forward the suggestion in the butcher's one Saturday morning that she wasn't but that Mary was. 'Ken these drugs they have noo, Mrs McGarrity!' Eventually, my dad put a stop to it by telling a succession of patients, one after the other for a full week – once they were in his chair and he had their full attention, as is his way – that there would be no new Blackstone prams in town for a while. And outside his house, never.

Our joint wedding made the front page of the local paper, and we'd have made the nationals too, if Mac the Dentist hadn't threatened the editor – another patient – with mortal agonies under the drill if he even dreamed of selling the story on.

It all happened so fast that only after the wedding did Jan and I get round to looking for a place to live. However, it didn't take us long before we found it . . . or did it find us?

Given our country upbringing, and our love of dramatic views, why the hell, one might ask, should Jan and I have chosen Glasgow, a hemmed-in hybrid city whose charm is mostly at ground level, in which to set up our first home as Mr and Mrs Blackstone? The answer began with the fact that each of us had excess emotional baggage, one way or another, through in Edinburgh. Much as we loved our Old Town loft, which had been in the past my home and Jan's refuge, we decided that we must have a new place for our new beginning. We were both self-employed, with clients spread across the central belt, so we could live as conveniently on the River Clyde as on the Forth.

And then, to seal the deal, there was the apartment itself.

Even on a horrible, grey November Saturday it called out to us as we drove along Sauchiehall Street with Jonathan and Colin in the back seat, all of us beginning the journey back to Fife after a fruitless morning of house-hunting and a trip to the Glasgow Transport Museum. 'Look up there,' said Jan, pointing to her left from the passenger seat. Normally I'm a firm believer in watching the road while I'm driving, but this was the wife who was talking to me, so for once, I risked a quick glance.

She was gazing at a tall, square, stone tower rising from a chunky, rectangular building up on the crest of the hill. It was one of the many treasures which stand out on the bumpy Glasgow skyline. I pulled the Ozmobile across the inside lane and stopped on the yellow line. We looked up at the imposing structure.

'Very nice, my love,' I said, 'but it looks like some sort of church to me.'

'In that case, why's there a For Sale sign towards the top of the tower?'

I leaned forward and took a closer look. As usual, she was right: Jan always did have long vision like a hawk. 'It looks interesting,' she said. 'Come on, Oz, get us up there. Let's take a closer look.'

It wasn't easy getting there, thanks to the one-way system,

but eventually we made it. I had to admit, the place looked really impressive close up. And yes, it had been converted into flats: converted from what, we could not tell, but in terms of size it looked more like a cathedral than a mere church.

The 'For Sale' sign was on the third of what appeared to be four levels in the tower itself. A hell of a long way up in other words, and there was no sign of a lift, but there was no holding Jan by this time . . . or me for that matter. We bribed the boys to stay in the Ozmobile with the promise of chips and stepped into the porch, which was at the other end of the building from the tower, and where we found that a row of entry buzzers and a video camera were set into the wall. Beside one we saw a note reading, 'For Sale, viewing 2–5, weekends.' I checked my watch; it was four o'clock.

Jan pressed the button, and after a few seconds a woman's voice crackled from the speaker. 'Come to see the flat? Just step inside, and I'll come for you. It's a bit awkward first time.'

She was right: I've been on shorter training runs than the walk from the porch to the front door. But as soon as we stepped inside we had forgotten all about it; we were sold. For the third time in my life, I fell in love at first sight . . . this time with a house.

The place was what the Edinburgh estate agents would call a 'double upper flat', meaning that it wasn't a flat at all, but on two levels. The small entrance hall was lit by glass panels in the main door, and by another fully glazed one at the far end. *A bit pokey*, we thought, until we stepped into the living room . . . and into the City of Glasgow itself.

The first thing to strike us were the tall, wide, insulated windows on three sides of the great apartment, reaching from the polished wooden floor almost up to the high ceilings. Even in the dying light of the winter afternoon, the view they gave was sensational. From where we stood, as we looked straight ahead, cars flooded incessantly over the Kingston Bridge, the Clyde crossing. To our right we saw the great baroque tower of the University, and set beneath it the Kelvingrove Art Gallery and Museum and the Kelvin Hall. To our left, Sauchiehall Street and Bath Street ran away up towards George Square and the City Chambers.

The owner didn't need to show us the recently fitted kitchen, or the three bedrooms at the top of the spiral staircase, the largest with its en-suite shower-room. She didn't need to tell us about the cable television and the private off-street parking places. We let her though, for she was dead keen. She was trying to sell the place even harder than we were trying to buy it.

'I'm sorry about the climb up here from the street,' she said, as she finished her tour. 'That's what puts people off, I think.' She looked at Jan hopefully, woman to woman.

I've never known any one who played their cards closer to her chest than my wife. On that afternoon she had them stuck right up her jumper. She was absolutely poker-faced as the lady handed her the specifications. 'Yes,' she answered. 'I can understand that.'

I did my best to follow suit. 'Thank you,' I muttered solemnly as we left. 'We'll think about it.'

We thought about it all the way to the car. Inside the Ozmobile, Jan looked at me, still unsmiling. 'Just one thing, darlin',' she said. Her rich voice, which was made to impart extra meaning to every word, was at its throatiest.

'What's that?'

'Absolutely no bloody iguanas. Okay?'

The deal was done inside a week. It's amazing how fast the professionals involved in house-buying can move if you really press them . . . or in the case of surveyors, if you promise them enough alcohol. The place was expensive, but nothing we couldn't afford. I still had a cash pile left from my share of an earlier adventure, and we sold the loft to my pal Ali, the demon grocer, without even having to advertise it.

I'll never forget the day we moved in. We stood there arm in arm, before the curtains went up, or the first of the furniture was delivered, looking all around us at the bright sunny morning outside, feeling like guardians of the city.

Jan was standing on the very same spot as I returned from showing the black giant down to the entrance door. Only she wasn't looking out; she was staring at me, still stunned by the sheer awesome presence of our visitor. 'Who the hell was that?' she gasped. 'Or what?'

'I introduced you, didn't I? That was Everett. He's my new client; I'm going to do some work for him.'

'That's a lawyer?' she asked.

I smiled as I slipped my arms around her waist, drawing her to me. 'As a matter of fact, he is. But that's not what he does now. I tell you, honey, our place in the affections of our nephews is secure.

'See the big fella down there?' I nodded at the window. 'He's their favourite wrestler!'

3

From the outside, the headquarters of the Global Wrestling Alliance ... 'The trading identity of Everett Davis Sports Entertainment plc,' as it said on the big man's business card ... looked like any other shed on the Craigton Industrial Estate.

Even the cars in the senior executives' parking area were similar to those in the unit which faced it across the street, a mix of BMWs, big Fords and Toyotas. The two exceptions were a gleaming new Range Rover, which I guessed was the only car there that could accommodate Everett Davis' bulk, and a plain white Winnebago camper van.

Inside, though, it was a different world. As soon as I stepped through the glass front door, I was face to face with my client, only this time he was in full wrestling gear. Life-size – maybe even larger than life – cardboard cut-outs of Daze and his fellow superstars lined the reception area, towering over the chairs and coffee tables set out for visitors.

Happily, the receptionist was real, and normal sized too, a pleasant dark-haired girl with a Glasgow accent. 'Can I help you, sir?' she asked.

'Yes please,' I answered, still feeling oddly intimidated by the two-dimensional bruisers. 'Oz Blackstone, here to see Mr Davis.'

'I'll let him know you're here.' She gave me a friendly

grin. 'Great name for a wrestler, that. You're maybe a bit on the lightly built side though.'

'I'll have you know I'm the middleweight champion of Pittenweem,' I retorted, as she left her office, through a door which it occurred to me was inordinately high, just like all the others I could see.

Less than a minute later, my client appeared in one of them. He had three or four inches clearance above his head so I guessed that seven foot six was the normal lintel height in his head office, and that the whole place had been designed around him. Unlike the day before he was informally dressed, in jeans and a tee-shirt . . . but not a Marks and Spencer job; this one had his own face emblazoned on it, above a slogan which read 'Ultimate Force'. Wearing that, the gentle guy who had sat in my home cum office the day before looked rather different. For openers, he seemed even bigger: his muscles seemed to be fighting for position inside the shirt. The designer specs had gone too. Instead his eyes shone in an odd way; tinted contacts, I supposed. Oh yes, and then there was his hair: for some reason flecks of gold dust seemed to have been combed through it.

The voice was the same, though, deep, warm and molasses friendly, as he thrust out a great hand. 'Hi, Oz. Welcome to the wacky world of the GWA. Come on through.' He caught me looking at his hair and laughed. 'Don't worry, I don't dress like this all the time, I just been shooting an insert.'

Without further explanation, he opened the door, standing aside to leave me room to step into a wide corridor. I should have known better by this time, but still I almost jumped out of my skin. The guy who stood behind him might not have been as awesome as Daze, yet he had his own aura, and it was plain terrifying. He looked to be around six feet eight . . . tall, wide and deep. His dyed blond hair was cropped short, just like his nose, which seemed to be flattened into his head, he had wee eyes which reminded me of something I once saw eating turnips in a field near Crail, and his pink ears looked as if they had been made out of plasticine by a drunk. He was in the same wrestling gear as his cardboard image in reception, black tights, gold boots and a bright orange vest, with white lightning flashes all over it, all set off by a piece of white leather headgear which looked more like a scrum cap than anything else. The only thing which didn't match the cut-out was the massive gilded leather belt which somehow made it all the way around his waist.

Everett laughed at my confusion . . . okay, at my terror. 'This is Jerry Gradi,' he said. 'AKA The Behemoth, the GWA World Heavyweight Champion.'

'Pleased ta meetcha,' rasped the cube on tree trunks, then turned to my client. 'What time am I due at that place, Ev?'

'Twelve midday. Are Max and Diane ready?'

'Yeah, they went out the side door, with Barbara.'

'Okay, you better hit the road. Time'll be tight travelling in that camper. Give them a good show, now.'

'Don' we always?' The monster grinned at me, grotesquely, then crashed through the double doors.

'They're doing a public appearance today,' Everett explained. 'It's at Murrayfield Rugby Stadium in Edinburgh. It's a promo for our pay-per-view event next month, in the exhibition centre in the Highland Show ground. It's the biggest indoor venue we could find there.'

I nodded. 'It would be.' I looked up at him, almost straining my neck in the process. 'I thought you were the champion?'

He laughed. 'Hell no! I'm only the boss. Daze had the belt until the last ppv event, but he got distracted by the Princess at ringside, so that The Behemoth blind-sided him and rolled him up for the pin.'

'The Princess?'

'Yeah, she's The Behemoth's ringside manager. That's Diane; she's going to Edinburgh with him. Max Schwartz is Axel Rodd – with two Ds – Jerry's tag team partner.'

'Who's Barbara?'

'Our publicity co-ordinator. An ace. I hired her from the opposition in the States.'

I shook my head. 'So Daze isn't so smart after all. He can be distracted by a woman.'

'He can by Diane,' he agreed, grinning. 'So can Everett. She's my wife.' He set off down the corridor. 'Come on. I'll show you around.' I fell into step, at his heels – well, I took three for every two of his – until he stopped at a grey door, on his right.

He pointed to the other side of the corridor. 'All that over there is office space,' he said. 'Our venue booking, ticket sales, and merchandising departments are all over there. Merchandising is very big business for us. Our Superstar replica figures are collectables, then there are the imitation championship belts, tee-shirts –' he tapped his chest '– like this one, and other things, such as big foam hands for waving on camera, inflatables, and scaled down copies of the Angel's wings.'

'Eh?'

'You'll meet him later.' The atmosphere of the place had got me. I wasn't even surprised when he said that.

'We're also into video games,' he went on. 'We have a copyright agreement with one of the big three players, but they do the marketing of those products.'

He turned and threw open the grey door. 'This is props. We store everything here; our ring, back-drops for television, wrestlers' costumes and other equipment, like the special chairs and steel bins we use to hit each other with in our matches.' He must have heard me gulp, for he added without even looking round, 'You know how they have glass in the movies that's made out of sugar? Same idea.'

He closed the door again and led me on down the corridor, until we stopped outside a second door. Alongside, were two lights; red, and green, which was showing. 'Come on in,' he said. 'No one's shooting right now.'

We stepped into what turned out to be a television studio. 'We shoot all our inserts in-house,' said Everett. 'If you watch our shows on cable TV, you'll see how we use them to build up the feuds between performers. Camera skills are worth a lot in this business; there are more than a few capable wrestlers who'll never be more than jobbers because they can't ham it up on screen for the fans.'

He reached down and pressed a button on a VCR player. 'Let's see what we got here.' The monitor alongside flickered into life, and there was Jerry Gradi, The Behemoth, in full battle gear, snarling and grimacing at the camera. 'Daze!' he roared, his voice at maximum decibels, the gravel grinding away. 'You want your belt back, punk? Well come on, try to get it. Bring all you got, but it won't be enough. Ain't dat right, Princess?'

And then she stepped into shot; the sort of woman who could start a fight in a seminary, just by being there. She had a tiara set in her lustrous auburn hair, and wore, technically, a tight-fitting sequinned evening number, with gleaming, coffee-coloured skin showing through a laced-up side panel which precluded any slight possibility that she might have been wearing underwear. On the day that bosoms were handed out, she had been at the head of the queue.

'Oh yes, monster,' she said, in a voice so sexy that it could have made a diabetic eat a cream egg omelette. 'That's right. We know what Daze's weakness is, don't we. You're looking at her.' As the camera zoomed in on her she flicked her red tongue along her top lip.

The screen went dead, but Everett kept on staring at it. 'She ain't kidding, boy,' he whispered. For a moment I thought that he had forgotten I was there. I coughed, just to remind him. 'Yeah,' he said, still softly. 'Let's go. The action's next door.'

We went back into the corridor and walked on until we reached the third door on the right. 'All men are different,' my dad told me once, 'yet in some respects they're all the same.' That piece of Mac the Dentist wisdom came back to me as my huge guide opened the door. When you've smelled one ripe gymnasium, in principle you've smelled them all. It's only the intensity that's different.

I looked around; it must have covered at least a quarter of the total floor area of the unit. An impressive array of exercise machinery lined the far wall, while nearer to where we stood, there was a row of heavyweight static cycles, and two treadmills. Off to our right two punch-bags and two speed-balls hung from steel supports. Half of the equipment was in use; I glanced around and counted a dozen people. Four were smaller than the rest; it took me a couple of seconds to realise that they were women. In the centre of it all there was a practice ring; its canvas floor was about five feet high, and the area all around was covered in matting. Inside the three ropes, two men were circling each other, threateningly.

'This is the work-room,' said Everett. 'This is where the boys train, and the girls too. The GWA is a team operation, and that's how we train, like a football squad . . . only harder.' He nodded towards the ring. 'Those two guys are in our headline match in the Newcastle Arena on Saturday. The big guy is Darius Hencke: ring name the Black Angel of Death. He's German. The small fellow is Liam Matthews, from Dublin: real name and ring name. His ring persona is a cocky little bastard. He's pretty much like that in real life too.

'They're choreographing their fight. It's for The Transcontinental Title, our secondary championship belt. Come on over and meet them.'

As we walked towards the ring, Matthews hurled a flying karate kick at the Angel of Death, who caught him in midair, lifted him above his head, and threw him out of the ring over the top rope, sending him crashing down on to his back from a height of at least ten feet. The smack as he hit the rubber mat echoed around the gym, but no one took the slightest bit of notice: except me. I winced, expecting the paramedics to appear automatically, but the Irishman simply picked himself up. 'I can take higher than that, Darius,' he called up to the Angel. 'As high as you can fuckin' throw me, I can take.'

'How about as high as *I* can throw you?' Everett's voice was hard all of a sudden. I had never heard Daze speak before.

Matthews grinned. 'You got to catch me first.'

'That time will come, my man.'

Then he was the bloke in the suit again, the fellow who had visited me up in our tower. 'Liam, Darius,' he said, nodding down at me. 'This is Oz Blackstone. I'm thinking about giving him a try-out as our new ring announcer.' As the two wrestlers glanced at me, I hoped that I had managed to keep my astonishment from showing.

Darius Hencke stepped clean over the top rope, and jumped down on to the gymnasium floor. 'Pleased to meet you,' he said, with a thick accent. He must have been at least six feet ten, a grim, glowering figure. Dark, I thought, for a German; but then he smiled, and all at once he didn't look like Death at all. Liam Matthews said nothing, he simply threw me the briefest of grins. He wasn't much taller than me, just over six feet, but in terms of muscular development he looked like a scaled-down version of Everett. He kept

26

bouncing up and down on the balls of his feet; clearly, this was the sort of guy who was incapable of standing still. He seemed to radiate energy in waves.

'Darius and Liam are two of our top attractions, Oz,' Everett went on. 'We're a European organisation so it's important that our squad is largely European too. Jerry, Diane, Barbara, Max and I are all Americans, and we have five others, including two of the women specialists, but other than that it's an EU operation. It has to be anyway, or we'd have work permit problems.'

He turned to the wrestlers. 'How you guys doing?'

'We getting there,' said Darius. 'You just saw the start of the climax. While Liam is on the ground, I climb on top of the ring-post and dive at him, but Dee Dee pulls over a crowd barrier and I land on that.'

Everett frowned. 'You sure you can do that? Even with one of the special aluminum barriers?'

The Angel nodded. 'Sure. The centre section will geev a little under my weight to cushion my fall, but it will still protect Liam.'

'Who's Dee Dee?' I asked lamely.

'Dee Dee Rocca,' Everett answered, 'Liam's ringside manager. Used to be mine too. Their job is to run interference with referees and opponents.'

He looked back at Darius. 'And that's end of match?'

'Yes, the referee disqualifies Liam, so he keeps the belt. The transmission fades with me on the barrier, him underneath and the medics rushing in.'

The big man grinned. 'Okay, you sold me. But rehearse it as often as you can. How many of those aluminum barriers do we have in stock?'

'Half a dozen,' said Liam, 'I checked.'

'Use at least three in rehearsal,' Everett ordered. 'But Liam, you don't go underneath till we see how the first one reacts to the hit from Darius. Understood?'

The Irishman grinned, dismissively. 'Sure, boss.'

The black giant nodded, and beckoned me to follow. 'Those two guys are just about the best in the business,' he said quietly, as we moved towards the door. 'They got all the wrestling skills, and they're unbelievable athletes too. Darius is as good a professional as you'll meet in any sport. But Liam's brashness, that I don't like. This is a dangerous business, and a casual approach can cause accidents.' He smiled, purposefully. 'Some day soon,' he muttered, in his Daze voice again, 'the kid's going to have a match with me. It'll do him good.' Somehow, I doubted that.

Everett led me out of the gym, down the corridor, and into his office. The room was carpeted, and the walls were wood-panelled, yet the feel was functional, rather than opulent. Clearly some of the furniture had been made with his size in mind, but the rest looked pretty ordinary. There were no ornaments in the room, and just a single photograph on the wall to the left. It showed a smiling, middle-aged black woman.

I pointed at it. 'My mamma,' Everett responded. 'She's been dead for a few years.'

The view from his window, facing the glass-topped table which served as his desk, was the blank grey wall of the unit opposite. Unexpectedly, part of me was inordinately pleased that there was one area in which I was one up on Daze. Jan and I had bought a big partners' desk which we shared for our respective businesses. We had positioned it against the wall of our living area, between two windows, so that each of us, if we chose, would have a view of Glasgow to distract us.

His sharp eyes caught my glance, and read my thoughts. 'Pretty uninspiring, eh Oz,' he grinned, as he settled into his swivel chair, and pointed me towards one on the other side of the table. 'The nerve centre of the mighty Global Wrestling

Alliance, overlooking a factory wall in Glasgow, Scotland. My competition thought it was pretty funny too, until they saw my first year's profit figures. Then I'm sure they took notice. This'll do us for now, till we've achieved the first stage of the business plan.'

'What's that?' I asked, knowing that was what was expected.

'Buy in the redeemable equity, so that we control the business from within. I want us to be able to do that in another year.'

'You keep saying "we". Who are the equity-holders in the company?'

'Diane and me, plus Jerry; that's all.'

I'll never be any good in business, for one reason above all others. I show my cards in my face: I can't help it. I've always been one of nature's astonished gulpers. This one was a beauty, though.

I know I'd only met Jerry Gradi briefly, in a corridor, and I know my dad's always lectured me about snap judgements. 'Look at their teeth, son,' said Mac the Dentist, 'before you come to conclusions about people. The state of the gnashers tells you a lot about a bloke.' But even without a quick dental inspection, The Behemoth did not strike me as a corporate player. Being an honest lad, and since I knew that it was written all over my coupon, I had to say so.

'Jerry's my best friend in the business, Oz,' Everett rumbled . . . fortunately with a smile; I still wasn't one hundred per cent sure of my ground with the big guy. 'He has twenty per cent. That ain't just for old times sake though. The Behemoth and Daze were the biggest drawing cards in the US before we came over here to start the GWA. I wanted to make sure he was tied in for stage three, and there's no better way than to let him in on the action.'

'So what's stage three, then?' I asked him.

'That's when the GWA goes truly Global. We go back to the States and take out our main rival, Championship Wrestling Incorporated, but not at the box office; in the boardroom.'

'Won't you have competition there? What about Triple W, the people you used to work for? Won't they be a bit pissed off if you pop up as their new rival?'

The gold flecks glinted in the neon light as Daze shook his head. 'It won't come as a surprise. Michael has been locked in a ratings war with Anthony Reilly, the Prez of CWI, for years, operating on rival cable networks. Their programming is timed in direct opposition to each other. Though not their pay-per-view events; the networks wouldn't allow that.

'When Jerry and I left, Reilly thought that he'd won the war. He hasn't, because Michael has other resources, but there's no doubt that CWI is top dog again. Triple W can live with that, though, because they know my long-term plan. Mike and I dreamed it up together.

'When I set up over here, and did my deals with the European broadcasters, I took some business from Triple W and CWI, but not enough to get their attention. CWI were probably grateful, for they'd been losing money running live events in the UK and Germany.' He grinned. 'They won't be grateful when I take GWA to the States and cut a deal to run shows on their network.'

'That's the plan is it?'

'Yup. It'll work too. Triple W will make sure that my name and Jerry's stay box office over there. The line on its programming is that we're on sabbatical. When I go in to cut the feet from under CWI, its network will snap me up, and they'll be out. Once I'm in the driving seat, I'll make Reilly an offer for what's left of his company and merge the two.'

'What if he won't sell?'

'If I get that far, he won't have much choice.'

I surprised myself by asking another sensible business question. 'Why hasn't Triple W tried to buy him out?'

Everett smiled. 'Organisations like ours are made and broken by television. Suppose Triple W did buy out CWI, what would it get for its money, apart from some wrestlers' contracts? Nothing. It couldn't operate on two networks, that's for sure. All it would do is help a smaller organisation make the step up to national television, and create a new and maybe an even nastier rival for itself.' He shook his great head again, and I began to realise that there was a pretty big brain in there too.

'No. Through his deal with me, Michael will get rid of Reilly without spending one cent.'

'Hold on a minute,' I said. 'You're the biggest draw in the game. Won't you be an even bigger threat to Triple W?'

'In theory yes; in practice, no, because as part of my network TV deal, I'll specify that our programming will no longer be in direct competition to Triple W. They've always gone live on Mondays. We'll switch to a Thursday slot. On top of that, Jerry will go back to Triple W for two years.'

'Won't you miss him?'

'Personally, yes, but America's seen our act before. On his own, Jerry will be on top dollar at Triple W, plus he'll still have his percentage of GWA. Professionally I can handle his departure. Darius and Liam have had no US exposure. When the marks in the States see the Black Angel and the Irish Devil they'll go crazy.'

'What about Diane? Will she stay with GWA?'

Everett nodded, so emphatically that he created a small breeze. 'Oh yes. We've discussed that.' He smiled, vaguely. 'We gotta start a family sometime soon, if we're gonna.' He glanced across at me. 'How about you, Oz? You got kids?'

'Bloody hell, no. Jan and I only just got married.'

'What the hell does that matter these days? You been living together for long?'

'No. We've known each other since we were kids, but we never did live together. The fact is, until fairly shortly before we decided to get hitched, I was living with someone else, and so was Jan. But our paths crossed again, and we realised that what we wanted most of all was each other. I don't feel very proud of leaving Prim—'

'Who?'

'Prim. It's short for Primavera.'

'She Spanish?'

'Christ no, she's from Perthshire. Her mother liked the sound of the word, that's all. As I said, I don't feel proud of leaving her, but the fact is, she'd fallen in love with someone else too.'

'She with him now?'

I smiled, in spite of myself, at the impossibility of that. 'No. He's dead.'

'Yet you still left her?'

'Yes. She realised how I felt about Jan; and how she really felt about me, I suppose.' Suddenly I felt awkward. 'It's all worked out for the best. I'm married and Prim's off in search of her next adventure. She's a magnet for them, believe me.'

I tried to fix a business-like look on my face. 'So, Everett; you've shown me GWA and you've told me all about it. Now, what's your problem?'

The big man had been looking idly out of the window. Now he spun round and fixed me with a sudden stare. 'Like I said yesterday, someone's out to screw me.' He paused, as a bizarre picture flashed momentarily in my mind.

'Our business is very profitable, but it also involves high risk. We guarantee to provide quality programming to our satellite customers. Two shows a week, Saturdays and Mondays, shot and screened as live, plus two one-hour edited segments for later screening. Everything is staged before live audiences in stadia around Europe. Also, like I told you, we do regular shows which are sold to satellite and cable subscribers on a pay-per-view basis.

'When I say "as live" that means that we shoot the events in one piece, then transmit them the same way. Everything goes down in a single take. There's little or no margin for error built in there, especially on *BattleGround*, the Saturday show. That goes out on network just over an hour after we finish shooting it. It runs for two hours; the *Monday Night Rumble* – that's what we call it – lasts for one. We tape matches for that on the Sunday, the day after *BattleGround*, in the same venue.

'Around four weeks ago, we were two thirds of the way through the taping of *BattleGround* in Dortmund, Germany, when the technicians discovered that they had been running for half an hour with empty video cassettes.'

'Jesus,' I whistled. 'So what did you do?'

'We stopped the taping, kept the audience there, and put the whole thing out live. We got away with it, by the skin of our teeth. I raised hell with our production contractors. They were full of apologies; they assumed that they'd been given duds by the tape supplier.

'I accepted their guarantee that there would be no repeats, and got on with business. Then, a week ago, in Nottingham, this happened.' There was a television set with an integrated video player in a corner of his office. He reached across, switched it on and pressed the play button.

A wrestling match sprang into life on the screen. 'This is a tag-team fight – that's two wrestlers on each side, one in the ring at any time – involving our hard-core guys, the Rattlers, and Chris and Dave, the Manson Brothers, who are really cousins. Watch it.'

I did as I was told. The Rattlers, big guys in jeans and

workshirts, seemed to be taking a real pasting from the non-brothers. As I watched, the Rattler in the ring was slammed across the ring into the padded corner turnbuckles, caught by the combatant Manson as he rebounded off and slammed to the canvas with a crash which seemed to shake the ring.

The referee began the count, until he was distracted by a small man in a grotesque jacket, who jumped up on to the ring apron. I had seen him before, in that Boxing Day match with Daze. The ref stopped counting and went across to the 'manager' with a show of remonstration. The winning Manson, who had 'Dave' emblazoned across his trunks, stood up from his flattened prey, and as he did, the other Rattler stepped through the ropes, a metal folding chair in his hands.

The wrestler swung his weapon at full force, slamming the seat into the back of the Manson Brother's head. There was no commentary on the tape, but there was sound. And what a sound. The bang rang out from the set, bringing a gasp from the crowd.

I was a novice at this game, but even I could tell that something was wrong. There was nothing theatrical about the way Dave Manson went down. He dropped to his knees first, then pitched forward, slowly, on to his face. As I watched, the referee turned and waved to the ringside timekeeper, who rang the bell.

Everett reached over once more and stopped the tape. 'We have special chairs for that sort of action, made of very thin metal sheeting, but looking just like the normal folding seats we use at ringside. That wasn't one of them. That was the real McCoy: Dave wound up in hospital.

'Someone switched the goddamn chair, Oz. In the middle of the fight, Sven, the Rattler, didn't notice the difference in weight.'

'Did you lose the recording?' I asked.

'No, we got away with it. We got the paramedics down there with a gurney, and took Dave outta there. That happens, every so often, as part of the choreography, so the crowd swallowed it. We didn't have to stop the taping.'

He shook his head and scowled. 'No, we didn't lose the show, but I lost one half of my biggest drawing tag team. Dave has a fractured skull, so he'll be out for months. On top of that, his shrewd little wife is looking for compensation. We have a form of insurance against accidental injury, but in these circumstances, it may not pay out.'

'But surely, since it was an accident—'

Daze, not Everett, looked at me. 'That was no accident, man. I questioned the roadies who set up the ring and put all the props in position. And believe me,' he repeated grimly, 'I sure did question them. Those guys were sweating bullets, but they swore on their mothers' lives that a trick chair was left there.

'For sure, Oz, someone switched them over. I guess it was the same person who switched the real tape cassettes in for duds in Germany.'

'But couldn't they both have been accidents?' I protested. 'Couldn't the first thing have been a supplier's mistake? Couldn't someone have picked up the spoof chair before the show and sat on it, then put another one back by mistake? Couldn't the whole thing just be coincidence?'

'If a kid sat on one of those chairs it would bend. A full grown adult would go right through it. That was not an accident, I tell you; any more than the thing with the tapes was. Someone is out to wreck my organisation, and me.

'I believe in the existence of extra-terrestrial beings, I believe in life after death, I believe in God and I believe in myself. But I do not believe in this sort of coincidence, no way sir; not when there's money involved.

'Look man, my contracts with the satellite companies have huge penalty clauses if I fail to deliver fresh product every week as promised. It happens once, it costs me one million dollars. Two million for a second breach. Three million for a third. Any further failures it's another three million, plus my customers give me one month's notice of termination, although I still have to supply during that period, subject to the same penalty rate.

'It would never come to that, though. I could take a million-dollar hit. I could take a two-million-dollar hit on top of that, just. But one more, and I'd be done. The GWA would be bust. Someone's trying to bring that about, and I'm damn sure I know who it is.'

'Who?'

'Tony Reilly. I reckon he's taking me seriously now. He's worked out my strategy and he's out to take care of the Global Wrestling Alliance before it takes care of CWI, and him. Somewhere in my organisation he has a mole, put here to start kicking in those penalty payments.'

I stared at him. 'Isn't that a bit extreme? Would the guy really go to those lengths?'

He . . . Everett, this time . . . looked at me again, without a flicker of a smile. 'Oh yeah. I reckon Mr Reilly would go to any lengths to break me.'

'But yesterday you said he made you an offer once to go and work for him.'

A shadow passed across the huge face. 'Sure he did; because he wanted to control me. There was money to be made out of Daze, and he was determined that no one but him was going to make it.'

'But why?'

Everett glanced at the wall. 'Reasons, man. Reasons.' And then he looked back at me in a way that precluded further questioning. 'It's him behind my troubles. I know it.

'I want you to help me find out who my enemy is; who Tony's man is, in my camp.'

'But how? You can't expect me just to walk in and start questioning people . . . especially not the sort of people you have here.'

'Of course not. I want you to be around when it matters, keeping your eyes open. To pull it off, you need to be a member of the team. But like I said earlier, I've thought of a cover story.' A huge grin spread slowly across his face.

The penny dropped. 'You mean you really want me to . . .'

4

I'll never forget the way Jan's eyes widened. 'He's asked you to be what . . . ?'

'Ring announcer. We'd call it Master of Ceremonies. The guy who calls out the names of the contestants, then the result.'

Even as a wee girl my wife was always very cool and resourceful, never getting rattled or flustered, always thinking before speaking, always weighing her words. In all the years since we were kids, I could count on the fingers of one hand the number of times I've seen her really incredulous. Looking at her across the bar table, I knew I was going to have to start using the other hand from that point on.

'Is he serious?' she gasped, almost choking as she fought to hold back her laughter.

'Totally. There's a vacancy for the job, and he couldn't think of a better cover for me.'

'But how does he know if you'll be any good at it?'

I put on my best hurt look. 'Don't you have any faith in me?'

'Unlimited faith, darlin',' she drawled. 'Faith beyond expression. You are bloody good at your job, you are very resourceful in a crisis, you are kind, you are thoughtful and you're great in bed. Now, I repeat: how does he know if you'll be any good at Mastering Ceremonies?'

I swapped my smug expression for the hurt look again. 'I

am good at it. Bloody brilliant, in fact. He gave me a try-out. In the video studio first, then up in the ring, with all the wrestlers watching me.

'Here, I'll give you a demo. Sit back and prepare to be impressed.' I made to stand, but she grabbed my arm and held me firmly in my seat.

'Don't you dare!' she whispered. 'Not in front of all these suits.' She glanced around the bar, which was full of men and women in dark business clothes. 'And you're really going to do it?' she asked.

'Five hundred quid a day, plus expenses. And if I catch Everett's mole, there's a success bonus of ten grand.' I flashed her a cheeky smile, across the table. 'You're my business manager. You tell me whether I'm doing it or not.'

'As your business manager, I have to ask you whether you're prepared to jeopardise your continuing, year-round business for the sake of a few thousand quid. You're in the process of rebuilding a client list that you put into cold storage when you pissed off to Spain to eat lotuses with Prim. Granted, they've been loyal to you, but if you disappear again, forget it.'

I shook my head. 'That's not going to happen. Everett shoots his shows on Saturdays and Sundays. Allow Friday afternoon for travelling sometimes: apart from that Mondays to Friday mornings are clear for my routine business.'

She looked at me, reassured but still questioning. 'Where are these events?' she asked.

'All over the place. We're in Newcastle on Friday evening, Saturday and Sunday. The weekend following we tape both shows here in Glasgow, in the SECC, then after that we go to Barcelona.'

'Oh yes? And what happens to the dear little woman while you're off ring announcing and detecting?'

'The dear little woman comes with me . . . on expenses.

That's part of the deal. I know we were supposed to be going up to Fife on Saturday, but I've sorted that too. I've got tickets for Dad and the boys for the Newcastle Arena event. You'll come with me, won't you?'

At last, she grinned. 'As long as I can go to the Metro Centre, it's a deal. For this weekend at least. A couple of my clients have audits coming up soon, and that means extra work for me. We'll play the other events by ear. Anyway, ace detective, you'll probably crack the case inside a couple of days.'

'Have you told the boys yet?'

'No. I'll phone them later on tonight.'

'Your dad's going to love you for messing up any plans he might have had for the weekend.'

'Ahh, he's a big kid at heart.'

She glanced up at the clock, which showed quarter to six. 'We having another?'

'Why not?' I stood up, and eased my way through the throng and up to the bar.

It's a funny thing about city pubs; some of them have really odd names. Few come weirder than Babbity Bowser's, in Glasgow's Merchant City. I suppose that in every town with a courtroom there are pubs to which lawyers and journalists gravitate, to trade in the vital currency of information. In Edinburgh, it's places like the Bank Hotel and O'Neill's, but in the Second City of the Empire . . . Glaswegians always did like to make big claims for them-selves . . . Babbity's reigns supreme.

It isn't all that big, and it certainly isn't flashy, but like all pubs it's made by the people it attracts. On this Tuesday night it was buzzing for sure. A big drugs-related trial, which had been running in the High Court for almost three weeks, had just ended with the conviction of all six accused. True to form in Scotland, the judge had sentenced the barons to a total of one hundred and seventeen years in jail.

Half of the Faculty of Advocates seemed to be in the place. The prosecution team from the Crown Office were sitting at a small table in the far corner of the bar, not even trying to keep the triumph from their faces. The various defence counsel and solicitors, and since there had been six defendants in the dock, that was quite a crowd, were gathered together fairly close to them. Only the youngest among them looked in the slightest upset by their defeat. The older ones had been there before, and knew the score. From the chat which had drifted over to our seats beside the door, I gathered that the consensus was that the judge had been ultra-careful in his charge to the jury, and that the only slim chance of success in an appeal was against the severity of his sentencing.

Finally, having been hailed on the way by a couple of advocates whom I knew, I made it to the bar and ordered a pint of lager for me and a gin and tonic for Jan. I paid for them, and was still wincing when the hand fell on my shoulder.

'Well, well, well. Fancy running into you again, Oz. And in Glasgow too. What are you getting away with these days?'

The last time I had seen Detective Inspector Michael Dylan, his crest had been more than a little fallen. Time had obviously healed that wound; from the beam on his face he was back to being the bumptious big arsehole I had come to know in Edinburgh. He wasn't perfect at the act though. In spite of all he did and said, I couldn't help liking him, just a bit.

'Hello, Mike,' I said, glancing in the process at his suit. Hugo Boss, I guessed. Dylan was the sort of guy who would leave the designer's label on the sleeve if he thought no one would laugh. 'I see you've been to Slater's again.'

Give him his due: he grinned. 'Not this time. I've been

giving evidence in the drugs trial. Star witness to the Edinburgh side of it. That was my swan song in the capital. I'll be through in Glasgow for a while, on secondment to the Serious Crimes Squad.'

That's bad news for us property-owners in the West, I thought. 'That's bad news for serious criminals in the West,' I said.

'So what brings you here, Ozzie?' Dylan went on. 'Last I heard you had fucked off to Spain and set up a business with that wee blonde bird of yours.' He grinned. 'Too hot for you, was it? Or was she?'

I shook my head. 'It was okay while it lasted. I found out that I missed someone, though. We're married now, and living through here, up behind Charing Cross.' I held up my two drinks, and nodded towards the doorway, where Jan was gazing at me, frowning slightly as if trying to remember Dylan's face. 'Look, I've got to get these back to the table.'

His eyes followed mine. 'That's the wife, son?' Dylan was in his early thirties, two or three years older than me. 'I can see why you hurried back; she's bloody gorgeous.

'Here, I see you've got a couple of spare seats. We'll join you.'

With a pint and a gin and tonic in my hands, I could barely say that we were just leaving.

'Who's he?' Jan whispered as I sat down opposite her. 'I know the face from somewhere.'

'Mike Dylan, a copper from Edinburgh. He used to be Ricky Ross's sidekick. He drinks in Whighams.'

'That's right,' she said. 'I remember seeing him there: talking to you, in fact. He looks a bit full of himself.'

'He's okay, really. Try to be nice to him. He's coming over.' I had been wondering about Dylan's 'we'. I had my answer at once as he emerged from the throng at the bar, carrying two pints of dark beer and followed by a short girl, in an even shorter skirt and with frizzy red hair.

'This is my girlfriend, Susie Gantry,' he said as he laid the pints on the table.

I reached out a handshake. 'Pleased to meet you, Susie. I'm Oz Blackstone, and this is my wife Jan.

'Gantry, eh,' I went on, idly. 'Same name as the Lord Provost.'

'He's my father,' said Susie, a touch apologetically, it seemed to me.

Christ, I thought to myself. *Typical bloody Dylan. He's hardly in town five minutes and he's shagging the Lord Provost's daughter.*

'And have you known PC Dylan long?' I asked her.

'Watch it, you,' said Mike, as the girl, not yet attuned to my waspish humour, shot him a quick frown. 'That's Detective Inspector.'

'Still?' I laced my tone with all the incredulity I could muster.

'Cheeky bastard, Blackstone. I shouldn't be for much longer, since you're interested. I'm expecting a promotion within the next few months.'

'How come? Are all your gaffers due to go up in the same dodgy aircraft?'

Dylan smiled at my wife. 'How did a sensible looking lady like you wind up with this?' he asked. He's the sort of bloke who can't help chatting up every woman he meets, even when he has one on his arm.

'Sunshine,' she drawled, poker-faced. 'I taught him everything he knows.' She looked across at Susie Gantry, and smiled. 'How about you? When did you draw this card?'

'About two months ago,' the red-haired girl replied, with an appraising glance at Dylan. 'I'm still deciding whether to shove it back in the deck.'

For once in my life, I began to feel sorry for him. 'How's your old boss these days, Mike?' I asked, by way of changing the subject.

'Ricky, you mean? He's off the force, and working as a security consultant to one of the big supermarkets. I saw him a few weeks ago.' He paused. 'Your name came up in conversation, in fact.'

'Asking after me, was he?'

Dylan grinned at me. 'More or less. What he actually said was "Do you know where that wee Something or Other Blackstone is these days?" Ricky still blames you for landing him in the shit, you know.'

'That's a good one.' I laughed as I said it. 'The guy was banging a murder victim's wife, and he got himself implicated in his own investigation. How did that all finish up anyway? I never heard.'

'The Crown Office decided there wasn't enough evidence to proceed, so all charges were dropped. Officially, the case is still open.'

'Does Ross still think I did it?'

Susie Gantry looked astounded. Her wide-eyed gaze went from Dylan to me then back to the detective.

'No, he's given up on that one, you'll be glad to hear. He's back to thinking that your girlfriend's sister did it, and that you covered up for her.'

'Well he can piss up a rope, then, for he's wrong on both counts.'

'Does that mean you know who did it?' Dylan smiled, in a sort of a sly way. *Caution, Blackstone*, the voice in my head whispered. *This bampot might not be as daft as he looks.*

'The only thing I know, Detective Inspector, is that if you haven't caught whoever did it by now, then you never will.'

He took a mouthful of warm ale. 'For once, you're right. Ahh, bugger it. It's no business of mine any more. So how are you liking Glasgow, Jan?' He switched back to chatting up my wife.

'Very much. We love it here. It's good for business too.'

'Christ.' He nodded in my direction. 'You're not in the same line as him, are you?'

She shook her head, sending her lustrous brown hair swinging. Then she laughed, deep as a note from a big bell. Dylan had been right about one thing. She was looking absolutely gorgeous. 'Certainly not, sir,' she said. 'I'm a chartered accountant. But I am like Oz in that I'm self-employed.'

'What sort of clients do you have?' Susie Gantry asked. I noticed that she was getting through her pint faster than her boyfriend.

'Small businesses, mostly,' Jan replied. 'A couple of advertising agencies, a design consultancy, a printing firm, a car dealership, two legal practices. I keep their financial affairs in order, and provide them with management accounts on a monthly or quarterly basis, whichever their bankers want.'

'What have they got to do with it?' Dylan asked. That was naive, even for him. Jan looked at him with the same expression that she wore when she was explaining something to our nephews.

'If you were lending money to someone's business,' she said, 'you'd want to make sure it was being handled properly. Business bank managers are just the same; their careers depend on the success of their funding decisions, so when they lend to small companies they need that assurance too.

'Most of my clients have come through introductions by bankers.'

Like me, Jan didn't like to be asked specific questions about her customers' businesses. To head Dylan off, I turned to his girlfriend. 'What about you, Susie?' I asked her. 'Are you in the same line of work as Inspector Clouseau here?'

Her laugh was the opposite of Jan's; high-pitched, nervous, a bit forced, I thought. She was attractive, but her quick, darting eyes, and her sharply cut features, gave her a highly-strung look. 'That'll be right,' she burst out. 'Imagine a Lady Provost in the CID. The Labour Group would just love that.'

I guess it must have been my turn to look surprised. I had been in Glasgow long enough to know all about Jack Gantry, Susie's father, and the post he held. The Lord Provost is Glasgow's First Citizen, elected for three years by the City Council from among its number, to chair its meetings but more important than that, to be its public face on all important occasions at home, and to promote it around the world. A Mayor, to use the English term, but much more so.

To some extent, the job is what the incumbents make of it. Some Lord Provosts have come and gone without making much of a dent in the awareness of the Great Glaswegian Public. Jack Gantry was different: he was Mr Glasgow. The theory of the office is that its bearer has no political power, but Susie's dad was power incarnate. He was in his late fifties, and he had dominated the city's Labour Party for thirty years, resisting all attempts to ease him from the Majority Leader's room into the Lord Provost's Office, until finally, he had decided to don the heavy gold chain of office. It was said that his successor as Labour Group Leader had enjoyed the illusion of power for three hours, before Gantry had called him in and had told him that when it came to political decisions, it was to be business as usual.

I knew all that, having read it in the *Herald* and the *Evening Times*, but the Lady Provost reference threw me. Susie spotted my confusion and explained. 'The Lord Provost is entitled to be partnered on all official functions; it's expected, so that VIPs' wives have somebody to talk to over dinner. Usually it's his wife, and that's fine; my mum's dead though, so I chum my dad. Lady Provost's a sort of unofficial title.' Her brittle laugh sounded once more. 'When the Lord

Provost's a lady they have a problem, mind you!'

'Is it a full-time job?'

Susie shook her head. 'No, although looking after my dad is. I'm working in his business during his term of office, and probably beyond that. He's a building contractor, among other things; I'm running the group for him.'

Dylan patted her hand, and glanced at his watch. 'Had we not better be going, Lady Provost?

'There's a reception at the City Chambers. We're due there at half six,' he explained to Jan.

I couldn't stop myself. 'Here, does that make you the Boy Provost, Mike?'

For some reason, Susie thought this was maybe the funniest thing she had ever heard. Dylan looked at me as if he wished I was parked on a double yellow line.

'Are you two doing anything after this?' his girlfriend asked us.

'We were going for a pizza, that's all,' Jan replied.

'Come with us, then. It won't be much of a do . . . it's for the Prime Minister of Estonia . . . but it'll give you a chance to see the City Chambers. If you're new in Glasgow, I don't suppose you'll have been inside yet.'

'That's great, Susie,' said my wife. 'Are you sure it's all right?'

'Course it is, girl, you're wi' the Lady Provost. And even if you weren't, you'd be with Jack Gantry's daughter.'

'But are we well enough dressed?' Jan asked. I was miffed by that. I thought my Marks and Spencer suit was at least as smart as Dylan's discounted designer.

'Overdressed if anything.' Susie smoothed down her close-fitting red dress as she rose. She was trim, although not nearly as well built as Jan. I looked at my wife, in her formal grey suit, and as always, was swept by an urge to take her home and help her out of it. But I could see she was sold on the reception. At least half a dozen lawyers' heads turned to look at us as we moved towards the door. I knew for certain that none of them were looking at either Dylan or me.

It was cold, dark and drizzly outside, turning colder too, but there are always plenty of taxis cruising around near to Babbity's. We hailed one, and five minutes later, were decanted onto the pavement in George Square, at the entrance to the City Chambers. We hadn't even made it to the door, when a dark-suited council officer emerged, to greet Susie effusively. Out there in the rain, he was wearing a tail-coat, a white shirt with a wing collar and a red bow tie, but he still managed to look imposing, a man of authority rather than a lackey. The Lady Provost whispered in his ear as he ushered her inside. The doorkeeper cast a quick look at Jan and me over his shoulder. He nodded, as if with approval, and muttered, 'Of course, Ms Gantry, no problem.' I glanced at his tie and wondered if the colour would change to blue with the election of a Conservative administration; then I told myself not to be daft. In Glasgow, there's more chance of an extra-terrestrial invasion than a Tory Council.

The seat of Glasgow's local government was built in the Victorian era, as a monument to its affluence and its stature in the Imperial economy. A decade or so back, when stone-cleaning was all the rage, its exterior was given a good scrub. Unfortunately the grim predictions of several architects have been proved to be true, as now the great George Square palace has taken on a faint greenish tinge in the glare of the sun.

It wasn't evident on that winter's evening though. Even if it had been, I would barely have noticed, given the opulence inside the place. Glasgow City Chambers is built largely of some sort of marble or polished stone, brownish with yellow seams running through it. The woodwork is all dark; great, varnished panels, probably mahogany. All of it is over a hundred years old, yet it looks pristine. Any modern administration which spent on its accommodation a quarter of the amount which the City Chambers would cost today would be voted out of office at the first opportunity, but the grandees who built it were hugely proud of it, as are thousands of their Glaswegian descendants.

'Come on and I'll show you round,' Susie offered, as our coats were taken by another of the many attendants in the entrance hall. 'I've got a couple of minutes before I'm on duty.' She rushed us up stairways and through corridors, in and out of empty offices and committee rooms, and finally, into the Council Chamber itself, wood-panelled, brightly lit and worthy of any legislature.

'Not bad, eh,' she said proudly.

'Not bad indeed,' I agreed. 'When was the last time there was a close vote in here?'

'Back when God was a boy. That's the way it is in Glasgow.'

I knew this too. The ruling Whips kept a grip on their members which was even tighter than their opposite numbers in Westminster.

'Come on,' said Susie. 'Time I was standing beside my old man.' She led us down a wide stone staircase and along to the Banqueting Hall. The council officer who had welcomed us had moved station, taking up a position in the big double doorway. Behind him, with his back to us, there stood a man in a grey suit with an ornate gold chain around his neck.

'Hi Dad,' said Susie, entwining her arm with his as he turned. 'Told you we'd be on time.'

Lord Provost Jack Gantry smiled at his daughter, with a resigned look on his face. 'Aye,' he sighed, 'but you don't half cut it fine.' He looked beyond her, nodding to Dylan. 'Hello Mike. I hear the case went okay then.'

'Couldn't have been better, Mr Gantry. Those six won't see the countryside again till they're old men.'

'Aye, sure.' His eyes narrowed as he flashed a shrewd look at the policeman. 'Of course you realise that there were boys out in the housing schemes taking their place before the trial even started. There's no more abhorrent a vacuum to some than a dried up drugs supply.'

'We do what we can to keep on top of the problem.'

'Aye son, but you're fartin' against thunder and you know it.

'The only way you'll ever put these drugs gangsters out of business is by taking the law out of it. Cigarettes and alcohol are bad for people too, but the government still makes money from them. If people want other forms of narcotics their demand will always create supply. Decriminalise, and at least that supply will be subject to proper market forces; regulation, quality control and competition-based pricing.'

Dylan smiled at him. 'Is that the Labour Party view, Jack?'

The Lord Provost's eyes narrowed. 'Fuck the Labour Party, son,' he said softly, between clenched teeth. 'That's the Jack Gantry view.'

'Dad!' Susie tugged her father's arm.

'Sorry hen,' he said, suddenly looking past Dylan, becoming aware of us for the first time.

'Well! You're not in the Social Club now.' She drew him towards us. 'These are Oz and Jan Blackstone; friends of Mike's. From Edinburgh originally, but they live in Glasgow now.'

Lord Provost Gantry treated us to one of the most professional smiles I have ever seen. 'Welcome to our city,' he said, extending his hand to Jan. 'Are you registered to vote yet?'

'We will be come the next election,' she replied, in a beautifully judged tone, which made it perfectly clear that nothing about us could be taken for granted. As I shook his hand, I looked beyond Jack Gantry's smile. I thought of the other people I had met that day: Jerry Gradi, Darius Hencke, Liam Matthews. It terms of sheer presence, they all paled beside this man. Behind all that civic bonhomie, the Lord Provost's eyes were as hard as the stone of which his palace was built.

He was an inch or two shorter than me, but he seemed twice as wide. Even the massive chain of office sat lightly on his shoulders. There was nothing threatening about him, not here, in his Banqueting Hall. But still, I could understand completely how he had come to have the keys of the City in his pocket for so long.

In the doorway, the first of his official guests had begun to appear.

'I'll look forward to speaking to you later,' he said. 'But we've got to go to work now. Mike, you make sure that everyone gets a drink, okay.'

Dylan nodded and led Jan and me off towards one of the white-aproned waitresses who stood around the big room. She took a few steps to meet us, holding out her tray of red and white wine, letting us help ourselves.

'I'll bet this was champagne in the old days,' said the detective.

'I'm sure you're right,' Jan agreed. 'But even now, what would the folk in Easterhouse and Castlemilk think if they could see this?'

'They'd think their rents were too high,' I muttered. 'They'd think that they'd rather have an extra copper on the beat.'

'Hey come on, Oz,' Dylan protested. 'We got a good result for the people today.'

'Sure you did, but you're only sticking your finger in a hole in the dyke, just like the Lord Provost said. How did you come to meet his daughter, anyway?'

'One of the Crime Squad guys introduced us in a pub one night. We just hit it off.'

'What does Mrs Dylan think about it?' I asked, casually, as the room began to fill up around us. His face clouded over. I could see that for the first time ever, I had got to him. To my surprise, I felt slightly rotten about it.

'Come on, Oz. You must know that Maxine walked out on me. Every other bugger in Edinburgh does.'

'Yes of course, Mike, I'd forgotten. I'm sorry; that was uncalled for.' I shot him a quick, let's make up, smile. 'The wee lass seems nice though.'

He switched back into the normal Dylan mode at once. 'She is that. Where she gets the energy from I don't know.' He grinned; actually, it wasn't far short of a leer. 'Fair wears me out, she does.' I didn't need to look at Jan to gauge her reaction. I could feel her bristling beside me.

A young waiter, brandishing a tray of canapés, intervened at just the right moment. Our detective friend grabbed three quails eggs, fried and served on circles of toast, plus two cornets filled with prawns. My wife and I declined, feeling guilty about the people in Easterhouse and Castlemilk, and with a thought to our pizza, which had only been postponed.

Dylan was halfway through his second quail's egg, when I saw him look up, his eyes widening. All of a sudden a shadow fell over me.

'Well hello, buddy. Hello again, Mrs Blackstone. I didn't know you moved in these circles.'

'We don't, Everett,' I said, accepting the huge – and mercifully gentle – handshake. 'We were arrested and brought here by our friend, Detective Inspector Dylan. You've just been greeted by his girlfriend and her father, over by the entrance.'

'Ah.' He looked down at the policeman, who seemed

totally stunned by the newcomer. 'So you're with Susie, huh. Lucky man.'

That's three of us who're lucky, in that case, I heard myself think, as I looked at the coffee-skinned woman who stood beside my newest client. I had seen her before, of course, mewing and taunting seductively, from the video screen in the GWA studio.

'You haven't met Diane yet, have you, Oz?' She looked at me with big, soft, brown eyes. There was something about her which told me, in the same instant, who was boss in the Davis household. But in the same moment it came to me that people probably thought the same about my wife.

The giant leaned down towards Dylan, in a half bow. 'Hi, I'm Everett Davis.'

'Better known as Daze?' the policeman ventured.

A laugh rumbled up, and surfaced. 'Probably: but it's okay, Daze ain't here tonight. Just Everett and Diane Davis, a businessman and his wife.' He turned to me. 'Jack Gantry invited us as a personal favour. I'm trying to cut a deal with an Estonian station, so when I heard about this reception, I had to be here.'

'So how do you come to know Oz?' DI Mike butted in. He sounded incredulous; it was my turn to feel a bit narked.

'We have a mutual friend,' the wrestler replied, without a sign of a pause or hesitation. 'He introduced us.'

'Are you a fan of the Global Wrestling Alliance, Mike?' I asked. I know; I'm a sod, but I just can't resist winding that man up. I could tell that he was the sort of bloke who would be a fan, but embarrassed to admit it.

He seemed to flush, slightly, telling me in the process that my guess had been spot on. 'I've seen it on occasion,' he mumbled.

Everett reached into the pocket of his jacket. 'Come see us in Newcastle on Saturday, then. Bring Susie and her father. These are for the VIP area.' He produced three tickets and handed them to Dylan. I recognised them, since he had given me four as I left his office.

'Are youse all enjoying yourselves, then?' The Lord Provost's easy, confident voice sounded from behind us, but his accent was noticeably different, now that there were more people around. It struck me that he must slip into Glesca' patois when he was performing for a wider audience. I turned and there he was moving towards us, all gold chain and Mr Glasgow smile, with a slim, grey-haired man following in his wake.

'Everett,' he said, his voice dropping to its former level, and his accent returning to normal, 'if you have a minute, the Prime Minister would like to speak to you.'

As he turned, the big man gave me a lightning fast wink. 'Of course, Jack.' He nodded towards the door. 'Where can we talk?'

'Come on through to my office. No one will disturb us there.' For a second, I thought he was going to try to throw an avuncular hand around Everett's shoulders, but he couldn't reach that high: instead he simply patted him, somewhere in the lower part of his back.

'See you tomorrow night,' the big man whispered to me, as he moved off with the Lord Provost and the Prime Minister. Automatically, without a sign from her husband, Diane went with them.

'Your dad seems pretty pally with Everett,' I said to Susie.

She nodded. 'He performed the opening ceremony at the GWA headquarters building. And he appeared at the ring at their first show in the SECC. Ever since they came to Glasgow, he's been telling people what a benefit they bring in selling the city abroad.

'Yes, you could say that he's a big Daze fan'

As Susie spoke a drinks waitress appeared at my shoulder,

54

as if the Lord Provost's departure had been her cue. She offered her tray to our group: our detective friend picked up two glasses at once, handing one to the Lady Provost, but my wife shook her head.

I took the hint. 'No thanks,' I said. 'Susie, it's been nice to meet you. It's even been good to see you again, Mike,' I slipped in as an aside. 'But we'd better be going.'

'Yes,' Jan added. 'It was great of you to invite us along: I wouldn't have missed it for the world. But I have some work to catch up on this evening.'

'My pleasure,' Susie Gantry replied. She gave us a smile, which vanished as quickly as it had appeared, with the slight frown which creased her forehead. 'Do you have time for any more work, Jan?' she asked, suddenly.

My wife looked at her, surprised. 'Just about,' she answered. 'It would depend how much was involved.'

The Lord Provost's daughter reached into her red leather shoulder-bag, and produced a card. 'Give me a call tomorrow, and we'll fix up a meeting. You can tell me a bit more about yourself, and I'll show you the Gantry Group.'

'Thanks,' said Jan. 'I'll take you up on that.'

I don't really know what made me do it. I suppose it would have been churlish not to, yet I've never had a problem being a churl when it's been necessary. I picked out my business card from the supply I always keep in my breast pocket and handed it to Dylan. 'Give me a bell yourself, Mike, if you fancy a pint sometime.'

He looked at me as if a show of friendship was an unusual experience for him . . . and I guessed that it probably was. 'I'll do that,' he answered, 'once I'm settled through here.'

'Where are you going to be living?'

'We're talking about that at the moment,' said Susie, with a worldly grin.

We left them to their discussion and went outside, into

the night. The drizzle had turned into steady rain, but there was a string of taxis across the street.

'Have you really got work tonight?' I asked my wife, half an hour later, as I laid the big square boxes holding our takeaway pizzas on the kitchen counter.

I knew the smile she threw at me. I'd known it since we were sixteen years old. She nodded towards our supper. 'D'you want that now, or re-heated in an hour or so?'

I've always liked the word 'rhetorical': I was taught the full extent of its meaning by Mrs Janet Blackstone, née More.

The master bedroom of our apartment is directly above the living space, with the same original windows, reaching down to the floor. All of our curtains were included in the sale price, but those in the bedroom had hardly ever been drawn. It looks out west and south over Glasgow, but its height makes it secluded, so Jan and I very quickly formed the habit of leaving the lights off and the windows uncovered.

We had forgotten all about the pizzas as we lay in bed an hour later, as happy and content as we had ever been in our lives, propped up on pillows, looking out at the traffic flowing across the Kingston Bridge, and at the headlight beams, distorted by the rain on the glass. 'Dylan isn't really as bad as all that, you know,' she murmured, suddenly. Her brown hair had fallen over one eye, as she reached over and traced her index finger down my chest, pausing to flick blue lint from my belly-button. 'He's made Detective Inspector, after all.'

I picked up the blob which her probing finger had freed and looked at it. Did you ever wonder why belly-button fluff is always blue? I held it up. 'He's got about as much substance as that, my darling.' I paused as an image formed in my mind. 'Do you remember Slimey Carmichael?'

She laughed. 'What, the Head Boy when we were in our fourth year at High School?'

'That's right. Since you do, you'll remember as well that he owed his position to being the biggest brown-tongue in the school. He was a complete tosser at games and in class, but he smarmed up to all the senior teachers, and joined all the right school clubs and societies, so they bought his act.'

'Don't knock it, my love. You can get to be Prime Minister that way.'

'Aye, maybe so. Anyway, Mike's a bit like him. The first time I met him I thought he was a real high flyer, until I realised it was all hot air. His balloon's been a bit deflated since then; some of Ricky Ross's mud splashed on him. I suppose this Glasgow transfer's a form of rehabilitation.'

'Still,' I conceded. 'As you say, when you get to know him he's not so bad.'

'Susie thinks so, obviously.'

'True. She's a lively wee thing, isn't she.'

Jan nodded, as she slid down from her pile of pillows, fitting herself alongside me. 'I wonder what her problem is?' she mused.

'Who says she's got one?' I slid down beside her.

'She has, believe me. People don't change their accountants otherwise.'

'Forget her problem,' I murmured, turning her towards me and nuzzling her firm breasts. 'Let's concentrate on our own.'

'And what's that?' she asked, smokily, being rhetorical again. I answered her anyway.

'When the hell are we going to eat those pizzas?'

5

In a lot of ways, Newcastle is like Glasgow. There's nothing quaint about it, but it has the same sort of grit – evolved, I suppose, through a century of building big ocean-going vessels. Like Glasgow too, the distinctive character and toughness of its people still shines through, for all its nineties face-lift.

Jan and I travelled down from Scotland by train on Friday afternoon, first class of course, courtesy of Everett Davis. He and his star performers had gone down to Tyneside that morning, to do television promotions for the live event, while the road crew drove down in their trucks, to begin the setting up of the arena.

As the express cut silently through the fields of East Lothian, many of them ploughed already in readiness for their spring seeding, I asked Jan whether she had taken up Susie Gantry's invitation.

'I called her this morning, while you were out doing that interview,' she replied. 'We had a long chat.'

'Why's she looking for a new accountant then?'

'Because she does have a problem. I was right. She thinks her book-keeper may be on the fiddle, and she wants someone independent to cast an eye over his work.'

That sounded a bit odd to me. 'Wouldn't the company's auditors do that?' I asked her.

'Normally they would. But Susie buys her book-keeping

and audit services from the same firm. They've just finished the audit for the last financial year, but they seem to have skated over some discrepancies that were worrying her.

'As a result, she doesn't trust any of them any more; she wants me to do some forensic work, either to confirm her suspicions or put her mind at rest.'

'Has she spoken to her father about this?'

'No. That's a bit of a touchy point with her. When the Lord Provost gave her control of the firm three years ago, he saddled her with an in-house accountant. He was an old mate of Councillor Gantry, who'd been doing the job for years, but very badly, according to Susie. She tolerated him for as long as she could, but finally a few weeks back, she'd had enough. She fired him.

'Her father wasn't very pleased about his pal getting the sack, although he didn't interfere. Against that background, though, the last thing Susie wants is for her appointees to be found wanting. She says her dad would never let her live it down. So, among other things, she wants help to find the right successor to his old mate.'

'Are you going to do it?'

Jan nodded. 'I'm having lunch with her in the Rotunda on Monday. We'll sort out the brief then.'

She glanced out of the window, as the train swept past a huge, grey, monolithic, menacing building, which I guessed had to be Torness Power Station. 'That's next week, though,' she said. 'What's the programme for this weekend?'

'We check into the Holiday Inn, then I have to go to the Arena. Everett's called a team meeting for five o'clock, to go through the running order for tomorrow's show. The roadies will start to build the ring and dress the hall this evening, while the rest of us are having a buffet supper back at the hotel.'

She threw me a mock grimace. 'You mean I have to eat

with a bunch of sweaty wrestlers?'

'They only sweat after their matches, my darling. Some of them even know how to use a knife and fork. You'll enjoy it.'

'If I must,' she grinned. 'What about tomorrow?'

'That's when you go to the Metro Centre. I have to be around the Arena most of the day, ostensibly rehearsing, but in practice nosing around and keeping my eyes open for potential saboteurs.

'The show begins at six o'clock. I told Dad you'd meet him and the boys outside the main entrance at five thirty. Once the thing's all over, and they're heading back to Fife, we're on our own . . .' I hesitated '. . . Except that Everett's invited us to have dinner with him and Diane.'

My wife grinned at me, and leaned across the table which divided our seats. 'You know, Osbert,' she whispered. 'I think you're as big a Daze fan as Mike Dylan. Just as well I sort of fancy him myself.'

6

We checked into the Copthorne Hotel, near to the station, to find that Everett's secretary had booked us into one of the best rooms in the place, overlooking the River Tyne and its iron bridge, a smaller version of the Sydney Harbour landmark, but one which, I'll bet, has seen as much action in its time.

I hadn't realised that the Global Wrestling Alliance had its own liveried bus, until I saw it parked outside the hotel as Jan and I arrived. It wasn't any ordinary tourer; it looked almost as tall as a double-decker, as if its roof had been specially raised, and I guessed it probably had. When I stepped outside at quarter to five after leaving my wife in our suite, it had begun to fill with wrestlers . . . very large wrestlers, each of them wearing a GWA tee-shirt.

The huge Daze . . . he had the gold in his hair once again . . . leaned out of the door and waved me on board. Even with the high roof he stooped slightly as he looked along the aisle. 'Okay guys,' he boomed. 'For those of you who ain't met him yet, this is Oz Blackstone, our new ring announcer.' He turned to me. 'Oz, I won't introduce you down the line. Most of these superstars have their names on their shirts, so you'll be able to figure out who's who.

'Grab yourself a seat, and let's get under way.'

I nodded. There was a spare seat halfway up the aisle, next to Darius Hencke; well, a spare half seat at any rate.

The huge German grinned as I squeezed myself in beside him.

As we swung out of the hotel drive, I could see the Newcastle Arena, on the same side of the river, not far away; so close indeed that I wondered why we hadn't just walked. In fact, I asked Darius that very question, but the driver answered for him, as he turned the bus in the opposite direction.

'We have to let the people know we're here,' the Black Angel of Death explained, tossing his long hair back from his forehead as he spoke and throwing a stage glower at a child who was gawping at him from the pavement.

The driver took us on a grand tour of the centre of the city, across the bridge, up into Gateshead, then round and back over the Tyne by another crossing, until finally, almost twenty-five minutes later, he drew the bus to a halt outside the venue.

The Newcastle Arena is a modern, purpose built place, a big shed with the flexibility to allow it to stage both sports events and rock concerts. As we stepped inside, I could see that Everett's roadies were a hard-working crew. The ring was in position already, although the canvas and surround were still to be fitted.

As the boss led his troops, me included, across the empty floor, I tried to imagine it twenty-four hours later, filled with seats and screaming spectators. For the first time, a wee bundle of nerves knotted in my stomach, as I thought of myself standing up there, calling out the matches.

The highest of the three ropes which enclosed the ring looked to be around five feet high. Everett jumped up on to the apron and stepped clean over, with ease. 'Okay guys,' he called out, 'listen up.' The wrestlers, two of them tall, strapping women, and half a dozen older guys whom I took to be the referees and in-house television commentators, gathered around the ring.

'We got eight matches on the bill tomorrow,' the giant boomed. 'You've all seen the running order, and you've all been working on your routines. Once the guys get the padding and the canvas down, I want you to run through them for me, as usual . . . without breaking any props.'

He looked at me. 'Meantime, Oz, you with me over there and we'll rehearse your ring announcements.'

I nodded, understanding fully for the first time, what Everett Davis and the sports entertainment industry were all about. The man wasn't a promoter after the manner of that American bloke with the big hair; he was an impresario, an actor director, and his presentations were an extreme form of dance theatre.

As the rest of the troupe split off into twos, or in one case, four, I followed him into a corner of the great hall, where a pile of speakers and other audio equipment stood ready for positioning. He picked up a cordless mike and handed it to me. 'Get used to handling it like it's not there,' he said. 'Hold it like I showed you the other day, chest height to give the cameras a clear shot of your face, about a foot and a half away from your mouth.' I nodded, dumbly.

'Okay. Now let's hear you.' I took the running order from the inside pocket of my sports jacket, and ran my eyes down it. The first match featured someone called Salvatore Scarletto (His real name was Johnny King: I had met him on the bus) fighting Tommy Rockette. (His gimmick appeared to be that he came to the ring carrying a guitar.) I ran through my intro, awkwardly. When we had tried it out first in Glasgow, I hadn't been holding a mike.

'Relax, man,' said Everett. 'Start slow and build up to a crescendo. Roll out each of the names, real slow, so that everyone can hear 'em loud and clear.' After half a dozen more attempts, he was satisfied. 'That's good. Just keep that tempo and you'll be fine, Oz. Now run through the rest of the card for me.'

I did as he asked. I must have been okay right enough, because his nods grew more emphatic and his smile widened as I went on. By the time I'd finished, I noticed for the first time an absentee from the list. 'Where's Jerry?' I asked.

'He's not appearing this week. We're using that video insert you saw the other day. It'll run for the audience on our big screen.'

'Is he okay?'

'The Behemoth? Okay? Man, he's indestructible. The fact is he's on a kids' television show tomorrow morning, as a special guest star.'

'Kids' telly? Won't he scare the life out of the poor wee darlings?'

Everett laughed. 'The opposite. He's great with kids; they love him.' He turned and looked across at the ring.

'The canvas is in place. I gotta go and rehearse the guys. You just stay here and keep practising.'

I did as I was told, facing into the corner and feeling only slightly daft as I ran through the card over and over again. I was just about ready to pack it in for the night when a hand fell on my shoulder, none too softly.

'Well now, Ozzie my boyo,' said Liam Matthews. 'How are you doing? Better than that last bastard, I hope.' I hadn't taken to the Irishman at first sight, but there was something in his tone which made me like him even less. The fact is it made me downright dislike him.

'I want you to remember something,' he brogued at me. 'All the other introductions, they can all go to ratshit for all I care. There's one you'd better get right, though, and you can guess whose that is.' He squeezed my shoulder for a second, hard enough for it to hurt.

'Sure'n let's be hearing you now.'

'If you want.' I raised my dead mike to the required level and began to call my intro, '. . . and his opponent, in this title match, all the way from Dublin, Ireland, the GWA Transcontinental Champion, Liam . . . The Man . . . Matthews!'

The Irishman's long, thick blond hair flew as he shook his head, vigorously. 'Christ man, where did the big D dig you up? You make me sound like a selling plater. I am the coming man in this organisation, and that's all you can do for me?'

'What more do you want?' I demanded.

'I want you to call out my name like you were introducing Jesus Christ, John Lennon and Muhammad Ali all in one. I want you to hang on to every letter, as if you couldn't bear to let them go. I want you to have those little girls screaming for me before you've even got halfway through.'

And why would they be screaming for you, you greasy Irish toe-rag? I thought. I decided against voicing it though. 'I'll work on it,' I said instead. 'I'll stay up all night working on it if I have to.'

'As well you do, Ozzie boy. Otherwise you'll come by the same injuries as the last fella.' He gave me one of the least pleasant smiles I had ever seen and turned away, trotting across to the ring where Everett and the Black Angel of Death awaited his pleasure, together with Dee Dee, the 'manager', dressed this time in a casual shirt, rather than his incredibly loud jacket.

I stared after him, pondering his threat, wondering whether to take it seriously.

'Don't you worry about that one, mate.'

The thick Glasgow accent came from behind me. I turned, to see a man standing beside the piled up speakers. He looked to be in his early to mid-thirties; he was fair-haired, wearing grimy jeans and a faded GWA tee-shirt, and his face was streaked with dust and sweat. He was tall, about six three, and brick-built. 'Liam likes to chuck his weight around. Just ignore him.'

I nodded. 'Okay. I'll enjoy ignoring the bastard, in fact.' I looked at the newcomer. 'You a wrestler?'

'Christ no. I'm one of the road crew. We're the really tough boys around here. Ma name's Gary O'Rourke, by the way.'

'Oz Blackstone.'

'How did you come to land this job, Oz?'

I took immediate refuge behind my previously rehearsed lie. 'I've done a bit of acting. A friend of mine introduced me to Everett, and he decided to give me a shot at it.'

Gary nodded. 'Aye, he's a good bloke, is big Daze. So's the other Yank, Jerry.'

'What are the rest of the wrestlers like?'

'Ach, apart from Liam who's a nasty wee shite, the most of them are okay. Yon Darius, he looks fuckin' terrifying in the ring, but he's a pleasant big guy outside of it. Even the lassies are fine.' He pointed across the arena, towards one of the women I had seen earlier: she was doing stretching exercises. 'Sally, over there, Sally Crockett: she's a real stunner. She comes from Manchester; the other women in the squad are Yanks.

'As for the boss's wife . . .' His voice tailed off.

'I know,' I said. 'I've met her.'

I paused and looked at him. 'How tough are these guys, really?'

Gary grunted and ran his thick fingers through his hair. 'Depends what you mean by tough. If you mean how are they in a real fight: some of them – the likes of Johnny King and Rockette there – wouldnae last two minutes in our local, but as for some of the others . . . Jerry Gradi, now, he's a fuckin' monster. So's Darius. He wears that loose ring costume, but you see him out of it. Man, he's so hard, the only bit of his body that moves is his dick.'

'What about Daze?'

The Glaswegian frowned. 'The Boss is brilliant in the ring. It's just so easy for him. He can even handle big Jerry like he was a wean. You look at him and you realise that he's holdin' so much back. As for how tough he is, the only thing I could say to that is that if he ever got mad at me, Ah'd send for the SAS . . . and even then Ah wouldnae expect to get anythin' better than a draw.

'The really impressive thing about these guys though is what they can do wi' their bodies. Look at that.' He pointed to the ring. I turned, in time to see Darius pick up Liam Matthews, lift him to shoulder height and choke-slam him down flat on his back on to the padded canvas.

'Liam weighs maybe a bit over fifteen stone. He and all the rest of them take that sort of hammering every week in life, but they just absorb it and come back for more. Now that's tough.'

'Is it a good crowd to work for?' I asked him, casually.

'Aye, it is. Big Daze tries to run this like a fitba' team. He goes out of his way tae make sure everybody's happy.'

'And are they?'

'As far as Ah can tell. It's the best place Ah've ever worked, Ah'll tell ye.'

'Where did you work before?'

'Buildin' trade.'

'What brought you here?'

Gary shrugged his impressive shoulders. 'Ah just fancied a change. Thought it would be nice tae work inside. The travel was an attraction too.'

The roadie bent and picked up one of the big speakers. 'Ah'd better get on wi' it.' He grinned. 'So'd youse, unless you want the pride of Dublin after you!'

I took him at his word and spent the next hour rehearsing, while Gary and the other five roadies worked around me, setting up the big Bose speakers on stands and building a ramp which rose from floor level at ringside until it stood about four feet high at the doorway which led to the changing area. When I asked one of the roadies what it was for he told me that it was to allow the crowd to see each wrestler as he made his way to the ring.

Make that 'her'. I had just surrendered my microphone to the sound man when the blonde whom I had seen exercising on the other side of the hall came wandering over in my direction. Gary had been right: she was a stunner, with legs that seemed to go on for ever.

'Hello there,' she said, with a smile. 'You're the new announcer, I hear. I'm Sally Crockett.'

I shook the hand which she offered. 'I know; Gary told me.'

'Ah.' The smile widened. 'He's a good lad, is our Gazza.'

A year before, I'd have launched into a serious pitch. Marriage had changed me, though. I left out the pitch, and scratched my nose instead, showing her my wedding ring as I slipped out a clumsy compliment.

'Thank you,' she replied. 'I saw you getting the Liam treatment earlier on.'

'It was nothing.'

'I'm glad you think like that. He's a bit of a bully, is our Liam. Thinks he's God's gift, too.'

Her accent was English, but without any regional twang that I could recognise. Her tone told me, though, that she didn't share Matthews' opinion of himself.

'How did you get into this business?' I asked her.

'I just fancied it. I used to be an athlete. I did the Heptathlon, but I wasn't up to Olympic standard – my hurdles were lousy – so I looked around for a change of sport, and found this. I love it.'

'Don't you ever get hurt?'

Her pretty face clouded over. 'Only once. I was in a mixed tag-team match with Darius, against Matthews and Anita Rose, one of the American girls.'

'What, did she clock you?'

She shook her head. 'No, Liam did. A couple of days before he'd been pestering me for a date, so much so that I told him to eff off. There was a part in our match, where I was supposed to wind up in the ring with him, hit him with a drop kick and then take a body slam. The drop kick went okay, but he mistimed the slam and broke two of my ribs.'

'Accident?'

'No way,' she said, bitterly. 'He's too good a wrestler for that. He claimed it was though, and Daze had to take his word for it.'

I was still pondering the character of my Irish pal, when Everett called out from the ring. 'Okay, folks, that's it; everybody back on the bus. Change at the hotel then meet up for dinner at eight.'

7

When I stepped back into our suite just after seven o'clock, Jan was sitting at a small table, working on a file of accounts which she had slipped into our case.

'I see you're enjoying Newcastle, then,' I said.

'Saves me having to do it tomorrow. So how did it go? Have you spotted the saboteur yet?'

'I've spotted a room full of them. It could be anyone . . . other than Everett. I met a nice lady wrestler, though,' I added as an afterthought.

My wife smiled. 'Ah, but is she as good as me?'

'Couldn't say. Try some holds on me and I might be able to tell you.'

'Best of three falls?'

I closed the folder on the table. 'Or a submission . . .'

We wound up being five minutes late for dinner, but it didn't seem to matter. When we found the reception room that had been set aside for us, the afternoon's cast of characters was milling around, talking shop. There was a free bar set up against the wall. As we made our way towards it, I noticed that all the wrestlers seemed to be on soft drinks.

Happily, it wasn't compulsory. I helped myself to a Holsten, and poured a glass of white wine for Jan. As I was handing it to her, Everett came wandering across. Although we stood a little distant from the rest, he still spoke quietly.

'Any thoughts, Oz, now you've seen the operation?'

'I don't like that bastard Liam,' I said. 'How's that for starters?'

The big man grinned. 'Not many do. I only hired him because he has some of the best moves in the business. No, I meant . . .'

'I know what you meant. It's too early for me to get a handle on anything yet. I've been getting to know the wrestlers as best I can, but I thought it best to start off talking to the road crew. I had a chat with that big bloke, Gary O'Rourke.'

'The new guy?'

My eyebrows rose. 'New, is he?'

Everett chuckled. 'Well, maybe four months ain't so new. He's a good worker, that's for sure. Earned himself a pay rise after three months. Did he say anything of interest?'

'Only that he likes his job. You're a popular guy with the roadies . . . which cuts across the notion that one of them might have been behind your two incidents.'

'Maybe so.' He fell silent and his eyes dropped for a few moments. I looked over my shoulder, and noticed that Jan . . . looking absolutely sensational, I thought, in her white blouse and close-fitting grey skirt . . . had drifted off, to strike up a conversation with Sally Crockett and one of the American women wrestlers.

'Hell Oz,' Everett continued. 'I don't see any of the road crew being involved in this. Tony Reilly would be far more likely to do a deal with someone in the ring team. "Shut down GWA and I'll give you a top man contract with CWI." That's the offer he would make.

'You come across anything odd this afternoon?'

I looked up at him, and shook my head. 'To be honest, nothing. I don't know how much I'm going to be able to help you here.'

'You're helping me already, man,' he retorted. 'Just being my eyes and ears on the shop floor. One special thing you can do for me tomorrow night too.'

'What's that?' I asked, a shade apprehensively.

'I want you to keep an eye on the prop that Darius and Liam are going to use in that last scene, the aluminum crush barrier. Your seat during the bouts will be alongside the guy who rings the bell. That special barrier will be a few feet from you.

'There'll be action outside the ring in a few of the earlier bouts. I want you to make sure that no one moves the damn thing in the confusion, like switches it for the one next to it. If Darius came down from that height on a real steel barrier, it could finish him. And after what happened with that damn chair, I'm taking no chances.'

'I won't take my eyes off it, I promise. Even when I'm announcing.'

'That's good.' Everett paused. 'Say, I got another announcement for you to make tomorrow. We got a special guest in the audience, thanks to Jack Gantry. Remember those tickets I gave to your buddy Dylan? He and Susie won't be able to come after all, so Jack's persuaded the Lord Mayor of Newcastle to come along with him.

'We invited him, of course, but his office turned us down. An invitation from Mr Glasgow, though, that's different.' He grinned. 'It always helps to have influential friends, don't it. I want you to introduce him at the start of the show. Okay?'

'Sure. Just give me the details tomorrow.'

As Everett nodded I looked back towards Jan. Sally and the other woman had moved to join another group, but Liam Matthews had taken their place. She flashed me a quick look over his shoulder, a 'get over here' look.

'Hello honey,' I said, as casually as I could manage as I moved towards her. 'Sorry about that.'

Matthews looked over his shoulder. 'Well, well,' he said. 'Sure and if it isn't little Ozzie.' I kept the smile fixed on my face.

The Irishman stepped sideways, his shoulder blocking my path to Jan's side. 'Now Ozzie, you wouldn't be about to do anything as stupid as to come between the Man and this lovely lady? You wouldn't, would you?'

There was a swaggering menace about him; I felt this unfamiliar swelling in my chest and realised, to my surprise, that it was anger. 'This lovely lady is my wife, Liam,' I said, as evenly as I could.

He laughed, out loud. 'She never is! Your wife?' As he turned back to Jan I stepped past him and stood by her side. 'My God, you poor darlin'. How lucky it is for you that Liam's come along to show you what you've been missing. Why don't you ditch Mr Skinny here for the weekend? Why take an inch when you can have a whole foot?' He leered suggestively at her and scratched his crotch, like a Spanish crooner.

Maybe I shouldn't have done it while his hand was busy, but I couldn't stop myself.

In extreme circumstances, I once kicked a bloke in the balls, but in all my life I had never actually thumped anyone, until that moment. I didn't really know how to do it, but it seemed to come quite naturally. I bunched my right fist into a tight ball and threw it as hard and as fast as I could with all my weight behind it, at the centre of the Irishman's smug, grinning face. It was first time lucky: my punch caught him square on the nose, sending him reeling backwards.

As he straightened up, looking at me with complete astonishment, the blood came spurting out, flowing freely over his chin, staining his white, frilled shirt. It was at that point that I began to question the wisdom of choosing the

GWA Transcontinental Champion as the target for my first-ever right-hander.

Matthews' face twisted into a snarl. Jan tried to pull me away, but he launched himself at me. I, of course, was all punched out. I have no idea what would have happened if a huge black hand hadn't appeared out of nowhere, catching the Irishman by the throat and lifting him clear off his feet.

His face turned bright red in an instant, as his hands grasped Daze's wrist, and his feet kicked in mid-air. I looked round and up at the giant; the expression of sheer fury on his face scared me far more than Liam ever could have.

'This lady is my guest.' He ground out the words as the Transcontinental Champ's face began to turn blue. 'I don't know what you said to make Oz slug you, but I can guess. You ever say anything like it again, or you give Oz trouble over this, then however good you might be, you are fired from this organisation. Understood?'

Somehow Matthews managed to nod. Everett dropped him, like something nasty he'd been obliged to hold against his better instincts. 'That's good. Don't forget it now – I meant every word. Go get yourself cleaned up.'

The bloody, purple Irishman shot me a glance full of hatred, turned on his heel, and headed for the door.

'I'm sorry about that SoB, Jan,' said Everett, his anger giving way to embarrassment.

Diane had come to her husband's side. Surprisingly she looked shaken by the sudden violence. 'Most of the people in this industry are gentlemen,' she said, in a soft accent which I thought might have been Southern States or even Californian. 'That one certainly is not.'

'That's all right,' Jan grinned. 'He's lucky I didn't hit him, instead of Oz.' She slipped her arm around my waist. 'He doesn't always do that, you know. Only when he's hungry.'

The big man laughed. 'We better go eat then!' He stood

back, ushering Jan towards the buffet table through the gathering, which was gradually recovering its assembled voice. 'I reckon he got the message, Oz,' Everett whispered, as we followed her, and as Diane appeared at his side. 'But just in case, don't turn your back on the bastard tomorrow.'

That was something I had decided already for myself.

8

The working day began at twelve noon. Before that Jan and I had time for a wander round the centre of Newcastle in the watery sunshine of a mild winter day. We found that the commercial heart of the city was smaller than Glasgow, or even Edinburgh, but it had a nice feel to it, regardless.

The Eldon Square shopping centre housed some pretty impressive stores, but the place was made for me when I found a branch of Slater Menswear, master tailor by appointment to the glitterati of Glasgow. I took it as a sign from someone, and bought a new red bow tie for my first ever television appearance. Somehow, it seemed to steady the nerves which were gathering in my stomach.

The taxi which was to take Jan to the Metro Centre dropped me at the Arena dead on twelve noon. I could see at once that the roadies had been hard at work. The GWA logo seemed to shout at the city from its position on the wall above the main entrance, flanked by huge likenesses of Darius and Liam.

With the bag containing my dinner jacket and trousers slung over my shoulder, I stepped into the hall, after showing my staff pass to the security men, who were on guard already. Inside, all the temporary seating had been put in place, much of it set out on floor space which on other occasions was used by the city's basketball and ice hockey teams.

Since I had left the place, four lighting towers had been

built, one in each corner of the arena. I looked around and saw television cameras at three fixed points and a fourth, a remote, fixed on a long boom. Above the wrestlers' entrance to the Arena, curtained off at the top of the ramp, the roadies had erected a huge TV screen, from which a still image of The Behemoth snarled down at the empty hall.

'Not bad, huh?' It was a gentle voice, one I hadn't heard before. 'Sometimes he even scares me.'

In civvies, without the battle-dress and the white leather scrum cap, even Jerry Gradi's voice seemed to be different. He was wearing a blue suit, beautifully cut from a sort of shiny material, which I guessed had not come off the peg at Ralph Slater's, and patent leather shoes. He was clean shaven and his ginger hair was neatly groomed, so neatly that he could have been taken for a television presenter – okay, a huge television presenter.

'I didn't think you were on this week,' I said, genuinely surprised to see him.

He grinned at me. 'I'm not. I got a hamstring tweak, so all I'm doin' is yelling from the sidelines on video.'

'But Everett said you were on kids' TV this morning.'

'So I was, but my slot was done by nine-thirty. I was gonna stay in London for the day, but I changed my mind. They drove me to the airport and I caught a flight. Looks like you and I beat the rest of the guys here.

'You all set for your first night?' he asked.

'Just about.' I paused. 'What happens this afternoon? Everett said there would be a run-through.'

'That's right,' Jerry nodded. 'A dress rehearsal, so that we can get the TV angles right. The guys and gals will go through the whole show, minus the high impact moves.'

'Why do you miss those out?'

'We never take a chance on someone gettin' hurt just before the show. Even if it is unlikely. Our guys are careful.'

He looked at me. 'This may sound odd to you, but career-wise the worst thing a wrestler can do is to hurt another wrestler. Word gets around, and he becomes a bad risk. I known guys could only get work in Japan, because they were too dangerous.'

'Is there anyone in GWA you don't like working with?'

The big man considered my question at some length. 'Rockette split my head open once with that guitar prop of his. It's made to give on impact, but he caught me with the edge of the damn thing. I had woids with him after, and he's been careful since.' I grinned at the thought of what those 'woids' might have been.

'There's the Irish guy, I suppose. Everything he does is on the limit. Daze and I would can him, only he's the best goddamn flier either of us have ever seen.'

I must have looked puzzled again, for he explained. 'In this sport, your body dictates your style. The big guys, like me and the British Bulldog, and Hogan and Big André, some of us might have one or two off-the-ground moves, but mostly we go for power – piledrivers, bodyslams, that sort of thing. The smaller, lighter guys like Matthews, and Snuka, and Savage, they go for more acrobatic stuff. Matthews can fly two thirds of the way across the ring off that top rope.

'I never worked with him yet. When we do we'll try a move where he flies that far and I catch him. If it works it'll be great. If not, one of us could get hurt.'

'What about Everett?' I asked. 'I suppose he's a power man.'

Jerry Gradi chuckled. 'You really got a lot to learn about this business. Daze can do everything. He's the best ever . . . and he never hurt another wrestler in his life.'

I almost said 'Until last night', but decided that I'd let someone else tell him that, so that word couldn't get back to Matthews that I'd been boasting about popping him one.

Just then, the big double doors, behind us, crashed open, and a buzz of sound invaded the hall. The Irishman was at the front of the crowd of performers as they made their way into the auditorium, each carrying a hold-all containing, I supposed, their ring gear. He headed directly for me. I looked around to make sure that my new friend The Behemoth was still there.

Matthews stopped, his face a couple of feet from mine. I was pleased to see that his nose was slightly swollen; I hoped I'd broken it. 'Daze said I should apologise,' he said. 'So I apologise. Let's forget it, okay?'

I looked at him, straight in the eye. 'You apologise to my wife, Liam. Then we'll see what's to be forgotten. Okay?'

Unsmiling, he nodded, then turned and headed for the changing rooms.

Jerry Gradi watched him go. 'Looks like someone slugged that bastard at last,' he grunted. A huge grin broke out on his face as he saw my embarrassment. 'You?'

'Shh!' I urged him. 'He might hear you.'

Still chuckling, the gigantic Gradi headed up the aisle towards Everett, who had arrived with Diane by his side. I stuck a thumb through the strap of my suit-bag and followed Matthews, to change into my working clothes.

There were several dressing rooms at the side of the arena. One had been signed 'Ladies'. I found a door marked 'Officials', guessed it might mean me, and stepped inside. A bench ran the full length of one tiled wall, with a row of lockers facing it. The sign on the door had obviously meant nothing, for I spotted Darius Hencke – not difficult, since he was nearly seven feet tall – among a crowd of half-naked wrestlers. There was a spare peg beside him.

'You ready for action?' I asked him casually.

'You want me fix Liam for you?' he asked, with a grin.

'Could you? Like for real?'

'Sure, in two seconds maybe. But only if I could catch him. He's very fast, very agile.'

'This stunt you're doing this afternoon. How dangerous is it?'

The big German looked down at me. 'You try it, you'd break your focking neck. Even if you could pluck up courage to make jump, you'd never land right. Liam and me, we're good. We know what we can do and we go through with it, full throttle. It'll be great finish.'

As he spoke, I noticed a big black bruise just above the elbow of his tattooed right arm (wrestlers are crazy about tattoos). 'How did you do that?'

'In practice. My arm catch the outside of the barrier. That not happen again.'

I was impressed by his confidence. I was pleased too, by the way he was talking to me, like one of the GWA family; as, of course, I was. I changed into my announcer's gear, and fastened my new bow tie around my neck . . . okay, I admit it. It was a clip-on job.

I checked myself in the mirror. Yes, I looked the part; but just to curb my growing confidence my old friend the hamster began to run around in my stomach once more.

Back in the arena, Everett, in slacks and a Rioja-coloured cashmere blazer gathered the team around the ring. He was carrying a remote mike, like the one with which I had rehearsed. 'Okay,' he began, once he was satisfied that the whole cast was assembled. 'As usual we'll do two dry runs, the first to let the colour commentators see what's happening, the second for timing.

'First match: Scarletto and Rockette.' As if in answer to a question the two contestants each raised a hand. 'Good; get backstage, then, ready for your entrance. Sound men, cue up the music. Commentators, behind your desks. Oz, get in the ring. Start the intro on my signal.'

The hamster was running flat out as I stepped through the ropes. I had written the details of each bout on a series of cards, small enough to fit into my hand without, I hoped, it appearing too obvious on camera. I sneaked a quick look at the first one, and decided to do it from memory.

I watched Everett as he checked the hall, until finally he nodded and pointed at me. I took a deep breath and stepped into centre ring, raising my mike. 'Ladies and gentlemen . . .' I heard my own voice booming around the arena, and found to my surprise that I liked the sound. '. . . Welcome to Newcastle Arena, and welcome to the GWA *Saturday Night BattleGround*!'

'Our first contest of the evening is a heavyweight clash between two of the GWA's most colourful superstars. First, may I introduce to you, all the way from Palermo, Sicily . . .' I let my voice rise to a pitch on the name. '. . . Salvatore Scarletto!'

I stepped back as the intro music began – each wrestler has his own – and a spotlight picked out the bogus Mafioso as he stepped through the entrance curtain. I was having so much fun that Everett had to cue me again when it was time to go on.

My first introduction over, I slipped through the ropes, to my appointed seat at a small table near the guy whose job it was to ring the bell.

'Hey, that was very good.' Diane was in the front row, directly behind me. She leaned forward. 'The guy who recommended you did right by us. My husband said you were an actor. I was in the business before I met Everett and got drawn into Sports Entertainment. I made a few movies. What plays have you been in?'

I hoped she didn't see me gulp. 'I've had a few jobs around Scotland,' I mumbled. 'Stock stuff mostly. Detective parts.'

'How about movies?' she asked. 'Have you done any?'

'I was involved with Miles Grayson's Scottish movie,' I offered. I hoped that would satisfy her, but it didn't.

'Oh yeah.' She laughed, lightly. 'That tartan and heather epic he did, with that new Scots actress. What's her name again?'

'Dawn Phillips.'

'That's her. I read they were living together now.'

'So I believe.'

'You know her too?'

'Yes. I know her sister better: I've done quite a bit of work with her.'

'Wow!' Diane was beginning to sound impressed. 'Who did you play in the movie?'

I sighed, a bit theatrically. 'My scenes were all edited out. You've been in the business; you must know how it is.'

'Too true.'

Fortunately, I glanced up at the ring at that moment where Tommy Rockette was miming caving in his opponent's head with his prop guitar. The referee waved frantically at the guy on my right, who rang his bell.

I picked up my cue. 'And the winner by disqualification,' I called into my mike, from my ringside seat. 'Salvatore Scarletto!'

As instructed, I let the Italian whose real name was Johnny King pose in mid-ring, feigning exhaustion. As he exited, under the bottom rope, I climbed up the steps for my second introduction . . . trying not to be distracted by the fact that Everett Davis had chosen not to let his wife into the secret reason for my joining their grappling circus.

9

As far as I could see the rehearsals went perfectly, apart from the occasion in the second run-through when Sally Crockett's opponent fleetingly broke free from her costume – although I wondered initially whether that had been part of their routine.

I had nothing to do between five o'clock and show time, and so as the half-hour approached I strolled out to look for Jan at the main entrance, where she would be waiting for the boys.

She was in there, all right, in conversation with Gary O'Rourke. The big roadie was wearing slacks and a GWA bomber jacket with the word 'Security' written across the back.

'Hello darling.' I slipped my arm around my wife's waist as I spoke and kissed her lightly. 'Had a good afternoon?'

'You've seen one M&S, you've seen them all,' she replied. 'I bought football tops for the boys, though.'

'This is Jan, my wife,' I said to Gary. 'Jan, this is Gary, the hardest working guy in the whole circus. He builds the set then takes it down afterwards.'

'Aye,' said the Glaswegian, smiling. 'And in-between times I guard it.'

'Are you out here during the show?'

'No. Ah'm around ringside then.'

Jan tugged my arm. 'Look, there they are,' she called out.

'Just at the top of the entranceway.'

Jonathan and Colin spotted us at the same time and began to wave, frantically, but just at that moment they were cut off from our sight by a black, chauffeured car which pulled up in front of us. The grey-liveried driver opened the passenger door in a flash, and Jack Gantry stepped out, followed by another man. Both of them wore heavy gold chains of office.

Ever the politician, he recognised us at once. 'It's Jan, isn't it,' he said. 'And Oz, Susie's friends. What brings you down here?'

'I'm involved with the show,' I answered.

'Ahh,' Gantry exclaimed, with what struck me as a slightly forced show of interest. 'I didn't know that. Maybe we can have a chat afterwards, but now I have to take my Lord Mayor to meet our host.' Unbidden, Gary O'Rourke pulled the entrance door open, and the two dignitaries, neither giving him the briefest nods of thanks, swept inside.

They were hardly gone before Dad and the boys were on us, wee Colin grabbing me around the knees, and Jonathan, who always has been an adventurous lad, leaping at his Aunt Janet and giving her a large hug. My father looked me up and down, appraisingly, with an amused, slightly quirky smile on his face.

'A bit over-dressed for this time of day, are you not, son?' He shook his head, and the grin turned into a chuckle. 'Oz, how the f . . . or goodness' sake did you get involved in this?'

I was suddenly and acutely aware that by now there were a number of team players gathered at the entrance, looking for families and friends just like us. The reason for my presence was not a subject I wanted to discuss with anyone, not even Mac the Dentist, in such a public place.

'A pal of mine knew I needed a job, and introduced me to

Everett Davis.' As I answered him, I shot him a quick frown, which he read.

'Ahh, I see. Jonathan and Colin have always wondered what their Uncle Oz did for a living. Now they know.'

My nephews were both looking up at me, with a look which I'd have liked to think was adulation but which made me feel somehow like a world-famous cartoon Duck. 'Come on, Huey and Dewey,' I said, ruffling their hair in an Uncly sort of way. 'Let's get you to your seats.'

'Will we get to meet Daze?' Jonathan asked. 'And Liam Matthews? And the Black Angel of Death?'

'And the Bee-Moff?' chipped in his wee brother.

'Afterward, lads, afterwards. Let's go, now.'

The VIP block was directly behind my appointed position during the show. Jack Gantry and the Lord Mayor of Newcastle were already in their places, just a little further along the front row from Jan, my dad and the boys. Beyond them, Liam Matthews was hugging a middle-aged lady with bottle-blonde hair. 'Look after yourself now son,' I heard her say in an accent which sounded more like Belfast than the wrestler's professed home town of Dublin.

'Sure, 'n don't I always, Ma,' he replied, in the same tones.

The soft Southern Irish tones were back in place as he strolled along the row, past Gantry, to our seats. 'Hello there, my friend,' he said, so smoothly that I could almost smell the snake oil. 'And who would these be?'

I didn't answer him. Instead, I nodded towards Jan. The Irishman dropped as courtly a bow as you'll ever see, took her hand in his and kissed it lightly. 'A thousand apologies, lovely lady,' he whispered. My wife gave him a brief, unconvinced smile, and a very slight nod. He turned to me again.

'These are my nephews, Liam: Jonathan and Colin. Great

fans of yours, both of them. Aren't you, lads?'

In unison, Huey and Dewey nodded, mute, mouths hanging open slightly. Matthews grinned, suddenly awkward. I guessed he had still to learn how to respond to his younger admirers. 'And this is my dad,' I went on. 'Mac Blackstone.' My father stood up and extended his hand.

It's barely credible that any professional sportsman would try to muscle a handshake with a fifty-something man, yet with his standard cocky smirk back in place, that's exactly what Liam did; out of still-smouldering resentment against me, I can only guess.

There are two things you should never do with a dentist. One is to annoy him as he's standing over you with the drill in his hand. The other is to engage him in any sort of test of hand and forearm strength. In his younger days, Mac the Dentist was once challenged to an arm-wrestling duel by a disgruntled fisherman patient in a pub in Pittenweem. Quite accidentally, he broke the man's wrist.

For the second time in two days, I watched the arrogance leave Matthews' eyes. Then I saw him wince. My dad let him off lightly.

'Christ almighty, man,' he said. 'Where did you get a grip like that?'

'Thirty years of pulling out teeth, son.' He leaned slightly forward, peering at Matthews' face. 'Yours look fine though. Whoever did those two crowns in the front made a bloody good job of them. How did you lose them?' He was genuinely, professionally, interested.

'In a match,' the wrestler answered. 'When I was learning the business on the independent circuit.'

'And what did that teach you?'

'Never to work with a wrestler I didn't trust, or whose moves I hadn't sized up first.'

So there is an acceptable side to Liam Matthews, I thought. I began to wonder whether his arrogance sprang from his unreal lifestyle, and whether, maybe, I had done him some kind of a favour by banjoing him the night before. 'Nice to meet you, Mr Blackstone,' he said with a second, gentler, handshake. 'Got to go to work now.' He smiled down at the boys, and along at my wife. 'See you after the show, guys, Jan.'

I glanced at my watch. It was five minutes to six: almost show time. At the thought, my hamster kick-started its treadmill. I picked up my mike from the bell-man's table, and took my seat, laying my arm casually along the top of the prop crush-barrier. I looked along at the three commentary teams, all in place at their tables: German, Spanish, and closest to me, English. I saw that Jerry Gradi, wearing his ring-kit, minus the white leather scrum-cap, had joined the UK team. I nodded to him; he scowled at me and I realised that Behemoths don't smile.

All of a sudden the arena lights went out, stilling the chatter and giving me my cue to climb into the ring. I stood there, facing in the direction of the main camera, and looking straight at its red light, glowing in the darkness. My hamster was whizzing round in circles. There was a crash from the speakers as the *BattleGround* theme music began to play. There was a blue flashing as the giant screen lit up with the opening video sequence. In the four corners of the arena, thunderflashes exploded.

Then the spotlight hit me, and I realised, maybe for the first time, what a poser I was. It was just me in that light; the thousands in the arena, the millions on the other end of the transmission didn't matter at all.

'Good evening, ladies and gentlemen, welcome to Newcastle Arena, and welcome to the Global Wrestling Alliance *Saturday BattleGround*!' I heard my own voice, rich and full, booming round the hall.

'Before we begin this evening, the GWA is proud to welcome two special guests.' I paused, giving the second spotlight time to pick up its cue. 'In his home city, the Lord Mayor of Newcastle, Councillor Daniel Dees, and all the way from our home base, Mr Glasgow himself, Lord Provost Jack Gantry.' A few people in the crowd cheered. More of them booed actually, but that didn't matter, for their noise was drowned out by the canned acclamation on the effects tape.

I waited until it died down. 'And now, our first contest of the evening: a heavyweight clash between two of the GWA's most colourful superstars. First, may I introduce to you, all the way from Palermo, Sicily. . .'

Scarletto/King and Rockette/Rutherford really did put on a show. For all the full dress runs-through we had done, the live action was different since it had the added ingredient of the powerful heat of the television lighting. The two wrestlers, fit as they were, still poured sweat long before the end of their bout.

Rockette's guitar seemed to explode into a hundred pieces as it smashed into the back of Scarletto's head. The referee waved at the bell-man, who did his stuff. Then it was me again. 'And the winner by disqualification . . .'

Even concentrating on my introductions, and on the spoof barrier by my side, I had to admit that *BattleGround* was a terrific show. The fans, or 'marks' in Internet parlance, certainly thought so. They cheered the faces, they booed the heels, on time and in accordance with a script unknown to them and unseen by them. With their signs, banners, GWA tee-shirts and merchandise, they were all, without realising it, extras in a multi-million pound television extravaganza.

The loudest cheer of the show, before the main event, went to Sally Crockett, the GWA World Ladies' Champion. The pleasant lass I had met the day before turned into a tigress as soon as she climbed through the ropes. Even with my limited experience, I could see that she was something special. She could fly like a bird, she had martial arts moves that would have graced any Kung Fu movie, and she finished her match with a power-slam that looked so hard it almost winded me at ringside.

We ran to perfect time. My watch showed eight minutes past seven, exactly on schedule, as I climbed into the ring to announce the headline match. The lights went out again as soon as I set foot on the canvas. Most of the crowd recognised the signal for the Black Angel's entrance at once; those who didn't were encouraged by some more taped cheers. As the applause took hold another sound began to build from the speakers. The howling wind noise grew in volume, reaching its height as a single green-tinged spotlight picked out the curtained entrance to the arena, and the enormous figure of Darius Hencke.

He was wearing an ankle-length robe, which was in reality a flexible frame for the huge plastic wings on his back. He seemed to glide down the ramp which led to the ring, without entrance music, only that howling wind, lit by only that pale green light. He reached the steps and climbed up on to the ring apron, then seized the top rope and vaulted high over it, in a flying entrance.

The lights came up as he landed, and the crowd erupted. I glanced down at the ringside and saw my nephews on their feet as their idol paraded round the ring, screaming, 'Angel! Angel!' with the rest. So was my dad. I stored that one away for future use.

The great thing about Darius was that he didn't need an introduction. So, as the din subsided and as Darius peeled off his winged robe to reveal the black combat suit underneath, I stepped forward to do my bit.

'. . . and his opponent, in this title match, all the way from

Dublin, Ireland, the GWA Transcontinental Champion, Liam . . . The Man . . . Matthews!'

I gave him the build up he wanted. The boy couldn't have done it better himself. With his little, loud-jacketed manager Dee Dee by his side, he swaggered his way to the ring in time with his music, a jazzed up version of something by Thin Lizzy, dressed in green satin tights with shamrocks picked out in sequins. His hair was tied back in a pony tail, and round his waist he wore his gaudy leather and gold championship belt.

He unbuckled it as he stepped through the ropes, to use it as a weapon as he flew at Darius, whose back was turned – stupidly, I thought, given that this was Liam Matthews. But it was part of the act and the crowd loved it.

I beat it out of the ring before I got caught in the cross-fire, returning to my ringside seat and renewing my grip on the special crush barrier which was soon to come into use. As I looked back up at the action, Darius had regained his feet, but Liam was still battering him with the belt, until at last, the Angel managed to rip it from his grasp and throw it over the top rope, conveniently in the direction of one of the roadies, whose job it was to recover all the props.

Having disposed of his weapon, he put the Irishman's pony tail to good use, by grabbing it and using it as a lever to send him tumbling across the ring, in a beautifully disguised somersault.

That was only the start of ten minutes of absolute mayhem. I could hear my nephews screaming behind me as the television warriors gave as fine an imitation as I have ever seen of two guys knocking ten extremely large bells out of each other. First, the Angel, apparently recovered from the treacherous attack with the championship belt, battered Liam from ring-post to ring-post, as Dee Dee screamed constant abuse at the referee. Just when the crowd thought the Irishman was done, he countered with a series of lightning-fast wrestling moves which seemed to bewilder his huge opponent, culminating in a flying drop-kick from the top rope which stretched him out flat on his back.

I glanced round at the boys. Pure horror showed on their faces, until the Angel thrust an arm in the air, defeating Liam's attempt at a decisive pin-fall. Beyond them the eyes of the Lord Mayor of Newcastle were shining, while on his left, Jack Gantry sat, shaking his head in what looked like bewilderment.

The Angel rallied, then Matthews came back, each of them seeming to soak up punishment. In fact, as I had learned, much of it was real. The drop-kicks and forearm smashes were pulled slightly, but the power moves were another thing entirely. Each wrestler's well-being depended on his technique in absorbing their impact.

At last the moment of the climax arrived. I had seen Darius throw Liam over the top rope before, but from a distance away. This time he was no more than three feet from me as his broad, muscular back smacked into the padded mat surround. As Darius climbed to the top of the ring-post for the finisher, he lay with his eyes closed and his chest heaving from the very real exertion of his unreal fight. The pony tail had long since come undone, and his sweat-soaked hair was plastered across his face and around his neck.

I looked up at the Angel, balanced carefully high on the top turn-buckle almost twenty feet above me. In the second before he launched himself into the air, and as Dee Dee approached, I let go of the crowd barrier. Darius was in mid-air, his right arm stretched out before him in a flying v-shape, as the little manager pulled it over, so that it covered Matthews' body completely, but without touching him.

The crowd on the far side of the arena, those without a

clear view of the live action, could see every detail of what was happening on the giant screen. They roared as the big German flew; through the din I could hear the voices of the commentators rise in anticipation and mock horror. I thought I could even hear Jonathan scream.

Not even that cacophony though, could drown out the noise of the impact as the Black Angel of Death landed on the shiny barrier, exactly on time and exactly on target. It was a mixture of sounds: a metallic creaking and cracking, a booming rush as the pent-up breath left the German's body in a great exhalation, and a loud, agonised scream – from Liam Matthews.

Close as I was, at first even I thought that it was part of the act. But then Darius rolled over slowly onto the matting, as if badly winded at the very least, and I could see that I was wrong. The Irishman's face was screwed up, mouth open, eyes shut tight as if that would drive away the pain.

Several of the vertical aluminium struts which made up the centre of the barrier had snapped clean through with the impact of the Black Angel's dive. Three of them had pierced Liam, one through his shoulder, one through his ribcage and one through his abdomen. Blood was pouring from the wounds.

Unaware of the disaster, the ringside cameraman moved in for a close-up shot. I had been frozen to my seat, but as he approached I jumped up and pushed him away. I grabbed my mike, not knowing if it was live or not.

'Medics,' I heard myself yell. 'Get the medics down here!'

10

'Was Matthews really hurt, or was it all just part of the act?' Jack Gantry asked me, in a quiet, almost conspiratorial, voice. He was still wearing his heavy gold chain of office, even in the privacy of the GWA hospitality room. It was an hour after the accident, and I had just emerged from a gruelling session with Everett and Jerry Gradi, who had questioned everyone around the scene of the accident.

'No, that was for real.' I winced as I spoke. I had watched as the paramedics sedated Liam then cut him free from the barrier, leaving the piercing spokes in place for removal by surgeons.

'Diane went with him in the ambulance. She called ten minutes ago from the infirmary. He's in surgery, but they don't think that it's life-threatening. This can be a dangerous game, but Liam knew that. He signed up to take risks, like all these people.'

The Lord Provost nodded. 'No serious damage, then.'

'I didn't say that, Mr Gantry. It could be serious enough to keep him out of action indefinitely, and that would knock a big hole in the GWA's next pay-per-view event. Tonight's match was supposed to have been a warm-up for that.'

'Ach still,' Mr Glasgow muttered. 'Everett's a resourceful big guy. He'll paper over the cracks.'

'Here, listen,' he went on, his tone changing. 'Before I forget; I'm hosting another reception next Wednesday in the

Burrell Gallery. It's to mark the presentation of the city's annual arts awards the night after. I'd be very pleased if you and your lovely wife would come along, as my personal guests this time. Susie and Mike'll be there, and I'm sure you'll know lots of other people, given your line of work.'

'Thanks very much,' I said, unashamedly delighted by the Great Man's patronage, and amused privately by the fact that he too clearly thought that I was an actor. 'We'd love to.'

'That's good. Ring my office on Monday and give my secretary your address. He'll send you an official invitation and send a car to pick you both up on the night.'

As I nodded, he patted me on the arm, as if for being a good boy, and headed back to rejoin his colleague, the Lord Mayor.

I turned and wandered across the room to find my family. My dad and Jan were chatting quietly, watching wee Colin as his idol, the Bee-Moff, lifted him in one huge hand and sat him carefully on his shoulder. Jerry shot me a quick stage scowl, then grinned. The Monster was back in friendly mode. Meanwhile Jonathan – a lad after my own heart – was showing remarkable initiative for one so young, by practising a belly-to-belly suplex on Sally Crockett.

'You keep it up while you have the chance, wee man,' I told him. 'If you were ten years older you wouldn't get that close.'

The Ladies World Champion smiled. 'I'm not so sure about that,' she said. 'He's got a gleam in his eye, has this one.'

'Christ, don't tell him that,' spluttered Mac the Dentist. 'He's full of himself as it is.' He reached out to take Colin from Jerry, as the wrestler lifted him down from his perch, his huge paw almost engulfing the wee chap.

'Come on, you two lads. Time we were off. I promised your mother I'd have you home by midnight, and I'd rather have Mr Behemoth here mad at me than have our Ellie.'

'How is my sister?' I asked, as I walked them to the door.

'Oh, she's fine. She's got a date tonight. Not with that teacher guy she's been seeing though; someone new. A journalist from Dundee, I believe.'

'As long as she doesn't get her name in the papers. You drive carefully now.'

I watched them as they walked up the drive away from the Arena. When I turned, Everett was behind me, with Jan, who was carrying my suit-bag. 'Let's go find dinner,' he said. 'Diane's meeting us at the restaurant.'

The taxi which arrived less than a minute later took us to Twenty-One Queen Street, which Everett had been assured was the best restaurant in Newcastle. His wife had beaten us to it. She was seated at a corner table, looking tired and worried.

'What news?' the giant asked her, at once.

'He was still in the theatre when I left,' Diane answered. 'His mother's waiting back at the Infirmary for him to come out of the anaesthetic.

'The shoulder wound was nothing much, but the next one skidded off a rib and lacerated his side quite badly. The third is the most serious: the receiving surgeon thought it might have pierced a kidney.'

Everett's face twisted in a grimace. 'Let's hope not. Liam may be an s.h.i.t. but he's a talent. How's Mrs Matthews handling it?'

'Is she going to cut up rough like Tricia Manson, you mean? She won't do that. She told me that Liam's father was killed by Loyalist paramilitaries. The way she sees it, being in our industry has kept him away from that sort of trouble, and she's thankful for it. She accepts that what happened tonight is an occupational risk.'

She frowned at her husband. 'We are going to sue the

people who made those barriers though, aren't we? The design was supposed to have been tested, plus, they guaranteed that those struts wouldn't break, no way.'

'We'll talk to them Monday, but let's drop it for now. This dinner is to welcome Oz and Jan to the GWA family. So let's change the subject.'

'What are you doing about tonight's transmission?' Jan asked him, suddenly. 'Wasn't the ending a bit chaotic?'

Everett beamed at her, with professional pride. 'The station will run it uncut,' he said. 'I reviewed the footage straight away. To those who don't know about the accident, the ending is absolutely terrific. When Oz stands up and gets in the cameraman's face, between him and Liam so he can't get a shot, he looks really shocked and threatening. Then when he shouts "Medics!" that's really great television. You couldn't plan it, or rehearse it.

'So tonight we make the best of it. We take that and we use it, then we freeze on Oz's face in close-up, and run the credits over that.'

He turned to Diane. 'You see, babe. I told you it was the right thing to hire an actor for this job.'

Under the table, I kicked Jan sharply on the ankle to stop astonishment showing on her face. But she was better than that. She treated me to a smile which let me know, among other things, that she'd see me later about the sore ankle. 'Didn't I tell you, darlin',' she said, 'that if you just hung in there, your big break would come?

'It looks like Everett's made you a household name overnight. Who knows, now you might even get on *Coronation Street*.'

11

It was late on Tuesday afternoon when Everett loomed on my doorstep again.

We had shot the Sunday matches in Newcastle without further trouble, and the day had been made easier by the news that Liam's kidney hadn't been badly damaged, and that he could be back at work in a matter of weeks rather than months.

However, I had no opportunity at all to speak to the big man alone that day, and there was something I had to ask him. So I was pleased when he called me on Tuesday morning and asked if he could come to see me at four-thirty.

I was by myself when he arrived, since Jan, after her discussion over lunch with Susie the day before to talk terms, was spending her first working afternoon at the offices of The Gantry Group plc.

'Hi Oz,' he said, on my doorstep. He was in his business suit and spectacles, as before, but I could see at once that his expression was different. The big man was subdued. 'Thanks for seeing me. I know you got other business to do, but I got a few things to tell you that I can't handle over the phone.'

'Come on in,' I told him. I was prepared this time. There was a pot of coffee on the table, together with two litres of water and a plate of iced doughnuts.

'Is Liam still on the mend?' I asked, pouring Everett a

glass of water and myself a coffee as he arranged himself on the sofa and reached for a doughnut – no, two doughnuts.

'Yes. He's still in pain, from his kidney mostly, but he should be fit to leave hospital come Friday. Diane stayed down there. She's coming home today, then going back to collect him and bring him home.' He made the first of the doughnuts disappear.

'Where does he live?' As I put the question I realised that I had never pictured any of the GWA team as ordinary people with private, domestic lives, not even Everett and Diane, with whom we had enjoyed a quiet, civilised dinner on the previous Saturday night.

'He's got an apartment in Kelvin Court, out in the west of the city.'

I glanced at him in surprise, unable to suppress a smile at the thought of the spangled superstar among the sober occupants of Glasgow's famous art deco residence. 'How about you, where do you and Diane live?'

'Not far from Liam. We have a big old villa in Cleveden Drive.' He touched the top of his head, with a fleeting grin. 'It has high ceilings and doorways, so it suits. When we came here I thought we'd have to build something to suit my size, but we found plenty of property that was okay.' He looked around our living room. 'This would be okay too . . . if the doors were a little higher.' The second doughnut vanished.

I sat facing him and picked up my coffee. 'So? What's happened since Sunday? Have you tackled the people who made the barrier?'

He frowned. 'Damn right I have, first thing yesterday morning. They put their technical director on the first plane up from Birmingham, knowing the depth of the shit they were in. He went over the thing with a magnifying glass, checked every weld and every strut, including those that were taken out of Matthews in the hospital.

'He did all that, then he showed me that every second strut had been cut half-way through, then painted over with silver nail enamel so it wouldn't show. Someone turned that barrier into a death trap, Oz. I guess they figured that if Liam had been killed, we'd have been forced off the air.'

Everett looked at me, Daze eyes; hard behind his soft framed spectacles. 'Whoever's out to get me is raising the stakes.'

'How would they know to fix that particular barrier?' I asked him.

'They didn't. We checked: found they fixed all the goddamned barriers. It must have been done after the guys had finished their practice.'

'So it must have been someone in the very heart of the team,' I muttered, voicing a thought.

'Why d'you say that?'

'Because whoever doctored the barriers must have *known* that they had finished practising, and that they wouldn't try another before the show.' He considered the point and nodded, slowly.

'Everett, who else knows about this?'

'No one.'

'And who knows the real reason why I'm in the team?'

'No one. Absolutely no one; not even Greg McPhillips. I spun him a story about theft of cash and products.'

'Tell me this, then. Within the organisation, who do you trust completely?'

He answered at once; clearly, it was something he had been over many times before. 'Jerry. That's it. But even he doesn't know about the barriers, or about you.'

I moved on to dangerous ground. 'So why don't you trust your wife? How come she thinks I'm an actor, like everyone else? You can't believe that Diane is Tony Reilly's saboteur.'

For a moment, I thought that the mountain flinched.

'When I met The Princess on the circuit, she worked with CWI. More than that she was Tony Reilly's girlfriend. She switched to Triple W after the two of us got serious.'

'Okay, so she made her choice. You're still together. Why should she betray you to Reilly now?'

As I looked at him a very surprising and distressing thing happened. All of the fire went out of his eyes, and he seemed to shrink. 'I'm convinced she's having an affair, man. With Liam Matthews.'

'Matthews?' I gasped. 'Matthews may be a cocky, over-sexed braggart, and he may be hooked on danger, like all of you guys seem to be, but I cannot believe that he'd be so stupid that he'd screw your wife. What sort of proof have you got?'

My mind, as it can, raced ahead of itself. After a few seconds, my mouth caught up with it. 'Everett,' I said, sharply. 'I do not touch matrimonial work. Absolutely not!'

He shook his head. 'I don't want you to. As for proof, I don't have any. It's just a feeling, on top of circumstances: times she hasn't been where she was supposed to. Times when I've been away and she and Liam have been in Glasgow, and I've phoned home late and she hasn't been there, but Liam's been at his place, not out in the night clubs . . . A whole lot of things, all leading to this scenario I have in my head. She shuts me down, gets paid off by CWI, and she delivers Liam Matthews, one of the four hottest properties in sports entertainment today, gift-wrapped to her old lover, Reilly.'

'Hold on there,' I protested. 'A few days ago you told me that the pair of you had plans to start a family.'

He looked at me and his eyes glistened. 'Those are my plans alone. Diane is not so keen.

'Dammit Oz, if she is involved with Matthews, I'm not even sure I want to know. I love her and I'd overlook just about anything to hold on to her. I just want you to tell me for certain that she isn't selling me out to that son-of-a-bitch Reilly.'

I picked up the plate of doughnuts and held it out to him. He took three. 'Everett, I'm bloody certain I can tell you that now. I saw the look on her face after I thumped Liam on Friday, and after you half-throttled him. If she'd been having it off with the boy, she'd have been scared for him. But she wasn't; she looked excited, as if she disliked him as much as everyone else and wanted to see him get filled in.'

'Sure, because he'd just made a pass at Jan!'

'She probably didn't realise.'

He grunted in disbelief. 'What! After you busted his nose? Anyway, on Saturday she jumped into that ambulance without anyone telling her.'

He had me there. 'Listen man, if you're as concerned as that, why not have it out with her?'

'Two reasons. One; I'm afraid I'd be right. And two; if I was wrong she would never forgive me for suspecting her.'

'Get Matthews out of town then. Once he's healing, send him and his mum to the Maldives for a month. After that, sell his contract to Triple W.'

Everett the businessman looked at me in mock horror, then laughed. 'I couldn't do that, man. He's too damn good!'

I felt relieved that he had snapped out of his depressive phase.

'Let's get back to Jerry,' I said. 'Why do you rule him out?'

'He's like my brother; my oldest friend in the business.'

'But wasn't he around when all three incidents happened?'

'Yes.'

'And on Saturday he shouldn't have been. He turned up from London unexpectedly, didn't he?'

'Yeah.'

'And he was at the Arena before any of us got there in the afternoon?'

'Yeah, but . . . oh shit, Oz, not Jerry.'

I shook my head, to reassure him as much as anything. I didn't like seeing Daze lay all his weaknesses before me. 'I don't think it's him either. He has a financial stake in the GWA, and he strikes me as a dead honest guy. All I'm saying is that if you want me to do this job, you have to be prepared to consider everything. Christ, you're just through telling me you think your wife's behind it.'

Everett sighed, wearily. 'Okay, I get the picture. I won't handcuff you, Oz. Treat everyone the same.' He chuckled. 'Yeah, even me. Maybe I've got more reason than anyone to kill Liam Matthews.'

12

My client, and seven out of the ten doughnuts, had gone by the time Jan got home at six forty-five. She found me at work in the kitchen with my old friend Mr Wok.

'Have you finished work for the day?' she asked.

'Yes, Boss. I did three interviews this morning, and transcribed them this afternoon, with a visit from Daze in between. My time sheets are all made up too.' Jan and I had made a deal when we married and set up home. She did all my invoicing, but on condition that I maintained a meticulous record of my work activity, on an hourly basis. Until then I had always operated on the basis of a fixed charge for a job; my wife, like the first-class accountant she was, made me change to a time basis, with expenses on top.

'What did Everett have to say? Is Matthews still on the mend?'

I tossed strips of white fish into the wok, adding them to the mix of yellow pepper, red onion, mushrooms and bean sprouts which I had fried until they were soft, and turning them quickly as they seared in the hot oil. Jan peered over my shoulder and nodded, approvingly. A few strands of her long brown hair flicked across my lips, and her breath warmed my cheek. God, how good she made me feel. God, how much I loved her.

'The luck of the Irish, indeed,' I answered. 'The boy Liam will be released from the RVI on Friday, into the tender care of Mrs Diane Davis, with whom, so big Daze suspects, he is having an affair.'

'Ah,' she murmured, as she chose a bottle of full-bodied Fat Bastard Chardonnay from our wine rack. 'That's why he exploded on Friday night. I thought at the time that he looked as if he'd like to kill the guy. And here was me, thinking that he was saving you from a doing, or defending my honour, or both.'

'Is she, do you think?'

'What? Having it away with that Irish ego-maniac? Not a chance. Diane's a classy lady: I can't imagine her being into rough trade, and he certainly fits that category.' She paused as she levered out the cork with our waiter's friend. 'Mind you,' she mused, 'I could see him thinking she was. The way he was all over her at dinner on Saturday shows that he's insecure with her. And that Liam does make a play for every woman he sees.'

She watched me as I spooned the stir-fry, and its dark, oily liquor, into two bowls. 'Is that all he wanted, then: a shoulder to cry on?'

'Oh no, far from it,' I told her, setting our supper on the table. 'He came to tell me that the barrier which caused the accident didn't just break. It was sabotaged. Somebody was after killing Matthews, or at least wouldn't have minded if he'd been killed.'

Jan whistled. 'Wow! Is he sure?'

'Certain. At the start of this thing I thought that Everett was maybe just a bit paranoid, and that the empty tape cassettes, plus the guy Manson having his head cracked, could have been unrelated accidents. Not this time, though, no way. The big bloke's right: someone's after the GWA.'

'That's three tries to put them off the air and three failures,' Jan pondered.

'Aye, and each one more extreme than the one before.

God knows what Everett's enemy will try next.'

She frowned at me. 'I'm not sure I want you to be around to find out.'

'I promised him, love . . . and the money's good.'

'Stuff that for an excuse. I earn good money too, but safely. Anyway, shouldn't the police be involved? This sounds like attempted murder to me.'

'I did try to suggest that to him, but he wasn't having any of it. He's afraid the publicity would scare the crowds away, and even worse, that it might frighten off his television networks. I said I'd go along with him for another couple of weeks. My best hope is that whoever's behind all this will give it up as a bad job.

'Come on now,' I told her, to end the discussion. 'I've been slaving for hours over this meal, and monkfish costs a bloody fortune. Give it some attention.'

She nodded and bent to worship my kitchen skills. When the devotions were over I asked Jan about her day. 'What does The Gantry Group look like from the inside?'

'It looks profitable,' she said. 'Susie thinks it should be more profitable than it is, in fact, and that's the problem. She reckons that there's either been incompetence or dishonesty. She's asked me to find out which.'

'Who owns the business?' I asked her.

'Lord Provost Gantry and Susie,' she replied. 'Lock, stock and barrel through a family trust which holds all the shares. They have in-house book-keeping and accounts staff, but until now, the Finance Director has been a man called Joseph Donn, the old pal of the Lord Provost's that I mentioned the other night.' She wrinkled her nose in a classic Jan gesture of disapproval. 'He's a part qualified accountant, not a member of the Institute, but he's looked after the books since the earliest days of the group, when it was just a small building firm on the South Side.

'Naturally when Susie fired him, Mr Donn didn't take it too well: he even appealed to her father, but Susie told the LP that if he tried to interfere, he'd better be ready to run the business again, because she'd be off.'

I grinned. I know I'd only met Susie Gantry once, but I could see her facing down Mr Glasgow.

'In time, the group will probably take on a new Finance Director, full-time. Before that happens, I've been called in to do a forensic job, finding out where any slippages may have happened.'

'Does Susie think that Mr Donn was bent?'

Jan chuckled; a deep throaty sound that she used to make even as a wee lass in primary school. Even in those days, it made my heart skip a beat. 'No, her assessment is that he's just stupid. She doesn't reckon he has the brains to be bent. She thinks that someone in the business may have been at it, though, and that Donn just lacked the skill to spot it.

'If she's underestimating him, I'll find out.'

'What does the group do?' I asked. 'Construction, is it?'

'That's the core business, alongside property and land holdings. Gantry Developments did this place, as a matter of fact, among many others. The group's well diversified now. It owns a portfolio of housing stock which it built for economic rent with public agency support. It has a dozen pubs in Glasgow and the West of Scotland, and a chain of ten private nursing homes. On top of all that it developed a major retail park on the east side of Glasgow and has another on the drawing board out in Barlanark.

'There's a lot to it, so I'm going to have to spend quite a bit of time there over the next couple of weeks. It'll mean I have to work weekends, so you'll be going to Barcelona on your own.' She topped up her wine glass, and mine. 'In net asset terms, the business is probably worth about thirty million. Across the group, Jack Gantry must employ, full-time and equivalents, upwards of a thousand people.'

'Jesus!' I whispered. 'The guy can afford to buy his own gold chain. He didn't need the city to give him one.'

'He did buy it, in a way. For the quick look I've had at the books, I saw that they show him as a major donor to the Labour Party in Scotland. I don't think that's where his influence comes from, though. He's been a councillor for over thirty years, Chairman of the Labour Party in Scotland, and president of the local authorities' convention.

'At civic level, he's the most powerful man in Scotland.'

'Why isn't he in Parliament?' I wondered.

'I asked Susie that very question. He doesn't want to be, apparently. He's interested in Glasgow, and he feels that he can do more for the city by staying in street level politics.'

'Quite a guy, is Mr Gantry,' I said. 'And we're in his good books too.'

Jan looked at me, puzzled. 'What do you mean?'

I reached across, picked up a big white envelope which had been lying on the sideboard, and handed it to her. 'This arrived today,' I told her.

She opened it and withdrew a heavy card, bearing Glasgow's coat of arms, and with an inscription in rich gold leaf. She frowned slightly as she read it. 'The City Arts Awards . . .' she began.

'That's right, my darling. You and I are invited to a night out with the luvvies, courtesy of Jack Gantry himself.'

13

I nudged Jan as we stood in the cloakroom queue. 'D'you think Dylan really fancies Susie, or is it just a career move?' I whispered in her ear. The Detective Inspector and the Lady Provost stood five couples ahead of us, he with his arm around her shoulders.

'He has to be on the level,' she murmured. 'Susie'd have seen through him in two minutes if he was on the make. And if it was a matter of her being into coppers, she could have someone higher up the tree than Mike.

'Anyway,' she went on, 'I quite like him. He may be a poser, but he's a friendly chap, and there's no harm in him.'

I grunted at that one, as old memories came back. 'There is if he thinks he can fit you up for something.' As I spoke, he and Susie handed in their coats and moved on towards the main hall of the Gallery where the reception was being held.

The Burrell Collection is the treasure of which the City of Glasgow is most proud . . . although for the life of me I cannot see why. It was left to the people donkey's years ago by one of its millionaires, as a sort of personal memorial. However the will wasn't straightforward. Sir William Burrell specified that his valuables should be put on show together, in a Gallery built by the council with money bequeathed for the purpose.

Since City Fathers tend to be childish on the whole, it took them a few decades to decide on a site and a design, by which time the bequest had dwindled in value and the public purse had to make up the shortfall. But as soon as it was up and opened, on a green field site in the Pollok Estate, the Burrell Collection became the showpiece that its founder had intended. For a brief period it was even trumpeted as the most-visited tourist site in Scotland, until someone realised that the smoking ban within the building meant that every time visitors nipped out for a fag they were counted as new entrants.

In our time in Glasgow, Jan and I had never visited the Burrell Gallery before. As I looked up at the great vaulted glass ceiling and took in the spacious design, I realised why Jack Gantry liked it as a venue.

The Lord Provost had been as good as his word. We had been picked up at the appointed time by a civic limo which we found we were sharing with the Convener of the Transport Committee and his wife. He was a pleasant, earnest, youngish man, with big glasses and a slightly awkward air, which was explained when he told us that he always felt guilty when using the Council Daimler rather than a bus. Jan and I, and the Convener's wife, said nothing. We were enjoying the ride.

Our travelling companions chummed us across to the bar. The event was being sponsored by a drinks company; I guessed that was why there were spirits available as well as the usual wine.

'What do you think of the new People's Palace then, folks?' There was a suppressed giggle in the woman's voice which came from behind me as I handed Jan her gin and tonic and picked up my own. Susie Gantry's red hair still had its electric frizz, but she seemed more relaxed than on our first meeting. I wondered whether behind her confident façade lived someone who was inherently shy with strangers.

'It's . . . er, very impressive,' I offered.

'Bloody should be,' she chortled. 'It took about forty years to build.'

'Not a Gantry job, then,' offered Mike Dylan, by her side.

She frowned at him. 'Cheeky so-and-so. Our slogan is that quality deserves time, my dear, but we're not that deliberate.'

'What's so great about the collection?' Jan asked.

'Judge for yourself,' Susie responded. 'Let's take a walk round.'

I could tell that she enjoyed her Lady Provost role as she led us around the Gallery. Truth be told, I didn't think much of the exhibits, apart from a couple of pictures and some Roman masonry which appeared to have been looted from the South of France. But the crowd was something else. It was like being on a television or movie set as we moved among the faces.

Everybody who was anybody in a Scottish showbiz context – and quite a few UK celebrities too – seemed to be there, and Susie Gantry seemed to know them all. 'Hello, Elaine,' she called out to one face. 'How're you doing, Ally?' to another. 'Nice to see you, Robbie,' to a third. And always she was acknowledged warmly. The beautiful people of Glasgow seemed pleased to be hailed by Jack Gantry's daughter.

Our circular tour brought us back – via the bar, of course – to a small dais set up in front of the enormous Warwick vase. 'What do you think?' Susie asked.

If diplomacy, timing and a sense of decorum are essentials for higher rank in the police service, as they are, DI Dylan can forget any notion of ever wearing a Chief Constable's epaulettes.

'I seem to remember,' he burst out, wearing a huge grin, 'that when this place opened, some Edinburgh councillor got himself on the Glaswegian death list by calling it

Steptoe's yard.' He looked around, still beaming expansively. 'I'd say he got it right.'

Unfortunately for Mike, the only direction in which he hadn't looked was immediately behind him, where Jack Gantry was standing.

'Indeed, Inspector,' the Lord Provost grated. 'I wasn't aware that you were an expert in antiquities. In fact from what my daughter's been saying, I wasn't aware that you were an expert in anything.'

Dylan turned three different colours in as many seconds. 'Just a joke, sir,' he offered, lamely, his grin turning cheesy.

'No it wasn't, son. It was an insult. An old insult, long buried, but dug up again.' Jack Gantry's voice dropped to a whisper, but it was probably the most menacing whisper I had ever heard. 'There's enough damned comedians here tonight, Michael. Okay?'

'I'm sorry, sir . . .' The detective's apology faded away as the Lord Provost turned on his heel and stalked off.

He looked down at Susie. 'Thanks for your support,' he moaned.

The wee firebrand looked up at him angrily. For a moment I thought she was going to explode too. 'Don't mention it,' she snapped. 'I thought you knew by now that my dad loves this city more than anything . . . even me.'

'Okay, but—'

She cut him off. 'But nothing. He's Glasgow's First Citizen in every respect. Daft he may be, but it's the cultural capital of his universe. My dad may be a hard man from the Gorbals, but he's no Philistine. This city's art galleries, museums, theatres, concert halls are his pride and joy. He loves opera, the theatre and music. He's an art collector. When I take you to his house on Saturday, you'll see half a million quid's worth of pictures hanging on his walls.

'As far as this place is concerned, he believes that Glasgow has done a great job for the nation in displaying the Burrell Collection; and by Glasgow he means the Council. When you mock this, you're mocking him.'

I thought it was time to lighten things up a bit. 'Eh Susie,' I ventured. 'Tell me what football team he supports, so I don't put my foot in it.'

She was still glaring as she looked round at me, until she caught my eye, and began to laugh. 'I'm sorry, people,' she said. 'It's not fair to involve you in our wee domestic.' She glanced up at Mike once more. 'You know Dylan, I must love you or something. It's the only reason I can think of for the fact that you're still standing.' He looked at her gratefully, like a big soft dog that's just been given a biscuit.

'As for football, Oz,' Susie continued. 'You're on safe ground there. The Lord Provost is an atheist in that respect. In private he actually believes that football's harmful to Glasgow's good name.'

'Judging by what I've seen of it lately,' I told her, 'I think he's right.'

She laughed again, then took my wife by the arm. 'How's things going?' she asked quietly. 'I'm sorry I wasn't in the office this afternoon. I was looking forward to catching up with you.'

'I'm getting through it,' Jan replied. 'But it's not easy. The construction and development side of the group is okay, that's quite certain. It's very profitable. The expected return on investment from the housing portfolio is very clearly defined too, and you're achieving it.

'The retail arm, the pubs and so on, that's not so certain. I'm having to analyse their performance one by one. It's relatively easy to bleed cash out of businesses like that, and it can be very hard to detect too. Once I've looked at individual profitability, I'll be able to see which managers are operating at one hundred per cent efficiency, and whether any are out of line.'

'What if they are?'

'If it's incompetence, that could show up easily. If not, that will be more difficult to nail down.'

'How do we go about it?' Susie paused. 'There are so many potential fiddles in the pub trade.'

'I know, but the most common is the one where the staff sell their own drink across the bar, in among the legitimate sales, but don't ring it up, so that it doesn't go through stock control. If we think that could be happening, we need to set traps.'

'Such as?'

'Put people in among the punters to watch and spot it. That's one way. Have spot raids by stock control teams to check the bar codes of all products on display for sale. That's another.' Jan smiled, grimly. 'Sack everyone on the staff. That's a third.'

'And maybe the easiest,' Susie retorted.

'Maybe, but I don't think your dad would like it if someone took the group to a tribunal for unfair dismissal. No, if the pub chain is underperforming overall, there's a fourth option.'

'What's that?'

'Call in all the managers, and give them profit targets to be hit on a quarterly or six-monthly basis. That way, if some of them are on the fiddle, they'll make damn sure that the group gets its profit before they start taking theirs.'

God, she's clever, I thought, as she looked at Susie Gantry. 'In my experience,' she said, 'if the staff want to skim a bit for themselves off a retail business – especially a busy pub – it's bloody difficult to prevent it. All you can do is set a tolerable limit and make sure they stay within it.'

'You could call us in,' Dylan suggested, tentatively.

Both women turned and stared at him in disbelief. 'What would happen to the CID if it was asked to investigate every potential pub fiddle in Glasgow?' Jan asked him. 'You don't have the manpower to investigate small-scale fraud, Mike, and you know it. Your specialists concentrate on the big stuff, and the rest gets left to sort itself out.'

He nodded his head, in reluctant agreement. 'Yes, I suppose you're right.' He grinned at me. 'Hang in there, Oz,' he said. 'There could be some business here for you too.'

'And what would that be, Mike?' asked Jack Gantry, jovially, his good temper restored as he stepped past the policeman and up on to the dais to address the City's guests.

'Nothing you'd approve of, I doubt, sir,' replied Dylan. 'We're discussing privatisation: in the field of criminal investigation.'

Gantry's chain gleamed as the light caught it. 'Don't sell me short, son. I'm one of the new breed. I'll privatise anything as long as it's efficient . . . and profitable.'

He drew himself up and beamed at the gathering of celebrities, a star himself in their firmament.

14

'Would you be interested in a bit more undercover work?'

I looked at her incredulously. She lay on her front on top of the duvet, propped up on her elbows, with one foot raised in the air. The summer tan still showed on her body, or at least was pointed up by the whiteness of her round, firm bum. God, she was gorgeous, was my wife.

'Again?' I gasped. 'What do you think I am? The Parish bull?'

Her breasts bounced lightly as she chortled. 'I know very well what you are, my love.

'Don't worry, I'm not expecting the impossible all of a sudden. No, I meant business-type undercover work; the same as you're doing for Everett. Remember that discussion with Susie last night? We may well have to make plans to put watchers into her pubs.'

I sat upright, and shook my head, as hard as I could. 'No. Definitely not. That's not what I do: I am a private enquiry agent, non-matrimonial, and that's the way I like it. I work for lawyers, not for publicans. The only reason I'm involved with this wrestling carry-on is because Greg McPhillips put me in the frame for it, and because he's a good client.'

Even when she was a wee girl, Jan's dismissive laugh was one of her trademarks. I had heard it thousands of times, usually directed at me. 'Aye sure, that's the only reason,' she drawled. 'Your mother was the only person I ever knew who could make you do anything you didn't want to . . . apart from me, that is.

'You're into the cloak and dagger stuff, and you know it. I remember when you and Thingy were off on the trail of that missing money, and on the run from Ricky Ross at the same time. You loved every minute of it. Even at the time I reckoned . . .'

She stopped suddenly; but I knew her as well as she knew me.

'You reckoned that it was excitement I fell for, as much as Primavera. I guess you were right, too.'

'No, I'm sorry: I was just being bitchy. I was in a relationship at that time as well, remember. We were ex's then, you and I, and she brought something different into your life. Prim's a great girl, and a powerhouse as well. I might have been secretly jealous of her, and secretly afraid that she was taking you away from me for good, but I've never disliked her.'

She smiled at me, in an intimate, gleaming way. 'Mind you, I can afford to be magnanimous, the way it's all turned out.'

'Maybe so,' I said. Since the morning of my return from Spain, Jan and I had never discussed Primavera Phillips, nor my relationship with her. Now that the subject had come up, it made me feel slightly uncomfortable. 'But you're still not going to talk me into acting as a snooper in Susie Gantry's pubs.'

'Why not? We'll need someone we can trust.'

'Which reason would you like? I'm too busy? Or will you settle for the fact that I just don't like wearing a dirty raincoat?'

She grabbed a handful of my chest hair. 'Daft bugger. You don't have a dirty raincoat. You don't have a raincoat, period.'

And then she paused, and gave me the Look. Although

we'd been together for most of our lives, I'd seen it only a few times before: for example, on Jan's sixteenth birthday when we made love for the first time, on my eighteenth when she gave me a signet ring, one time in Jan's flat, with our respective partners present but happily unaware, and a few months before, when she said, 'Okay, I'll marry you.'

I looked back at her, and I waited. 'Speaking of periods,' she said, 'I don't know if you've noticed, but I haven't had one for a while.'

I gulped, so hard that I almost choked. 'How long?'

'Seven weeks. I bought a tester kit yesterday. You're going to be a Daddy, Oz Blackstone.'

Sometimes your brain just cuts out. Know what I mean? I think I might have gulped a few more times, but otherwise I just sprawled there and stared at her. I don't know why I was surprised; Jan had been off the pill for a couple of months. Mind you over the years, and even when she was living with Noosh, we had taken a few chances, so maybe I had just assumed that making a baby was something we'd have to work at for a while, and hope that we got lucky.

There are times that live for ever, during which everything done and said burns itself into your brain. In such moments, you'd imagine that everyone would choose words which were weighed, meaningful and appropriate to the occasion. Not us Blackstones.

I stared at my amazing, pregnant wife, open-mouthed. 'Fuck me!' I whispered.

She beamed, and pulled herself towards me, across the bed. 'How could I refuse such a generous and spontaneous offer?' she said.

15

'Cherish every moment, son,' my dad told me when we phoned Anstruther to break the news. 'The expectation of your first child is one of life's great times. It's exciting and frightening all at the same time.

'It's a great test of patience too. Come next September you'll think she's been pregnant for ever, and to be able to feel the baby moving about, yet not know what it looks like ... my son, I can't find the words. You'll just have to experience it yourself.'

'Chances are we will know what he or she looks like. Jan will be scanned, I suppose.'

At the other end of the line, Mac the Dentist grunted. 'Hmph! There are some areas in which medical science has gone too far,' he growled. 'I remember when our Ellie was born. Not that I was there, mind you. Our consultant didn't approve of fathers being involved at any stage of the process, bar one.

'But the moment when I was allowed in to see your mother and she said to me "Mac, we have a daughter." Och ...' He paused, and in that moment my eyes went misty. 'It was one of the greatest moments of my life, and the revelation was part of it. I don't think my medical colleagues should deny that to people.

'If the Lord had meant you to know whether it was going to be a boy or a girl He'd have put a window in there somewhere. Just don't let the buggers tell you. Mind that now!'

I didn't realise it, but I was still smiling as I walked into the main arena at the Scottish Exhibition and Conference Centre, just before one on Friday afternoon, the designated gathering hour for the first run-through of the weekend's *BattleGround*.

'Hey guy,' The Behemoth called across, as I turned into the doorway, 'was it that good?'

I strolled across to join him. He was wearing jogging bottoms, and a grey zipper top which made him look even more like a small mountain.

'As a matter of fact it was, Jerry. Jan's having a baby.'

The rugged face cracked into a smile, and a laugh came rumbling up like a volcano. 'That's great, Oz. Ain't it amazing what you can do, even with limited equipment.'

My 'Cheeky bastard' response jumped out before I had time to think just who I was calling a cheeky bastard. Happily, Jerry was my firm friend; and in any event he was the sort of honey monster who was as gentle in private as he could be ferocious in public.

'Hey Everett,' he called across. I turned and saw Daze behind me, vast in his training gear. 'Our ring announcer's gonna be a dad.'

The giant smiled, stretching out his hand as he walked across, but I could detect a look in his eyes that could have been a mixture of pain and jealousy. He kept it out of his voice though. 'Congratulations, my man. I don't need to ask whether you're pleased. Did you plan to have a baby this soon after you got married?'

'Planning isn't something Jan and I have ever been too strong on,' I replied.

Suddenly I felt self-conscious. I hadn't really wanted to share the news with anyone that soon. It had escaped in an unguarded moment. 'How's Liam doing?' I asked, to change the subject.

'He's healing up fine,' Everett replied. 'Diane just called me from her car. She expects to deliver him back home within an hour.'

'She comin' here for the run-through?' asked Jerry.

'Eventually.' I wondered why the big man was so casual, given the fact of his wife delivering the man he suspected of being her lover back to his pad in Kelvin Court – stitches or not – but he answered me straight away. 'Liam's mother is waiting there for them. Diane was given nursing notes by the hospital and she has to go over them with her. She'll be back here for our rehearsal though.'

'Are you guys wrestling this week?' I asked.

'I am,' said Daze. 'Jerry's still nursing that muscle strain; but we're going to have a confrontation.'

'What d'you mean?'

'I'm fighting Rockette tomorrow. The Princess will distract me again . . .'. He grinned suddenly and disarmingly. 'I'm dumb, see . . .

'While I'm looking at Diane, Tommy will break one of his trick guitars across my back. I'll lose my cool at last, pick him up by the throat and throw him over the top rope, straight at her.'

Christ, Everett, I thought. *I know you suspect her of being Mata Hari, but chucking a seventeen stone wrestler at her might be a bit extreme.*

'However,' he went on, looking at me as if he was reading my mind, 'Jerry will be doing colour commentary at ringside. He'll jump up and catch Rockette in mid-air, then he'll climb into the ring with Diane behind him. The show will fade just as he and I are starting to get it on.

'How does that sound, Announcer?'

'It sounds fine, but what's it about?' I knew enough about the GWA by this time to understand that all their 'confrontations' fitted within a wider story-line involving the characters.

'The purpose is to promote bookings for the Edinburgh pay-per-view event, where Jerry and I are in the headline cage match.'

I frowned. 'What's a cage match?'

'Hell on earth,' Jerry growled. 'We build a fifteen foot high steel cage all around the ring, so that no one else can get in and so's the wrestlers can't get out. The winner is the guy who manages to climb over the top of the cage and land on his feet on the other side. Havin' the cage there lets you do all sorts of manoeuvres that just ain't possible in the ring. Only the very top guys can do cage matches. I hate 'em.'

'Why?' I asked him. 'You're one of the very top guys.'

'Don't like heights,' he mumbled, sheepishly.

'Oz,' interrupted Everett, smiling at his friend's confession, 'I've told Jerry about the barriers. And about you. I know we agreed that it would be our secret, but I couldn't have stood The Behemoth here finding out and thinking I didn't trust him.'

Of course, by that time I was convinced of his innocence too. 'Fair enough,' I said. 'What do you think of the situation, Jerry?'

'I agree with Ev. It has to be that SoB Reilly. He's gotta have someone on the inside.' He looked at me, and I saw for the first time the sharp intelligence in his eyes. 'You see, Oz, the only people who care about our business enough to try to do us harm, or do us good, are other people in our industry.

'We're unique. There's no other branch of sports or entertainment like us. We've grown up over the years because we've traded on a basic human instinct, lust for violence. A hundred and fifty years ago, folks used to watch executions. Today they come and watch us pretend to kill each other.' He jerked a thumb towards Daze.

'We're like elephants, him and me, and I don't mean in size. We don't prey on anyone and we don't have no one prey on us. The GWA is a new young bull elephant among the herd, and CWI is the old bull. Reilly's out to do us in before we get too strong for him.'

I tried to push it away, but I couldn't. A vision of Jerry Gradi servicing a cow elephant came into my mind. I smiled, but managed to stop short of laughing. 'I see,' I managed to say, then felt that a slight change of tack was called for.

'What are you going to do about Liam's championship belt?' I asked.

'Good question,' said Everett. 'We're having an eliminator tomorrow. Salvatore Scarletto, Johnny King, that is, fights Chris Manson; winner gets a match with Darius for the belt at the pay-per-view.'

'Has Johnny got enough flair for that?'

Everett nodded approval. 'Another good question. Yeah, he has. The babes like him well enough, and he has good skills. He's a coming boy. Not yet, though. He'll give the Angel a battle, then he'll go down. Darius is ready to move up; Jerry and I need someone else on the top shelf.'

He turned to his colleague. 'So let's get to it. And Oz, while you're not announcing you be looking out for trouble. I'm cutting down on the high impact stuff this week and on the props, but I want you to try to spot anything else, anything at all, that might go wrong.'

'What about Rockette's guitar?' I asked him, at once. 'That's a prop.'

'You're right, it is: so this is how we handle it. Tommy

brings it to the ring as usual, he hands it to you, and when he's ready, you hand it back to him. That should be okay . . .' He shot me a grim smile. 'Unless someone puts a bomb in it, that is.'

16

I was beginning to feel like a seasoned pro as we did the Friday run-through. None of the wrestlers showed all of their routines, but even the limited moves which they practised were slick, powerful and impressive.

Whatever my nephew, wee Colin, might have felt about his idol, the Bee-moff, I had my own favourite, and she was Sally Crockett. It struck me, as I watched her rehearse her match with Linda Lashe, a French girl with significant attributes, that pound-for-pound the GWA's top woman superstar was as fine an athlete as I had ever seen.

She had speed, she had daring and she had considerable physical strength; on top of all that, it seemed to me with my limited knowledge that she was a pretty good wrestler too. I said as much to Jerry as we stood at ringside, watching her work.

'Yeah, ain't she just,' my giant pal murmured. His voice had an odd, dreamy sound, which made me look up at him. He was gazing at the ring with a look of pure adoration, as the GWA World Ladies' Champion leapt from the top rope, caught her opponent's head between her feet and flipped her across the ring.

'Here,' I said. 'You fancy her, don't you?'

He didn't react at first, then he looked sideways at me. 'She's one of the most talented wrestlers I've ever seen,' he answered, well on the defensive.

'Of course she is, but you fancy her as well. Don't tell me otherwise.'

The monster's shoulders seemed to slump. 'Okay, so I do. A gal like Sally isn't going to look twice at an ugly lump like me. All I can do is pretend to beat people up. I ain't no smoothie like that Liam guy.'

I looked at him incredulously. 'Matthews! A smoothie? Liam's as smooth as a porcupine. He thinks he's God's gift, but his chat up lines are marginally less sophisticated than "Me Tarzan, you Jane." Smoothie! Christ, that's rich.'

Then the truth hit me, and was out in the same instant. 'You're afraid of women, Jerry, aren't you?'

He shook his head. 'No. I'm afraid of the power they have.'

'What's that?' I asked him.

'The power to turn you down. The power to reject you.'

I was amazed by the hidden complexity of my new friend. 'How many times have you been rejected by women?' I asked him.

He shook his head again. 'Not the point. Anyway, plenty of women come looking for me. You might be surprised but some chicks get the hots for The Behemoth.'

'Yet when The Behemoth sees someone he really likes he's afraid to do anything about it, in case she turns him down?'

'That's about it. It happened to me all through High School, and all through College. It's an old American truth, Oz: the quarter-back gets his choice of the cheerleaders, the defensive line get the broads from the bleachers.'

'Sod that for a game.' I looked up at the ring, where the Ladies' Champ had just rolled up Linda Lashe in a difficult move called a small package, for a very neat pin. 'Hey Sally,' I called to her, as she stepped through the rope and jumped down to the floor. She waved and headed towards us. As she approached, the big man laid a hand on my shoulder and squeezed but, potential broken collar-bone or not, my mind was made up.

'Hi Oz,' said the Mancunian lass, cheerily. 'What's up?'

'My big pal here, Mr Gradi, once he's finished grinding my shoulder to dust, has something that he wants to say to you. It involves going for dinner to One Devonshire Place tomorrow night, after the show.'

She looked at me, and gasped, slightly. 'What was your last stage role, Oz?' she said in her soft English accent. 'Cyrano de bloody Bergerac? Let the bloke speak for himself.' Her gaze swept upwards. 'You want to take me out, Jerry?'

Blushing bright red, the man mountain shifted his weight from one foot to the other. 'That would be nice,' he mumbled.

Sally nodded and smiled. 'Yes, it would. A table at nine-thirty should give us plenty of time to get there.' Turning to head for the dressing room, she stopped after a couple of paces, and looked over her shoulder. 'I thought you were never going to ask,' she said.

I watched her as she trotted away from us across the arena, until Jerry's great paw settled on my shoulder once again, more gently this time. 'Just as well for you she said yeah,' he growled. 'Every so often I get to beat up a ring announcer.'

He paused, frowning. 'Where's One Devonsheer thing?' he asked. 'What is it?'

'Just off Great Western Road,' I told him. 'It has a claim to be the best restaurant in Glasgow. It has a quiet atmosphere: very discreet. Just right for the occasion.'

The great face fell. 'If it's that good, how will I get a table for tomorrow night at this notice?'

'You've got one. I had one booked for Jan and me. Use my name and take it over.'

'But won't Jan kill yah?'

I thought about that one. 'No,' I told him, hoping I was speaking the truth. 'Jan's a sport. She'll be okay when she realises it's a sacrifice made in a noble cause. Besides, we'll have plenty more Saturdays in One Devonshire. I'll take her to the Ubiquitous Chip instead. She'll like that just as much.'

I turned back to look at the ring. Suddenly it seemed smaller, a lot smaller than the twenty feet square which I knew that it was. I had never seen Daze in there before, ready for action in his wrestling gear. He seemed to fill it with his great black towering presence. I glanced across at Tommy Rutherford, aka Rockette, as he stood in the far corner, beyond the referee. I suppose I expected him to look scared, but he didn't. Like a good pro, there was an expression of confident aggression on his face. He began the sparring by circling Daze, very fast for a man of his size, kicking out at his ankles, calves and the back of his knees.

'You fight a guy much bigger than you,' Jerry muttered, 'you gotta try to take him down to the floor, to give yourself a chance.' As he spoke, Rockette changed those tactics. He was a stocky guy, but he sprang from a standing position to deliver a two-footed drop kick to the centre of Daze's chest. But as it landed, the big man simply puffed out his torso, and his opponent seemed to be propelled away from him, landing heavily on his back.

'I gotta get into position now,' said The Behemoth, moving round to the far side of the ring, and leaving me completely focused on Daze as he swung into action. I had never seen anything like it. I had been impressed by Sally Crockett, but the huge Everett was in a class by himself, even though he was simply sketching out his moves rather than slamming through them with full force. He was lightning fast, smooth, supple, and tremendously strong, building the pressure on Rockette so that even in the play-fight the Londoner, a big man in his own right, soon wore a look of genuine desperation.

And then The Princess made her entrance. 'Why y'all, Daze,' she called out as she sidled towards ringside, positioning herself in front of Jerry. 'Is that the best you can do against a fat little man like him?' He had been holding his opponent shoulder-high ready for a finishing move, but at her taunt, he simply let him fall to the ring floor.

In line with the script, he moved slowly across to the ropes as if he was hypnotised; and in his turn, Rockette mimed a scramble across the ring floor, the grabbing of an imaginary guitar, and its swing, to crash against the huge back. Everett shook his head and turned, almost in slow motion. A great arm shot out and seized the other man, then with no apparent effort he picked up the bulky wrestler, turned and threw him casually over the top rope.

It looked for all the world as if he had simply chucked two hundred and fifty pounds of Tommy Rutherford at his wife. And as Jerry stepped in front of Diane and caught him in mid-air, across his great chest, it looked for all the world as if he was handling nothing heavier than a basketball. He held him there for several seconds, although I noticed that Rockette's arms were clamped on to his shoulder and back, to spread the weight, then slammed him down into the ringside mat.

'That's great,' Everett called down from the ring. 'Let's do it again.' I looked at the Rockette man as he said it, and had to smile. It was clear from his expression that he could live without another flight into the unknown.

Rehearse they did, though, three more times. Finally, the ring-master was satisfied that the performance was foolproof, and that Jerry's dodgy muscle would stand up to the flying wrestler's bulk. 'Okay,' said Daze, as he stepped over the rope and jumped to the floor. 'That'll do it for tonight.

Dress rehearsal tomorrow midday as usual. Let's hope this one's trouble-free.'

I moved round the ring to join them as they headed for the exit. 'How's Liam?' I asked Diane.

'Chastened,' she said, with a smile. 'He may think that he's a chick magnet, but his mom thinks he's a little boy. And for the next week at least, she's in charge.'

I sneaked a glance at Everett, and saw a very faint smile flicker around the corners of his mouth. Just for a moment, I felt a strange cold tremor, as an obvious possibility finally forced itself into my impressionable brain.

17

'You don't seriously think that, do you?' She was standing by our living room window, looking out across the night-time cityscape.

I knew from that response that Jan was taking it seriously too. If she'd thought that my proposition was completely daft, she'd have blown me right out of the water, as she had done often enough in the past.

'Why not? For a start, Everett doesn't like Matthews; he'd fire him if he wasn't such a bloody good wrestler. You saw yourself how he reacted when Liam and I had our disagreement. On top of that, he's convinced himself that Diane and the boy are having it off.

'The thing that amazes me is why I didn't suspect him of rigging the barriers in the first place.'

She smiled. 'But you wouldn't, would you. To use their language, Daze is a face. He's a hero, and heroes don't do that sort of thing. You're part of their world now, you think like them. You even wanted to believe that it could be Jerry Gradi, because he's a heel.

'Ask yourself this though. Would Everett have been so devious that he staged the two earlier incidents just to cover his plan to get Liam?'

'Maybe those two other episodes were genuine accidents. Maybe he took advantage of them.'

'Why involve you?'

'So that I could volunteer that story to the police investigating Liam's death . . . if he'd been killed that is.'

'But he wasn't, and the police aren't investigating. So why are you still involved?'

'Who decided against calling the police in Newcastle? Everett did. As for me, he could hardly change his new ring announcer after only one week, could he? Anyway, I'm a bloody good ring announcer, I'll have you know.'

She shook her head. 'No, honey, I don't buy it. Everett just wouldn't do something like that. He's too nice a guy.'

'You'd have said that about Prim's sister's pal,' I countered, 'but he had a damn good go at killing us.' And then I stopped in my tracks. Neither Prim nor I had ever told anyone the story of what had happened in Geneva.

'What!' she said, astonished. 'Miles Grayson? How?'

I did some fast thinking, and a wave of relief at being off the hook washed over me. 'Bloody awful driver. Absolutely lethal on those roads up in Argyllshire.'

'Achhh, stop avoiding the argument, Blackstone. What would it have cost Everett in penalties if he had lost last Saturday's show because of Liam's accident?'

'A million dollars.'

'Do you think he hates him that much?'

I must admit she had me there. I argued on for a few minutes more, but eventually I had to agree that I was being paranoid. Everett Davis had too much wrapped up in GWA to risk it all by killing one of his top performers. And yet . . .

'Can I tell you my news now?' Jan asked.

'Of course, love, sorry.'

'I registered with a doctor today. She checked my blood pressure, heart, blood sugar and everything else she could find. I'm in prime condition, I'm glad to say. She ran a pregnancy test too, just for confirmation, and she gave me a delivery date.'

'You make it sound like he's coming by DHL.'

'I wish she was! September 20, Oz. Try to keep your diary clear, will you.'

I took her in my arms. 'Be sure of it. When do you get issued with your bump?'

'In about three months, I guess. That's the bit I'm not looking forward to; going through the summer looking like the side of a house, all hot and sticky, and running to the toilet all the time.'

'What, you mean you'll be peeing for two?'

'Daft bugger! No, when you get really big the baby presses on your bladder. Makes you a bit subject to wind too, so the doctor said.'

'What did she mean by that?'

'Farting, Oz. She said I might, on occasion.'

I beamed at her. 'What's new about that? You've been farting in your sleep for years.'

'Rubbish!'

'No. It's true; but gently, lady-like.'

'You never said before.'

'I was afraid you'd stop sleeping with me.' I held her to me, but carefully. 'Oh God, Janet Blackstone, *née* More, how I love you.'

'Just as well,' she whispered, giving me her most delicious grin. 'Seein' as how you've got me in the club.'

'Come into the kitchen, and I'll begin to spoil you. I'll cook dinner. Speaking of which, I've booked a table at the Chip for tomorrow.'

'I thought you mentioned One Devonshire,' said Jan. I nodded, then explained about my match-making enterprise earlier in the day.

'And you gave them our table!'

'Yes, but the Chip's great too, and it's lively, and I thought they'd be better somewhere quieter, and so . . .' I looked at her, uncertainly.

My wife laughed. 'I never imagined that when we decided to settle in Glasgow it would be to start a dating agency for bashful wrestlers. What do you think wee Colin would say if he knew that his favourite monster was too shy to do his own chatting up?'

She followed me into the kitchen, where two steaks lay ready to go on to the griddle which I had heating on the hob, and watched as I dropped them on to its hot non-stick surface, searing them quickly on either side.

'On the subject of dinners,' she said, 'I've invited Susie and Mike here next Tuesday. Is that okay with you?'

'Sure. How did you get on at Gantry's today?'

She frowned as I glanced across at her. 'I've finished my analysis of all the pubs,' she said. 'It's almost too good to be true. Some do better than others, but there isn't one of them that doesn't give a decent return on investment. I've had a few licensed trade clients in my four years as an independent, and the Gantry pubs do better than any of them.'

'So is Susie wrong? Is the business doing as well as it could?'

'No, it's not. The way that old fool Donn handled the finances of the company was a real buggers' muddle. He could only have got away with it in a private company. Everything just went into one big pot. There was no divisional structure, no separate VAT accounting, nothing, just localised books kept in each division. They're what I'm having to take apart.

'But looking at that overall picture, the profitability, the return on resources utilised, is well below reasonable expectations. I'm nearly done now. I've only got one place left to look, the health care division, as they call it, but that's going to be the most difficult of all, because it's the most complex and labour intensive of all the group businesses.'

'You're loving it, though, aren't you.'

She smiled, her long, slow, intimate smile. 'Yeah, I'm loving it. Who says accountancy can't be fun?'

I looked at the steaks on my griddle, at the chips in the electric fryer, and at the eggs which I had cracked into a skillet. 'Well, put it to one side for tonight,' I told her, 'and prepare to enjoy your last good fry-up till the end of September. I doubt if you'll find too much of this lot on the pregnant ladies' diet sheet.'

18

Where the SECC had been only moderately full on rehearsal day, mostly with business people attending trade exhibitions in two of its smaller halls, the Global Wrestling Alliance *Saturday BattleGround* brought the crowds flocking in.

There were signs of the throng to come even as I arrived at midday by taxi, carrying my suit-bag. A small group of fans was gathered near the arena entrance. They were teenagers mostly, some of them carrying hand-painted signs supporting their favourite superstars, to wave at the cameras during the show. I had almost reached the entrance to the main hall when I was stopped by two of them.

'Hey Mister! You're the announcer, urn't yeez? Ah saw youse last week, when Liam goat hurtit.' I looked at the girl, and at her pal. They were both around twelve or thirteen years old, with heavy black eye make-up and the beginnings of figures showing under their boob tubes and tight trousers: harmless now, but in a couple of years they'd be real jail-bait.

'That's right,' I agreed.

'Gie's yer autograph, then.' Both of them thrust thick-bound books in my face; the girl who spoke offered me a pen as well.

The only people who'd ever asked for my signature before were creditors. But as I looked down at the girls, I managed to hide my astonishment, I kept my cool. 'Of course,' I said, as casually as I could.

There was a table beside me. I took the books from them and leaned on it to scrawl my signature.

'Will Liam be wrestling this week?' the other one asked. She seemed less pushy than her pal. 'We love Liam. He's oor fav'rite.'

Well just you stay away from him, I thought, *or you could all get into big trouble.*

'No, he's not here today,' I said. 'You were watching last week, you said you saw that he was hurt.'

'What, he really did get hurt!'

'Quite badly. He'll be out for a few weeks.' The girl's face fell, and tears came to her eyes. 'He will be back though,' I reassured her, 'don't worry about that. He's just got some healing to do.'

'Whit aboot the Black Angel?' the first girl demanded. 'We love him too.'

'Dar . . . The Angel is okay. He's not on today either though. We've got Scarletto against Manson, the Rattlers in a tag-team match, Sally Crockett and a few others, and Daze in the main event.'

That seemed to cheer the quieter one up. She smiled as she wiped the back of her hand across her eyes, smearing her damp make-up. 'Who's he fightin'?' she asked.

'Tommy Rockette.'

'Rockette!' said her pal, scornfully. 'He's a fuckin' tosser!'

Maybe I should have given her a lecture on the standards of language and decorum which gentlemen expect of young ladies, but I didn't fancy being harangued in a public place by a pre-teen. Anyway, her assessment of Rutherford, while a little harsh, was not entirely unfounded. So I simply wished her, and her tear-streaked chum, a good afternoon and went into the hall, with a quick hello to Gary O'Rourke, who was on security duty at the door.

The road crew had done their work as well as ever. The

battleground was decked out in full military colours, light and lasers in place and thunderflashes – checked personally by Everett – primed to go off at the opening of the show and at the entrances of the main players. The dressing room was well decked-out too, full of performers; the entire male cast, in fact, apart from Daze. I found a space next to Tommy Rockette.

'Ready for your short flight?' I asked him.

He turned to me, his dyed blond pony tail swinging. 'You think this is a fucking gaime?' he snarled, in a thick East London accent. I had never spoken to the man before, so I was taken aback by his hostility.

'I think it's a very professional operation, and I have great admiration for all you guys,' I said. 'I'm not trying to take the piss, honest.'

'Just as fucking well for you, mate.'

I left him to get on with it, and changed into my dress suit and my Newcastle-bought bow tie. When I was ready, I put my discarded clothes, and bag, into a locker. Pocketing the key, I turned and saw Jerry in a corner, his forehead furrowed in a deep frown. I guessed that he was more preoccupied by his date with Sally than with his part in the performance, and I smiled at the thought of him slamming Rutherford onto the ringside mat.

I was first to leave the dressing room and go outside into the arena. Once there, I did as I had been instructed by Everett: I wandered quietly around the ringside area, kicking the barriers, testing the firmness of the ring posts, glancing under the apron for suspicious packages, walking round the ringside matting, feeling with my feet and looking for any signs that something might have been placed under it.

My client, still in his street clothes, came over to me as the wrestlers began to emerge from the changing room. 'Everything look okay to you?' he asked, quietly.

'It looks clean.' I wondered for a moment whether to mention Rockette's sudden aggression, which seemed out of place in the GWA family – especially with Liam Matthews *hors de combat* – but decided that it would be unfair. Clearly, the guy was concentrating on a risky manoeuvre, and I had rubbed him up the wrong way.

'That's good. I've checked all the pyrotechnic stuff. Let's do the first rehearsal, then.' He put his hand to the side of his mouth and yelled. 'Commentators in position, first match prepare, music ready. We run in five minutes.'

The rehearsals went as smoothly as they had done seven days before in Newcastle. As the day unfolded, the only thing that was different about the Glasgow experience was the crowd. Where the Newcastle audience had been slightly curious as the Arena began to fill, as soon as the doors opened, the people flooded into the SECC main hall, buzzing with excitement and bedecked with corporate products. Where GWA had been a novelty to the Geordies, it was part of their city as far as its Glaswegian loyalists were concerned. Their cheers were ten decibels louder than their English counterparts: these were committed, knowledgeable Sports Entertainment fans.

I suppose that was why the stage-fright hit me twice as hard as it had the week before, as I stood up in my spotlight, shouting to make myself heard over the roar which greeted me, even before the lights and the sound-effects started. I realised very quickly that in Glasgow, my job was virtually irrelevant. The crowd cheered or booed, as appropriate, as soon as each signature music began, for they knew them all, by heart. The Rattlers were first out into the spotlight, to a crescendo of jeers as befitting the number one heel tag team. On the other hand, when a chorus of treble voices sounded over the PA, the cheers for their opponents, the

Choirboys, almost took the roof off.

Sally Crockett, wearing a belt of gold and with a body to match, won the biggest response of the afternoon, especially when, after her match, she flattened Joe Anderson, a jobber who had been featured as a heckler who stalked her matches from ringside and who this time had jumped through the ropes to mock her skills into a hand-mike. The crowd went wild as she hit him with a lightning fast stunner, picked up his mike, and yelled at him as he lay on the floor. 'You want a real fight? Let's have one!'

I knew they would, too, at the next pay-per-view; the GWA's first ever mixed singles match, the GWA World Ladies' Champion versus The Heckler.

They cheered for Johnny King too. He wasn't as slick as Matthews, but he had much of his charisma, and a good finishing move. There are some very successful wrestlers who don't have more than two or three moves. Jerry had told me of one world-renowned grappler who, in his words, 'wouldn't know a wrist-lock from a wrist-watch'.

The cheers died when the lights went out. The hall fell, if not silent, then into a single excited whisper. And then the thunderflashes boomed, the lasers speared the sky, and with them a great roar boomed; the ten-thousand-strong crowd cheering with a single voice. Daze was the one superstar in the GWA who was never introduced. He didn't need it. Not at all.

I had thought that the Black Angel's entrance was impressive, but it was understated compared to that of the giant. The lights went out again, all of them save the low voltage emergency exit signs; the special effects fell silent, and all we were left with was the smell of cordite in the pitch-dark hall.

Then suddenly flame spurted from four canisters taped to the top of each ring-post, and he was there, inside the squared circle, having been lowered from the roof on a cable in the darkness. I had been warned to stand in the corner, and I did, but it still startled me as the huge black shape came out of the heavens.

He went to the four corners of the ring, arms raised, glaring out, milking the applause. Ten seconds after the fourth corner was my cue. I raised my mike. 'And his opponent . . .'

Rockette sashayed down the aisle to a chorus of boos, the least popular man in Glasgow at that moment. Dressed in a high-collared, sequinned blue jacket and matching tights, he strummed his heavily varnished acoustic guitar all the way to the ring, until he stepped through the ropes and handed it to me.

I had seen the battle several times before, so I didn't wince too often as Tommy Rutherford was battered all around the ring. I didn't care in fact; after his rudeness in the dressing room I had come to agree totally with the twelve-year-old autograph hunter.

I had seen Diane before too, and twice that afternoon in costume, but she still gave me a buzz as the light picked her out at the top of the walkway, and as she made her way steadily down towards the ring in her tight-fitting evening dress, her brown skin gleaming through the laced-up side-panel.

'You still strutting your stuff up there, big man?' her taunt began, as she moved round the ring towards the English language commentary table where Jerry was seated. 'Bet you wish you could strut it for The Princess, don'cha.'

Daze dropped Rockette and stepped towards her as if hypnotised. As he did, the Londoner crawled across the ring, beckoning to me. I did a little mime for the crowd and the cameras, to confirm that he wanted the guitar, then passed it to him through the ropes.

Acting as if he was still half out of it, he hauled himself to his feet and lurched towards his opponent, who stood staring out of the ring. The crowd screamed a warning, but the giant took no notice as Tommy Rutherford took a full swing and crashed his instrument as hard as he could across his shoulders and against the back of his head.

I had seen one of these spoof guitars in Newcastle the week before; it shattered into a thousand pieces on impact. This one didn't; instead it broke in two, at the point where the fret-board joined the chamber. There was no sound of splintering, only a ghostly twang as the strings vibrated with the force of the blow.

Daze stood there, swaying for a moment, then turned, on cue, towards Rockette . . . and hit him, just once, very fast, very hard, with his right fist – a short, boxer's blow to the middle of the forehead.

I'm a country boy. I know potatoes; I've seen them in sacks, big ones too. That's what Tommy Rockette looked like as he went down; a great big sack of potatoes. 'Now that wasn't in the script,' I whispered. Fortunately, my mike wasn't live.

Daze dropped to one knee and picked Rutherford's dead weight clean off the canvas. As the crowd, who had no idea what was in the script and what wasn't, roared its approval, he hoisted him up to shoulder height, as rehearsed, looked at Diane, saw Jerry coming to stand beside her, and threw him.

Catching an unconscious man must be much more difficult than catching someone who is awake and co-operating, but The Behemoth managed it. He staggered slightly as he made the catch, but he held on. Very quickly though, he laid his burden on the mat, then as he had done twice that afternoon already, rolled under the bottom rope, jumped to his feet and squared up to Daze.

As the first of the mock blows were thrown, and as the referees rushed into the ring en masse to separate the two, I heard the commentators talk us through the end of the show, and out of recording time. At the same time I looked at Tommy Rockette, still lying on the floor. He wasn't hearing anything.

But me; already I could hear Everett backstage, in about five minutes' time. I wasn't looking forward to it.

19

It took longer than five minutes for him to get round to me, but when he did, he was not pleased.

'Look man, I've never held one of those spoof guitars,' I protested, as he glowered at me in the small office. 'I've never held any sort of a bloody guitar. I'd barely know a Gibson from a glockenspiel.'

'Christ, Oz,' he bellowed, 'the prop is made from balsa!'

'Yes, but it's varnished so that it looks pretty much like the real thing, so if you don't know what it should weigh . . . Everett, I took the guitar that Tommy handed me, as instructed, and I never let go of it, as instructed, until I handed it back to him. I'm sorry you've got a lump on your head, but like they said at Nuremberg, "I was only obeying orders".'

My protest of innocence seemed to be working, for his expression softened a little. 'I take it that Rockette knew it was a real guitar,' I said.

'Oh yeah,' Everett muttered. 'He knew all right.'

'So he's the saboteur? Did Reilly promise him a deal, or what?'

He shook his head, frowning. 'It's not that easy. The bum has nothing to do with Reilly, and he had nothing to do with the earlier stuff. Once he came round, Jerry had a talk with him, in private. The Behemoth can be very persuasive, and he was in a hurry for some reason he wouldn't tell me, so he didn't mess around.

'Tommy realised very quickly that he either 'fessed up there, or wound up in a hospital ward. He told Jerry that this stunt of his was strictly personal. Essentially, the Rockette character is a jobber at the top level, but Mr Rutherford has a big ego. He thinks he should be a mainliner, one of the guys who gets to wear the gold.

'He told Jerry straight out that he should have been going in with the Angel for the Transcontinental belt. And he said that when I gave the shot to Scarletto instead, he didn't like it at all. He tried to make out that the thing was almost an accident, though. Said to Jerry that he picked up the wrong guitar in the dressing room, and that he was on his way to the ring when he realised it. Said that he almost went back to change it, but he was so pissed at me that he decided to give me a whack with the real thing.

'Of course, I don't believe that for a minute. He decided right back in the dressing room.' Everett rubbed the back of his head. 'Son of a bitch knew exactly which guitar he was picking up.'

'Why did he have a real one anyway?'

For the first time since, still in his ring gear, he had marched me into the small room and in the process had given me claustrophobia, Everett smiled. 'The guy can play it for real, and he thinks he can sing. So every so often, like tonight, we let him go outside and warm up the crowds while they're waiting for the doors to open.'

'That was some shot he caught you with the thing. Are you okay?'

Daze grinned again. 'Thing you gotta learn about me, little buddy. I really am as tough as I look.'

'So is that the end of Rockette?' I asked him. 'Have you fired him?'

The big man stretched himself, his head almost touching the ceiling. 'I can't afford to, Oz. With Liam out of action, and Dave Manson, the roster's depleted enough. I need the bum.' He held up his huge right hand. 'So I put the fear of God in him with this – and with the threat of another chat with Jerry.' As he spoke he extended his left hand, palm up. 'At the same time with this, I gave him an incentive. I told him I'd put him in a tag team with Chris Manson and give them a shot at that title, against the Choirboys.

'But no more guitars. Phoney or real, they're out from now on.'

20

The Ubiquitous Chip is a sort of Glaswegian oasis. We'd heard about it not long after we came to the city, and we'd gone there once, for lunch in mid-week when we were feeling flush, but dinner on a Saturday evening was a new experience for us.

The place has a courtyard style, although it's watertight. Just as well; it had started to rain just as Jan picked me up from the SECC, and as we sat there we could still hear it battering off the roof. It's a bit showbiz too. This may be simply because it's very close to the headquarters of BBC Scotland, but a couple of months as a citizen of Glasgow had given me the distinct impression that the whole place is culture-chic crazy. The Burrell reception had underlined that; not long before we left, Susie, Mike, Jan and I were photographed by a girl who said she was from *Hello* magazine. My wife and I had been astonished, but the Lady Provost had assured us that it was an everyday occurrence in Gantry-land.

From our small corner table, I glanced around the lower dining area and was almost relieved to see that – apart from a woman who presented a heavyweight television news programme – I didn't recognise anyone.

'Penny for 'em,' drawled Jan as she dissected her thick venison steak. From our youngest days, I had always been impressed by the way she ate; carefully, sensually, regarding her food as a pleasure to be savoured.

'A miserable bloody penny!' I retorted. 'My thoughts do not come cheap, I'll have you know.' There was nothing sensual about me as I stripped the top layer off my skate wing: I was just pacing myself, so that we finished at more or less the same time. I learned to do that when I was a kid. Ellie and I played this very serious game, where the winner was the one who had the last mouthful.

'Okay, fifty pence.'

'Throw in index-linked increases for future transactions and you're on. I was just thinking that Glasgow's a real goldfish bowl. Through here it's as if everyone's looking at you all the time, whereas in Edinburgh, everyone averts their eyes.'

She nodded, stopping her fork halfway to her mouth. 'You and I adapted right away then. We live in a bloody goldfish bowl. Fortunately it's too high up for anyone to look in on us.' The fork moved on, then stopped again. 'I know what you mean though. You're no one in this city if you're not famous.'

We ate in silence for a while. The meal was expensive enough to deserve our complete attention. 'That was excellent,' said Jan, when she was finished. 'I'm glad you gave Jerry our table at the other place.'

'Yeah, although that's very good as well. It's quieter though, and maybe better suited for the purpose of – how will I put it? – sexual negotiation.' I glanced around. 'Everyone in here knows exactly where they're going afterwards.'

'So that's what Jerry's doing, is it,' my wife whispered, with a smile.

'Christ no. It'll be Sally who does the negotiating. The big guy's so terrified I'm not sure that they'll sign the treaty, though.'

'What's he scared of?'

'Her. The Behemoth is in love.'

Jan's smile disappeared. 'I hope she lets him down easy. Jerry's such a nice guy; he was so good with Colin last week.'

'Don't worry about it. I got the impression that she was quite keen too.' I took a sip of the Rawson's Reserve. 'I don't know what Jerry's small talk will be like though. I just hope he doesn't say anything he shouldn't.'

'About Tommy what's-his-name, you mean?'

I shook my head. 'No. The whole crew knew that Rockette hit Daze with a real guitar as soon as they saw the way it broke. They saw the way the guy went down too. Jeez, you should have seen it. I bumped into him just as I was leaving the hall: he's got a lump as big as a golf ball on his forehead.

'No. I meant that I hope Jerry doesn't say anything about the sabotage, or about me.'

'Why not? Is Sally a suspect?'

'I don't see it. She's relatively new to the game. I don't see the man Reilly recruiting her. But I got involved in this thing on the basis that only the immediate circle, by which I meant Everett and Diane – who still doesn't know about me, by the way – were in on the operation. Suppose word got around that I was a plant; Christ, I might become a target myself!'

Jan stared at me. 'I hadn't thought of that one. I agree, let's hope they don't get down to pillow talk.'

She fell silent as the waiter arrived to hand us the sweet menu, and to clear away the empty dishes. 'How much longer are you going on with this, Oz?' she asked me, as he left.

'I'll give it another couple of weeks,' I told her. 'I've been doing some constructive thinking about this, at last, and I've come up with an angle we can investigate positively. If Tony Reilly of CWI has recruited a saboteur, it's likely to be a

Yank. Apart from Everett, Diane and Jerry, there are six other Americans on the payroll.

'Of those, two were back in the States on holiday when the barrier was fixed. Barbara, the marketing girl, was in Europe doing advance work for future events. Dave Manson is a victim, and his cousin Chris was involved by accident in his injury, so he's ruled out. That leaves Sonny Leonard, the foreman roadie. Everett thinks that he's okay, but he'd say that about every member of the team, except Liam, if you put it to him. So he's agreed that we concentrate on him.

'Leonard has one of the company's mobile phones, which he uses all the time. On Monday, that being his day off, I'm going to GWA to look with Everett at the itemised bills for that number. We'll see if that throws up anything.'

'If it doesn't, are you still going to Barcelona?'

I smiled at her. 'I have to. I'm the star ring announcer, remember.'

As I spoke, Jan looked up and over my shoulder. I followed her gaze and found a stocky, balding young man looking down at me. He was wearing a crumpled suit, a sure sign that it was a designer job and very, very expensive. 'How goes it, Marlowe?' Greg McPhillips, my lawyer pal, asked. 'You've got Glasgow well sorted, haven't you.'

Greg and I were friends at university. Afterwards, as I went briefly and disastrously into the police force, before finding my niche as a Private Enquiry Agent, he joined Glasgow's leading firm of general solicitors and became a partner at the age of twenty-eight: not surprising since the firm was called McPhillips, and had been founded thirty years earlier by his old man.

'We're finding our way around. Pull up a chair and have a drink with us.'

He glanced over his shoulder at the blonde behind him. He had a string of them, every one as designer as his suit.

'Sorry Oz, we can't. Poppy's talked me into going to see a band at King Tut's Wah Wah Hut. We're struggling for time as it is.

'No, I just came over to congratulate you on being such an insinuating bastard.'

Jan had met Greg before. She didn't like him: something to do with his attitude to women. 'Pardon?' she said, in a tone which indicated that a shot in the mouth could follow shortly.

He smiled his way out of trouble. 'No offence Jan,' he boomed, in his big hearty voice. 'I just meant that I gave your husband a recommendation to Everett bloody Davis as the very man to sort out his petty cash fiddler, and the next thing I see he's talked himself into a job as GWA's ring announcer.

'I'm taping tonight's show. I take it that you're on again.'

'Starring role, man, starring role. It's a great show tonight, as well.'

'I'll look forward to it, then. Must rush now. Goodnight, Jan.'

We watched him as he headed for the door, dragging Poppy behind him, the girl teetering on her unfeasibly high heels.

'That settles it,' said my wife, emphatically. 'You are getting out of this thing as fast as you can. With that idiot shooting his mouth off all over Glasgow, your actor cover's going to be blown in no time.

'Get this sorted, Oz. A lady in my condition doesn't need to be worrying about her man.'

21

I had a brainwave on Monday morning, before I left to meet Everett. I don't have them very often, but when I do they can be real crackers.

On the stroke of nine, I called Greg McPhillips at his office. I should have known better; he was a partner in the firm after all. However he had arrived when I called back fifteen minutes later.

'You're an early bird,' he said, as he took my call. His voice sounded hoarse and strained.

'Not especially. What's up with the throat? Got an infection?'

'No,' he croaked. 'It was effin' noisy in King Tut's. I had to shout at the bird all night to make myself heard.'

'It should have worn off by now.'

'Aye, but I was at the Garage last night as well.'

'Poppy likes the bands, eh.'

'This wasn't Poppy, it was Hayley.' A busy boy, is our Greg.

'I did have a chance to watch you on telly, though,' he went on. 'Big Everett didn't half level that bloke at the end, after he gubbed him with the guitar. For a minute I thought it was for real.'

'Daze can be very convincing.'

'I liked your performance too. Am I on a percentage of this?'

I laughed; I knew Greg well enough to realise that he was half serious. 'I'll buy you a big drink; I promise.'

'Champagne would be nice.'

'Christ Greg, but you're a natural born solicitor, aren't you. Champagne it is.'

'Krug?'

'Moet.'

'Deal.'

I paused to let him stop chortling. 'Speaking of performances,' I said, eventually, 'after you left the Chip on Saturday night, a bloke came over to our table. He introduced himself as the Assistant Secretary of the Law Society of Scotland, and he told us that he had recognised you.'

There was a grunt from the other end of the line.

'He asked me as a friend, to have a very friendly word with you on his behalf, to say that if Mr Everett bloody Davis, whose name you shouted all over the restaurant, happened to be a client of yours, then you have a duty of confidentiality towards him, which was surely breached by telling the entire dining population of Byres Road that he has a problem in his office involving dishonesty.

'He said I should tell you that if anyone made a complaint to the Law Society about behaviour of that sort, it would be liable to come down on you like a ton of bricks. He gave me a list of the things it could do to you, but I expect you know them all. He didn't mention thumbscrews specifically, but the hint was there.'

I let my words sink in for a few seconds. 'To tell you the truth, Greg, I wasn't too happy myself. Glasgow's a great big village, and word spreads.'

'All right, all right, all right.' The last 'all right' was distorted beyond recognition into a strange, wheezing squeak. 'Thanks for the tip, Oz. I was a bit pissed, as you'd have realised. I just hope the guy doesn't phone my old man.'

'I asked him not to, and he said that he wouldn't this time, if I passed the word on.'

'Maybe I should phone him.'

Here, Blackstone, a voice whispered in my head. *You really should have been an actor.* 'No,' I said, emphatically. 'The best thing you can do is keep your mouth tight shut about the whole business from now on.'

'Aye, maybe so,' Greg agreed, painfully.

'How did you land that job anyway?' he asked.

'I was in the right place at the right time, that's all. It's great fun. We're off to Barcelona this weekend.'

'Lucky bastard! And how about the pilfering? Have you sorted that out yet?'

'We're on to someone. This very morning, in fact. Keep that to yourself, mind.'

'Don't worry,' he croaked. 'I will.'

22

'I try to run this company on a tight budget,' said Everett, almost mournfully, as we sat in his office looking at a pile of mobile phone bills. We were virtually alone in the head-quarters unit. Monday was a day of rest for most of the crew.

'If there was an alternative to these goddamned expensive things, I would take it. They just eat up money, especially when the guys use them around Europe.'

'Do they all have company phones?' I asked him.

'Diane and I share a hand phone, and I have one wired into my car,' he replied. 'Jerry has one that fits into an adaptor in the BattleBus. Barbara has one because she travels a lot, I gave one to Darius, because his father is sick in Germany and likes to be able to talk to him, and to Liam, because he found out that Darius had one. Then there's Sonny's.

'Those are just the company phones of course. Quite a few of the roster have their own. I've seen Sally Crockett using one, for example.' He paused. 'Say, what's with her? She's a happy kid normally, but yesterday I thought she was going to burst into song.'

'Sounds to me like there's a man involved,' I said. What I didn't say was that when the cast had gathered at the SECC twenty-four hours earlier to shoot the action for the Monday night programme, I had seen Sally and Jerry arriving together in the BattleBus. They looked as if they had enjoyed their first date.

Everett frowned. 'As long as he doesn't take her mind off the job. I've never seen a woman worker who gets as big a pop from the crowd as she does.'

'I don't think there's a chance in hell of that happening. I've been talking to Sally; she's one hundred per cent committed to the GWA.'

I pointed to the pile of papers on the desk. 'What have we got here?'

'These are the itemised mobile accounts for the last six months. I pulled everyone's account; Sonny Leonard's bills are in here somewhere. His number's 0735 951775.'

I picked up the invoices and began to go through them; they were all in the name of the company and differentiated only by the line number. I sorted through them and separated them out into seven lots, six bills to each, and handed one to Everett. 'These are Sonny Leonard's.'

We each pulled up chairs and sat on the visitor side of the CEO's glass-topped table. I felt as if I was Gulliver, in that place he went to after Lilliput. Everett gave me back three of the invoices. 'You go through these; I'll look at the rest. Let's see what we get.'

I took out a pen and looked at the first invoice. In the course of the month Leonard had made around fifty calls. Most were to the GWA number, from different locations around Europe according to the dial codes shown.

'Where's CWI based?' I asked.

'Philadelphia, PA, City of Brotherly Love. The city code is 215.'

There was one call to the US shown on the first bill, to number 00 1 314 732 6578. 'Everett,' I said. 'Can you remember where Leonard comes from?'

'Yeah. He's from St Louis, Missouri. I believe his mom

still lives there.' I reached across, picked up the telephone directory which was lying on the glass table, and flicked my way to the international codes section. The city code for St Louis Missouri, showed as 314.

I looked at the second bill, which was five months old. Again, most of the calls were to the GWA headquarters, and to other Glasgow numbers. Again, there was one call to the St Louis number. 'It looks like he calls his folks, once a month, on the company phone.'

'Can't object to that,' the big man drawled. 'I call mine once a week.'

I looked at the third invoice, a month more recent. The St Louis number was there again. I had almost finished my check when I looked back at one of the numbers. The national exit code, which I had passed by at first, came back to me. 'Why would Sonny be in Spain four months ago?'

'He did an advance trip to check out the Barcelona venue. Why?'

'Because he made a call from Spain to a US number. 00 1 215 671 4307. What's the CWI number?'

'Dunno,' said Daze, in a voice like ice. 'But three months ago he made three calls to that number. Two months ago, he made five. Last month he made seven.'

He stood, towering above me and walked round to the speaker phone on the desk. I watched him, as he punched in thirteen numbers; 0-0-1-2-1-5-6-7-1-4-3-0-7. As he hit each button a tone sounded from the speaker, each one singing into the silent room. After a few seconds the phone began to ring; one, two, three, four times.

After the fourth ring, there was a click, and a sunny, 'Have a nice day', female voice came on the line. 'Hi,' she said. 'You're connected to the offices of Championship Wrestling Incorporated, the world's premier Sports Entertainment company. We open for business at eight am, Eastern

Standard Time, but you can leave a message now, if you wish. Please speak after the tone . . . and have a nice day.'

Before the message tape could start to run, Everett punched the cut-off button with a huge finger. 'Son of a bitch!' he hissed.

'Aye, and a stupid son of a bitch too, not to know that all calls from a mobile are itemised on the bill.'

'Let's see if someone else is a stupid SoB.' He leaned across the table, scanned the piles of invoices, then picked up another. I didn't need to ask; I knew that they were for Liam's phone.

'For fuck's sake, Everett! You don't need to do that.'

He ignored me and went straight to the third invoice from the top. 'There! Look at that!' he called out, pointing. 'November 14, I was in Frankfurt, he called our number from his mobile, seven thirty. I called later from my hotel, Diane wasn't home; I got that smug woman's voice on the answer service. I called Liam after that; made up a story about something I had to say to him. He picked up the phone all right. I'll bet she was with him.'

I tried to keep an even tone, and not to laugh at him. That wouldn't have been wise. 'And I'll bet that Liam got the answering service too, when he called. Did you ask Diane where she was?'

'Yeah, she said she went to a movie.'

'So believe her. She's your wife; you owe her that.'

'She's my wife, but she don't want my kids.'

'*Yet*, Everett. From what you've told me, she doesn't want them *yet*.'

'Why'd the son of a bitch phone her?'

'For some innocent reason, for sure. He wasn't at home when he called her, or he wouldn't have used his hand-phone. Maybe he thought she'd like company for dinner. Listen – your conspiracy theory's gone by the board. Diane can't be sabotaging the company so that she can deliver Liam and herself to Tony Reilly. Liam's accident knocked that daft idea on the head.'

'Don't mean they ain't having an affair though.'

Finally I lost patience with the poor, insecure, big sod. 'No,' I barked at him, 'but it doesn't mean that they are! You've got nothing more than unfounded suspicion; no evidence at all. Concentrate on the proof you do have, that Sonny Leonard is in regular contact with CWI head office. What are you going to do about that?'

Everett slumped into his chair, his chin resting on his chest, and sat silent for a full minute. 'I'm going to watch the bastard in Barcelona next weekend, like a hawk; and so are you. If he steps one foot out of line, I'm going to break his back and send him home to Tony Reilly in a wheelchair.'

I looked at him and I was scared. Sure I'd heard him make a physical threat before, after my altercation with Matthews in Newcastle. But that had been said to frighten Liam, and to embarrass him before the team. This time there was a cold anger about him which made me worry that he might do exactly what he said.

'I don't think so,' I said quietly. 'You hurt this guy, and they've won, because you'll be in the wrong. You'll wind up in the courts, and that will be the end of your career and of the GWA. If we establish for sure that Leonard is Reilly's plant, that's the point at which we talk to Mike Dylan.'

He glared at me. 'I told you. I can't have cops in this. The publicity could ruin me.'

'No, Everett. This is British law we're talking about. As soon as someone is charged, whether it's in Scotland or England, their case is sub judice. There can be no publicity until it comes to court. When it does – and if it's in England, that could be a year away – chances are Leonard will plead guilty: even if they don't extradite Reilly, and he isn't in the dock himself, no way will he allow the story to be dragged out in open court.

'Go with me on this. When we have hard evidence, we take it to Dylan.'

His sigh could have blown out all the candles on a centenarian's birthday cake. And then he smiled. 'You're a persuasive SoB yourself, Blackstone. I'll think about it. But that's as much as I'll promise for now.

'See you on the flight to Barcelona.'

23

'Jesus, Oz, this is tremendous, you can see the whole city from up here.' For once Mike Dylan meant exactly what he said. There wasn't a trace of his customary flippancy in his voice as he stared out of the window into the evening, down towards the Kingston Bridge.

'What's that bright light over to the west?' he asked.

'That's Ibrox. Rangers have a UEFA Cup tie tonight. I thought the whole city knew that.'

'Not me. I'm a rugby man.'

'Ah,' I said. 'An atheist.'

'Who did the conversion of this building?' he asked.

'Need you ask?' Susie interrupted in her high, brittle voice, from the kitchen doorway. 'This is one of Gantry Developments' finest achievements. Six years ago we won a Saltire Society award for this project.'

'How come you live in a semi-detached in Clarkston, then?' Dylan shot back at her.

She laughed. 'I couldn't afford one of these at the time. But we've got another big conversion on the drawing board at the moment, a big redundant church at the top of St Vincent Street. It's grade A listed, but it's derelict. If we get planning permission, I'm having the best of those.'

'*If* you get planning permission . . .' I didn't try to hide my incredulity.

'Come on, Oz. My dad can't pull any strings for his own company, or we'd get crucified. But we've consulted the City planning officials, and the Historic Scotland people about all the things we'd need to do for the conversion to be acceptable. We think we can meet all their conditions and still have a viable development.'

'Make sure you put a lift in it, will you?' said Jan, emerging from the kitchen with a tray loaded with plates of toast and paté, our first course. 'That's the one drawback about this place.'

Susie nodded. 'I know. We couldn't do that in here because of the layout of the building. This is listed too. But in the new one, we'll be able to build a lift-shaft inside the main tower without the machinery being seen from outside.' She took her seat at the table, facing Dylan. 'I'll show you the plans next time you're in the office. When will that be?'

'I've got other things to do tomorrow afternoon and Thursday, standing commitments to other clients,' Jan replied, 'and I want to work here on Friday. I could come in to see you tomorrow morning.'

'Can't do morning, I'm afraid. I'm doing my Lady Provost act, accompanying my dad to an official opening, and there's a lunch afterwards.'

'Oh well, I'll just have to hold on to my patience until Monday.' She shot our guest a sudden, meaningful glance. 'I can barely wait, I tell you.'

Susie's eyebrows shot up in one of her classic nervous gestures. 'What! Are you on to something?' she burst out.

'Could well be,' said my wife, pausing before biting into a piece of toast, layered thick with paté. 'I'm looking into the health care division, the last on my list, and I've found something which is beginning to look very interesting. I'll need to go over it again, and then I'll need to consult a few people.'

'What is it?' Susie demanded, eagerly.

'I don't want to say just across the dinner table, so please don't press me.' Dylan was attacking his starter, so he didn't notice her quick gesture, the tiny nod of her head in his direction. But Susie and I did. 'I expect to be absolutely sure of my ground by Monday. After that, you'll have to decide where we go.'

'Anything I can do in the meantime?'

Jan nodded. 'You could look out the personnel files of everyone employed at management level in that part of the business. Now please, don't let's discuss it any more.'

Dylan reached across and tapped me on the arm. 'Let's talk about you then, Oz. What the hell's all this wrestling stuff about? How did you get into it? All that big Davis said at the City Chambers was that a mutual friend introduced you.'

I decided that the tall grass of the truth was my best hiding place. 'That's right. Greg McPhillips, an old university mate. He's Everett's lawyer.'

'But why did he put you in the frame for that job? You're a detective, for Christ's sake, not a fairground barker.'

The tall grass was on fire. I found fresh cover in a total fabrication. 'When we were at university, Greg and I worked on Sundays for a guy who had a market stall. I was good at it; when Everett told him about the announcing job, Greg remembered that.'

I looked him in the eye and waited for his comeback line. There was always one with him. He gave me a big, slow, cheesy grin. 'What did you sell, then?'

'Lucky knickers.'

All three, Mike, Susie and Jan, stopped eating and looked at me, wide-eyed.

'Lucky knickers?' said Dylan.

'That's right,' I shot back, hitting him between the eyes with the appalling punch line. 'Every girl who bought them got done.'

24

The GWA logistics manager had done a deal with the airline, booking a block of business class seats on the Manchester–Barcelona flight for the price of economy class. The staging had been sent out three days earlier in trucks, the journey planned so that its arrival would coincide with ours.

I didn't know at the time whether Everett had fixed it, or whether it was just a coincidence, but when we boarded the flight after a three and a half hour coach trip from Glasgow, I found myself in a window seat next to Sonny Leonard.

All the way down on the bus I had been thinking about Jan; how perfectly we had made love the night before, how beautiful she had looked that morning when I kissed her goodbye, how rich in quality our life had become, and how much we were looking forward to being parents. The reality of her pregnancy was just coming home to us both, and it had a strange effect.

'What are we going to do, Oz,' she had asked me, dreamily, as the winter moonlight streamed through our bedroom window, 'when we don't have anything else to wish for, because we've got everything we've ever wanted?'

I remembered how I spread my fingers and placed my hand gently on her warm belly, my thumb in her navel and the end of my little finger in her thick mat of dark hair. I had tried to imagine that I could feel the baby move, although of course it was far too early. I gazed down at her and as I did,

I realised that something strange was happening to me; something called growing up.

'I'll tell you what we'll do,' I told her. 'We'll build a new set of ambitions for this chap, or chapess, in here, and we'll do our best to make them happen as well. After that's done . . . we'll still have each other, decrepit old buggers though we may be by then; and who could want for more? Not me.'

I closed my eyes as the bus drove smoothly down the M6: once again, I saw Jan's beautiful face in the moonlight, heard her throaty laugh, bathed in the warmth of her smile, and sank down once more into her loving arms.

I was still thinking of her as I took my seat beside Sonny Leonard on the aircraft. We had spoken a couple of times in Newcastle and at the SECC, but on a 'Do this for me, please', basis rather than personally. I glanced at the American as I fastened my seat belt; he didn't look to be in a talkative mood, and frankly neither was I.

Show me a man who says that he actually likes travelling by air and I will show you an idiot. Okay, I know that our world has been revolutionised by the invention of the heavier-than-air flying machine, but that doesn't mean that we can afford to uncross our fingers when we are thirty thousand feet above the ground, our lives depending on an apparatus built and operated by man and subject therefore to human error.

Take-off is the part of the flight I hate most of all. I can cope with landing because the sight of the ground getting closer – not too fast – is comforting in a rocky sort of a way, but I have always loathed the experience of being shoved into the sky by a pair of bloody enormous engines, listening all the way through for the slightest change in their tone which might intimate disaster. It doesn't do to let it show, though.

I could tell from the whiteness of Sonny Leonard's knuckles as he gripped the armrests that he felt the same way as me, although he turned his head to look across me and out of the window, as the DC9 broke into the low grey cloud which hung, as predicted, over Manchester. Neither of us spoke, though, until the plane levelled off, and the cabin crew appeared with the bar trolley.

'Where are the rest of your guys?' I asked the American, to break the silence. He was a stocky guy in his early forties, with grizzled hair, wide shoulders, a broken nose, and the suggestion of a beer gut.

'Back in Glasgow,' he replied. 'The Spanish are awkward when it comes to foreign labour. They insist on us using local people whenever we can. Don't know whether it's their trade unions or their government that's behind it, but that's the way it is. I'm essential to the operation, so they accept that I gotta be there, but Gary and all the others are being replaced by locals for this show.'

'Won't you have a language problem? As a nation, the Spanish are bloody awful at English.'

Leonard shook his head, then nodded very quickly as an immaculately made up stewardess offered him a small bottle of Freixenet cava. 'Nah, that's okay,' he said. 'My Spanish is pretty good. It has to be, working in the US. LA and New York are pretty much bilingual.'

He had given me an opening. 'Have you been with GWA from the start?'

'Yeah. When Everett first started planning the company he asked me if I'd set up his road crew, and run it for him. He didn't tell me it would be in Glasgow, though.'

I grinned at him as I took a tin of San Miguel from the stewardess. 'What's wrong with our fair city, then?'

'It's cold, it's wet and it's goddamn miserable – and that's in the summer. I'm a St Louis boy – I like my summers hot.

I tell you, I thank the Lord for this Barcelona gig. I was beginning to freeze to death back in Scotland.'

'I don't imagine it'll be all that hellish warm in Barcelona either at this time of year.'

He pointed towards the ground. 'Warmer than down there, buddy, bet on it.'

'We'll see,' I said, as I opened my beer.

'What did you do before GWA?' I asked him.

'I was with Triple W. I was number two to the head honcho there.'

'What's Triple W like?'

'It's a damn good operation. It has the top roster of performers in the US right now. A lot of people thought it would take a ratings nose-dive when Everett and Jerry left, but it's held up pretty good.'

'What about the other lot, CWI? Have you ever worked for them?'

He looked at me, sideways from his seat. 'The company line here,' he said, his voice lowered almost to a whisper, 'is that CWI sucks, and that Tony Reilly – the guy who runs it – is an asshole. You don't have to look too far to figure out why that should be.'

'I don't understand.'

'The Princess was Tony Reilly's girl, before she met the Boss. Mr Reilly didn't like it when she left him. The Boss doesn't like Mr Reilly, 'cause he said a few things about her afterwards. I better say no more than that.'

I chanced my arm. 'Do I get the impression that you don't agree with the company line?'

'Mr Ring Announcer,' Sonny Leonard drawled, with a smile, 'I always agree with the company line.'

I didn't push it any further. Instead I let our discussion drift on to the logistics of the GWA operation, and on the quality of the Spanish workers who were waiting for us at our venue, up on the Olympic hill of Montjuic. They had been recruited by our hosts, who had promised that they would have all the skills the job required. Finally, after our lunch trays had been cleared away we lapsed into silence, and in Leonard's case, to sleep.

Although I had spent some time in Catalunya, and still owned fifty per cent of a property there having agreed with Prim, my ex-partner, that I would cash in my half only when she chose to sell, I had never been to Barcelona Airport until I touched down with the GWA party. The greater part of it was built for the 1992 Olympics, and was designed to foster the illusion that air travel is a pleasant experience. It works; the place looks more like a shopping mall than an air terminal. Its only downside is a crazy system in the baggage hall which requires a 100 peseta coin before a trolley could be freed from the rack. I wonder if the bright spark who introduced it asked himself how many people disembark from an international flight with the local coinage in their pockets.

We made it through passport control and customs somehow, to the bus which was waiting for us outside. As I was boarding Everett tapped me on the shoulder and pointed to the two seats immediately behind the driver. We sat together, silently as Sonny Leonard climbed on board and made his way to the back of the vehicle.

'Did you get anything out of him during the flight?' the big man asked as we pulled away from the kerb. So the seating arrangement had been no accident.

'Maybe,' I said. As I thought about his question I realised something about myself: I suppose it's the reason why I'm a very good Private Enquiry Agent but a bloody awful Private Detective. When I'm interviewing someone who knows what the purpose of our conversation is I am completely relaxed, but when I have to resort to any sort of deceit, I am stricken with guilt. 'I got the impression that Leonard's a mercenary. He doesn't care about the rights and wrongs of a situation, he cares about who's going to give him the best deal. You offered him the chance to be head honcho, as he put it, and I think he was grateful. But I don't reckon you have his undying loyalty.'

'So you reckon he could be bought?'

'I think that as an operative, he'd go to the highest bidder. But whether he'd get involved in sabotage, I could not possibly say. I do know that he doesn't see Tony Reilly as a monster, though. He was very respectful, in fact. It was Mr Reilly this, Mr Reilly that.'

Everett growled. 'If he is selling GWA out, he's gonna learn some respect for me – the hard way.'

Barcelona Airport isn't very far from the city centre. The bus pulled up outside our hotel in no more than fifteen minutes. The driver waited as we checked in, then drove the team to the BattleGround venue, a big, elegant upturned bowl. If there is a European city with better sports stadia than Barcelona, I've still to find it.

The GWA trucks were parked at the side, backed into loading bays. As we approached we saw several young men in overalls, some heading into the tall vehicles, others heading into the stadium, carrying items of equipment and scenery. 'What the . . .' Sonny Leonard exploded, a few rows behind me. 'I told these guys not to begin unloading until I got here.'

As the bus drew to a halt he jumped from his seat and tore down the aisle, leaping out onto the tarmac even before the doors were fully open. I heard him swear in heavily Americanised Spanish as he strode towards the labourers.

'Sure and don't be bursting a blood vessel, Sonny.' The familiar, laughing shout came from inside the nearest truck as the rest of us followed on his heels; and a second later,

Liam Matthews stepped out, onto the unloading ramp.

'What the hell are you doing here?' Everett boomed. 'You're supposed to be convalescing. I told the back office to book you and your mom a holiday, starting next week.'

'Sure, so you did,' the Irishman agreed. 'In the meantime, all my stitches are out, I'm healing fast and my old lady's giving me no leeway at all, so I decided to come down here with the trucks and give Sonny the benefit of my experience.' He beamed at the red-faced foreman. 'Don't you worry either, fella. We haven't broken any of your gear. It's all inside, ready for you to start setting up.'

I looked at Everett, then at Diane. He was frowning, like a huge black cloud. She was grinning, from ear to ear.

25

I had never watched the roadies set up from scratch before. Under Sonny Leonard's shouted directions – clearly, his Spanish was up to the job – they began in the centre, by raising the ring.

I stood with Jerry Gradi and watched them work. 'Why does your ring only have three ropes?' I asked him.

'Because it always had three ropes,' he replied. 'So did boxing rings, until about forty years ago, when a fighter died after being hit back of the head by a whipping bottom rope. After that, their authorities switched to four.

'The ropes in a boxing ring are tighter than ours too, so that fighters can't use them to lever more power into their punches. We like 'em loose, to help us build momentum. The other difference is in the turn-buckle padding.' He pointed to Leonard, up in the ring. 'In boxing, the steel rings in the corners that turn the ropes are covered by a single pad, from top to bottom.

'We got separate pads on each turn-buckle, on account of one of our standard moves is to grab the other guy and slam him into the corner, hard. The top pad is the thickest, 'cos that's where the biggest impact is. It's the foreman's job to fix 'em on, to make sure they're secure.'

As we watched, Sonny Leonard was working on the corner nearest us, fastening on the pads, which were covered in red leather, and looked a lot like boxing gloves. Jerry pointed at him. 'You make sure those is tight,' he called out, meaningfully. 'Daze is going to be tossing me into that corner tomorrow night, and I don't want to wind up hittin' no steel.'

'Check 'em yourself, then,' Leonard snarled back at him.

'Okay, okay, okay,' The Behemoth replied, holding up his hands in a mollifying gesture. 'Don't get so touchy. It ain't your ass gonna get stomped in there – unless you screw up those turn-buckle pads, that is!'

'I didn't know you and Daze were on tomorrow,' I said. 'I thought you were keeping that for the next pay-per-view event.'

'We are, really. Tomorrow's just a warm-up. Rockette and I are taking on Daze in a handicap match.' He grinned. 'Tommy's gonna get stomped again. Ev hasn't quite forgiven him yet for that guitar stunt.'

I looked at him. 'You're looking happy this week. Are things going all right with Sally?'

'Yeah, great, thanks. Don't need you to speak for me no more. I'll need to watch out for looking happy, though. That ain't The Behemoth's angle. Gotta do some work on bein' ferocious again.'

26

I missed Jan like crazy, all that night. She'd have loved being with the crew in Barcelona, especially to see me being interviewed by a reporter from the Catalan television station. They were looking for Spanish speakers, so Daze took me along to the studio with him. His grip of Castillian was much better than mine, but I think I scored more points with the presenter by managing a few words in Catalan.

We were happy to do the slot, since there were still a couple of thousand seats left in the big arena, and Everett was keen to have a full house.

Jan would have loved our night on the town too, at a long table in one of the Catalan capital's most famous restaurants, a big galleried place with some seats which let diners look down into the kitchen, with its huge, original, cast-iron range.

Eventually I couldn't restrain myself any longer. I dug out my mobile phone and called her, from the din of the restaurant. 'What the hell are you doing?' she asked.

'Having dinner.'

'In the street, by the sound of it.'

'Naw, honey, the street's quieter than this place.'

'Well lucky you. Me, I'm still working on Susie's papers.'

'Turn it in love. There's always tomorrow. You're sleeping for two now, remember.'

The satellite link was clear, but I could barely hear her against the background noise. 'I suppose so. I've got the hairdresser in the morning, and I'm shopping in the afternoon, but I can always work in the evening, before your show.' There was a roar from a table near ours, and I had to strain even harder to make her out. 'I'm getting there, Oz. I'll let you see what I've found when you get home.'

Jan would have enjoyed the next morning too; a tour of the city on our chartered bus, with stops at the Sagrada Familia, Gaudi's great cathedral, which has been under construction for over a hundred years and is still nowhere near completion, at the Ramblas, for coffee in one of the dozens of street bars, whose tables are set under the trees between the avenue's twin carriageways, and at the enormous Camp Nou, home of Barcelona Football Club and a place of worship for most Catalans, where a light buffet was set out in a hospitality suite.

By the time the bus arrived at the Arena, dead on one pm, I had decided to spend some of my windfall income from the GWA commission on a surprise spring weekend trip to the city for the two of us.

Sonny Leonard was standing at the performers' entrance to the stadium, smoking a cigarette, as we dismounted from our vehicle. 'Everything ready?' Daze called to him.

'Yeah, boss,' the foreman replied. 'These Spanish guys know what they're doing okay. The CWI crowd did a couple of tour events here last summer, so they had a good idea of what our business is like.'

'That's good. Take a break, Sonny. You and the bus driver take a cab back to the hotel, go into the five-star restaurant and have some lunch. Get back here for six.'

'Yeah, okay. I'll do that.' He dropped his cigarette and ground it into the tarmac with his right foot, then headed towards the bus.

Watching him go, Everett grunted. 'CWI, huh?

Guess we'd better show these people how a real wrestling promotion should be.' He turned to the team. 'Come on, Ladies and Gentlemen, let's get inside and into the run-through.'

He beckoned to me. 'Oz, while I get changed into my ring gear, you go find Barbara and ask her how the tickets have gone since Channel 33 broadcast our interviews last night. If there are any left, tell her to let them go half-price.

'After you've done that, with Leonard off patch, I want you to do what you did last week. Go over the staging and look for problems – anything that shouldn't be there.'

I did exactly as he asked – everyone always did exactly as Everett asked – steadily through the afternoon; during breaks in the run-through action, and while I wasn't polishing my minimally bilingual introductions for the show itself. As I checked the staging, I was careful to ensure that I wasn't noticed by Liam Matthews, who had joined the commentary team for the event. However the Irishman seemed to be well on the way back to top form, which meant that if it wasn't female, he didn't notice it.

'All clear, Everett,' I told the giant as he stepped out of the ring after his last run-through with Jerry and Rockette, a heavily curtailed affair, with only the speed moves but none of the power stuff being rehearsed. It looked like a good match; I had never seen Daze and The Behemoth go at it before, other than that one time on television in Anstruther, and I was looking forward to it.

'You didn't find anything unusual?'

'Nothing at all; everything seems fine. Did you check the whiz-bangs?'

'We ain't using them here; they're against regulations. Just lasers, lights and noise . . . lots of noise. I'll put four of our hired Spanish security guys on duty at the ring before we let the crowd in, to make sure than no one – marks or otherwise – goes anywhere near it.

'With luck, we'll get through this show clean.'

27

Because of Central European Time, we were running an hour later by the watch than usual, and so it was after six when the doors were opened and the first of the curious public came filing in. I had just checked with Barbara: the last of the tickets had gone; it was a full house.

The feeling from the crowd as it grew was different from either the languid Geordie curiosity of Newcastle, or the proprietorial buzz of the Glaswegians. The Catalan marks were full of Latin excitement, shouting and laughing among themselves, singing football songs and waving the home-made banners which seemed to be obligatory at all televised wrestling promotions. By six-fifty-five, as show time approached, they even had a Mexican wave going.

It was on its third circuit of the arena when my own private wave swept over me. It seemed to begin in the pit of my stomach and radiate outwards. I felt my heart hammering, I seemed to explode into a cold sweat, my head swam, the arena seemed to fade to red, then back again, and I felt overwhelmingly weak. I had experienced stage fright before, but never anything like the pure dread of those moments.

Fortunately, my attack vanished as suddenly and as completely as it had visited me. The lights dimmed, the wave stopped, the audience fell silent, and we were in business. I climbed into the ring, the lighting director found me, and my silver spot winked on. Wrestlers are judged, to a great extent, by the acclamation of the crowd. I'd guess there's nothing new about that; I imagine the same was true in the Coliseum of Ancient Rome. Today's gladiators call it a 'pop'. I'll swear that in my third week as the GWA ring announcer, when the spotlight hit me, I got a 'pop' of my own. Or at least I thought I did; that's how tightly my new role had taken hold of me.

I got through my few welcoming words of passable Spanish, repeated them in English, then got on with introducing the first match. That was easy; it featured Sally Crockett, the first genuine, pan-European ring superstar.

As usual she was superb as she worked over a beefy Swedish girl who wrestled under the name of Valkyrie and who came into the ring wearing a horned helmet and carrying a huge brass shield. At the end of the match, two of our Spanish roadies carried her out of the ring on that shield and up the ramp towards the dressing room, leaving Sally to milk the adulation of the crowd for all it was worth.

As she stood perched on the middle rope I sneaked a glance towards the wrestlers' entrance. Jerry was there, in a track suit and without his helmet, adulating with the rest of them. For a moment, I wondered how he would take it when the time came – as it would, in accordance with the laws of unpredictability which govern pro wrestling story lines – for her to lose.

The crowd's enthusiasm for Sally's show carried on through the programme. I was still learning the game, and my lesson for the night was that sports entertainment is to a great extent about firing up the crowd to a point just short of hysteria, to the level at which it has an addictive effect on the viewing audience. *They'll be well hooked tonight*, I thought as the excitement reached fever pitch with the entry of The Behemoth, flanked by Tommy Rockette and Diane, The Princess.

She was wearing a specially made, skin-tight, nipple-pointing, ass-clinging, no-underwear number in the red and yellow stripes of the Catalan flag. Small wonder Everett was jealous, yet, I reminded myself, it was he who allowed his wife to appear in public dressed like that. As she approached the ring, I looked down at Liam Matthews, at the commentator's table. He was gazing at her with a look of undisguised lust . . . but then so was every other man at ringside.

And then the roof rose a couple of feet in the air, before settling back into position. There was no aerial entrance for Daze this time, since the structure of the arena ruled it out. Instead his music played and he marched slowly down the ramp in his ring suit and cape, looking like a small – no, medium-sized – army under a single red spotlight. Reaching the ring, he disdained the steps, leaping instead from a standing position up onto the surround, then stepping over the top rope. Arms raised high, he circled, facing each quadrant of the screaming audience in turn, as a pattern of sharp red and yellow laser beams flickered across his body, creating a flame effect.

The television lights were still coming up, and I was barely out of the ring before Jerry hit him with a spearing shoulder-first football tackle, just above the right hip but below the rib-cage, bearing him across the ring and into the ropes. But as they were catapulted back, by their own weight and momentum, Daze caught the top strand, steadying himself as Jerry went flying across the ring to the ropes on the other side. The force of his impact sent Tommy Rockette, who had been standing on the apron holding the tag rope, crashing down on to the floor beside my table, and rebounded The Behemoth back towards the centre.

The black giant caught him in mid-ring, all close on four hundred pounds of him, swept him off his feet and round into a power-slam which sounded like the collapse of a large building. The referee knelt beside them and began to count; 'One,' pause 'Two'. Theatrically, he mouthed the third and winning call, but the sound died in his throat as Jerry thrust his right shoulder off the canvas.

Daze jumped to his feet, hauling The Behemoth upright after him and pushed him into the ropes once again, as if to set him up for another slam. This time, though, it was Jerry who used the top strand as a brake. He grabbed his opponent's arm and made to hurl him into the corner, but the big man simply braced himself, reversed the hold and sent him, instead, flying backwards with impossible speed into the corner of the ring.

The helmeted monster hit the red turn-buckle pads above me with a 'Bang!' which was so loud it was heard even above the howls of the crowd; so loud that it drew a great collective gasp. *No wonder they don't rehearse those*, I said to myself. Daze followed up his advantage, sprinting into the corner to crash a lariat blow to the side of the other man's head, then he stood back, waiting for him to fall forward.

Fall forward Jerry did, but not according to the script, not in the exaggerated way I had seen them rehearse. Instead, his knees seemed to buckle; he began to topple to the ground, but Everett caught him first, turning him on to his back and laying him gently on the canvas.

'Doctor! Now!' he roared, as the crowd began to fall silent. 'Medico! En seguido!' I had my doubts. Two weeks earlier, when Matthews had needed one in Newcastle, there hadn't been a single doctor in the house.

I scented it as I ran up the steps into the ring; a sharp, burning smell, strong enough to make its presence felt even over the other odours which hung in the air; sweat, liniment, and humanity in general.

There was yet another smell too. As I looked at Jerry, lying there on the floor I saw the blood as it welled from beneath him and began to spread; I saw it as it began to bubble on his lips. My dad has a thing about first aid. He believes that everyone should learn it, and he made damn sure that Ellie and I did. I knew what that bubbling meant.

'Turn him over on his face!' I shouted to Everett, who was kneeling beside his grey-faced friend. 'I think his lung's been punctured. Turn him, or he could drown on his own blood.'

He didn't look up at me, but stared out of the ring, his expression frozen, with shock, I guessed.

'Do as he says!' another Scottish voice called out. 'I'm a nurse! Do it now!'

The evening had become totally surreal. I blinked. It couldn't be Primavera, there in the ring: but it was. She was tanned; her hair was longer than it had been when I had left her. And blonder; more bleached by the sun, yet it was Prim all right; blue eyes sparkling fiercely, trim little body encased in denim shirt and jeans. She stood beside Everett. Even kneeling he looked almost as tall as she was. Then she slapped him, hard, across the face. 'Do it!' she screamed at him.

He snapped out of it at that, leaned over Jerry and rolled him over as gently as he could, Prim kneeling beside him, in the blood, helping him. The Behemoth's tunic was saturated, but once he was lying face down I could still see the ragged wound in his back, just below the right shoulder-blade.

As I watched I felt a hand on my shoulder; I looked round to see Sally Crockett, with tears streaming down her face. 'What's happened?' she whimpered.

'It looks as if he's been shot,' I answered; cruelly blunt, I know, but I was stunned too. At once I tried to reassure her. 'Don't panic though. Prim's worked in a war zone. She knows what she's doing.'

As I spoke, my former lover turned and stared up at me.

'Oz,' she said, 'give me a credit card.' Her tone was so commanding that at that moment, if she'd asked for my right arm, I'd probably have unscrewed it and given it to her. Without a word, I took out my wallet and handed her my Tesco loyalty card.

She took the stiff plastic and pressed it against the hole in Jerry's back. 'Thanks. This guy has a sucking wound,' she explained to Everett. 'We have to keep the air out.' A pair of paramedics had appeared in the ring and stood, gazing down at her in professional admiration. She spoke to them in Spanish, astonishing me again, for she had very little when we had split. One of them replied. 'Nada,' he said, shaking his head.

'Bloody magic,' she muttered. 'Oz, these guys have no bandages. I need something to pack this.'

Sally was wearing a white silk shirt. Without a word she unbuttoned it, slipped it off, and handed it over. 'Thanks,' said Prim. 'Now I need something to make it secure.'

I looked across the ring. Matthews was standing on the apron outside the ropes, grim-faced, watching. I called across to him. 'Liam, there was a roll of gaffer tape on the commentary table earlier. Find it and give us it in here.' The Irishman nodded and called down to the commentators, who were still in their seats. A moment later, one of them tossed a thick roll of shiny brown tape up towards him. He caught it, threw it on to me, and I handed it down to Prim.

'That's good enough,' she said, then looked at Everett. 'You. I need you to get him into a sitting position, so I can strap this up. After that they can take him in the ambulance.' She was in total command.

Jerry Gradi in normal circumstances was a huge guy to handle. Unconscious, as a dead weight, he should have been virtually impossible, but Everett Davis was superhuman. With Prim still pressing the plastic card tight against the wound, he turned him over again, then lifted his great trunk off the bloody canvas.

'Oz,' she called. 'Get down here and take over pressing on the card while I tape him up.' Wincing as the blood soaked into my trousers, I knelt beside her, balled Sally's shirt into a pad as she showed me and used it to force the card as hard as I could against the hole in Jerry's back, staunching the flow. I held my thumb on it until she had covered the packing completely with the gaffer tape, winding it as tight as she could around the huge wrestler's rib-cage. Finally she tore the tape free from the roll with her teeth and spoke to the ambulance crew once again. One of them jumped down from the ring, and ran off. 'Gone for a wheelchair,' she explained.

She went with the paramedics when, eventually, Jerry was loaded into their chair, and wheeled out of the arena. It was only then that I remembered the crowd: to an hombre and señora they had stayed in their seats, watching the scene, or as much as they could see, in silent fascination.

I was still carrying my mike. I switched it on, and apologised in my best Spanish for the delay, and asked them to stay seated. 'Might as well send them home,' said Everett despondently, as he stood in the ring beside me as I made my announcement. 'I'm screwed. The stations are gonna have to show back-up material. Bang goes one million dollars in penalty payment.'

'Not necessarily,' I said. 'You can still shoot the match with you and Rockette. There's still time. But right now, can we try to figure out what happened?'

'This happened.' Liam Matthews' voice came from the corner of the ring, the one into which Jerry had been slammed. We stepped across to join him.

He had his hand on the top turn-buckle pad. As we looked at it we could see that it was ripped, that the padding was protruding, and that some of it was blackened and scorched.

'I was watching from the side as Jerry went into the corner,' said Matthews. 'It just seemed to burst, but looking at this, I'd say there was some sort of explosive charge inside it, and it went off when The Behemoth hit it.'

'But other people have been posted in that corner tonight,' Everett protested.

'None as big as him,' I reminded him. 'Or as hard as that.' I sniffed the pad, and remembered the burning smell, as I climbed into the ring. 'Liam's right; this thing was rigged to take out either big Jerry, or you.'

I shoved a finger into the rip, then pulled it out, fast. There was metal inside, and it was still warm. I reached behind the turn-buckle, found the cords which held the pad in place, and untied them.

'That's the answer,' I said to Everett, waving it at him. 'Now, are you going to rescue this show?'

The big man was still struggling to focus on the reality of the situation. 'What time is it?' he asked at last.

I looked at my watch. 'Ten past nine, local time; an hour earlier GMT.'

As he frowned, Diane came to stand beside him. Her costume was damp with sweat, and almost transparent. I looked down and saw that there were blood streaks around the hem.

'They've downloaded the first hour of the show to the station,' she said, her voice still steady. 'We have to send them the second half inside the next twenty minutes.'

'Then we're screwed,' said her husband. 'We don't have time to fill the gap.'

'Yes we do,' she snapped. 'They break for commercials before the last match. We can download what we have right now, then follow up later with tape of you and Rockette.'

Everett shook his head. His expression was agonised. 'Just what the hell do you think I am, bitch?' he snarled at her. 'That guy in the ambulance, that guy who could be dead right now; he's my best friend in the world. I knew him long before I knew you. When I joined Triple W out of college, it was Jerry who taught me what this game is all about, even though he knew he was probably making me the main man, at his expense.

'You think I can just step back up to the plate and perform? Stand in his blood and perform? No way.'

She stepped in front of him, hands on hips, glaring up at him. 'That's exactly what Jerry wants you to do. He owns a chunk of this company, remember. You want him to wake up and find that you've cost him a couple of hundred thousand dollars because you've acted like a pussy?' She spat the last word at him.

He sighed, and nodded. 'Yeah, okay. I'll do it. Oz, you hold on to that pad. Di, tell Rockette he's on in five minutes. Tell the camera ops not to shoot the blood on the floor unless they got no other option.'

'You've got another option,' said Liam Matthews, quietly.

'What do you mean?' Diane asked.

The Irishman looked at her. 'Daze and Rockette as a main event, with no gimmicks, just will not work. We all know that. We need an edge . . . and you're looking at him.'

'You can't wrestle,' I heard myself protest. 'You had a kidney injured two weeks ago.'

'I don't have to wrestle,' he shot back. 'You'll see.

'Trust me on this, boss. You begin your match with Rutherford, string it out, then go along with whatever happens.'

Everett was beyond arguing. He nodded and headed back towards the dressing room area.

I switched on my mike again, and told the crowd, in

broken Spanish, what they knew already; that The Behemoth had been injured. Then I told them a small lie; I said that he wasn't badly hurt. Finally, I announced that Daze would be back in the ring in five minutes. The buzz of conversation turned into a cheer; not as loud as before, certainly, but a pop none the less. By the time the lights dimmed, and the spotlight picked up Tommy Rockette, guitarless, making his way down the aisle, they were as excited as they had been before.

I announced him, in English, then Spanish, and jumped down from the ring to await the arrival of Daze. Diane had found a chair and was sitting at my table, wrapped in a roadie's jacket. As I took my place, Sally Crockett, who had gone back to the dressing room to find a GWA tee-shirt to replace her silk shirt, came and knelt beside me. She was shaking; I took her hand and gave it a squeeze.

'Don't worry,' I told her. 'He's going to be all right. I know it. You can't kill Behemoths.'

She looked up at me. 'But what happened, Oz? Was it someone in the crowd?'

'No. I can't tell you for sure, but it wasn't that. Just you concentrate on being thankful that my ex was there to take charge.'

So much had happened, so fast, that I had barely had time to consider Prim's cameo reappearance in my life. I had just begun to wonder why, when the lights dimmed again, and threw me back into the midst of the show.

Everett's match stank, I have to say. He fumbled at least three moves as he and Tommy Rutherford hammed it up in the ring above me, but the Spanish crowd were there to see Daze, and damn few of them knew the difference between a power slam and a polka.

The pair had been in listless action for three minutes, when Liam Matthews, back at the commentary table, took off his head-set, stripped off his jacket to reveal muscles bulging out of his short-sleeved shirt, picked up a hand mike and trotted up the steps into the ring.

The first clue Tommy Rockette had of his presence was a karate kick which caught him on the left temple and turned him into the same sack of potatoes which he had imitated so well a week earlier. Daze looked on, genuinely astonished I guessed, as the Irishman, a foot shorter than him, shook his hair out of its pony tail and stepped up to him, poking him with his right index finger in the centre of his huge chest.

'Big fella yerself,' Matthews drawled in his best adopted Dublin brogue. 'Have oi got a bone to pick with you. Two weeks ago, in England, I picked up a little scratch.' He paused, not for the crowd, I knew, but so that the viewing audience could follow him. 'Next thing I knew, I wasn't the Transcontinental Champion any more.' He nodded. 'That's right, when I was injured, they stole my belt.

'Now everyone knows that you're the ringmaster of this here circus, and that everything that happens in the Global Wrestling Alliance has to be okay with you. So I guess that when the suits in the back office took away my belt, you didn't argue about it.'

He poked Everett in the chest again. 'So here's what I've got to say, Mr Daze, sor,' he yelled into his mike. 'The hot news in the GWA, is that the Champ, The Behemoth, is on the injured roster. That means the suits will have to forfeit his belt too. So little Liam is here to make a challenge to the mighty Daze.' The spectators didn't have a clue what he was talking about, but as his voice rose, so their excited buzz began to build into a cheer.

'At the next pay-per-view, in Edinburgh, it'll be me against you, big man for the GWA title – assuming you've got the guts to face me, that is.' The cheer grew into a roar.

'And when you do, I'm going to . . .' He hit Daze across

the chest with a blow which looked like a karate cut, but was in fact a loud slap. '. . . chop . . .' Another blow. '. . . you . . .' A third blow. '. . . Down!'

The roar had grown into a single shrill scream, as Daze picked Liam up by the throat, as I had seen him do once before. But this time, the Irishman kicked out, with the side of his right foot, appearing to catch him significantly below the waist. The giant released his hold . . . and as he did, every light in the arena went out.

When they came on again, five seconds later, only Daze and the still-prone form of Tommy Rockette remained in the ring.

Watching the story unfold, I had forgotten that Diane was sitting beside me, at my small table. 'And roll credits,' she whispered in my ear. 'Terrific. The clever little bastard has saved the show. And at the same time, he's given himself the big push he was after, right to the top of the totem pole, up beside Daze.' She stood, then walked around across to join her husband as he waved goodbye to the audience and vaulted over the ropes and down to the floor, in a single jump.

As Matthews crawled out from underneath the ring he winked up at me. 'Don't know what you've got to grin about, son,' I whispered to myself, so quietly that not even Sally could hear, although she was still kneeling beside me. 'You've just talked yourself into a match with a monster, who thinks you're shagging his wife. There's a fair chance he's going to bust the other kidney as well!'

28

Diane had gone, presumably to change out of her provocative
Catalan flag dress, but Everett was waiting for me at the top
of the ramp. 'We got some business to do, Oz,' he rumbled.
I was wrong; it wasn't quiet gentlemanly Everett who stood
there, it was Daze. All the shock and uncertainty was gone
from his eyes, replaced by fiercely blazing anger.

'That bastard Leonard set this trap,' he said. 'We stood
and we watched him. Take two security guys and arrest his
ass. Then find a room where he and I can talk, once I've
changed.' He looked down at me. 'You might not want to be
there when we do.'

'Wrong, mate,' I retorted, even though I was, frankly,
scared stiff by the strength of his fury. 'I will be there. If only
to stop you from killing him.'

The giant shook his head, slowly. 'I'm not going to kill
him, man. But I guarantee he's going to tell me everything
about how Tony fucking Reilly hired him to sabotage GWA
and to cripple or kill its people.'

'No, Everett,' I told him, as firmly as I dared. 'I'm the
investigator here, not you. Leonard's going to tell me all that
stuff in a formal interview, on tape; then I'm going to have it
transcribed and he's going to sign it, with us as witnesses to
that signature. In his statement I'll ask him to specify that he
was not forced by physical violence or the threat of it, to
make his confession.

'Now I'll go and find him like you want. But in the meantime, you go and change out of your monster suit. Find a white shirt and wear that, so that after we've interviewed the guy, everyone can see that there are no bloodstains on you.' I paused and looked at him. 'You know what happens after that though, don't you?'

'Tell me,' he said.

'We have to hand him over to the police. And this.' I gave him the burst turn-buckle pad, which I was still holding.

'Hell, no! We deal with this in-house. Once I have Leonard's confession I'm gonna take it to Tony Reilly and beat him to death with it. Son of a bitch is going to sell me his GWA holding at a knock-down price or I'm going to sue his ass off!'

'Okay, but Leonard still has to be handed over. Look, Jerry's just been admitted to hospital with what to all intents and purposes is a gunshot wound. They're going to do just the same as they'd do in Glasgow, London or New York – tell the cops. You won't have a choice.'

'Maybe not. We'll see when they come looking. But now, you go get the bastard.' His head seemed to droop. 'While you're doing that, I'll try to find out how Jerry's doing.'

I nodded, and headed off to the main door of the Arena, where I commandeered two security guards to back me up in detaining the foreman. Inside, we found the local installation crew standing around. They were waiting for something, clearly. One of them had a different coloured uniform jacket from the rest. Guessing that this might mean that he was in charge, I called him over, in my dodgy Spanish.

'Have you seen the GWA foreman?' I asked him.

He told me that they had been expecting Leonard. He had told them that after the show was over, he would need them to make the changes to the set which were needed for the next day's shooting of the matches for the Monday broadcast. They were waiting for him: but he had not appeared.

'Let's find him, then,' I told him. 'You people must know all of this building; you work here all the time. Get your men, join us, and let's look for Señor Leonard.'

Look for him we did, outside in the trucks, and all over the arena: on the floor of the hall, in the walkway round the perimeter of the roof, in the public toilets, male and female, and in the storage and basement areas. I knew long before we were finished that we had more chance of finding the Phantom of the Opera.

'He's gone,' I told Everett, who was waiting for me in the changing area, having changed into khaki slacks and a white tee-shirt. 'Mr Leonard has done a runner.'

'Goddammit! We should have grabbed him right then, Oz.'

'I know. I asked the television director when he saw him last. He said that he saw him by the ring while Prim was treating Jerry, but that he can't remember seeing him after that.' The 'idea' bulb flashed in my brain. 'What about his passport? Maybe he's gone back to the hotel to collect it, and his gear.'

Everett shook his head. 'He's an American, Oz. He probably carries his passport with him all the time. As for his gear; hell, he's a roadie. They hardly carry any.'

'Could we have him stopped at the airport?' I ventured.

'Where's he going? Not back to Scotland. The US eventually, sure, but he could get there from anywhere. My guess is that he'll get out of Spain and take it from there. What would you do if you were in his shoes?'

It didn't take me long to answer that one. 'I'd phone Reilly and have him send me a plane ticket to the States, for collection at an airport of my choice: – Perpignan, Montpellier, Toulouse, Bordeaux, Lyon . . . any one of those or another, either direct or routed through Paris.

'Mind you, we could catch him wherever he tries to fly out from . . . if you tell the police about him.'

'Hah! And what would we have after that? Press stories all over Europe about GWA, and about the hits we've taken in recent weeks. I do not want my customer stations to know what happened to Jerry, that Dave Manson isn't on sabbatical, and that I'm having to wrestle a guy in my next pay-per-view who's still passing traces of blood every time he pees.

'If that sort of stuff hits the fan, the way is open for Reilly to move in on me. CWI supplied those stations before; at a loss, sure, but I bet Tony would take some more losses to put me out of business. Unless I have Leonard's confession that he was Reilly's man, bought and paid for, I can't do much to head him off.

'So no, Oz. Even if the Spanish police do come asking questions, like you reckon they will, I will not tell them about Sonny Leonard . . . and neither will you. If I have to, I'll smash up a turn-buckle and tell them it was equipment failure caused the accident.' He waved the red leather pad, which I had given him earlier. 'They ain't gonna see this.'

'What if this turns into a murder investigation?' I shot at him. 'Are you still going to conceal evidence?

'How is Jerry anyway? Did you get through to the hospital?'

Everett sighed. 'Saturday night is not the best time to call a hospital emergency unit in any city. There wasn't no one there could speak to me. I'm gonna have to go down there to find out for myself.'

I nodded. 'Yes, we should. Let me change out of this bloody penguin suit, and I'll come with you.'

29

I expected him to be waiting for me at the performers' door when I emerged in my civvies; slacks, my black suede bomber jacket and a Behemoth tee-shirt which I had scrounged from the merchandise people.

But he wasn't. She was there instead: Primavera Phillips, with dark blood staining her jeans all the way up to the knees, and smeared on the long sleeves of her denim shirt. She looked tired, not far short of exhausted, but she was beautiful nonetheless, with her tangled, sun-bleached blonde hair flicking against her shoulders, something I had never seen before.

'Hi.' She spoke softly, almost tentatively, as I approached.

'Hi, yourself. Come here.' We closed the gap between us in a moment and hugged. As I pressed her to me, the tension within her exploded into tears.

Her face was buried in my tee-shirt, which bore the image of Jerry Gradi. For a moment the symbolism of it made me fearful. 'Prim, he isn't . . . Is he?'

'No,' she mumbled into my chest. 'I spoke to the doctor who admitted him, after he'd been X-rayed and sent up to surgery. He's going to be okay, they reckon.'

Relief flooded me, finding its way out in laughter. 'In that case,' I said, 'since you saved his life earlier, don't bloody drown him now.'

She looked at The Behemoth's face on my shirt for the first time, and grinned.

'You're a heroine, my dear,' I told her. 'I'm going to make sure, damn sure, that the GWA recognises what you did tonight.'

'What? Are you going to get me free admission for life to all your shows? Thanks, but I'll settle for a steak from you, although I don't doubt it'll be on expenses.'

'It's a deal; Everett can afford it. But hold on, I've got to meet him here. We were going to see Jerry.'

'Everett's your large friend, yes? Looks a bit like a tree, goes by the name of Daze?' She shook her head. 'I've seen him already. I told him about Jerry, and also that there's no point in anyone going to see him till tomorrow. Even after the surgery, they'll keep him under for a few hours at least. He said to tell you he was going back to the hotel to catch up with Diane. Who's she?'

'His wife. You probably saw her; Catalan flag dress.'

'Saw her?' Prim exclaimed. 'Everybody saw her; bloody near all of her! Some of the women around me in the crowd weren't too keen on what she was doing to their flag, I should tell you.'

'I'll mention that, quietly, to the big man,' I promised.

'And who was the girl with the big tits? The one who gave me her silk shirt so quickly.'

'That was Sally; the GWA Ladies' Champ. She's Jerry's girlfriend.'

'A lady wrestler! Really? I've never met one of those. I thought they were all bruiser types; big bull dykes and such.'

'Nah, they're athletes. Just like the girls on that television show back home.'

She stepped back, took her arms from round my waist, and looked up at me. 'Oz, how the hell did you . . .' She stopped in mid-sentence. 'No, save it for dinner. I don't suppose you'll want to use this in the restaurant, but you might want it back anyway.' She reached into her hip pocket and handed me my Tesco loyalty card. 'Trust you to give me that one.'

I took it from her. 'Thanks. I'll pass it on to my pal The Behemoth, as a souvenir.'

'When you do, you can tell him he owes his girlfriend a new shirt. That one was a write-off.'

She pulled the tail of her own shirt from her jeans, used it to wipe the tear-streaks from her face, then shoved it back into her waistband. I took her by the hand and started towards the taxi rank at the front of the arena, where the last few spectators stood. 'Come on, let's grab a cab and go down-town.'

She pulled me back. 'No; my coche's down there, in the park.'

It took us less than three minutes to reach Prim's car. It was a Seat Ibiza hatchback, in what looked, even under the car park lights, a sickly orange colour. She unlocked it with a remote device. I climbed into the passenger seat, but Prim slid into the back. I looked at her, waiting: not surprised, for I was beyond being surprised by anything she did.

So I didn't bat an eyelid when she slid out of her jeans. 'Sorry,' she said, 'but I can't go into a restaurant looking like this. There's a pair of scissors in the glove box. Pass them over, will you please.'

I did as she told me: they were big, heavy dress-making scissors. Knowing her as well as I did, I guessed that she kept them there for security. She took them from me and as I watched, never thinking to avert my eyes from the sight of Prim in her knickers, she cut off the blood-stained trouser legs just above the knees. Next she unbuttoned her shirt, and slipped it off. I breathed an inward sigh of relief; she was wearing a bra. Invariably the sight of her without one had a certain effect on me. She trimmed the sleeves off the garment just above the elbows, then dressed quickly and jumped out of the car.

'There,' she said, modelling her new-look outfit on the tarmac. 'A bit skimpy for this time of year, I'll grant you, but at least we won't be arrested.' She opened the driver's door and slid into her seat, beside me.

'Like it?' she asked, grasping the steering wheel.

'It looks fine from inside, but were you blindfolded when you bought it? I mean, the colour, Prim . . .'

She laughed: not her normal, easy laugh, but high-pitched, not unlike Susie Gantry's distinctive giggle; as if for the first time in our lives she was unsure of herself with me. 'I got a deal on it, didn't I. Anyway, most of the time it's so dirty that you can't tell what colour it is.' She turned the ignition key, and the engine thrummed into life. It certainly sounded okay. 'I know a place where we can eat,' she said. 'I've been exploring Barcelona.'

'What else have you been doing?' I asked. 'Improving your Spanish for one thing. I was impressed, back there.'

'My job has a lot to do with that. I'm nursing again, in the big hospital in Girona. You know, the one you see just as you drive into the town from the north.'

'Yes, I know it. How did you get in there? I thought they'd have recruited Spanish only; you know what they're like.'

'I had help,' she said. 'Ramon put in a word for me.'

'Ramon?'

'Ramon Fortunato. Remember the Guardia Civil captain we met?' I nodded in the dark. 'He's not Guardia any more, he transferred to the Mossos Esquadra, the new Catalan national police force, and he's based in Girona. He heard about a supervisor job that was going in the A & E department and he asked me if I'd be interested. I hadn't thought about going back to nursing, but equally, I didn't intend to sit on my arse working my way through our capital. So I thought, what the hell.'

'Good for you,' I said. 'For big Jerry's sake, it's as well you're up to speed on emergencies.'

'That stuff back there?' she exclaimed. 'Pure meatball surgery: I learned that trick on chest wounds when I worked in Africa. Out there I used my Mastercard so often, then steam-sterilised it, so that the signature was obscured. I had to report it lost and get a replacement. That procedure would make great television, but I'd be sacked from any hospital in Europe for doing anything as unhygienic.'

'Don't worry, kid,' I said softly. 'I won't report you.'

I stared at her profile as she drove us down from Montjuic and into the city, thinking of the last time I had seen her: when we had split that morning in St Marti d' Empuries; the village where we had lived together for a while until I had an encounter with Jan which made me realise where I really belonged. And until Prim . . . but that was still too painful a memory for me to dwell on for long.

I had left her there, with a last kiss for luck. One way and another we had amassed a fair bit of money in our short time together, but we had agreed that we would do nothing about dividing it for a year, to give Prim a chance to decide how and where she wanted to live her life.

So I had driven off into the autumn afternoon, knowing that I would have to see her again at some point, but never dreaming that it would be in such bizarre circumstances.

The place which she knew was a restaurant in a side street about half a kilometre from the Columbus Monument. She found a space in one of the city's many underground car parks and led me to it. There were tables available, since it was still only around nine-forty-five, early on a Spanish Saturday night.

I let her order for us both: anchovies and escalivada, followed by two T-bone steaks, with two beers for starters and a bottle of Faustino III.

I watched her as she took her first mouthful of Estrella, and thought to myself that for all the tiredness which still showed on her face, and for all that she looked to have dropped a pound or two, I had never seen her looking lovelier.

'What else has Ramon been doing for you, then?' I asked her, casually.

She arched her eyebrows over the top of her glass. 'Nothing in that respect, my dear,' she said. 'Not that it would be any of your bloody business. He's a friend, that's all. He and his wife live in Albons, and they eat in Meson del Conde every so often. I saw them there and we all sort of got to know each other.'

She looked down at the table-cloth. 'There's been no one else, Oz. Not so far. In the last year I've had the two most memorable relationships of my life, both of them all too brief, sadly. I've always been aware of the dangers of rebound flings, so I've made a point of declining all offers.' She grinned. 'There have been more than a few, by the way. Junior doctors the world over would shag themselves into oblivion, given half a chance.

'So much for my non-sex-life, though. What about yours?'

I made a hole in my beer. 'Did you get my letter?' I asked her, as casually as I could.

'The one where you told me that you and Jan were getting married?' She nodded. 'I got it. Thanks for not inviting me, by the way. That would have been pushing it.' For the first time, I caught the faintest trace of bitterness in her voice.

'We're living in Glasgow,' I went on, quickly. 'Dad and Auntie Mary got hitched too, Ellie and the boys are fine, I'm back in business, Jan's carrying on with hers, we're both making plenty of money . . . and Jan's pregnant.'

She gasped slightly. 'When you went back, Oz,' she asked, after a moment, 'she wasn't, was she?'

'No, no, no,' I assured her. 'I'd have told you that. We only just found out.'

'The icing on the cake, eh.' She tried to hide it, but I saw her chin tremble.

'Prim, love, I'm sorry.'

She shook her head, and smiled, but her eyes were shining. 'Don't be, my dear. We talked it all out, remember. It wasn't just you who made the decision. As for Jan, I was never convinced that you were over her, even if you believed it. Why d'you think I wouldn't marry you when you asked me?'

'You said you wanted more time to think about it.'

'Yes, but what I meant was that I wanted you to have more time to think about it, so that both of us could be sure that it was me you really wanted. Brilliant tactician me, eh. Bloody backfired on me, didn't it.'

'But you didn't want to marry me either! You told me.'

She finished her beer and signalled for two more. 'Bollocks, my darling. Given the job that you do, I'm amazed that you always believe everything a woman says to you.'

She reached across the table and grabbed my hands. 'I'm sorry. I didn't mean to say all this. I didn't want to marry you if you were in love with someone else. That's the truth. Let's just be thankful it wasn't me who got pregnant and leave it at that.

'Quick, change the subject. Tell me, exactly how the pluperfect fuck did you get involved in this carry-on?'

'I'm doing a bit of undercover work for Everett,' I explained. 'Someone's been trying to sabotage his operation. What happened tonight is the culmination of a series of events. The big Daze fella hired me to help him find who was behind it.'

'And have you?' Prim asked.

'We have now. The road foreman: an American called Sonny Leonard. We suspected him before tonight, and now he's done a runner. The device that shot Jerry was hidden in the top pad in the corner of the ring. It was triggered by the impact of twenty-seven and a half stone of wrestler hitting it at high speed. It was Leonard's job to fit those pads; we even watched him do it.'

'I see. Are you sure he knew about the device?'

'There was other evidence against him; also, like I said, he's vanished.'

I finished my first beer, just as the second arrived. 'But how about you? How the hell did you come to leap up into that ring tonight like Florence fuckin' Nightingale?'

'Simple. I was in the English lady's bar in L'Escala last night, having a drink after work, the telly was on and all of a sudden, you were on it, speaking dodgy Catalan, and talking gibberish about this thing called the Global Wrestling Alliance. I have never fallen off a bar stool in my life before, but I was so surprised last night that I did just that.

'At the close of the item, the presenter said that there were still tickets available, and gave a number to contact. So I called it. The rest, as one says in Auchterarder, is geography.' She paused.

'I had quite a good seat too, overlooking the ring, When Jerry went down, I could tell from the way Everett reacted that it wasn't right, even before he yelled for assistance. Then I saw the blood. I had to argue my way through security to get to the ring, but I made it in time.'

'Thank heaven,' I said, sincerely. We both sat silent for a while, contemplating the outcome that might have been.

'Tell me,' I asked her, eventually. 'If there hadn't been an emergency, would I ever have known you were there?'

'I don't know,' she answered. 'I hadn't decided. You tell me. If I hadn't seen you on Canal 33, would I ever have known you'd been here?'

'I don't know either. I'd been thinking of calling you.' I

took my mobile phone from my pocket, and in that instant it rang.

'Probably Everett,' I said. But it wasn't.

'Oz? Is that you?' I didn't recognise the voice on the other end; not even after he'd told me who it was.

'Of course it is. Who's that?'

'It's Mike here.'

I held the phone away from my ear for a second and stared at it, astonished. 'Dylan? What the fuck are you calling me here for? Are you drunk or something?'

Prim stared at me across the table, as surprised as I was. The name, Dylan, meant plenty to her too.

'No, Oz, I'm not drunk.' The voice seemed to steady. 'I have something to tell you. Where are you?'

'In a restaurant.'

'Are you in company?'

'Yes. Now will you please tell me what this is about.'

'Okay.' His voice cracked again. 'Oh Christ man, I'm sorry.'

To this day, I still don't remember the moment he told me that Jan was dead; that my wife and my child were dead. What I do remember is the sensation of a blow within my head; the sudden overpowering dizziness, the phone slipping from my hand on to the table, Prim looking frightened as she reached to pick it up, and the cold beer splashing over me when my hand caught the glass and upset it, as I slipped from my chair to the floor.

30

I wanted my dad, very badly. I sat there, on a chair in the wine cellar of the restaurant, where Prim and the owner had taken me as I began to recover from my faint.

I was aware, yet unaware. I knew that something very bad had happened, but my mind refused to tell me what it was. All I knew was that I wanted Mac the Dentist with me, just as I had wanted him when I was four, when I had fallen out of a tree and broken my wrist.

Primavera was sitting next to me. Her head was on my shoulder, she was clutching my arm tightly, and she was crying. She was shaking like a leaf, too.

A man stood facing us. He asked me in Spanish if we would be all right. I looked at him blankly. 'How the fuck would I know?' I said, in English. He must have thought that I had meant 'Yes', for he nodded and disappeared back up a flight of stairs, to the restaurant.

I looked down at Prim again, and I saw my phone in the breast pocket of her shirt. I remembered, and I knew. My mind still wouldn't form the words, 'Jan is dead', but I knew all right. Mike Dylan's cracking voice on the phone, the look of unprecedented fear on Prim's face as she had picked it up, and now her racking, helpless sobs, far different from the tears of relief which she had shed earlier.

Horror. It was a word you saw in bookshops over a rack of shelves filled with names like Koontz, Barker and Stoker.

It was an adjective used with movies. It was a concept from wars long before my time. It wasn't a word that was meant to figure in my chaotic, but comfortable, life.

Yet now it did; now it consumed me. I sat there, in that dingy, musky, dusty cellar and I felt myself becoming cocooned in it: in a chrysalis of pure horror. It was numbing; it brought out beads of sweat which clung to my forehead like little chips of ice. 'Where are my tears?' I demanded of myself as Prim sobbed beside me, but it was too, too cold for weeping.

I closed my eyes and, clear as day, Jan's face swam into my vision, her dark hair shining as if moonlit, her head tilted back slightly, her eyes giving me her knowing look, light laughter on her lips. 'It's all right,' I told myself, 'it was a dream.' But then, as if to mock me, red blood began to froth from her mouth. It ran in thick lines from her nostrils, and from her ears, down her cheeks and chin to form a river round her neck.

I opened my eyes again, to drive away the vision, but it would not go. Whatever I did I had to confront it. I twisted my head, this way and that, but still it was before me, until at last I felt my mouth twist, and I heard myself scream, 'No! No! No!'

Then Prim was on her feet, still crying, but wrapping her arms around my head, pressing my face against her. 'Oz, oh Oz,' she whispered. 'This can't be happening.'

But she couldn't break through my chrysalis, through my cold carapace. Nothing could crack that. I seized her arms above the elbows, near the shoulders, in my hands, gripping hard enough to bruise, and forced her away from me. I held her at arm's length and I spoke to her in a voice that I had never owned before.

'You talked to him? You talked to Dylan?'

She nodded, helpless in my grip.

'Tell me what he said.'

'Let me go, Oz. You're hurting me.'

'Tell me.'

'I will, but Oz, you're breaking my arms.'

'Tell me.'

'Oz,' she wept. 'Please don't punish me for being alive.'

At last, her pain got through to me: I let her go, noticing the furious red and white weals which my madman's strength had left on her skin, noticing, but dispassionately, still not caring much.

'What did Mike say, Prim?' I asked her yet again, but patiently this time. 'I remember he was talking to me, but that's all. Then we were down here.'

She sat down again beside me, in her dining chair, with its bentwood back, and she began to stroke my arm, with her right hand, gently; up, down, up, down, ruffling the soft blond hairs, then smoothing them down again, ruffling, smoothing. I watched her, knowing that I didn't really want her to speak.

She did, though, as I had demanded of her, more fool me. She spoke, and changed my life.

'Dylan told me that Jan is dead, Oz. He said that she was found this evening. He couldn't say any more, he was too upset. But he gave me a couple of numbers for you to call, when you're ready.'

Her tears came again. 'Oh, Oz. I am so, so sorry.'

I was still numb, and by now I was taking relief in it. I looked at her, and I said, 'I'll bet.'

She looked at me as if I'd slapped her. I saw her hurt, but I was impervious to it. No, nothing got through my cocoon.

A small part of my rational brain knew all this, and made me realise that I had to use my horror as a shield. It wouldn't hold for ever, I knew, but while it did, I could be functional. Once it gave out . . .

So I cherished my coldness, and I hung on to it. To read that sort of book, they say you must suspend disbelief. In my need, I did it the other way round; I suspended belief.

'Come on,' I told her, standing as I spoke. 'We can't stay here. We have to go. I have things to do.'

She nodded, wiping her tears with the back of her hand. 'Okay. Do you want to go back to your hotel?'

I hadn't thought that far ahead. I hadn't thought my way past the top of the staircase, in fact. I handed the controls to my ice-cold auto pilot, and let myself go by instinct. 'No, I can't be with them. They're friends but they're strangers too. I need privacy for what I have to do. Take me to the apartment.'

Primavera looked at me. 'Are you sure? Is that—'

'Right and proper, you were going to say? I don't give a monkey's about that. What Dylan said isn't right or fucking proper either. I need privacy if I'm to deal with it. So come on. I'll drive.'

The man in the restaurant wasn't going to take any money, but I insisted on paying for what we had ordered. The Faustino III was on the table, not yet uncorked: having paid for it, I took it with me.

The hamlet of St Marti d' Empuries, in the municipal district of L'Escala, lies just over an hour and a half away, by the Autopista, from the centre of Barcelona. Prim's car had a sporty engine, and so I did it in an hour and fifteen minutes. Neither of us said a word all the way up the road. I was aware that my speed was making her nervous, but I didn't care, comfortable as I was within my icy state. Once she reached for the temperature control on the heater panel, turning it into the red zone, but I twisted it back to the blue minimum straight away.

The lights were still on in Meson del Conde when I drove into the square and parked beyond the church. Even before

I switched off the engine, Prim jumped out, ran to the ground level entrance to the apartment, opened it and pounded up the stairs to the living area. I followed her, carrying the Faustino; as I stepped inside and closed the door, I heard loud retching sounds coming from the bathroom.

I raised the shutters, opened the glass door and stepped out on to the terrace, gulping in deep lungfuls of the cold night air, as if it was fuel for my mood. I don't know how long I'd been there, looking out at the sea, when her voice sounded behind me. 'I'm sorry about that, but all of a sudden . . .' I shrugged my shoulders, my back still to her.

'I'll put on some coffee,' she volunteered.

I stretched out my left hand, behind me, offering her the Faustino. 'Open that too, and let it stand for a bit.' As she took it from me, I said, 'Remember the last time I stood here, and I told you that I was going back? Back to Jan?'

An indistinct murmur came from behind me.

'God works in mysterious ways, eh Prim. Let me tell you something, love: something you can believe. There is no God; he chucked it years ago. I think he probably gave up in disgust back in the thirties. Now there's only the other fella, and he's got the monopoly.

'I'll tell you something about Hell too. They say it's hot. Wrong: fucking freezing, you take that from me.'

I turned towards her. 'You got those numbers Dylan gave you?'

She nodded, took one of the restaurant cards from her shirt pocket, and handed it to me, together with my phone. 'Oz,' she asked me. 'Why was it Dylan who phoned you?'

'He and his bird are friends of ours in Glasgow. He works there now, like us.'

I took the numbers from her, and sat down on the couch, beside Prim's phone, but before calling Dylan, I retrieved the charge card for the hotel restaurant from my jacket and dialled the number. The night porter grumbled for a bit, but eventually he did as he was told and connected me with Señor Davis's suite.

Daze lived up to his name as he took the call; he sounded as if he was still three parts asleep. He soon woke up the rest of the way, though.

'Everett,' I said, coldly and evenly. 'Listen up, please. It's Oz. I've had a message from home and it's bad news: personal. I'll tell you all about it when I know all the details myself, but I have to go back as early as I can tomorrow. I need Barbara to get on to Iberia and pull some strings to get me to Glasgow as fast as they can, by whatever route.'

'Sure man,' he rumbled. 'Oz, what sorta news is this?'

'Don't ask, mate. I'll tell you when I can. I'm sorry you're stuck for an announcer for tomorrow's matches.'

'Don't worry. I'll have Liam do it.'

'Aye, he'll love that. By the way, I'm not in the hotel just now. This is where you'll get me.' I gave him the apartment phone number. 'Thanks. I'll be in touch.'

I hung up, and picked up the restaurant card, just as Prim placed a cup of strong black coffee in front of me. 'There, drink that,' she said. 'Don't worry about going to sleep. I've got some pills here that'll do the job.'

'You don't have enough,' I told her. 'Anyway. I never want to sleep again. Just you keep the coffee coming.'

I looked at the card: one number was for a mobile phone, and the other was Glasgow, prefix 0141; Susie's, I guessed. It was two-twelve local time, an hour earlier in the UK, but somehow I guessed that they wouldn't be out clubbing. I called the second number.

Susie picked up the phone on the third ring, and she knew who it was. 'Oh Oz,' she cried, as soon as I began to speak. 'I'm so sorry. Mike's here, hold on.' I was surprised by the speed with which she handed on the phone, but I didn't know then that some people are afraid to speak to the bereaved. I do now: I guess they're afraid it might be catching. Have I got news for them; it is.

'Oz, how are you?' Dylan asked as he came on line.

'I'm okay, Mike. I'm sorry for what happened when you called, but I've got it together now. I need you to tell me what happened. Was it her heart? A cerebral haemorrhage? A road accident?' As I mentioned the third scenario, my vision of Jan from earlier threatened to slip inside my shield, but I was strong enough now to force it away.

'It was a domestic accident, Oz. She was electrocuted.' He paused, waiting for me to faint again, perhaps.

'Go on,' I said, curtly.

'From what I've been told it was your washing machine. It was faulty. It must have gone live when she switched it on to do a wash, then next time she touched it – she was killed instantly. She wouldn't have known a thing, the doctor said.'

'When did this happen, Mike?'

'Just before six.' Something tugged at my brain but I ignored it.

'How was it discovered?'

'When it happened it blew out all the power in the building. The Scottish Power guys isolated the problem to your flat. When they got no reply to the doorbell they forced an entrance; in case there was a fire risk, as much as anything else.'

'How did you get involved?'

'Our people found Susie's number on a notepad. They called it to see if she knew where you were. I had your mobile number, on that card you gave me, so I said that as a friend, I'd deal with it.'

'Thanks, Michael,' I told him, not because I felt any

gratitude, but because I knew he expected to hear it. 'It took guts, I know that.'

He grunted something. I thought it might have been, ''S'okay.' It wasn't of course.

'Has anyone been in touch with Jan's mother?'

'No,' he replied, at once. 'They wouldn't know how. It's our job to inform next of kin, and that's you.'

'Has there been anything on radio or television?'

'Clyde carried a piece about the accident, but we haven't released the name. I told our press people not to, until I'd heard from you that it was okay.'

'I'd rather they didn't,' I told him. 'If that's allowable.'

'That'll be okay. I'll fix it.'

'Good man. Listen, I'll contact you when I get back tomorrow. Meantime . . .' I knew what I had to ask next, and my shield of disbelief cracked for a moment as I approached it. Until now, this could all have been fantasy: now we were getting close to the point at which there could be no denial.

'D'you know where she is?' I asked him.

'They took her to the Royal, Oz. She'll be in the mortuary there.'

'They won't have done a PM or anything, will they?' I tried to stop myself from trembling.

'No. Not unless the Fiscal orders one, and in these circumstances, he probably won't, unless you ask him to.' I sighed with relief, then concentrated again. The worst was still to come, and I had to be able for it.

'Okay. Mike, we'll speak again tomorrow.'

'Sure, Susie sends her love, by the way.'

'Yeah. Thank her for us.' The plural still seemed entirely natural to me.

As I hung up, Prim topped up my coffee. I told her, in summary, what had happened. She went as white as a sheet and shuddered. 'As simple as that,' she whispered.

'I wouldn't call that simple at all,' I barked at her. But I was shouting for the sake of it now. My cloak of disbelieving horror was becoming threadbare. Beneath it, there was anger and I knew that it would sustain me for a while, but afterwards . . .

'Okay, okay,' she murmured, ruffling my hair with her fingers as I sat there, mollifying and comforting me as best she could.

'How am I doing?' I asked her. 'Come on; you're a nurse. You must have seen hundreds of people in this situation. How am I handling it?'

'Too well,' she responded. 'You've got to let it go soon, Oz. Otherwise when the dam bursts . . .'

I stood and walked out to the terrace, carrying my mug, as she followed me. I turned, leaned my back against the railing, and looked down at her. 'I know that, Prim,' I said. 'But I have to hold it together while I do one more thing. I guess you know what that is.'

She nodded.

'You do one more thing for me, then. Let me be alone while I tell him, and afterwards. Take a couple of your pills and go to bed. Leave me the Faustino, and a key to get back in. I may go out for a while.'

She reached up, took my face in her hands, drew it down, and kissed me on the forehead. 'Is there a perverse law of nature, do you think,' she asked me. 'One that abhors perfection?

'That's what you two were, you know, you and Jan. I knew it in my heart of hearts that day up in her flat in Castle Terrace, when she helped us give that man the slip, and sent us off in her car. I remember looking at the two of you as you said your goodbyes and thinking, *This is crazy. The perfect couple and they don't even realise.* But I was in love with you too, and at that point I had you, so I was selfish, and put it out of my mind.'

Her eyes had filled with tears again. 'I am so sorry, my love,' she whispered. 'You did not deserve this.'

I shook my head. I knew that the dam was cracking, and that a sea of grief and despair was barely being restrained. 'No, Prim. She didn't deserve it. Now go, please, and leave me to make this last call, while I still can.'

I took my mobile phone from my pocket as soon as she had left the terrace, turning to face the sea as I dialled the number. I knew that there was no chance at all that these two would be out clubbing. The phone rang for a while until, eventually, I heard it lifted. 'This better not be a wrong number,' a gruff voice growled.

'It isn't, Dad, it's me.'

'Eh? I thought you were supposed to be in Spain, son. In fact I know you are; we watched you on telly tonight. What is it? Are you pished?'

I steeled myself to reply. My senses were heightened as never before, so that I could hear my own voice, hard and controlled. 'Yes, I am in Spain, Dad, and no I'm not drunk . . . yet. Is Mary awake?'

'Yes, she wakened with the phone ringing.' I had never sensed fear in Mac the Dentist before, but there on Prim's terrace, I did.

'In that case, you're going to have to tell her something that's going to break her heart – into as many pieces as mine.'

31

After destroying my dad's happy life, I took the Faustino, and a glass, and went down to the beach below the hamlet. I climbed up on the old Greek wall, a relic from the time before Christ – whoever he might have been – and I sat there in the pale moonlight, drinking toast after toast to Jan, and one or two to the child that we never had.

When the bottle was finished, I threw it into the sea, and the glass after it, then lay down on my back on the wall, and, looking up at the stars, I let the dam burst. I cried through all the hours of darkness, shouting the occasional pointless 'Why?' into the night, as I stretched out there with a great slab of grief pressing down on my chest.

My weeping had barely subsided as the first light of the new day began to creep into the eastern horizon. To this day, I don't know what made me do it, but I clambered down off the wall, stripped off my clothes and ran into the sea. I swam three hundred yards across the cove to the jetty which marked its limit then, turning, swam back.

When I strode out of the Mediterranean, and back up the beach, I felt no better – the griefstone was still unbearably heavy – but I knew that I had cried myself out for a while. I slipped on my boxer shorts, gathered the rest of my clothes into a bundle, and ran barefoot up the steep road which led back to the village, back to Prim's apartment.

Inside, I walked straight across to the sofa, and spread

out my clothes, as neatly as I could. When I turned she was standing behind me, in the kitchen doorway, wearing a towelling robe which had once been mine, and with a faint, tired smile on her face.

'Changed your mind, did you?' she asked.

'What d'you mean?'

'You look as if you chucked yourself in the sea, then thought better of it.'

'Maybe I did.'

She came towards me, holding out another mug of coffee. 'How d'you feel now?'

'To be honest, I wish I was dead,' I told her, frankly. 'But I can't afford that luxury, not yet anyway. I got a lot of stuff out of my system down there though; enough to let me get home and do what I have to do.'

'Mmm. How was Mac?'

'As you'd expect for someone who's lost a daughter. I can't bear to think of Mary, not yet.'

Primavera looked me solemnly in the eye. 'You'll never be a boy again, my poor Oz. You've aged ten years overnight.' It wasn't the most comforting thing anyone had ever said to me, but it was certainly among the most honest.

'In that case, I'm ten years nearer . . . whatever there might be.' I cut off that line of conversation, firmly. 'How's the hot water situation?' I asked.

'Plenty. I've just showered. Have a bath and get some heat back into you. You look frozen. Go and soak in there for as long as you like.'

I took her at her word, so much so that when she knocked on the door an hour later, she woke me. I found myself lying in the small bath in tepid water. I had been afraid to fall asleep, afraid of what I might dream, and afraid, I suppose, of waking for the first time into a world without Jan in it.

'You ready?' she called. 'Because there's a call for you.'

I climbed out of the bath, wrapped myself in a towel and dripped my way across the living room floor. The caller was Everett, with news of my flight. 'Barbara's got you booked on an Iberia flight from Barcelona to Paris at eleven thirty-five, connecting with an Air France flight at two fifteen through Birmingham. You'll be in Glasgow by four thirty. That okay for you? It's the earliest she could do.'

'That's fine, Ev. I can make that.'

'Good. I'll have her get into your room and pack your stuff. Your passport there?'

'Yes.'

'Okay. I'll have her put it in your bag and leave it at the hotel reception. You just pick it up on the run. And collect your tickets at the Iberia desk, Terminal A. Don't worry about payin' for them, that's done.' He paused. 'Can you tell me now what this is about?' he asked.

So I did; and was left marvelling that my wife had such an effect on people that a seven foot two inch man, who could turn Parmesan to Danish Blue just by looking at it, who had met her on only three occasions, could be struck speechless by her death. He whispered, 'Oh my,' then there was silence. The line was still open, but there was silence. I could picture him staring at the phone, then looking at Diane, open-mouthed, then back at the phone.

'See you in Glasgow,' I said, and hung up. Half an hour later, we were en route for Barcelona.

We made it to the airport, via the hotel, in plenty of time, even though Prim insisted on driving. I was happy to let her: all the icy horror of the night before had gone. Instead I felt weak and dog-tired, partly from lack of sleep, partly from the strain of bearing my burden of grief. She drove me right up to the Iberia terminal.

'At the risk of having you shout at me again,' she said, 'you will be okay, won't you?'

I made myself smile at her. 'I will now. I'm sorry I was a bit scary last night, Prim. It was pretty tough keeping control of myself for a while.'

She chuckled. 'Listen, I've seen scary. You weren't that bad.'

'Whatever I was, you being there helped me. I wouldn't have wished that on you for the world, but still I valued your presence.' I leaned across and kissed her on the cheek. 'Got to go now.' I started to climb out of the car, then paused. 'Can you do one more thing for me, pal? Phone the hospital where Jerry is, and find out how he's doing, then give me a call to let me know.'

'Of course I will, but there's just one problem – I don't have your number.'

'That's not a problem at all.' I took a card from my wallet and handed it to her. 'See you,' I said, closed the car door and headed into the terminal.

32

My dad was waiting for me when I walked out of the International Arrivals gate at Glasgow. I had phoned him from Barcelona to let him know my travel arrangements, and had told him that I would drive up to Anstruther next day, as soon as I had done everything that had to be done.

I knew that he would be there, though. As soon as I saw him, I remembered coming out of my faint in the restaurant, and my need for him. My dad has always been there for me, as indeed, I have been for him, for all of our lives. But when I saw him at the airport my instant reaction was one of fear. Mac the Dentist had always been a brawny, powerful, vibrant man, yet now he looked old, drawn, shrunken, and I, with all my certainties blown away for ever, had a sudden vision of the day when he would not be there either. Death is a mugger in an alleyway, in a strange city, at night.

I hugged him; we were equals now. For the first time I knew, truly, how he had felt when my mother died. Although no one has a monopoly on grief, it has levels and shades, and it is experienced in differing ways and to different degrees.

'God, son,' he said, once we were able to speak to each other. 'You look forty if you look a day. I was worried about how you'd hold up, until Primavera called, just as I was about to leave home. She explained how she came to be with you when you found out, and she told me that you were okay. She said I'd find you changed, but I knew that for myself.'

'How's Mary?' I asked him.

'Sedated,' he replied. 'Your sister's looking after her.'

'What about the boys? Have you told them what's happened?'

'I thought that you might want to do that.'

'Aye, I think I do. I'll have to tell wee Colin what happened to his idol, The Behemoth, as well.' I explained about Jerry Gradi's wounding, and about Sonny Leonard's disappearance.

'Did Prim tell you that she saved his life?' He looked at me, puzzled. 'No, I don't suppose she would.'

I took him by the arm. 'Come on. I've got things to do.'

He knew what I meant, at once. 'That can wait until tomorrow, son.'

'Oh no it can't. You're taking me to the Royal Infirmary, right now. The police can wait for ever for all I care, but I have to see Jan.' I turned and stared at him, hard. 'I have to see for myself, Dad, otherwise I won't really believe it.'

'I know, lad,' he said. 'I know.'

33

'Why d'you have to do the bloody washing at six o'clock on a Saturday evening, love? Why the hell didn't you leave it for me to do when I got back?'

I tried to be angry with her, there in the room which the kind-hearted, sad-eyed attendants had prepared for us, but my heart just wasn't in it. My childhood sweetheart, my wife, my soulmate, lay there on her bier, eyes closed, her mouth slightly open, not rising to my bait at all. I looked at the wall-clock and saw that just over twenty-four hours had passed since . . . it . . . had happened.

Her skin was pale and translucent and her hair had lost its lustre: but she was still my Jan. For all the world she looked as she had less than three days earlier, when last I saw her asleep in the night. They had clothed her in a white gown, and her hands were folded across her chest. She still wore her wedding ring, and I promised her there that she always would.

They had given me a chair, and had told me that I could stay for as long as I wished. Nice people: chosen well for their awful job. I sat for half an hour, weeping for most of the time, speaking to her between the tears; telling her that I loved her, telling her that she had been all the life I wanted, telling her that I wished it was I who lay there, not her. All of them useless, empty words, all of them vain wishes, but every one straight and true from my heart.

At last, I had talked myself out. I sat there in the silence, all the more awful for its lack of the sound of Jan's breathing, and the thing which had niggled at my mind when I had spoken to Dylan earlier that same day came rushing back to me.

She had died, Mike had said, just before six . . . or just before seven in Barcelona, the moment at which I had experienced that strange, unprecedented attack of dread and panic. 'Was that it, Jan?' I asked her. 'Were you calling out to me? Was that your cry for help?'

I felt my heart racing as I tried to deal with the possibility. I leaned back in my chair, let my head fall forwards and closed my eyes. I sat in that position for at least a couple of minutes. Gradually, my heartbeat slowed down, and as it did, I felt my mind clear, settling slowly like the surface of a pond after a rock has been tossed in, ripples gradually dying away.

As it did, I felt a strange, light pressure across my forehead, just above my eyebrows, as if something tangible was passing into my brain. It lasted for ten seconds or so, and then it faded. I opened my eyes, and I smiled; I felt a strange, inexplicable easing within me, and a surge of a kind of contentment.

I was full of a great certainty; that Jan had spoken to me, not to tell me that everything was all right, but that everything was as it was, and as it should be, and to tell me also that however lonely I might be through the rest of my life, I would not be alone.

I stood, and I looked at her body once more, and I saw it for what it was; a remarkable vessel, designed for the containment of something miraculous. Already, her face seemed to have taken on a different aspect. A transition had taken place; Jan just wasn't there any more. I thought of a term which had been in my mind earlier: soulmate. Now I knew, truly, what it meant.

I left the makeshift chapel, thanked the attendants, signed

a formal identification, and rejoined my father who was waiting in the corridor, outside.

'Let's go back to Fife for tonight,' he suggested. 'I'll bring you back down in the morning.'

'No, Dad. You go back and look after Mary; she needs you. I'll stay at the flat tonight, do what I have to do tomorrow, then come across.'

'Christ son, you can't stay there,' he protested.

'Of course I can. It's our home and I belong there. I'm not afraid of it.'

He took me back there, but he wouldn't come in. I understood that, so we said our farewells in the street. 'Tell Mary I'll be with her as soon as I can,' I told him.

I waved him off in his trusty, beloved Jaguar, and went inside. I was pleased to see that the police had made my front door secure after the Scottish Power break-in, and that my electricity supply had been restored.

The hardest part was going into the kitchen. Our lethal washing machine, a German-made monster, had been taken away. I was glad about that, yet disappointed too, for I had been entertaining thoughts of taking my heavy hammer and reducing it to its component parts.

I had eaten two aircraft meals, so I wasn't hungry, but I made myself some tuna sandwiches and a coffee, just to be doing something, and opened the first of what I intended to be several lagers. I was halfway through my second, and the dishes were in the washer, when I phoned Susie Gantry's number. The annoying BT woman answered, so I left a message asking Mike to call me.

I was playing a Jacqueline du Pré CD, one of Jan's favourites, when the phone rang. I assumed it would be Dylan, but in fact it was Prim.

'How are you doing?' she asked, sounding like a little mother hen.

'I'm doing okay. I'm playing music, and getting slightly drunk. I've been to see Jan, and I feel better, in a way that I can't explain to you. Did you do what I asked?'

'Yes,' she said, quickly. 'Jerry came through the surgery well. I spoke to the doctor who admitted him. He said that they removed a piece of metal, but that they were puzzled by it since it seemed to be covered in leather.

'He's suffered damage to the base of his right lung, but nothing that's going to leave him disabled. He'll probably even be able to wrestle again before the end of this year.'

'Did your doctor say anything about the police being involved?'

'The hospital didn't call them in, so I don't imagine that they are.'

'That's good. That means that Everett stays in control of the situation. Now that we've rumbled the guy Leonard, his crisis should be over.'

There were a few seconds of expensive silence. 'Where are you now?' I asked her.

'At home. I've got work tomorrow, so I'm having an early night. What do you have to do next?'

'I'll have to go and see the police tomorrow, then make funeral arrangements – if it's okay with the Fiscal.' As I spoke I heard a 'call waiting' bleep, but I decided to ignore it. 'There's a guy up in Fife, a patient of my dad's. He's a good man; I'll ask him to take care of everything.'

'Mmm,' Prim murmured. 'I think I'd prefer the personal touch too, at a time like this.' I could sense her hesitating. 'I saw Shirley Gash tonight, down at Miguel's,' she went on. 'Out of the blue, she asked if I knew how you were doing, so I had to tell her what had happened. She was just appalled, as you'd expect.' I knew Shirley well; she was a pal from my days in Spain.

'She asked me to give you her deepest sympathy, and she

said that once the funeral's over, if you wanted to get away for a while, you can have her summer-house for as long as you like.'

I smiled, as if she could see me. 'Jesus, Prim, kind as it is of big Shirl, that summer-house is just about the last place on earth I'd want to stay.'

'I thought you might say that,' she said, 'so here's an alternative. Would you like to come out here, to the apartment? I wouldn't be here, of course,' she added quickly. 'I'd bugger off for a couple of weeks, maybe back to Auchterarder to see my folks, or maybe to the States, to visit Dawn and Myles.'

I closed my eyes and I was back on the beach below St Marti, lying on top of the old Greek wall. The idea of going back there should have been appalling, yet somehow, it wasn't. It was comforting; it gave me a feeling of belonging. 'I'll have to think about that, Prim,' I answered, slowly. 'Let me get past the funeral, and see that the family's okay, then I'll think about it. I'll have to consult, too,' I added.

'One thing I know already; every decision I make in my life from now on, everything I do, will depend on the answer to one question. "Would Jan approve?" That's the way it'll be.'

'And quite right too,' she said. 'For now, just you carry on getting slightly drunk. I'm sure she would have approved of that.'

34

As I expected, the 'call waiting' signal which had bleeped while I was talking to Prim had been triggered by Mike Dylan. Over the next few days, and weeks, I found out what a good friend that loud-suited, loose-mouthed imitation of a detective could really be.

He picked me up next morning and took me straight to the Divisional police office in Baird Street, to meet the officers who were preparing the report on Jan's death for submission to the Procurator Fiscal. He sat with me as I gave them a brief formal statement confirming that Jan had been in good health when I left for Spain, that we had lived in the flat for a few months and that we had never noticed any problems with the washing machine or with any other electrical appliance. They asked me for the address of the previous owner, which I couldn't give them, so instead I pointed them in the direction of the selling solicitor.

Next Mike drove me to the Fiscal's Office, where he had a pal, a guy he had known in Edinburgh who had been posted to Glasgow, like him. The file on Jan's death was still empty of everything but the medical examiner's report and a copy of the death certificate. Since both said clearly and unequivocally that death had been caused by cardiac arrest due to electric shock, Mike's friend agreed that a post mortem examination would not be necessary and wrote a note instructing the mortuary that Jan's body could be released to the next-of-kin.

Finally, he drove me to the District Registrar's Office, and helped me through the unimaginably painful experience of registering my wife's death. 'Age?' the assistant registrar asked. 'Thirty,' I said. In all my worst nightmares, in the most pessimistic of moments, not that I had many of either, I could never have dreamed up that scene.

And that was it. All of the death-related business which I had to do in Glasgow, was transacted in two hours. I packed a case, tidied up the flat and cleaned the bathroom and the kitchen; something Jan would have done, but not necessarily Oz. I was about to leave, when the phone rang. I thought that it would be my dad, but it wasn't. It was Greg McPhillips; Everett had called to tell him what had happened, but somehow he needed to hear it from me before it could become reality. The poor sod was so distressed that I wound up comforting him. I thought this was strange at the time, but I was to find out over the next few days that it was par for the course.

I told Greg that I would be in touch with him after the funeral, said goodbye, and hung up. I was actually turning the door handle when the phone rang again. It wasn't my dad this time either; instead it was a pushy, boyish-sounding reporter from a news agency, on the trail of a scoop. I confirmed that my wife had died in a domestic accident and told him that I had nothing more to say.

He wasn't the sort to be put off that easily. 'I understand from the police that Mrs Blackstone was electrocuted by a washing machine,' he wheedled.

'Yes that's correct,' I agreed.

'What make was it?' he went on, hungrily. 'This could be a story for *Watchdog.*'

Suddenly I understood why Everett Davis was paranoid about the media. This bastard was excited by my wife's death; he saw profit in it. Before my rage could overwhelm me, I hung up the phone and walked out of the door.

I dreaded the thought of returning to Anstruther: I dreaded the thought of confronting Mary's grief; I dreaded the thought of trying to explain death to Jonathan, my nine-year-old nephew; I dreaded the conversations with the undertaker and the Minister; and I dreaded most of all the prospect of being chief mourner, the man in black in the front pew at an obscenely premature funeral. I dreaded them all, but I did them nonetheless.

I saw Mary and, with my dad, tried to show her – and numb-struck Ellie too, to whom Jan had been as a sister – that all we could do was to be good to each other, in her memory.

I took Jonathan to St Andrews, bought him an ice-cream from Janetta's, then walked him through the ruined cathedral and into the cemetery, where I tried to explain to him that each of the headstones there told the story of a life which had come to an end, as had that of his Auntie Jan, and that while this was sad, it was also natural and inevitable, and had to be seen as a passage to something else. He looked at me with his old eyes, 'Is there a Jesus, Uncle Oz?' he asked.

'It's as good a name as any, my man,' I told him, and we left it at that. There was nothing I could have said to wee Colin that he would have understood, so I left the comforting of him to his mother.

Jan's funeral took place on the Friday following her death, in the Parish Church. The service was conducted by the Minister who had married us a few months before. Every pew was packed as our small family group filed in: me, in the lead, my dad and Mary next, Ellie and Allan Sinclair, her estranged husband, who had flown in from France the night before, and finally, Jan's father and his second wife.

Believe me, in these circumstances, one does not scan the

congregation for faces; but some things you can't miss. I was immensely gratified to see on the left of the church towards the rear an enormous black figure, and frankly astonished when, a few rows further forward, the light glinted on a heavy, ornate gold chain, around the neck of a thick-set man.

The service was conventional, but rather than have Bible readings, my dad and I had decided that we would each read a poem. He chose 'Remember' by Christina Rossetti. My selection was Jan's favourite; a much more obscure work, in which a woman contemplates the future by declaring that when she grows old, she will rebel in her way, by wearing purple.

It's about growing old together disgracefully, a prospect which had been far in the distance for Jan and me, yet which had been denied to her, and to us, by that bloody washing machine. Tears were blinding me by the time I reached the end, but I knew it by heart anyway. 'Of course,' I told the packed congregation after I had finished, 'we all of us know that Jan had the courage to wear purple all her life.'

The morning rain had cleared when we buried her – dressed in her finest and wearing her wedding ring and a gold necklet I had bought her – in the cemetery nearby, in the lair next to my mother, west-facing so that every night the sun would go down on them both. We lowered her into the ground, me at her head, my dad at her feet, and six others. I have difficulty now in picturing the scene, but with an effort I can recall that Allan Sinclair, Greg McPhillips, my pal Ali the demon grocer, Mike Dylan, Johnny Wilson, our best childhood friend, and the mountainous Everett Davis all helped us in our task.

As the Minister spoke the words of the ritual, I took the red rose from my button-hole and dropped it into the grave.

As I did, the rain began to fall again, lightly, onto the coffin and the brass plate with its inscription, 'Janet Blackstone'.

35

There was much that I had to ask my dad; much that I
would ask him in time, about his thoughts, and his experi-
ences, after my mother's death. However we both knew it
was too soon. So, after I had spent the weekend following
the funeral answering as many letters of sympathy as I could,
and after my brave sister had spent a day in Glasgow packing
clothes and cosmetics – I've never asked her what she did
with them – and taking them away in Jan's Fiesta, which
Mary had agreed with me she should have, I went back to
my high tower flat to pick up my life.

My first call was to Greg McPhillips, to check what work
was awaiting me. There was plenty, but there were other
things too; personal things that he had undertaken to handle
for me. Jan hadn't left a will – Hell's teeth, she was only
thirty – but her insurance policies were either joint life or in
my name, and all our accounts, other than our separate
business accounts, were joint. Claim forms had to be signed,
mortgage lenders to be advised, bank details to be changed,
but none of it would be a problem. I told Greg that I would
take care of all that the next time I was in his office, which
would certainly be within the next two days, as a result of
some of the work he had given me.

'Fine,' he said, 'but there's something else. I sort of
assumed an instruction from you last week. I got the name
of the manufacturers of your washing machine, plus its serial

number, from the police. It's a German company.

'I wrote to them, on your behalf. I advised them of the accident and said that as your solicitor I would await their observations. I had a letter in Friday's mail from their UK office. They said as the machine was well out of guarantee they had no liability or obligation in the matter. However in the circumstances, they are prepared to offer you a replacement as a gesture of goodwill.

'What d'you think of that?'

By now, you know I'm naive in certain respects. Although I'd shielded myself behind my anger in the period after the accident, it had never turned itself in the direction of the company which had made the lethal machine. That changed in an instant. Within me I could hear Jan's voice, and when I spoke, it was for us both.

'I think you should decline their offer,' I told my friend, coldly and evenly, in that tone which I hadn't owned ten days before. 'I think also that you should advise them that we will be obtaining a copy of the police report on the machine, and that if it shows that my wife's death was caused by a fault in its manufacture, then we will pursue every remedy open to us, both civil and criminal, in Scotland and in Germany.

'How does that sound?' I asked him.

'It sounds like something a real hard-arsed lawyer like me would say. I've already asked the Fiscal's office for a copy of the police report. I'll let you know as soon as I get it. My guess is that the Germans will want to examine the machine themselves to confirm what the police say, but that very soon they'll make you an offer of compensation.'

'How much?' As soon as the words were out, I was swamped by a wave of guilt for asking the question. Jan's death couldn't be quantified in financial terms. 'No, forget that. I don't want their fucking money. I just want them to agree to withdraw every single machine of that type.'

'They'll do that anyway,' Greg forecast. 'Take their cash,' he urged. 'Give it to your nephews if you like, but take it. If they're culpable, they should pay.'

'Aye, I suppose you're right. Let's just wait for the report.'

After I finished my call to Greg, I phoned a few other contacts, to let them know I was back in business. They all seemed glad to hear from me, and they all had work. I began to wonder whether there was a conspiracy among my business friends to keep me occupied. I spent another hour at my desk planning a work schedule, then arranged two interviews for that afternoon.

When I had no other options, I was finally forced to turn to the task I had been dreading. I moved round to the other side of the partners' desk, and sat in Jan's chair. I had gathered all her mail together; now I began to open it. There were two cheques from clients, and a couple of letters from the Inland Revenue, but most of the envelopes contained the usual junk; the stuff that annoys recipients but makes serious money for the Royal Mail.

Jan's filing system was simple and efficient. The papers relating to each of her clients were all kept together in sequence. I filed the material in her out and pending trays, then switched on her computer, and found her directory. That was neat too, with her clients listed as such, with address, phone, fax and e-mail numbers and name of principal contact in each one.

I phoned them, one by one and told them formally what they knew already. They were all upset, and two of them even offered to pay me a termination bonus. I declined, but said that if they wanted to make a donation to their favourite charity in Jan's memory, that would be okay with me. Once I had finished, I boxed each client's papers, wrapped them securely and called a delivery service to return them all.

The only exception was The Gantry Group. Jan's relationship with her newest client had been of such a short duration that she had not had time to develop a file, or amass papers. I called Susie anyway, at her office. I had seen her at the funeral, and afterwards, with her father and Dylan, at our reception in the church hall, but she had been too upset to say much.

She was still solemn when I spoke to her that morning; she mentioned money too. 'Jan did a lot for us, Oz. I'll work out the time she spent here and send you a cheque.' I gave her the same answer I had given the others. When she protested, I told her, 'Look Susie, that work is all abortive now. You'll have to get someone else to start again. Any idea who?' I asked.

She treated me to a flicker of her laugh. 'I've been worn down on that one, I'm afraid, Oz. I'm going to have to take old Uncle Joseph back. Dad said we couldn't afford to go back to scratch again, so we'd have to make do with the Devil we know.

'Actually, from the work that Jan did, I may have been wronging the old bugger after all.' That didn't square with what my wife had told me before I left for Spain, but I supposed that she must have come to that conclusion later.

Susie invited me to dinner on the following Thursday. For a moment I wasn't going to accept, until I realised that it would mean one less evening that week in the flat, on my own. So I thanked her, and accepted.

In the silence that remained I sat at our desk, looking at the only substantial block of Jan's files that were left; the only client I hadn't terminated. They were my papers: invoices, receipts, tax returns, Revenue correspondence and all the other things which my wife and business manager had done for me. For the first time, I began to wonder how I was going to manage myself.

I was still brooding on this as I made my solitary lunch, and also thinking irrationally about adopting a cat, when the phone rang. It was Everett. 'Hello man,' the brown voice rumbled. 'You hanging in there?'

'What choice do I have?' I asked him.

'None, my friend. You do it for her.' He paused then jumped straight to the point. 'Oz, Liam Matthews is just insufferable as a ring announcer. When you comin' back?'

I was astounded. 'I didn't think you'd need me back. With Leonard in the frame as your saboteur, my job's done, isn't it?'

'It looks like that job's done, sure, and by the way, I owe you your bonus, but that doesn't obscure the fact that you're a damn good ring announcer. And I need one. Thousand sterling a weekend, Friday evening through Sunday, plus your VAT, plus expenses.

'Amsterdam this weekend, then Manchester, then the Wednesday after that it's the live pay-per-view event in Edinburgh. We got heavy subscription for that already. I need you Oz, my friend. Diane needs you. Our partner Jerry, he needs you. Don't let us down now.'

I laughed. I laughed for the first time in nine days. 'Who am I to reject all that need,' I said. 'I'll do it. It's what Jan would want. What time's the plane on Friday?'

36

Greg had just received the police report from Dylan's pal the Assistant Fiscal when I called in to his office in West Regent Street, to drop off a couple of witness statements and to sign the various forms which he had for me.

We were both pushed for time, and so he gave me a copy to take away with me. I had a series of interviews for another lawyer scheduled that morning and early afternoon, and so it was well into the day before I had a chance to pick it up.

I managed to read it all the way through on the fourth attempt. On each of the first three readings I made it as far as the description of Jan touching the live, water-filled appliance, then broke up.

The report was concise and unequivocal in its judgement. It said that the machine had been halfway through a wash cycle when the accident had happened. It pointed out that Jan must have loaded the machine, selected and switched on the programme. Therefore it surmised that the powerful vibration of the machine must have shaken loose a live wire from the power supply to the motor. This, it argued, had come into contact with the casing of the machine, stopping its cycle and turning it instantly into a death-trap.

Since the investigating officers had found a partly sliced pepper on the chopping board it presumed that Jan, 'the victim,' had been in the kitchen when the mishap had occurred, that she had stopped what she was doing and had attempted to restart the washer. On touching the lethal appliance she had received a massive electric shock which had killed her instantly. She was barefoot and the tiled floor was wet, but even without that added conductivity, she had no chance of survival.

The report said that its finding must remain one of extreme probability rather than fact, since the faulty wiring had been melted and fused together by the extreme heat generated as the current had earthed itself through Jan's body. However the police examiners had called in Trading Standards Officers to test their findings, and they had agreed whole-heartedly with their conclusions.

When I was finished, I phoned Greg. 'It looks pretty damning for the manufacturer, doesn't it?' I said to him.

'Aye,' said my friend. 'As I guessed, they've asked for permission to have the machine tested independently. But they sound pretty well convinced. They have Scottish solicitors acting for them now, and one of them called me this afternoon for a preliminary chat about the quantum of your claim.'

I looked up at him. 'Give me that last bit in English,' I asked.

'It means how much they're going to pay you,' he said. 'If their tests bear out the others, and it seems that they should, it could be big; six figures.'

'I don't really give a toss, Greg.' As I spoke, I was visited by an unbidden memory of Jan in that makeshift mortuary chapel. 'They can't give me what I want,' I added.

'No, no, of course they can't. I do have some good news for you, though. I had a talk with the Assistant Fiscal and I got him to agree that in the light of the report, there's no need for a formal Fatal Accident Inquiry before Sheriff and jury. He accepts that it's clear no criminal offence has been committed, and that since the matter could wind up in the civil courts, it's better that his office doesn't muddy the waters.

'So the file will be marked "Accidental Death", and closed. That'll be a weight off your mind, Oz.'

'Sure,' I said, with more bitterness than I intended. After all, Greg really did think he had done me a favour. 'I can't tell you how happy that makes me.'

37

I had been dreading dinner with Susie and Mike, and I'm quite sure they had been too.

However it wasn't as bad as I had feared. Sure, I felt a bit like a spare part, and I was painfully aware of the extra chair all through the evening, but Susie managed the really difficult bit perfectly.

As Mike handed round the drinks – I had come by train and was going home by taxi – she sat down opposite me, and said, 'Oz, tonight we can talk about Jan if that's what you want. But if it's too painful for you, we can talk about other things.'

I looked at her, feeling enormously grateful. I knew that somewhere in me there was a need to talk about my wife, our life and her death, with friends from outside my family circle. But I hadn't known Susie for long, and Mike for not much longer; kind and solicitous as they were, they simply weren't close enough. As I thought about it, I realised that there was only one person in the world who was.

So I told her. 'I need to come out into the world again, Susie. Let's talk about life.'

And that was what we did. We talked about Dylan's career shift and his prospects in Strathclyde, a much bigger force than Lothian and Borders, with more ladders and career opportunities. We talked about Susie's plans for the St Vincent Street development and her new apartment.

Over dinner, I told them about my exciting alternative career as a ring announcer. I mentioned Jerry's mishap in Barcelona, but stuck to the official story that it had been caused by an equipment failure. 'They want to watch that,' said Dylan. I looked at him, inwardly concerned that his copper's nose might be twitching. I needn't have worried; it would have taken a good-sized pinch of pepper to make Mike's hooter twitch. 'That's two accidents recently,' he went on. 'They'll have the Health and Safety people after them if they're not careful.'

Of course, since we were in Glasgow, we talked about football as well. It was true that in Edinburgh, Dylan had been essentially a rugby man, but that is politically incorrect in Glasgow, where the round ball rules almost unchallenged and where, no matter how hard the clubs try to change the pattern, allegiances are determined still by religion and ancestral prejudices.

'Your father must be invited to every big game in Glasgow, Susie,' I said. 'But does he hold a season ticket anywhere?'

She grinned. 'You're right about the invitations. He could be at Ibrox or Parkhead every Saturday during the season if he wanted. He's much too cute to hold a season ticket, though. The other side's supporters would notice, and they're voters after all. The group did make a donation to the Save the Jags campaign, and we bought some Partick Thistle shares as well. But that was politically okay, you understand.' She smiled again.

'He doesn't go to a match every Saturday, of course, or anything like it, although he does make sure that he visits Rangers and Celtic alternately. He makes a point of being at all the European matches, but that's because the visiting sides usually bring their Mayor in the party, so he feels he has to.'

She looked at me. 'The truth is that my father hates

football, for the image it's given this city over the years. Privately, he gets terribly angry that for all that Glasgow has invested in the Burrell, in the Royal Concert Hall, in the Kelvingrove Art Gallery and Museum, and in all the other museums and show-places that we can boast of, Edinburgh is still internationally famous for its Festival while we're best known for our football teams.

'Give him a few drinks in private then sit back and listen. You'll get a tirade about how we can bring the world's most famous orchestra to Glasgow, yet the only cultural coverage we ever get is when some character pretends to play the flute at a football match.' Susie chuckled. 'Mind you Oz, all that's a family secret.'

'And safe with me. I can't tell you how much our family appreciated your dad coming to Jan's funeral.' I smiled at her, and to keep the conversation light-hearted, added, 'Especially since there are no Glasgow votes in Anstruther.'

'If there were,' said his daughter, 'he'd know who they were and where they lived!'

'How's his old pal Mr Donn settling back in?' I asked.

Susie made a face. 'Smugly,' she replied. 'He's even installed a new book-keeper; his nephew, would you believe. The boy's efficient, I have to say, but that won't save him though.'

'You have plans for revenge, I take it.'

She nodded. 'Oh yes. When my father steps down as Lord Provost, if he ever does, he's promised himself that he will go on a long cruise . . . with the other Lady Provost.'

'Eh?'

'His mistress, but we don't talk about her at all. Shouldn't have mentioned her: must be the drink. Christ, I don't even know her name, he keeps her that tight. I only know for sure because he told me always to phone before calling at the house. Me! His daughter!' She bristled with a mixture of Amarone and indignation.

'Anyway,' she muttered, with a grim smile, 'as soon as that bloody boat leaves the dockside, Uncle Joseph and young Stephen are out on their arses. See if I'm not my father's daughter!'

In case his girlfriend's indignation slipped out of control, Dylan, sensibly for once, switched the subject back to the GWA. 'So you are going back to that, Oz?' he said.

'Amsterdam tomorrow,' I confirmed. 'Then sunny Manchester, then the big event in Edinburgh. That'll be a live transmission, so there'll be no scope for any more accidents.'

'Will the big chap be fit by then?'

'If the big chap's fit for Christmas, he'll be lucky.'

We chatted on about not very much, until my taxi arrived, by which time I was quietly sloshed, as I had been every night that week. It was raining, par for the course for the beginning of April, so I paid the guy inside the taxi and sprinted for the entrance to my building.

A funny thing happened as I opened my front door and switched on my hall light. The three tracked ceiling spotlights came on, then one went out, not in the quiet, now-you-see-it, now-you-don't way, but with a loud bang. I swore quietly and walked through the living area to the kitchen, with thoughts of another beer. There too, I switched on the light, three floods set on a circle. The same thing happened again; all three came on, then one went out; with a bang.

I changed my mind about that beer. Instead I sat in the dark and looked out at the city, asking myself what were the odds against two light bulbs – in separate fittings, in an apartment whose electrics have just been checked out as thoroughly as humanly possible by the guys from Scottish Power – exploding, one after the other.

I reached my own conclusion. I didn't feel spooky as I sat there, not a bit. I didn't feel alone, either. 'Hello, darlin',' I said, smiling into the shadowy room. 'Looking out for me, are you? Don't go too far though. Those bulbs are expensive.'

It had worried me, that during all the nights since Jan's death, I had never dreamed of her. That night I did. It was a grey dream; she came to me through a mist. She didn't smile and she wasn't happy, and yet . . .

I can't remember what she said; maybe she didn't say anything. But she told me nonetheless that while she missed me as much as I missed her, and while there was nothing good in what had happened, it would be all right. I would have to be patient, and to live my life out, but once I had done that, however long it took . . . it would be all right.

38

The plane to Amsterdam was a Fokker – yes, I know that joke. For a passenger plane it seemed to me to be very small, and seated next to Everett in the front row, I couldn't help but wonder about the effect of his size on its stability.

'Is Diane not coming on this trip?' I asked him, once we were through the white-knuckle part of the flight and the pretty Dutch girls had appeared with the drinks trolley.

'No, she said she has things to do in Scotland. Anyhow,' he added, quietly, glancing over his shoulder, 'Matthews is back on the commentary team this week.'

'Jesus, man. Are you still nursing that one?'

He shrugged his shoulders. For a moment I thought that the Fokker lurched a little. 'Sorry, Oz. I guess that was an insensitive thing to say to you, of all people.'

'Yes,' I told him, but with a smile, 'I rather think it was.'

'I'm trying, man, I really am. I love her so much it makes me crazy, that's all.'

'It seems to me that you only have one problem with Diane. What are you going to do with her in the organisation while Jerry's out of action?'

'We've thought about that one,' he grinned down at me. 'Diane's going to become the handmaiden of the Black Angel.

'Jerry leaves a very big gap in the roster in every respect. We really got only one guy who can take his place in the short-term, and that's Darius. He's our only worker who's big enough to be really convincing in matches with me.

'Liam will get his shot at the pay-per-view, sure. He earned that when he saved the show in Barcelona. But Daze can't job to a guy his size, no way. He'll go down, then we'll start to position the Black Angel as the main contender. Having The Princess alongside him will make that easier.

'For the longer term, we're signing an ex-Triple W guy called Al Hendrix. He wrestles under the name of Cyclops because he's blind in one eye and wears a mask. He has commitments in Japan just now, but he'll be with us in a week. I'm bringing in a Jap tag team as well, all of them on six month contracts. It breaks my Europeans first policy, but I'm replacing Jerry and Chris Manson and they're both Americans, so . . .'

'Sounds exciting,' I said; to please him as much as anything else. To be honest, I really wasn't sold on the GWA to the extent that I could be as enthusiastic as him.

'Yeah,' Everett murmured, lost in his art. 'Diane's working on some new costumes to match the Black Angel's rig. She says they're slinky, but not as provocative as Barcelona; that went a bit far.'

'And annoyed the locals.' I told him of Prim's comments about Catalan sensitivity when it comes to their flag.

'Thanks. I'll tell her to keep that in mind.' He paused. 'Say, she really is something, that friend of yours. I was in a complete panic back in that ring after Jerry was hit. If she hadn't sailed in and taken charge, I don't know what would have happened.'

'I do,' I whispered.

'Yeah.' He caught my meaning. 'Look, I want to let her know how grateful I am. Should I send her flowers – orchids or something?'

'Prim? No, I don't think so. I'd say you should write to

her, to thank her. Then you or Jerry send her a case of French wine; good stuff, mind, no crap.'

'We'll do that, Jerry and I.' He smiled. 'I was thinking, I might offer her a job as a GWA superstar too, after the way she got my attention back in that ring.'

'Better not do that,' I warned him. 'She might accept.

'By the way,' I went on, 'did you have that turn-buckle pad examined?'

He nodded vigorously, then glanced over his shoulder to make sure that the people in the seats behind us were all engrossed in magazines. 'I sure did,' he said. 'I took it apart myself, and I found a device inside, stitched right into the padding. I took it to a firm of private security consultants. They told me that it was one of those key-ring gun things, but that it had been adapted so that the cocking ring became the firing pin as well. Like we thought, the thing was triggered by a heavy blow, someone the size of Jerry being slammed against the pad, driving the firing ring against the turn-buckle and – bang.'

'And Jerry and I watched that bastard Sonny Leonard strap the thing on,' I muttered. 'What have you done about tracing him?'

'Nothing. Let him run back to Tony Reilly and tell him that his plan failed, and that I'm on to him. We won't hear from them again. Leonard's history; Gary O'Rourke is the new head honcho.

'Anyhow,' he added, 'what could I do without bringing the police in on it?'

'Let me think about that,' I told him.

We had an uneventful flight to Amsterdam, and, as it turned out, an uneventful weekend. Considering everything that had gone on in Newcastle and Barcelona, the show was top class. Sally Crockett's audience ratings in Holland were very high, so Everett gave her the headline spot, after Tommy

Rockette's second showing in a tag team with Chris Manson, against the Rattlers. Watching them all through rehearsal, I thought that Rutherford looked the most relieved man in the team, knowing that he would not be facing Daze.

The big man's own slot was a handicap fight with the Choirboys, interrupted once again by a confrontation with Liam Matthews, who left his commentary chair to jump up on the ring apron and harangue the giant. This time he ran for his life up the ramp, pursued by a mock-serious Daze forfeiting his match with the Tag Team Champions.

The plane was almost ready to land in rainy Glasgow on Sunday evening, when a possible answer to Everett's two-day-old question came to me. He and I were in the same front row seats, and so I tapped him on the arm.

'Hey, remember that phone bill of Sonny Leonard's?' He nodded. 'The other American number; the one in St Louis. We reckoned that could have been his parents, right?' He nodded again. 'He looked a dutiful son, didn't he. What's the betting he's been in touch with his folks again within the last two weeks?'

The great dark face broke into a grin. 'Could be, could be,' he said, softly. 'Why don't you drop by the office tomorrow just after five and we'll check it out.'

39

I had finished my day's work and was about to head for the GWA headquarters when the phone rang. It was Greg McPhillips, and I could tell as soon as he opened his mouth that he was not a happy boy. Inevitably, that meant that I wasn't going to be happy either.

'I'll give you the bad news first,' he began, 'since there isn't any good news.'

'Greg, pal,' I told him. 'Right now there isn't anything you could tell me that I'd class as good news, so don't be bothered. What is it?'

'Well,' he said, as if he really didn't fancy his job at that moment. 'These German washing machine makers have moved very fast. I have just had a visit from their lawyer, who only happens to be a partner in the biggest firm of ambulance chasers in Scotland.' I knew that lot. You never heard good news from them, unless you were their client.

'The independent testers the Krauts employed turned out not to be very independent after all. They arrived in Glasgow on Friday, and they worked all weekend, taking the machine apart, looking at the wiring, scraping bits off, sending samples for lab analysis and so on.

'They reported this morning. Essentially they agreed with the police guys and the Trading Standards people that the accident could have been caused in the way they said. However, they came up with an alternative solution.

'They said that it would have been possible to rig a small incendiary device to the housing of the wiring that would have melted it and allowed the wiring to fall against the casing of the machine, rendering it live. It would be a very simple device, they said, triggered by a mercury-filled rocker thing, which would go off as soon as the machine started to spin. That's an old terrorist and Special Forces trick, apparently. They use it to blow people up, but the principle's exactly the same.

'The mercury would vaporise with the heat, and the fuel element, which is similar to plastic explosive, would burn itself out too; the rest of the device would be identical to the casing of the wiring itself, i.e. rubber. So all you'd have left once the thing had done its business would be slightly more melted rubber than you'd expect to find.

'They say that they found slightly more melted rubber than usual, so their scenario is a possibility.' Greg paused, probably waiting for me to explode, but I held it together.

'What our ambulance chaser friend had to say was that his clients were very interested by this. He pointed out that on the face of it, since there was no reported break-in to your place – indeed since the Scottish Power guys had to break in themselves – the only person who was in a position to lay such a device was you.

'Now my professional colleague is clever. He told me that he wouldn't dream of making this allegation to the Fiscal, because you would immediately sue for huge defamation damages, with at least a fifty per cent chance of success. However if you press ahead with a civil action, then under the privilege of the witness box, he will enter his experts' theory as a defence, and invite the jury to reject your case.

'In other words, Oz, he's saying that if you sue his clients, you'll be accused of murdering Jan.'

That did it. I have never experienced such a red, howling,

venomous rage in all my life. 'I want his name, Greg,' I roared. 'I want to know who this bastard is, because I am personally going to tear his fucking heart out!'

'I don't blame you, Oz. That's why I've no intention of telling you who he is. Anyway, there's a whole queue of people waiting in line to do much the same thing to this guy.

'I want you to calm down, and take time to think this over, rationally.'

'Raise the action Greg,' I shouted at him. 'Sue the bastards until they bleed. I don't care what it costs.'

'Oz,' he said, patiently. 'My father and our partners are not ambulance chasers. I'm not going to accept that instruction from you, or any other, until you've had at least a week to think about it. Come and see me next Monday. We'll discuss it then.'

40

I was still steaming mad when I drew up in the GWA car park. In the next bay, Sally Crockett had just started her little yellow sports coupé. She was facing out and I had parked nose in, so our faces were only a few feet apart.

She wound down her window, and I wound down mine. 'Hey Oz,' she said, with a cheery sympathetic smile. 'How are you doing? You look a bit down today.'

'Sorry, Sal,' I replied. 'I was lost in thought there – thoughts of killing a lawyer.'

She laughed. 'Need any help?'

There was something about the Ladies' Champ which always brightened me up. 'You, on the other hand,' I told her, 'look as sunny as that flying banana you're about to drive. What's made your day?'

'The boss has just given me next weekend off, that's what. So I'm just going down to see my mum, then tomorrow I'm catching a flight to Barcelona. Jerry got out of hospital yesterday, so he and I are having a few days in a place called the Hotel Aiguablava, just a bit up the coast.'

She chuckled. 'I've planned out some new moves for my match with the Heckler at the pay-per-view. I may try them out on him.'

'I reckon he might like that.'

'What he'd also like to do while we're there, he told me, is to visit that friend of yours, the girl who treated him in the ring. I was going to phone you tomorrow morning to get her address.'

'No problem.' I scribbled Prim's address and phone number on a page of my notebook, tore it out and handed it across to her. 'There you are. Tell the big fella I was asking for him.' I paused. 'Does he know about Jan, by the way?'

'Not yet.'

'If you visit Primavera, you'd better tell him first.'

She nodded. Feeling a lot calmer than when I'd arrived, I waved her goodbye, watched as she drove off, then climbed out of the Ozmobile and walked into the building.

Everett was in his office, waiting for me, with Sonny Leonard's phone bill lying on his glass-topped desk. As I walked in he poured me a mug of coffee from his filter and handed it to me, together with a coaster from which Tommy Rutherford's professional face grinned up at me.

'How we going to play this thing?' he asked.

'By ear seems like the best way.' I picked up the invoice from the desk and found the St Louis number. 'Show me how to switch your phone to hands free.' He pressed a button and the dialling tone sounded into the room. I sat on the edge of the table and keyed in the number.

We waited for several seconds as the US ringing tone sounded, insistently. Then it stopped as we heard the call answered. The line was as clear as a bell. 'Yaiss?' It was an old woman's voice, quavery and nervous.

'Hello,' I said, speaking more slowly than normal. 'Would that be Mrs Leonard?'

'Not any more,' she answered. 'Mr Leonard died 'bout twenty-three years ago. It's Mrs Zabrynski now. 'Course Mr Zabrynski's dead now too.'

'I'm sorry to hear that.' And of course, I really was. 'You are Sonny Leonard's mother, though?'

'Oh yaiss,' she chirped, brighter at once. 'He's my boy. Fine son, too.'

'I can imagine. My name's Oz Blackstone, Mrs Zabrynski. I'm calling from GWA in Scotland. Is Sonny there, by any chance?'

'No, Ah'm afraid not. Sonny's in Philadelphia, Pennsylvania, right now. But he'll be back here on Thursday,' she added, helpfully.

I did some quick thinking, and took a chance that Sonny didn't confide in his dear old Mom. 'Listen, Mrs Zabrynski. Sonny decided to leave GWA very quickly. He has a lot of friends here, and we didn't have a chance to wish him a proper goodbye. We'd like to send him a surprise gift from all of us. Could we deliver it to him personally, at your home on Thursday?' Everett, who was watching me intently, nodded vigorously.

We could almost hear her beam on the other end of the line. 'Why how naice of you all,' she exclaimed. 'Of course you can do that. I'm expecting him back by twelve midday. Let me give you the address: it's thirty-four seventy, Andrew Hamilton Drive, Saint Louis, Missouri.'

I wrote it down on my notebook. 'That's great, Mrs Zabrynski,' I told her. 'There's just one thing, though. We really do want this to be a surprise. You won't say anything about it to Sonny, will you; not even if he calls you before Thursday?'

'Mr Blackstone, Ah love surprises. Ah won't breathe a word.'

'Thank you very much, Mrs Zabrynski. Till Thursday then.'

'Yaiss. Goodbye, and thank you for calling.' I hit the stop button and the phone went dead.

I stood up from the edge of Everett's desk and looked at him. 'There you are, sunshine. On a plate.'

'Sure,' he said, 'but what do we do now?'

I shrugged my shoulders. 'Simple. You hire a couple of Pinkertons, or whatever, they go to see Leonard at his Mom's on Thursday, apply the thumbscrews and get a statement out of him implicating Reilly.'

'I can't do that,' he growled. 'Hire a PI in the States and he's almost bound to have a connection with the cops, or worse, the DA's office.'

'In that case send him a kiss-a-gram with a note that says, "Hello Sonny, I know where you live. Don't let me hear from you again, ever. Love Daze." He'll get the message.'

'No,' said the giant, vehemently. 'Leonard's a loose end. He has to be tied off. You go to St Louis. You go visit him Thursday.'

'Bloody hell, I can't do that! I don't have a licence over there; I can't just roll up and start interviewing people.'

'What you need a licence for? You're just delivering a message for me, and I'm a US citizen. You go talk to him, deliver my message, then get a reply in the form of a signed statement.'

'I still couldn't do that, not on my own. What if he cuts up rough?'

He looked at me. 'You're not scared of Sonny, are you?'

'I'm not scared of anyone, pal, not any more. But if he and I get into a rammy – that's Scottish for ruckus, by the way – in his old lady's house, she could call the cops, then what? No, I couldn't do it, not without back-up.'

'Why don't you go?' I asked him, forgetting for a moment how bad an idea that could be.

'I'd love to,' he answered, 'but I got next weekend to take care of, plus the final preparations and television promos for the pay-per-view. I can't go. Look, you want back-up, you find someone. Cost ain't a problem.'

'It's not that easy,' I protested. 'I can't just grab someone off the street. Whatever you say this is dodgy, so I could only take someone I trusted absolutely. There's my ex-partner Jimmy, who does the odd interview for me, but he runs a pub these days. No way could he get away. There's mad Ali, but he's got an open all hours shop.

'There's my dad, but even if he didn't tell me I was a bloody loony and wanted to come, his patients can't be postponed just like that.'

'Jesus Oz,' Everett grumbled. 'There has to be one person in the world you know and trust, and who's got the balls for this job.'

Of course, when I really thought about it, there was.

41

'Can this be for real, d'you think? You and I, sat here in some bloody bar in Chicago, off on yet another daft mission. Honestly, what the hell made you call me?'

'I told you before, I needed someone I could trust absolutely to back me up on this job. When I ran down the list, there was only one person – you.'

'But would you have called me if Jan was alive?'

'If Jan was alive, she'd be sat right where you are. But she isn't. The point is that I needed you and you came. Thanks.'

Prim had been a bit hard on our surroundings. 'Some bloody bar,' was in fact the cocktail lounge of a pretty decent restaurant on Michigan Avenue, not too far from our hotel, the Clarion Executive Plaza, on State Street – 'that great street', as The Man used to sing. We had jetted into O'Hare on separate flights that afternoon, she from Spain, I from Glasgow, and had met up in the arrivals area.

By US standards, St Louis isn't all that far from Chicago, and so we faced only a short shuttle flight in the morning. It was evening and the light was going, but as I looked out of the window and up, I could still see the great needle that was the Sears Tower, now just one of many buildings that had once been the tallest in the world.

I turned at the sound of a classically discreet cough. 'Your table is ready, sir,' said our waiter. He escorted us into the restaurant, where he placed us beside another window which looked along the great boulevard.

'You're looking very well,' I said to Prim as he went off to fetch the wine and mineral water which I had ordered. 'I didn't get a chance to tell you that in Barcelona.'

'Thank you, sir,' she replied. 'I wish I could say the same for you. You still look on the high side of forty. Haven't you been sleeping?'

'Fitfully, you might say. To tell you the truth, I've been feeling homesick for the last couple of days. I had planned to go up to Anstruther tomorrow night, to see my dad and Mary. They're still pretty numb, according to Ellie.'

'What about Noosh?' Prim asked quietly. 'Have you heard from her?'

'I tried to get in touch with her,' I replied. 'Her firm told me that she's running their Russian office in St Petersburg. I asked them to pass a message to her, but I haven't heard anything since. I don't really want to, truth be told.

'Look, Prim, let's talk about something else. How about business in hand? You got off work no problem?'

'Easy. I've got a couple of weeks owing. I've changed my flight back, in fact. When you go to Manchester on Friday, I fly to Glasgow. I'm off to see the folks for a week.'

'I wondered why you had that bloody big suitcase.' I grinned at her, and for the first time since Barcelona, I began to feel a sense of the guy I had once been. Okay, when it came to the crunch, it was Jan who had been for me all along, but I really liked Prim; she lifted my spirits.

'What about this man Leonard?' she asked, as the wine waiter opened our Turning Leaf, while another set two enormous prawn cocktails before us. 'He is the guy, yes?'

'Has to be.' I explained the pattern of calls showing on the mobile phone statement, and told her about the way the barrier in Newcastle and the turn-buckle pad had been rigged. 'We reckon that after Jerry was shot, Leonard was out of the arena before the ambulance.'

'So what are you going to do with him tomorrow? And why do you need me there?'

'I'll decide how I'm going to play it when I see him. I want you there as a corroborating witness to whatever he tells us, but also I reckon you'll put him more at his ease than if I went in alone, or with another guy.'

'But if he's made it back home, and he can't be prosecuted, why should he tell you anything, other than to piss off?'

I smiled at her across the table. 'Primavera, my dear, I realise that you haven't seen the man at his best, but do not underestimate the persuasive power of Everett Davis – even from four thousand miles away.'

42

I don't know why, but I'd expected St Louis to be bigger. As our 737 cruised alongside the convergence of the Missouri and Mississippi, the city – set on the western bank of the great united river – looked to be much smaller than Glasgow, or even Edinburgh.

Prim and I had retired to our respective rooms in the Carlton Executive Plaza – *Why are American hotels obliged to have at least two and preferably three names?* I had asked myself – almost immediately after dinner, but the time-shift had meant that neither of us slept much. We had been bleary-eyed when we met up in the lobby at seven thirty to take a cab to the airport.

We noticed as soon as we stepped out of the plane that without the cooling wind blowing down off Lake Michigan, St Louis was milder than Chicago. In fact for April, it was downright warm, and both of us felt over-dressed. From the look he gave us our taxi driver agreed with us.

'Thirty-four seventy, Andrew Hamilton Drive,' I told him as we climbed in, glancing at my watch as I did. It was just after midday; I hoped that Sonny Leonard's mother's patience would hold and that he still wouldn't know that we were coming. We were lucky. Mrs Zabrynski's home was in a suburb on the same side of the city as the airport, and so the taxi journey took us no longer than fifteen minutes.

Andrew Hamilton Drive was long and straight, one of

many in the flat, grid-like community. As I paid the cabby and turned towards number thirty-four seventy, I saw that it was a single-storey house with a smart, white-painted wooden exterior, built on a raised deck which stood on stilts five feet tall, and with a railed terrace running all the way around.

'Okay,' I said to Prim. 'Follow my lead.' Together we trotted up the steps to the deck. I rang the bell.

The portly figure of Sonny Leonard opened the door. 'Surprise!' I said.

'Oh shit!' said he.

'I don't think you're pleased to see us, Sonny,' I went on, quickly, trying to keep the roadie on the back foot. 'Now why would that be? We only want to talk to you. You might not remember my friend Prim, or maybe you do. She was in Barcelona; she jumped into the ring to give emergency aid to Jerry Gradi after he was shot.'

A look of terror flashed across his face.

'Can we come in, Sonny?' I asked. As I spoke, an old lady appeared behind him in the hallway. She looked like a really nice old dear, which didn't make me feel too good about having deceived her.

'Your surprise arrived, I see, son,' she said.

'Yes, Momma,' Sonny replied. 'It's friends from Scotland. Listen, I'll just talk to them out here on the deck for a bit. We'll be in directly. You put some coffee on now.' She waved and nodded. Leonard closed the door on her and pointed to four wooden seats off to the right.

'Let's sit down here.'

We followed him, and took seats on either side of him. 'How is The Behemoth,' he asked at once. 'Did he make it?'

'He's making it even as we speak, Sonny,' I told him. 'With Sally Crockett in a nice hotel in the Costa Brava. He'll be pleased you were concerned about him, but that won't stop him from tearing your head off when he catches up with you.'

I took my small tape recorder from my pocket and switched it on. 'Let's get to it. Everett sent us across to see you, to have a talk and get a signed statement. He was going to come himself but I managed to persuade him that wasn't a good idea . . . for the moment.' I paused, to let him consider that.

'However, if we're not happy when we leave here today, you will have a visit from him. Believe me, you really do not want that.'

Sonny Leonard shifted in his chair. I had got through to him. He looked at Prim, as if for relief. 'What does he want?' he asked her.

She smiled at him. 'He wants you to tell him how Mr Reilly of CWI hired you to sabotage Global Wrestling Alliance events . . .'

I leaned forward and tugged at his sleeve. '. . . specifically how you rigged the barrier in Newcastle, the one that injured Liam Matthews, then placed a miniature firearm in a turn-buckle pad in Barcelona, almost killing Jerry Gradi.'

Sonny Leonard threw his head back and looked up at the eaves of his mother's house. 'Oh shit, I knew the boss would think that,' he moaned. 'Listen, Oz. I'll tell you the gospel truth. I had nothing at all to do with those things. I never met Mr Reilly personally, and I never took any money from him.' As he paused, beads of sweat formed on his forehead. 'I guess I know why Everett thinks I did, though.'

'Tell me,' I said, not in the slightest convinced.

'The Monday before the Barcelona gig, the day when normally there's damn few people in the office, I went in to do some stock-checkin' of our equipment and props. I reckoned we was a bit light on some things, and I knew

Everett had been in, so I went to his office to talk to him about it.

'He was gone, but there was this pile of mobile phone bills on his desk, with mine right on top, and lines drawn on it underneath this one number. Maybe you can guess what it was.'

'I know what it was, Sonny.'

'In that case,' he said, 'you'll know how I felt. Like I told you on the plane, it ain't no secret how the boss feels about CWI and Reilly. I guessed I was in trouble, but I couldn't say anything till he did, case he fired me for rooting around in his office.'

He took a deep breath of the warm Missouri air. 'Then that thing happened in Barcelona. I knew something was wrong as soon as Jerry hit the pad. Then I heard the boss yell in Spanish for the medics. I saw the blood, and I saw the busted pad – the one I had fixed on.

'I was at ringside when Daze turned around and looked at me. It was like he was in a trance, and I tell you, Oz, looking at him I saw my own death.' He turned to Prim. 'Then you jumped into the ring, miss, and started yelling at him, till he forgot about me and looked at Jerry again.'

He stared down at his hands bunched together in his lap. 'It was as clear as day; whatever had been done to that turnbuckle pad, I had fixed it on, I had been calling the CWI number, and I was taking the rap.

'I ran for it, Oz, simple as that. I was scared shitless and I ran for it. I took a cab back to the hotel, picked up my passport and the rest of my gear and went to the bus depot. I got on the first bus out for anywhere. That happened to be Madrid. The next day, Sunday, I caught a plane to JFK. That's the God's truth.'

I have interviewed a fair few people over the years, and during that time I've learned to spot the difference between liars and those who are telling the truth. As I looked at Sonny Leonard, all my experience and instinct told me that he wasn't lying; still, I couldn't fly in the face of the evidence.

'But what about those calls to CWI, man? And on a company phone, too.'

'Yeah I know, that was stupid. But I wasn't phoning Reilly.' He paused and smiled faintly.

'When I was at Triple W, I had a girlfriend there. Her name's Sandra. She worked as a secretary, but she did all sorts of stuff. Now Reilly, he'd do anything to hurt Triple W. So when someone told him about Sandra, he made her an offer to come to work for CWI in his promotions department.

'She should have asked me about it, but she didn't; she just took the job. As soon as she got there, she knew she'd made a mistake and the longer she was there, the unhappier she got. All those calls were to her, just trying to give her a lift.'

'So what were you doing in Philadelphia this week,' I asked him, 'when I called your mother on Monday?'

The smile became a grin. 'Well, first I was getting her out of CWI,' he replied. 'And second, we was getting married.' He stood, stepped over to the front door and threw it open. 'Hey Sandy,' he yelled into the house. 'Come on out here and meet these guys.'

She stepped nervously into the door-frame. 'Hello,' she whispered.

'Sandy, honey,' said her new husband. 'This is Oz, from GWA in Scotland. And this—'

Prim thrust out her hand towards the girl. 'I'm Oz's business associate,' she explained.

'I'm trying to persuade them,' Leonard went on, 'that I ain't been sabotaging Everett's operation in Britain for Mr Reilly.'

Her mouth fell open in horror. 'Sonny wouldn't do that, mister, honest,' she burst out.

I looked at her. 'Would it surprise you to learn that someone has been?'

She shook her head. 'No. Nothing would surprise me about Tony Reilly,' she said, in a light Eastern seaboard accent. 'He's a dangerous man, if ever I met one.

'I wasn't with CWI when Diane left him for Everett Davis, but those who were said he went ballistic. He said he'd kill them both. The story was, that was why Daze left the US.' She paused. 'I heard there was history between them before that, though.'

'What sort of guy is Reilly?' I asked her. 'What does he look like?'

'I can show you,' she said. 'I got a CWI marketing brochure inside.' She stepped back into the house, reappearing a few seconds later, with a glossy folder. She opened it, took out a red-covered A4 booklet and handed it to me. 'Page one,' she said. 'That's him.'

I opened the brochure. It was my turn to be shocked. I know there's no reason why it shouldn't be the case, but given my Celtic roots, I just hadn't expected someone called Reilly to be black.

43

'Sandy Schlitz?' said Everett, still stunned by my story. I had
called him straight away from the airport in St Louis. 'Sonny
Leonard's married Sandy?'

'That's right. We talked to her, and she confirmed that all
those calls were to her, or at least that he made that number
of calls to her at the CWI office.'

'In that case, Sonny's telling the truth,' he said. 'I know
Sandy from my Triple W days. She always struck me as
slightly dumb, but she's a good girl, and honest too.

'That's good work, you two.' He grunted. 'Even if it's not
what I wanted to hear. Because you know what it means.'

'Oh yes,' I said. 'It means that you've still got a problem.'

Since we didn't fancy a sightseeing tour of the St Louis
soap factory, Prim and I caught the first flight back to
Chicago. We were faced with another night in the Windy
City, so we made the best of it, with a quick visit to the Adler
Planetarium and the Shedd Aquarium in Grant Park, before
dinner in a very good Italian restaurant in the heart of the
Loop, listening to the rattle of the elevated trains as we ate.

'You're still homesick in spite of all this around us, aren't
you?' Prim said as I said goodbye to my Minestrone starter.

'I don't think so,' I said. 'I think I take this with me
everywhere I go.'

'For how long?'

'All my life, I reckon. It may not show as much but it'll

262

always be there. Sorry, Prim; I'm lousy company.'

She smiled. 'But I know you, so that makes it all right. I'd much rather you were like this, than pretending to be the old Oz. All wounds take time to heal: those as bad as yours may take a long time. But I like the man you are now just as much as I liked the old one.'

'Listen.' I paused to sip my wine. 'Once you've touched base with your folks, what are you going to do?'

'Go back to Spain, I suppose, go back to work. For a while at least.'

'Promise me one thing then. Don't head off into another war zone without telling me. No one has so many friends that they can afford to lose touch with even one.'

'I promise.' She reached over and squeezed my hand. I couldn't help it, I recoiled; I pulled it back, very slightly, but she couldn't mistake it. 'Sorry,' she said.

God, was I a mess. Feeling guilty, I took both of her hands and squeezed them hard. 'No, I'm sorry; there I was going on about friendship, too. It's just that . . . How do I put it? . . . there are lots of bridges I'll have to cross, but in my own time.'

We said our goodbyes at O'Hare Airport next morning. Prim's flight to Glasgow was due off just before mine, so we sat together in International Departures until it was called, then I walked her to the gate. I thought about kissing her goodbye; just a friendly peck on the cheek, but I couldn't. Too soon, Oz, too soon; maybe never. So I smiled, ruffled her hair, and said, 'Give me a call from Auchterarder. Say hello to your folks for me.'

My body clock was totally confused, so I tried to keep it ticking all the way back to Manchester, to get it on an even keel, but once or twice I dozed off. The second time . . . at least I think it was . . . I had the grey dream again, only this time Jan was in our living room standing by our partners' desk.

I snapped awake, with a very clear picture in my head. It was of Jan, just before I left for Barcelona, the last time I saw her alive. It was still early morning, but she had been working on some papers at the desk, as she had through most of the previous evening. They were strewn all over it. And at the same time, her eyes were shining – the way they always did when she achieved some personal triumph. She had looked so good, I had felt incredibly horny, and had had to force myself towards the door.

As I sat on the plane, coming back to reality, I thought about that moment and wondered just what the hell had happened to those papers.

44

Everett was waiting at the International Arrivals gateway at Manchester Airport when the flight came in, just before eleven pm, BST. I was still preoccupied with my dream on the aircraft, but he took it for jet lag.

His Range Rover was in the short-term car park, which was almost part of the terminal. He handed me a copy of the *Saturday BattleGround* running order. I glanced down it and noticed that Darius was in action in the opening match against Le Baron, a French jobber, then was surprised to see Daze in the middle of the order, against Cyclops; Al Hendrix, the import from Japan.

'He's going straight in against you?' I said.

'Yeah. We've been running promos on him all through this week's programming. He's costing enough so I'm gonna get full value out of him. We'll run a little play where I'm supposed to be fighting Axel Rodd . . . that's Max Schwartz, remember . . . till Al takes him out and goes at it with me. We'll play it even, until we're interrupted by Liam.'

'Is Matthews going to be fit for the pay-per-view?' I asked him.

'Yeah, he's okay. The doctor signed him off on Wednesday, and he's back doing full gym work, with high impact manoeuvres. He and I have even done a run-through of our match for next Wednesday. It's going to be good; the guy's fast, very fast. I could be wrong but his attitude seems a bit different since his accident; a little less arrogant, maybe.'

I smiled at him. 'Does that mean you're beginning to give up your theory about him and Diane?'

Everett grunted. 'Yeah, I guess you were right about that. He couldn't be that stupid. Anyway, if Diane was going to play around, I don't reckon he'd be her type.'

'What's her type, then?'

He grinned at me, sheepishly as he fitted himself into the Range Rover. 'I guess I am.'

'So,' I asked him, as he drove out of the park, 'am I back on watcher duty for this weekend?'

'Yeah, you sure are, now that Leonard's in the clear.' His grin returned. 'Hell, I must have scared him, looking at him out of that ring, mustn't I. Scared him outta town and outta the goddamn country! I suppose I better send him a severance payment after all.'

'Funny, he never mentioned that. He's got himself a job anyway, as road crew foreman with a touring rock band. Sandy's on the team too, in charge of catering.'

The big fellow laughed. 'From what I remember of the kid, I hope the guys like steak. Enthusiastic but limited just about sums her up.'

I unzipped my flight bag and took out the CWI brochure which Sandy had given me. 'You never told me Reilly was black, Everett,' I said.

He looked at me, taken aback. 'Fucking honky,' he said eventually, with an attempt at a grin. 'Why shouldn't he be?'

'No reason at all,' I conceded. 'But you never told me about the history between you two either. You told me no way you'd ever let him control you, but you never really told me why. The first time I saw this photograph, something clicked in my head. It came to me on the flight back home.' I gazed at him hunched behind the wheel of the big vehicle.

'That photograph in your office, Everett, of your mother.

Tell me if I'm wrong, but doesn't Reilly bear a striking resemblance to her?'

All of a sudden, he looked at me, in a way that made me hold my breath and keep on holding it. His eyes were unblinking as they held me. 'You clever bastard,' he whispered at last. I was pleased just to be able to breathe again. 'Not even Jerry knows that; only Diane.'

He frowned. 'You got it right. Tony Reilly and me, we're half-brothers. Tony's dad was a Philadelphia hoodlum. My dad was a lawyer; he handled their divorce and afterwards he married my Mamma.

'Tony's dad never forgave him. He poisoned him against my dad, and against me from the day I was born. One day, when I was nine, my dad was crossing the street in Austin, where we lived by then, when he was knocked down and killed by a car. It was a hit and run. They never did find the driver, but my Mamma and I always knew the truth.'

'So that's why you're out to break CWI? To get even for your father?'

Everett shook his head. 'No. I don't hold nothing against Tony. But that don't work the other way. When CWI made me that offer, I knew if I signed, I'd be the highest paid jobber in the business. Tony would have made me look like a chump.

'When I met Diane, I didn't make a play for her because she was my brother's girl, it just happened that I fell for her, and she for me. When we set up the GWA, Tony thought we were clearing out, to get away from the heat. But as soon as he figured out this business was for real, it was inevitable that he'd come after us.

'I knew that. I always knew that the GWA would have to take out CWI, to ensure its own survival.

'I'll be honest; I was pleased when we came up with Leonard as the fall guy. Now it turns out not to be him, I'm more scared than ever.'

I frowned. 'I have to tell you, Everett. Sandy doesn't think that Reilly is behind this thing. She said he still laughs at the GWA around the office; that he doesn't see it as a threat.'

'Maybe he does. But he's my brother and his father's son. I got to assume that he's out to get me, just like his daddy got mine. So to hell with Sandy. I'm still looking for a mole.'

'In that case, it could be a blessing, Sonny being in the clear, you know,' I said.

'Why's that?'

'Sort of cuts down the list of suspects. If you're right about your brother being behind this – and I agree, when you look at the whole picture it can't be anyone else – you have to look at the sort of person he'd buy to help him.

'Let's say he went for an American, with an offer of money and a job with him afterwards. Jerry's obviously in the clear, and I'll say Diane is, even if you won't.'

He shook his head. 'No. I'll say that now.'

'I'm glad to hear it. So, with Sonny Leonard out of the frame as well, that cuts the field down. It leaves Max, Barbara, your two women specialists, and two guys who are basically jobbers.'

Everett scratched his chin. 'Forget Max. He was back in the States on injury vacation when the Newcastle thing happened. Forget Barbara. She wasn't with us the night Dave Manson got whacked, and she'd have had to be, to switch that chair. The same's true of the two women. They're a tag team and I don't use them that much.

'The other guys? Ronnie Snell and Dick Ostermeyer? I suppose they could be candidates, except . . . no, Ronnie wasn't there either when Dave got it. That leaves Ostermeyer.'

'Which one's he?'

'He wrestles as Dragon Davies, from Tiger Bay, Cardiff.'

'Oh yes,' I recalled. 'I've announced him; in Newcastle

and in Barcelona. He's an American?'

'Yup. He's a damn fine wrestler, the best jobber we have. You see him go down, you think he'll never come up in this life. He has a speech impediment, though, so he can't go on the mike to develop his persona like the rest of us do. I recruited him from Japan, where that wasn't a problem.'

He frowned. 'I can't see Dick being bad, but I suppose we have to look at the possibility. He ain't on the programme this weekend, though, as you'll see.'

'How old is he?'

'Mid thirties.'

'What did he do before he became a wrestler?'

'He was in the US Marines. Why do you ask?'

'Because whoever rigged that miniature pistol in the turn-buckle pad must have had pretty good knowledge of handling firearms.'

'Shit yes, that's true.'

I looked at him as we passed under a sign for central Manchester. 'Can you remember anything about Darius Hencke's background?' I asked, quietly.

'He's an ex-soldier too; he was in the German special forces for a couple of years. Did a tour on a UN peace-keeping force in Africa. Why d'you ask about him?'

'Because it doesn't have to be an American. Apart from you and Jerry – and Liam, because he got squashed – who'd be the biggest prize for Tony Reilly?'

45

The Nynex Arena isn't as impressive as the stadium in Barcelona, but it's big nonetheless. And we filled it, on two consecutive nights – two more trouble-free nights as it turned out.

I met Al 'Cyclops' Hendrix at the Saturday run-through. On that first encounter he was almost as scary as Jerry, but without any of The Behemoth's redeeming out-of-character features. There was something about his attitude I didn't like; it was as if he knew that Everett needed him and was prepared to screw every personal advantage out of that situation.

After seeing him in action I had to admit that he was able to back up his expectations with performance. He wasn't as muscular as Everett, or as bulky as Jerry, but he had real wrestling skills, and his timing was superb. He made his first appearance from behind the curtain, ambushing the unfortunate Max 'Axel Rodd' Schwartz, then, carrying a great rough club, marched over his fallen body and down to the ring to confront Daze.

The big man's flame canisters, strapped to the ring-post, shot to their usual impressive height, but even before he entered the ring he was met by a pounding from Cyclops. As I had been told to expect, they fought it out evenly, until Liam jumped up on the ring apron. Daze, distracted, went for him as per the script and was hit from behind by his opponent, with that club, which he had handed to the bell-ringer on his way into the ring, and which was really made of plastic. I knew, because I had checked.

As I watched the story-line unfold, it struck me that Daze might be more than a little gullible, but that's the way it is with pro wrestling. Only the bad guys get to be cunning.

Darius Hencke's match went smoothly too. Everett had been sceptical about my worries. He had reckoned that Tony Reilly would barely have heard of the German, who was still an up-and-comer in most people's eyes.

'Never underestimate your enemy, mate,' I had warned him as we drove into the entrance-way to the Holiday Inn Crown Plaza. I spoke from bitter experience; I still felt as if life itself was my enemy.

Everett gave me a lift back to Glasgow in the Range Rover once we were finished on the Sunday, leaving the rest of the troops to strike camp. My mind was somewhere else again, worrying away at thoughts of what I was going to do once I got home, so our conversation was fairly sporadic and trivial at the start of the journey.

We were well north of Gretna before we got back to the subject of the conspiracy which had taken over his life. 'Oz,' he asked, out of the blue, 'If you were my brother Tony, would you give up now? Or would you have something else up your sleeve?'

We had reached Lockerbie before I had worked out an answer. 'Everett,' I said. 'If I was Tony Reilly I wouldn't have started in the first place. The whole thing's got way out of control. He may be a corporate pirate and everything else you say he is, but what happened to Liam and to Jerry is at another level. We're talking attempted murder here – and I have to tell you that I'm still shitting myself that you're concealing that from the police.

'Obviously I've never met Reilly, so I don't know what his

limits might be. But you know him; Christ, you're his blood. You've got to ask yourself: would he go that far?'

For the first time a grain of doubt flickered behind the designer spectacles; but not for long. 'His old man killed my old man; my Mamma was certain of that till the day she died, and she sure convinced me. His old man was a hood, and Tony still has some of his connections. He'd go that far.

'Look at the pattern. The thing with the tapes didn't cost us. The Manson incident didn't put us off air, nor did the Matthews business. So the stakes were raised. If Jerry had died in that ring, the networks would have dropped me like a hot potato.'

'Okay, if you're convinced,' I went on, 'let's say that he hasn't chucked it, he's just told his man to lay off for a bit. Ask yourself this. How did you manage to get away with it in each of the four incidents so far?'

'Luck, I guess.'

'Sure but as well as that, you were able to stay on air because the Saturday show is recorded shortly before transmission . . . shot as live, but not actually shown live.

'Next Wednesday will be different though, won't it. The whole deal will go live as it happens. Yes?'

'That's right.'

'In that case, if I was Tony Reilly it's bloody obvious what I'd do next. I'd hit the pay-per-view event.'

46

The flat was silent when I opened the door and stepped inside, but to me it wasn't empty. 'Hello,' I whispered. 'I'm back.'

I dumped my duty-free Jack Daniels in the booze cupboard, chucked five days' washing into my new Phillips machine, then checked through my post and my voicemail. When I had finished there were several cheques in my in-tray, and a number of new interview bookings in my diary. Apart from the business stuff, my phone messages included a call from Prim, from Auchterarder, letting me know that she had arrived safely at her folks' place; one from Dylan, asking if I fancied a drink after work on Monday; and two from my dad, the second sounding more tetchy than the first: 'Wondering where the bloody hell you are now, son!' I had forgotten completely to tell him that I was going to the States.

I called him straight away to make up. When I told him where I'd been, he was impressed. 'One of my favourite movies,' he said.

'What's that?'

'Judy Garland – *Meet me in St Louis*. They don't make them like that any more.' He sounded more like the old Mac the Dentist. 'What did you think of the city?' he asked.

'It's got a nice airport, and that's it; but Chicago's impressive, though. How's Auntie Mary?'

'She's getting there, but she worries about you a lot. So do I of course,' he added, casually. 'How're you doing, son, really?'

'I'm okay, Dad. I'll never get over it, but I've come to terms with it. I don't know how to explain it, but I've found something . . . not faith, stronger; a sort of certainty.'

'I understand, Oz. You and I belong to the same club now, although it guts me to think about it. Tell me something; have you had the dream yet?'

I paused. The grey dream was my greatest secret. 'Yes,' I admitted at last. 'A few nights ago. It was distressing, but since then everything seems, I don't know, not to hurt quite so much.'

'Uh-huh,' he said softly. 'That's how it was for me too.' I felt a huge surge of warmth, standing there, beside our desk. My dad and I had never been closer.

'Come up and see us soon, Oz. So long for now.'

I hung up the phone, and turned to the thing that had been bothering me since the flight: those papers which Jan had been going over, and the excited, quietly triumphant look in her eyes.

'What was it?' I asked myself out loud. And right then, in my head, Jan answered me; something she had said over the dinner table with Susie and Mike came back to me, word for word.

'I'm looking into the health care division, the last on my list, and I've found something very interesting. I'll need to go over it again, and then I'll need to consult a few people.'

Exactly that. She had still been working on those papers on the afternoon I left; yet when I had arranged her business affairs after the funeral, I couldn't remember seeing them at all.

I opened the desk drawer in which she had kept her most recent files. I had been on autopilot when I had cleared her desk, but I knew I hadn't sent anything back to Susie Gantry. The only papers which I had retained in each client file were rough working notes which Jan had made over her years in practice, and retained because they held some significance for her. I had kept them only because I could not bear to throw away anything that had been of her, created by her hand.

I checked The Gantry Group folder again. All it contained were those plain white pages, covered in her strong, clear script; nothing else. Yet I had left her working on those papers on the morning before she died.

I couldn't stop myself. It was late in the evening, but I phoned Susie's number. Ostensibly it was to arrange to meet Mike in the Horseshoe Bar next day after work, but as soon as that date was fixed, I asked him to put Susie on line again.

'When was the last time you saw Jan?' I asked her.

'When we were at yours for dinner,' she said. 'I never saw her after that. Remember, she said she'd come and see me the following Monday.'

'Yes, that's right.' I paused as I thought back to that evening. 'Listen, can you do something for me first thing tomorrow? Could you check and see whether those papers she was working on, the ones relating to the health care division, are back in your office?'

'Sure I will. But I had assumed that you still had them.'

'Not as far as I can see.'

'Okay. Leave it with me. I'll call you first thing.'

47

Susie was as good as her word: the phone on my desk rang at ten minutes before nine. I was sat in my captain's chair, chewing my way steadily through my muesli and reading the *Herald* at the same time. It was another slow news day, which meant another photo of Lord Provost Jack Gantry on the front page.

'I've checked those files,' the First Citizen's daughter told me. 'Twice, just to be sure. As far as I can see, everything's there.'

'Is that right,' I said. 'I suppose she must have gone to your place in the afternoon and put them back.'

'If she did,' said Susie, 'someone's getting the sack. I have a standing rule here that everyone on the premises, staff and visitors, must sign in and out. It's a fire safety thing. Maybe she took photocopies,' she suggested.

'No way. Jan never took copies of her clients' confidential papers. She worked on the originals, then returned them as soon as she was finished. Can you remember which papers she'd have been working on then?'

'Only that they had to do with our health care set-up; that's all I can tell you. Now, unless there's anything else, I'm off to read the Riot Act out in my front office. If Jan put those papers back on that Friday afternoon, as she must have, I'm going to want to know why her name isn't in the book.'

I nodded absent-mindedly as she hung up. I had noticed changes taking place in the face in the mirror over the previous three weeks, and I could feel my new frown lines as I stared at the desk-top. Jan had still been working on the papers on the Friday morning, and she hadn't even begun to consult the people she had talked about when we had Susie and Mike to dinner. Why would she take them back to the Gantry office that day? I was confused, a bit dazed; something was tapping at the back of my brain, trying to work its way to the front.

I went round to Jan's drawer once more and took out her working notes on the Gantry project. There were several pages, quite a thick bundle of manuscript; I went through them one by one. They began with a summary of the financial position of the development division, then moved on to look over the construction business. The bulk of the pile of notes reflected Jan's detailed analysis of the profitability of the public houses, with a summary page listing them all together and stating her opinion that all of the licensed premises were being operated properly.

And that was all there was. There were no notes on the health care division. None at all. Yet when I had left on that damnable Friday morning to catch the flight to Barcelona with GWA, they had been all over the place. Christ, I even remembered chiding her, in fun: 'That's supposed to be a partners' desk,' I said to her, less than five minutes before I kissed her goodbye . . . without knowing that's what it was. 'How much of it do you need?'

The thing looked huge now, as I put the pages back into their original order and replaced them in the filing drawer. I sat down once more in my captain's chair, staring blankly at the remains of my muesli, my heart pounding as I fought in vain against facing up to a frightening truth.

If Jan hadn't put those papers back into The Gantry

Group filing system – and I was sure she hadn't – then, sure as God made wee sour apples, someone else had.

There was only one answer to that, of course: someone had broken in and retrieved them. But when? I reached across and picked up Jan's lap-top – we each had one – and switched it on. It was powerful and booted up quickly. I selected her electronic diary and opened it at the date in question.

The only entry for Friday read, 'Work at home'. Saturday's listed priorities were 'Hairdresser', ten am, and 'Watch *BattleGround*' at nine-thirty pm. From the Sunday entry, she'd decided to go to Anstruther; only for her, Sunday had never happened.

As I looked at the page, the thing that had been working its way through my cluttered brain finally broke surface; my wife spoke to me again, inside my head. Our last conversation, the last time I had ever heard her voice: on the mobile phone, me in the chaotic restaurant in bloody Barcelona, Jan sitting opposite where I sat now, working.

'*I suppose so,*' she had said. '*I've got the hairdresser in the morning, and I'm shopping in the afternoon, but I can always work in the evening, before your show.*' I strained to remember what she had said after that, as I had strained to hear her words against the Spanish shouts all around me. '*I'm getting there, Oz. I'll let you see what I've found when you get home.*'

Of course she hadn't taken those papers back to The Gantry Group office. She'd been keeping them to show to me.

There could only be one answer to the riddle: someone had been watching the flat on Saturday morning, had seen her drive away, and had made an unnoticed entry to recover the files, which I knew would have been tidied away by then. Jan and I had a strict rule; we never allowed our jobs to mess up our home, outside working hours.

Of course, this led on to a further conclusion. Whoever broke into our flat would have had ample time to roll out the washing machine and fit a booby-trap device, just as the manufacturer's 'impartial' experts had suggested.

And who, apart from me, knew that Jan was working on those papers, and about the thing which she had been anxious not to discuss across the dinner table under the ears of Detective Inspector Mike Dylan? Only Miss Susie Gantry, that's all.

48

When I sat down and thought about the situation rationally, Susie Gantry made no sense at all as a suspect. She had hired Jan in the first place and had asked her to research the profitability of the business.

Unless of course my wife had been a far better accountant than she expected. What if, I asked myself, Susie had simply expected Jan to give the business a clean bill of health then pick up the reins from old Joseph Donn? What if Jan had stumbled on something that was buried really deep, something that she was never meant to find?

What if she had signed her own death warrant by dropping that hint to Susie across our dinner table?

'No way, Oz!' I said aloud, as Jan would have. 'Trust your judgement on this. Susie Gantry is not the sort of person who sends people to break into houses and rig deadly devices. No fucking way!'

'But someone did,' I shot back at myself. 'Even if the accident was just that, a fatal one in a million fault, someone took those papers and put them back in the Gantry files. Somewhere in the Gantry office there's someone who didn't want Jan to find whatever was hidden in those records.'

It was as if she was there with me; the other half of my brain, as she had become, slipping in points to the argument. 'So why did that someone take the chance of putting those papers back into the files, having taken them, and the notes, from our place?'

'Because if they knew that you were dead, Jan,' I whispered, 'there would be no threat. The Gantry Group is a private company, but the records of the business have to be kept for Inland Revenue purposes. There would have been an element of danger in simply throwing those files away. So whatever this deadly secret is, it must be there still, buried deep in the books, where only a clever girl like you could work it out.

'But now that Mr Joseph Donn and his nephew are back in control of the company accounts, there won't be any more clever girls looking them over, will there.'

I felt my eyes narrow as the cold anger which had overwhelmed me in Barcelona took hold of me once more.

'Time to talk to the police, Osbert Blackstone,' I said, in that voice of someone else's. 'Even though you'll be putting the policeman in question right on the spot.'

49

I had arranged with Everett that I would meet him at midday on Monday to discuss how to protect the pay-per-view event, but before I left home, I called Greg McPhillips.

'Hi Oz,' he greeted me, affable as ever. 'Have you had a chance to think rationally about taking action against the Germans? I'll tell you now; you don't need the money.

'I've sorted out all Jan's insurance policies: your mortgage, such as it was, is paid off automatically, there's an additional endowment policy that pays eighty grand in the event of accidental death, a death in service arrangement as part of her pension plan, the fund value itself, and a straight life policy. There's a lot of cash there – I'm not going to say how much over the phone – but the tax planning was done very well, so you should be exempt from estate duty.'

It went straight over my head. 'You're not going to give me back my wife though, are you, Greg?'

'No, pal. That I can't do.'

'Well in that case you just sort everything out, pay all the funeral expenses, take your own fee, and put the balance in some sort of account. Tell me when it's all done, 'cause right now, I don't give a shit.

'As for the Germans, I want another week to think about that. If I do take action against them, it won't be about money, believe me.'

'No, of course it won't, Oz. I shouldn't have said that.'

I couldn't help but laugh at his contrition, since I'd heard it so often before. 'Greg, my dear old friend, a list of all the things you shouldn't have said would stretch from here to Edinburgh and back.'

I hung up and headed across the river to the GWA headquarters, where Everett was waiting for me with fresh coffee in the pot. I welcomed it; I was still cold with anger from the aftermath of my conversation with Susie, and was having trouble switching my attention to my client's business.

He offered me a doughnut from a plate piled high before him. I took two, and left the rest for him.

'I just checked with the networks; our advance booking figures for the pay-per-view have set a new record in Europe for any event. Counting the UK, Germany, Holland, Poland, Italy, France and Spain we have three and a half million buys.'

'What's that in cash?' I asked him.

'Seventy-two million dollars, my man, of which sum a shade over twenty-five million comes to the Global Wrestling Alliance.'

I stared at him; for all the weeks I had been working for Everett, I had no idea that his business could generate that sort of cash.

'Taken together, the European market's still not as big as America. Now you understand what Tony Reilly has to lose?'

For the first time, I did. 'With that at stake,' I said, 'whatever it takes to protect this event, you do it.'

'And what do you say that is, Mr Detective?' he growled, guessing my answer in advance.

'First, we tell the police what's been happening. Either you agree to that or I'm out the door now. I've been playing hide and seek with the law on this assignment for long enough. I know a guy on the Serious Crimes Squad – Mike Dylan, Susie Gantry's boyfriend. I'm seeing him tonight, and I want your authority to tell him what's been happening.'

He looked at me doubtfully. 'I mean it, Everett,' I told him. 'You let me tell Mike or you're getting yourself a new announcer for Wednesday.'

He shrugged those great shoulders. 'Fair enough,' I said. I stood up, turned and walked to the door. I was in the act of turning the handle, when I heard him sigh behind me.

'Yeah, okay,' he conceded. 'You can talk to him. But ask him to be discreet, please.'

'Thanks. Of course I will.' I went back to my seat, and picked up what was left of my first doughnut. 'Next, I think you should hire a good security firm to do a complete check of the arena, before the spectators are admitted. I take it that you'll have a full house?'

'Hell yes! We sold out this one a month in advance. This Ingliston place ain't the biggest arena, but it'll look great on screen.'

'That's good. Third, every piece of equipment that's going to be used on Wednesday has to be checked personally by you. No more lethal turn-buckle pads, please.'

He shook his head. 'No, that I guarantee. I'll go over everything with Alex Kruger, the special effects controller.'

'Who's he?'

'You never seen him? He works for our television contractor; it's his job to make sure all the whiz-bangs go off exactly on time. Our road crew install them, he fires them with remote devices.'

I frowned at him. 'Are you sure he's okay?'

'Yeah, no doubt about it. He couldn't possibly have had access to the barrier that hurt Liam, or to the turn-buckle pad. Don't worry about him.'

'Listen mate,' I told him, 'until this show's over on Wednesday, you should worry about everyone.'

50

The Horseshoe Bar is one of the last great unreconstructed pubs in Glasgow; not a plastic saloon with a list of designer beers and no draught worth the name, not a surplus-to-requirements banking hall staffed by smart young people in suits. No, the Horseshoe is a genuine, well maintained boozer with a polished wooden bar-top, a ripping good pint of lager and the best pie, beans and chips in town.

Dylan was there before me; ten minutes before me, he complained, but I had seen him stepping through the door as I turned the corner out of Renfield Street. No matter; since he was there first I let him buy the first round.

It being early on a Monday evening, the place was nothing like busy, but I took my lager nonetheless and motioned Mike to follow me to a table in a quiet corner near the door. 'You changed your habits?' he said. 'I thought you were a stand-at-the-bar type.'

'So I am,' I told him. 'But I want to talk to you, professional-like, and I don't want anyone ear-holing us.'

He looked at me, suddenly suspicious. 'Professionally? I can't talk to you about my job, Oz. You know that.'

'No, Michael,' I said patiently. 'I talk, you listen. Got it?' Mollified, he nodded.

'Good. What I have to say to you is on behalf of my client Everett Davis. I've been working for him undercover for the last few weeks. That's what the ring announcer stuff has been all about.'

Dylan stared at me, in a mixture of mock amazement and outrage. 'Have you been playing coppers again?' he asked. It was surprisingly near the mark for him. A few weeks before I would have joked along with him, but I didn't have the patience any more.

'Don't be fucking stupid, man,' I snapped at him. 'I've been working on a confidential basis, trying to determine whether certain suspicions which Everett had were justified. There's no longer any doubt that they are, and so, acting on my advice, my client has now agreed that I should tell you, as a member of the Serious Crimes Squad, what's been going on.'

I paused. 'That's how your report will begin, right?' He smiled gently and nodded.

'Okay, here's the position. Everett is convinced that an American rival, Tony Reilly, of an organisation called Championship Wrestling Incorporated, has suborned someone in his employ to sabotage GWA shows and ruin his relationship with the television networks which are his customers.

'There have been four incidents in all; two of them deliberate acts beyond doubt.' I described the incidents in detail, from the rigged tape cassettes to Jerry Gradi's near-fatal shooting in the ring in Barcelona, leaving nothing out, not even Prim's sudden life-saving appearance.

All the flippancy had gone from my friend by the time I had finished. 'Didn't the Spanish police react?' he asked.

'I thought they would, but the ambulance crew told the surgeons that it was a wrestling injury. No one thought to take it further.'

'It's been a few weeks since then, though. Big Daze has been a bit backward in coming forward – and so have you, mate.'

I shot him a look that would have cut steel. 'Sorry, Oz,' he said at once. 'You've had other things on your mind.'

'Of which more later,' I grunted. 'Everett is very sensitive about this. His business is high-risk, but it generates millions of whatever currency you'd like to name, and billions of some of them. For a while we thought we were going to be able to hand you the whole thing on a plate.

'I was in the States last week checking out our prime suspect, but we were wrong. It wasn't him.' I told him about Sonny Leonard and my trip to St Louis. 'The guy is off the list, Mike. It just wasn't him.

'Which means,' I concluded, 'that we're scratching around for a culprit. Everett's convinced that it's an American.'

'And you?' asked Dylan, 'What do you think?'

'It's not me, that I can tell you. And it's not Everett, or Jerry Gradi, or Liam Matthews – or Sally Crockett. Other than that, to be honest, I haven't a clue. The only things I do know are that we've got a fully live event coming up on Wednesday evening and that the person behind these four incidents is still out there.'

The detective nodded. 'Yes, and we also know that he's got some skill with firearms, as well as access to a nasty wee piece of hardware. There are far more of these mini-pistols in circulation than you'll ever hear us admit.'

He looked at me, suddenly sharper and more serious than I had ever seen him. 'What does Everett want from us, Oz?'

'The ball's in your court,' I told him. 'I've told you about the situation; you're the copper.'

'Okay,' said Dylan. 'Suppose I go in tomorrow and tell my boss all about this. Has it occurred to you that there's a possibility that he might have the Wednesday event called off?'

'No it hasn't. Why would he do that?'

'Threat to public safety.'

'But there hasn't been a threat to the public.'

'Jesus, you've had a guy shot in the ring. That sounds threatening enough to me.'

'Mike, they have sold seventy million dollars' worth of pay-per-view subscriptions so far. If this show is called off Everett is a dead man with the television networks, and GWA is bust. Whoever's been out to get him, that person will have won, thanks to you. Do you want to explain that to Everett's pal, Lord Provost Gantry – or his daughter?'

He gulped; a quick swallow of air. 'No,' he admitted. 'Maybe not.'

I seized an advantage. 'Look, we're hiring extra security for Wednesday, specifically to protect the public. You tell your boss, of course, and have a presence there, but don't let him or anyone else dream of calling the thing off.

'Try this one on. If I gave you details of everyone on the GWA payroll, could you feed them into the police national computer and see what it tells you?'

Dylan nodded. 'Name, date and place or country of birth, National Insurance number, passport numbers for the foreigners: give me that sort of stuff and I should be able to come up with something.'

'Now we're talking. I'll speak to Everett and get as much as we have to you as soon as possible.'

I finished my lager, walked over to the bar and ordered another round. Mike was grinning when I got back to the table. 'I knew you were up to something with the big man. Ring announcer, my arse.'

I decided to wipe the smile off his face. 'Since you're the great detective, Michael,' I said, 'try this one on.

'The night before she died, my wife was working on papers from the files of The Gantry Group; health care division. I know this because she told me when I phoned her from

Barcelona. It was the last thing she ever told me in fact.' I watched his face, saw my voice slice into him.

'Next morning, she went to the hairdresser's, as she usually did every second Saturday. Afterwards she went shopping; for Jan, that would mean the St Enoch Centre, a bit of lunch, Princes Square, maybe Habitat or somewhere else for household stuff – an afternoon's worth.

'Then she came home, and she was killed. She switched on the fucking washing machine and she was killed. You with me so far?'

'Yes, Oz,' he whispered, discomfort all over his coupon.

'That's good. In that case, I'd like your help with something. I'd like you to tell me who took the Gantry papers from Jan's filing drawer and put them back into the company records, and who took her notes on the health care division and made them disappear. Because I didn't, and I know Jan didn't.

'While you're working that out, maybe your experts can have another look at that bloody appliance, and tell you whether they agree with the manufacturer that it could have been rigged to kill my wife the moment she went to empty it.'

Dylan looked at me. He tried to speak, but went into a fit of coughing and spluttering. 'Do you realise what you're saying?' he asked me.

'Yes Mike. I'm saying there's a chance that my wife was murdered because she had found out about something that's going on within The Gantry Group – the company your girl-friend runs.

'The company where Mr Joseph Donn has just been re-installed as Finance Director,' I took a deep breath, and stared at him, 'over Jan's dead body, you might say.'

I was an expert in the task of breaking bad news, so putting my friendly detective inspector on the spot didn't bother me one bit.

For a few seconds he was absolutely speechless. 'You're not saying Susie's involved, are you?' he gasped, as he began to recover himself.

'Not for one minute, Mike. But someone in her company is, of that I'm certain. Also, I would love to know what our friend Joe Donn was doing on the weekend Jan died.'

'What the hell am I supposed to do about it? Why tell me about this, Oz?'

'Well for one thing, if I go to any other copper; say, for example, the boys who investigated Jan's death; they'll investigate hard, they'll walk all over Susie, and you'll be seriously embarrassed, maybe even out of a job. Remember Ricky Ross?' As I looked at him, he did, and he shuddered.

'For another thing,' I continued, 'you might be a flash bastard, but I trust you. Now ask yourself this. What would you do if any other company was involved?'

He answered without a second's thought. 'I'd go to my boss and ask permission to seek a warrant to seize the documents involved.'

'Well in this case, why don't you go to your other boss? Ask Susie to let you have those papers back.' I checked myself. 'No, on second thoughts, ask her for photocopies. We don't want anyone to know that we're still looking into this.'

'But what'll I tell her when she asks why I want them?'

'Tell her what you like, mate, but make damn sure you tell her to keep her mouth shut.'

51

'You can trust this buddy of yours not to make too many waves, can you?' Everett was still not reconciled to the idea of bringing the police in on his problems.

'He understands the situation okay, and the sort of money involved. I spoke to Mike this morning before I came here. He's advised his boss of the situation and he's got the green light to handle it himself. He'll be there tomorrow night with a couple more CID men, but there'll be no heavy uniform involvement, nothing like that.

'Have you hired the security firm, as we discussed?'

The big man nodded. 'Yeah, I did that yesterday afternoon. I went for the biggest and best. They've promised me a specialist team on site all day tomorrow.' He paused. 'Will you still make it through tonight for the first rehearsals?'

'Sure. No reason why not.'

'That's good. Everything's gotta be word and move-perfect tomorrow; there's no scope for mistakes, so everyone has to rehearse as often as it takes – including you.'

I threw him a look. 'I could shove a brush up my arse and sweep the floor at the same time,' I offered.

Everett grinned. 'I'll bear that in mind, should the need arise. Meantime, let's go and sort out this information your policeman friend needs.'

The GWA contractual work was all handled by the McPhillips law firm, but Everett employed a personnel manager to deal with the routine aspects of people management. He led me straight into her room. 'Want to look at the files, Hazel,' he said.

He crossed to one of three steel filing cabinets which stood against the far wall, opened a drawer, pulled out a file, apparently at random, and handed it to me. It belonged to Diane, and listed her birthplace, Decatur, Illinois, her date of birth, which was one day after mine, her maiden name, Boone, her US and UK social security numbers and her permanent address and telephone number.

'That be enough for you?'

I nodded. 'Looks ideal. Are they all in this format?'

'They're all computer stored, so I guess they will be. Hazel, I need you to do something.' The dark-haired woman, who was in her mid-twenties, looked up from her desk. 'Print out the top sheet of every file and bring them to me. Don't ask why, and don't tell anyone.'

She nodded, without a word, and we went back to Everett's office. One mug of coffee and two doughnuts later – he had five – she knocked lightly on the door, stepped inside and laid a brown A4 envelope on the glass table.

'That's whit yis wanted,' she said, in a broad Glasgow accent, turned on her heel and left. I watched the door as it closed.

Everett was grinning as I turned back towards him. 'Hazel doesn't say a word she doesn't have to, but she keeps tabs on everyone in the business. I like her, like her a lot. I'm just waiting for the day she smiles at me.'

I was back home by midday, half an hour before Dylan arrived to pick up the documents. I spent the time glancing through them; they were completely up-to-date, for they included forms for Al Hendrix and the unpronounceable Japanese tag team.

'How long will that lot take to process?' I asked Mike, as

he flicked through the thick bundle.

'Depends on access to the computer,' he replied. 'We'll have to do some checking across the Atlantic and in Europe, and that'll take time. I hope it'll be wrapped up by close of play tomorrow, but I can't promise anything.'

'Touch and go,' I said. 'We need this before the event, don't we?'

'If your client had brought us in earlier that would have been no problem.'

'*Touché*,' I conceded. 'Have you talked to Susie about the other matter?'

'As soon as I got back to her place last night.'

'How'd she take it?'

'Badly, as I'd expected. She exploded at first, but when I got her to calm down, and explained what had happened and what it might mean, she got frightened. She's terrified by the very idea that someone in her business might have been involved in Jan's death. Of course she's worried too about the effect on Jack's political career.'

'Fuck Jack's political career,' I snapped at him. 'Is she going to get those photocopies for us?'

'Calm down, Oz. She's going to do it as soon as there's no one else in the office to see her. She hopes she'll manage it tonight, but she did warn me that the new book-keeper's been working late a lot, getting to know the business and getting ready to do his first VAT return.

'I asked her about Joseph Donn too. She said that he couldn't have been in your flat that day. When she fired him, he went off in a huff to his apartment in Marbella. Jack had to call him there to get him to come home, back to the business.

'First things first,' said Mike. 'Let's concentrate on the GWA situation first. On Thursday, once that's resolved, you and I will sit down and see if we can pick up whatever it was that Jan found. I've got plenty of leave due, so I'll take a day off. We can work here.' He hesitated. 'As a matter of fact, Oz, you couldn't put me up for a few days, could you? Susie sort of feels – and I agree with her – that if I'm investigating her company, it might be better for me professionally if I wasn't living with her.'

'What you're saying, Mike, is that she's chucked you out.'

'Not exactly. Just till things are sorted out.'

I smiled, and nodded. 'A few days then; just a few. It might even make it easier for us to work on this thing. The sooner we get started, the better.'

'Thanks mate,' he said. 'I'll move my gear in tonight.

'There is one other thing I'd like to do though,' he added. 'I've got a pal in the scenes-of-crime unit. I want him to dust this place down for fingerprints, especially the area around Jan's desk and in the kitchen where the washing machine was. I'll even ask him to dust the machine.'

'What good will that do?' I asked him.

'Maybe a hell of a lot of good. Even in this day and age, we still catch more criminals through prints than through DNA.'

52

Getting to Ingliston from Glasgow was a damn sight easier than getting to Barcelona. Without breaking any speed limits (well, not too many; it's difficult to tell with the different restrictions on the cross-Glasgow motorway), I made it to the pay-per-view event venue from my flat in just under an hour.

When I got there, the ring was in place. Darius Hencke and Johnny King were inside the ropes working through their title match, and Everett was supervising the installation of the special effects by Gary O'Rourke and his team. He spotted me as soon as I walked through the door and waved me across to join him.

As I reached him, I saw that there was another man with him, hidden completely from my sight by the giant's bulk. 'Oz,' said Everett, 'this is the gentleman I told you about, Alex Kruger, the special effects co-ordinator. Alex, Oz Blackstone, ring announcer; you'll have seen him in action often enough.'

Kruger nodded and offered a handshake. 'Pleased to meet you at last. You handle yourself well in there.'

'Thanks,' I answered, deciding that mutual adulation was in order. 'Your special effects ain't too shabby either.'

'Ah, I just plan them,' he said. 'Gary and the road crew put them together.' His English was very good; maybe too good for a German, I thought. Then I saw his small metal Belgian flag lapel badge. 'My job is to trigger them in order, as I'm cued by the television director.' He pointed to a scaffolding tower at the back of the arena. 'I sit up there, at a little console, with my headphones on.'

'That's them all in place, boss,' came a voice from behind me, one that I had heard before; Gary O'Rourke's unmistakable Glaswegian tones. 'Hello mate,' he said, catching sight of me. 'How're you doing? Sorry to hear about . . . you know.'

'Thanks Gary.' I was touched by the genuine sympathy in his voice, as I barely knew the man, but I had been with the GWA long enough to realise that by and large it really was the family that Everett had set out to create.

'Everything's ready to roll?' the big man asked.

'Aye, lights, lasers, whiz-bangs; the lot. Ready for the telly boys tae do their run-through.'

'Okay. Hey Ted,' Everett bellowed, in the direction of a raised booth behind Alex's dais. 'We're ready to run the light show for you.' In the distance, a man stood up, waved, showed a thumbs up sign, then held up his right hand, fingers splayed.

The giant turned towards the ring. He waited until Darius and Johnny had finished the move on which they were working then called up to them. 'Five minutes guys, then we dim the lights for the FX run-through.' The Black Angel of Death, breathing slightly heavily after being tossed, impossibly, acknowledged him with a nod and a wave. As he did so, Alex Kruger ran to his tower and climbed a ladder, up to his position.

There was a different effects sequence for the opening of the show, and for each major wrestler's entrance. The overture was the most spectacular thing I'd seen in the GWA so far: a dazzling array of lights, whirling blue lasers, the yellow stars of the EU flashing in and out on the giant television screen and a series of wire-guided silver flares which seemed to drive right into the ground beside the wrestlers' gateway.

As always, though, the most dramatic curtain raiser was reserved for Daze. The same light sequence that I had seen used in Barcelona was augmented by the superstar's face flashed up on the screen and projected onto the arena roof, and onto the ring floor by powerful, crimson-tinted lights. It was crowned finally by the explosion of four geyser-bursts of sparkling red firework flame from canisters strapped to each ring-post.

'Wow!' said the big man, when it was all over. 'You guys really excelled yourself this time. I never saw those corner flares go so high.'

Gary O'Rourke beamed with pleasure at the accolade. 'D'ye like them then, boss? Ah told the factory to stick a bit mair powder in for this show.'

'Then they got it just right,' said Diane, appearing beside us as the road crew foreman spoke.

'How do you like this, boys?' she asked us. 'It's make-over time for The Princess.' Gary, Everett and I turned simultaneously to look at her.

I heard Gary gulp, Everett gasp and me whisper, 'Jeez!' as she twirled before us.

She was dressed in a black leather costume . . . or rather about one third of a black leather costume. If she had told Everett that it would be less provocative than the Barcelona outfit, she had been kidding. It reached from her neck to her ankles, yet it was just about the most naked piece of clothing I had ever seen. All of the sides and most of the back had been cut away, and the remainder was bound together with a few tight leather straps. Even the inside legs had been scooped out from an inch above her ankles to an inch below her . . .

Altogether, it was the stuff to make old men weep and young men lock themselves in the toilet for some time.

'There's a black leather cap to go with it as well,' she said.

'Oh yes, and a whip. I've decided that the Black Angel needs a Satanic handmaiden.' She dropped into character. 'Ain't that right, Daze?' she purred.

'We talk about this later,' Everett growled.

'No we don't, honey,' his wife drawled back at him. 'I wrote my own contract with this organisation. It gives me creative control over my costumes. Me and no one else.'

'Yeah, but I plan the shows, and if I say that you and that fucking peep-show are out then that's the way it is.' I had never heard Everett swear at anyone before, far less his wife. I wished dearly to be somewhere else, and I could see that Gary felt the same. Quietly we drifted into the background and left the Davis family drama to play itself out.

Diane had changed into a shirt and jeans by the time I left, but clearly the flames were still smouldering.

My temporary flatmate was in when I got back to Glasgow just before eleven. So were the boxes from a takeaway Chinese which I found in the kitchen.

'If you're going to live here even for a day, Dylan,' I grumbled, 'the watchword is tidy.'

'Sorry Oz.' He sounded genuinely apologetic. 'I was going to clear them up, but Susie called.'

'Does she want you to move back in?' I asked hopefully.

'As a matter of fact she does, but I reckon it's best this way, till we get things sorted.' My heart sank once more.

'Any news on those copy documents?'

He nodded. 'Yes. The boy was working late again this evening, so she couldn't do anything. But the good news is that he always plays football on a Wednesday, so she'll be able to do it tomorrow night for sure.'

'Aye,' I countered. 'If we can both still see after tomorrow night. I tell you, boy, if those flares of Daze's don't blind you, then his wife's cossie will!'

53

The private security firm which Everett had hired were not there to mess about. There were none of those fat, tired, bleary-eyed, middle-aged men, the sort you see sometimes on doorkeeper duty in public buildings, slumped inside ill-fitting uniforms. These guys were all young, fit, sharp-creased and hard, with clear eyes and a bearing which told you they were all ex-servicemen.

I stood beside Daze in the ring. He was in wrestling gear, since we had just completed the final run-through, and in a grim mood; partly because of the sheer tension of the day, and partly, I guessed, because he had lost his argument with Diane.

She had appeared by the Black Angel's side in her black leather gear . . . or what there was of it . . . parading round the ring, helping Darius to take off his winged gown and passing it carefully to an attendant. Normally, only the commentators and the television people stopped to watch the dress rehearsal. When Diane was up there in that suit the only sounds to be heard in the arena were the shuffling of Darius' boots on the mat and a low, strangled moan from somewhere behind my table.

I raised my mike and spoke into it. 'Listen up, everyone. Stop what you're doing. The boss has something to say.' I handed the mike to Everett. He had just been through an energetic rehearsal of his fight with Liam, but he wasn't even breathing hard.

'Okay people,' he began. 'You'll have seen we have some extra staff with us this afternoon. This is a very special event that we're staging tonight; a hell of a lot of families are paying a hell of a lot of money to watch it live on television, so we can't afford any more "accidents" like those that happened to Liam and to Jerry.

'I want this whole arena cleared right now, so the security team can begin a complete sweep of the building. After that the hall will be sealed, and no one will be allowed back in unless and until they have business to do.' He dropped the mike and whispered to me, 'what time is it, Oz?'

'Ten past five.'

'We go on air in under three hours. Doors open to the public at seven fifteen, and I want everyone back on site then. So get changed and get on the bus. It'll take you along to the airport hotel where there's a light buffet laid on. We'll all eat properly after the show.

'Remember people, this is a big one tonight, our biggest yet; so be fast, be strong, be skilful and most of all . . .' He grinned for the first time that afternoon. '. . . be-lievable. Thank you all and good luck.'

He switched off the mike. 'When do the police get here?'

'Dylan said they'd be here at six. I'll wait here for him.'

'Hell no, you come along to the hotel. We'll leave a message with the security guys; tell them to join us there.

'You know if that computer's come up with any result yet?'

'It hadn't when I called Mike at midday. Let's hope he's bringing a report with him.'

He didn't, though. 'There's heavy demand on the system today,' he said, as he joined me in the reception room at the Stakis Hotel, 'and the American checks are taking time. They promised me something by nine pm latest. When does the show begin?'

'Eight,' I told him, grimly aware that I had talked up the efficiency of the police for Everett. 'We run from eight till eleven.'

'Oh Christ, that's not too clever. But I've left instructions that as soon as it comes in it's to be biked through to me at the arena.'

'Fair enough, pal. There'll probably be nothing in the report to help us, but if there is, let's just hope that when it gets here, we're not standing in the midst of the wreckage!'

54

Everett was less than delighted by Dylan's news, but he didn't make an issue of it; he was becoming completely absorbed in the *BattleGround Special*, so much so that he accepted Mike's offer of a lift back to the Ingliston arena without stopping to wonder whether he would fit into his car.

Fortunately, it was a Saab, fairly high in the back, and so, by lying a little sideways, he made it.

He had barely straightened his back after getting out, when the security team chief came marching up to him. The man, in his late twenties, wore an immaculate black uniform with a peaked cap. There was something about his bearing which made me think that sixty years earlier he would have fitted well into a similar suit with SS flashes on its lapels.

'The arena is clear, sir,' he said. 'Cleared and secured. We put sniffer dogs in, the lot.'

Everett glanced at his watch. 'That's good. We open the doors to the public in fifteen minutes; that gives my road crew time to load the special effects flares. From opening to the start of the show, the only people from my staff allowed inside the main arena are those with these orange badges.' He waved a plastic photographic pass at the man. 'That's the television people, the match commentators, road crew, Oz, here, and me.'

'Yes sir, I was aware of that and my men are all briefed

accordingly.' He glanced at Dylan. 'What about this gentleman, sir?'

Mike produced his warrant card and held it up. 'This is my floor pass,' he said with a grin. 'I'm the fuckin' polis, son. I go where I like; so do my sergeant and my detective constable. They should be at the main entrance right now.'

'Very good, sir,' the security man snapped.

'Okay,' Everett boomed. 'Let's go with that.' He turned and looked over my shoulder, and the GWA troupe who were disembarking from the transfer bus.

'Gary,' he called across to the foreman roadie. 'The hall's secure; you can load those whiz-bangs now. Make sure you tell Alex Kruger when they're in place, so he doesn't go pressing any buttons on his console.'

He turned back to me. 'Oz, do me a favour, will you. We've got a hospitality room designated for special guests; they're a couple of local radio disc jockeys who've been plugging the show for weeks, plus a couple of old Scottish rugby stars, and the managers and captains of the Hearts and Hibs football sides.

'Barbara's setting it up now. Could you go and make sure everything's okay, and be there to greet guests, just in case they arrive early. Diane and I will join you there, just as soon as I've had a chance to give a final pep-talk to the wrestlers.'

I nodded. 'Sure I will. But with Hearts and Hibs both coming, don't you need two hospitality rooms?'

I was in the main entrance area, about to open a door labelled 'GWA guests' when my mobile phone rang. I took it out, puzzled. 'Yup?'

'Oz? It's me.' Primavera.

'It's your big night, isn't it? I just thought I'd give you a ring to wish you luck . . . and to see how you're doing; how you're coping.'

I couldn't help it; my hackles rose of their own accord.

'Prim, my dear, I can say this to you because I know you'll understand, but over the last few weeks I have grown to hate the word "coping". People who ask me that mean well, but, I don't know, it just makes me feel demeaned. Somehow, they make it sound as if I'm having to learn to wipe my own arse.' I paused, sorry now for having let go. 'Or am I being hypersensitive?' I said in a doomed attempt to turn my irritation into humour.

'Maybe you are,' she said. 'But you're entitled. I've never thought about that word before; it's just a term you use.'

'Yes, flower. Until it's used at you.'

'Of course.' I heard her draw a breath. 'Listen, I've obviously called at a bad time. In fact I shouldn't have called at all. Good luck tonight. 'Bye now.'

'No, Prim,' I called into the phone. 'I'm sorry. I shouldn't have taken that out on you.' But she was gone.

I did my best with the dee-jays, the footballers, and the blown-up ex-rugby stars, but my heart wasn't in it. I had snubbed Prim, who was, after all my best pal, and I felt rotten about it. I was glad when Everett and Diane – not in her ring gear – arrived to relieve me, and I could use the excuse of slipping off to smarten myself up for the cameras.

Once I had done that I went out to the arena floor, using my orange pass, to do a sound check on my hand-mike, and to check that my table was in position. I had just said hello to the English language commentators, when Mike tapped me on the shoulder.

'We forgot one thing,' he said. 'Or you did. This thing's a sell-out and I haven't got a seat.'

'Not a problem,' I told him. I looked around until I saw Gary O'Rourke on the other side of the ring. I waved to him, and he came running round. 'Gaz, can you get one of the lads to put another folding chair at my table? DI Dylan needs somewhere to sit.'

'Aye, Ah'll do that no bother,' he answered willingly, glancing at the detective. 'Ah'll get one masel'. Here,' he added, grinning, 'what d'ye think of thae boys in the uniforms, Oz, eh? We should have them wi' us every week. Whether they're any use or not, they fair smarten the place up.'

Still smiling to himself, he bustled off to find the additional chair. 'Don't worry if the camera hits on you where you'll be sitting, Mike,' I said, as he left. 'Just act as if it wasn't there. Look out for stray wrestlers though. Quite often the action leaves the ring and spills over onto the surround. If you see one of these guys flying towards you – duck.'

'I'll bear that in mind . . . unless it's one of the women, of course. Now I must make sure that the guys on the door know where I am, for when that biker shows up.'

Wondering what would be left of him if he was hit by one of the meaty GWA ladies, I watched him as he made his way along the aisle to the entrance, through the mounting excitement of the crowd. The arena was full; full of people in tee-shirts, waving banners, showing off GWA merchandise for the cameras which were circling the arena filming stock colour footage for use on future promos and broadcasts. It was ten minutes till show time.

Dylan was back from his errand and in his seat when the lights dimmed. The noise in the hall was stilled. Until the opening sequence began, when it simply exploded. The lights whirled, the lasers cut the gloom, the yellow stars shone, the music roared out and the wire-borne flares rushed and crashed into the floor by the superstars' entrance. I held my breath, waiting in spite of myself for some unknown and unimagined disaster. But finally the spotlight was on me, Oz Blackstone, up there in the ring, on live television. The words, 'On with the motley,' flashed through my mind. Then I raised my mike.

'Ladies and gentlemen, GWA fans all over Europe, welcome to Ingliston, Edinburgh, and welcome to *Battle-Ground Special!*'

As instructed, I allowed twenty seconds for the boom cameras to swing round the cheering, waving crowd, then called out my intro for the first match, which featured the newly imported Japanese tag team.

I was aware of Dylan staring at me as I slipped quietly into my seat. 'Here,' he said in a hoarse, astonished, and not unimpressed whisper, 'you're not bad at that.'

The show was spectacular – the best, I knew: but for every minute that it stretched out I was tense; through every introduction I grew more and more scared. Yet to spite my fears, everything came off flawlessly.

The Japanese tagsters were the most acrobatic team I had ever seen. Big Al the Cyclops looked awesome as he pounded the daylights out of poor old Max Schwartz. The Princess all but stopped the show, and a hundred thousand male pulses across Europe, as she swung down the aisle ahead of the Black Angel of Death. Yet Darius made everyone forget her . . . almost . . . as he put on a terrific acrobatic battle with Johnny 'Salvatore' King, finishing with an aerial move which he had developed specially for the occasion.

We were within a few minutes of the penultimate match, Sally Crockett against The Heckler, when the police biker arrived. I found myself hoping that he wasn't in shot as he stepped up to Dylan and handed him a thick brown package. Mike took it from him without a word of acknowledgement and tore it open.

'Fuck,' he swore quietly as he looked at the report. 'This hasn't been filtered at all. Christ knows how long it'll take to go through it.'

'Don't worry too much about it,' I told him. 'We're more than half-way through the show and everything's been fine.'

'Still,' I heard him say to himself, as I rose to declare the Choirboys the winners of their tag team title defence. 'It's got to be . . .'

Sally Crockett looked terrific as she vaulted into the ring. The crowd thought so too; even without the sexy uniform she drew an even bigger pop than Diane, second only to the Angel. She looked terrific as she swung into action against The Heckler. The guy was a fair light-heavyweight wrestler . . . I had seen him fight behind a mask in earlier shows . . . but Sally had too much for him in every respect. Their mixed gender match could have looked phoney and too obviously staged, but it didn't, because as I had realised when I saw them rehearse, Sally had insisted that her opponent didn't hold back on her.

She took some genuine thumps up there in the ring, but shook them all off, to counter with a series of drop-kicks and powerful leg throws. Finally, she locked her man in an unbreakable submission hold. Theatrically, amid the screams of the crowd, the referee waved to the time-keeper, who rang the bell.

I didn't have to jump up into the ring to announce the results. So I simply stood to call out, 'And the winner of this bout by submission, the GWA World Ladies' Champion, Miss Sally Crockett!' As I shouted into my mike, I felt its namesake tugging at my arm.

'What the hell is it?' I snapped as I sat down, annoyed by his interference. Dylan didn't reply; instead he stared at me, bug-eyed and speechless, and shoved a page under my nose, pointing, jabbing at it. I snapped back to reality and looked at the sheet. It was a one-page report. I read it quickly.

Arrested in Glasgow in connection with possible third party involvement in a shooting. Released. Case dropped by Crown Office for lack of evidence.

Background history. Age thirty-three, born Glasgow. Educated, Shawlands Academy. Completed vocational training in Royal Army Medical Corps, before transferring to special forces. Specialised training in firearms and in all forms of sabotage, including explosives.

It was only then that I looked at the name at the top of the page. 'Gary O'Rourke,' I gasped, my eyes now as wide as Dylan's.

'What's his job here?' Mike asked.

I didn't answer him; instead my mind swam through treacle to reach the obvious. I was aware that Liam's music had started, that he was already at the foot of the ramp, about to vault into the ring, where I should have been ready to introduce him. I didn't give a damn, as I mouthed the word, 'explosives'.

I thrust the page back at Dylan and dropped my hand-mike on the table, then turned and ran round the ring. I used to be pretty quick on my feet, but I hadn't done much sprinting since I had left Edinburgh going on for a year before. Still, I felt my shoes almost dig into the concrete floor of the arena as I took the corner into the long aisle which led to the back of the hall and the television control towers.

I sensed, rather than saw, the dimming of the light. I was barely aware of the start of Daze's music. But I knew where he was. Without looking I saw, pace by huge pace, his march down the ramp, towards the ring where Liam was waiting. My lungs were bursting as I reached the foot of Alex Kruger's tower. I caught sight of him up there, poised over his console, his eyes shining. The crowd noise was so great that my loudest bellow would never have reached him . . . even if he hadn't been wearing headphones.

There was a ladder at the side of the scaffolding, up to his perch. I grabbed it, at first almost pulling it backwards on top of me, then steadying it and finding a footing. I tried to run up it, but my shoe slipped at once, making me bang my forehead into a rung. Scrabbling at it, I gained momentum at last, and pushed and hauled my way up as fast as I could.

A change in the sound of the crowd told me that Daze was stepping over the ropes and into the ring. I knew what would happen next.

I had reached the top of the ladder. I threw myself on the floor of the cage. The little Belgian was standing, over the console, both thumbs raised, looking like my nephew Jonathan at his PlayStation.

'Alex,' I screamed at him. 'Don't fire those flares!'

55

They told me later that the headline match between Daze and Liam was one of the finest technical displays ever seen on pay-per-view television. They told me that it alone would have made the whole show value for money, never mind any of the earlier great performances that I had seen.

They told me that Liam Matthews placed himself unshakeably on the top tier of wrestling superstardom by the way in which he attacked an opponent at least a foot taller than he was, almost wearing down the giant until he made his one fatal mistake, delivering himself into Daze's Spear, the most awesome finishing move in wrestling history.

They had to tell me this afterwards, for all through the bout I lay sprawled on the floor of Alex Kruger's booth, gasping for the breath to explain to the FX operator that the flares on the ring posts might have been booby-trapped. All the time he stared at me like I was nuts, openly resentful that I had ruined his big moment.

All the sounds of the action floated up to me, until finally, I heard the single sustained roar which told me that it was over. Then the breathless, but still booming, voice of Daze filled the hall. 'Ladies and gentlemen, wrestling fans everywhere; thank you for being with us for this *BattleGround Special*. Till Saturday, in Frankfurt, Germany, from Ingliston, Edinburgh, goodbye.'

I gulped, a touch fearfully now that the panic was over.

That should have been my announcement. I climbed off the floor of the booth and stood, looking at the crowd below as the hall emptied. Everett and Liam were still in the ring; it was full of youngsters and they were signing autographs.

I yelled at the big man, but he couldn't hear me above the continuing babble, and the taped walk-out music which was still playing. I waved frantically until at last I caught his eye. He shot me a huge questioning frown. I tried to work out a gesture which meant, 'Clear the ring, for fuck's sake.' I couldn't, so I yelled my message, as loud as I could.

I couldn't tell at first whether he had understood, until he raised his mike again and said, 'Ladies and gentlemen, boys and girls, the GWA superstars will all be happy to sign more autographs for you outside, but meantime we have to ask you to clear the hall as fast as you can, so that we can strike the ring.'

Telling Alex to follow me, I climbed down from the tower, and pushed my way through the departing audience. 'What the hell's up, Oz?' Everett asked as I reached him. 'What happened to my flares?' he barked at Alex.

'I want them examined,' I told him. 'But very carefully. If I'm wrong, fire me, but until then, stick with me. Alex, can you dismantle these installations?'

'Of course I can,' said the Belgian, and set to work. Laboriously he stripped off the black insulating tape which secured the flare canister nearest to his tower, and lifted it into the centre of the ring. Carefully he reached into it and lifted out something looking like a large firework; which it was.

'It's okay,' he announced. He moved on to the next corner and repeated the process. 'All right again.' And the third.

My heart was in my boots as he removed the fourth and last canister. I was beginning to feel like the biggest idiot in Edinburgh . . . well, the second biggest, after Dylan. My heart resumed its normal position in my chest as Alex recoiled from the container.

'Tschaaah!' he gasped.

'What is it?' asked Everett.

'This one's loaded with gelignite,' the technician replied.

'How much of the stuff?' the big man ground out, eyes narrow. Standing beside him, I felt myself begin to tremble. Standing on his other side, I saw Dylan's face quiver.

'From the weight of it, enough to blow you, big as you are, clear out of the ring, and probably to kill Mr Matthews if he'd been close to the thing when it went off. Enough to do serious damage to the commentators, the timekeeper and the people at the announcer's table. Enough to injure the spectators nearest to the ring.'

As Mike sagged, I noticed that he was still holding the report on Gary O'Rourke. I reached over and took it from him and handed it to Everett. 'Guess what the PNC check showed,' I said.

As he finished reading the page he crumpled it in his huge hand. 'Gonna find the son of a bitch,' he growled.

But Dylan had recovered himself. 'No, sir. This is a police matter now. We'll find him.' He turned to his two colleagues who were standing at the side of the ring, together with the stiff-suited security chief.

'The man's name is Gary O'Rourke, road crew foreman. Find him and arrest him.'

The security man raised a hand. 'Is he the fair-haired chap, by any chance? Glasgow accent, powerfully built?'

'That's the man,' I confirmed.

'He left during the last bout. I was checking outside and saw him come out from the staff door, carrying a motor cycle helmet. Just after that I saw a bike ridden out of the car park.'

'Magic,' Dylan groaned. 'I should have lifted him as soon as you tore off to that tower, Oz.'

I looked at him, feeling sorry for him once again. 'I won't tell anyone if you don't, Mike.'

56

Naturally, Dylan circulated a description of O'Rourke's motor cycle, together with its registration number, which the national computer system spat out a lot more quickly than it had volunteered his curriculum vitae.

Just as naturally, there was no trace of him.

'Bastard's disappeared,' Dylan grumbled as he came back into my flat just before noon, after picking up Susie's photocopies from her place before she left for work, and checking into his office to file his report on the night before.

'He had more than an hour before the stop order went out. That's plenty of time to get under cover. Christ, on that bike of his he could have been well into England by then.'

'What are you doing about this guy Reilly in the States? Are you going to ask the Americans to interview him?'

He screwed up his face and shook his head. 'No chance, on what we've got. I tried that on my boss and he nearly blew me out of his office. Before we can ask the Philadelphia police to go anywhere near Reilly we have to show them good cause. The way things are at the moment there isn't the semblance of a case against the man.

'Your big pal might be dead certain about him, but until we've had a chance to talk to Mr O'Rourke in a room with walls that move about, there's no way we can prove it. And maybe not even then; our boy Gary does not strike me as a soft touch.

'When he was questioned about that shooting thing he was involved with a security outfit; the sort that provides bouncers for pubs that really need them. He was one of their top men.'

'What was that about?'

'Some guy in Garthamlock got himself kneecapped, for reasons unknown. No one ever suggested that O'Rourke did it, but he was fingered as having ordered it. However, when they nicked the guy who actually did it, he said he'd never heard of him.'

I shrugged and got up from my captain's chair. I had been working at the desk; on Jan's side. I had decided that from now on, for ever more, that would be my work station.

'Sod him, anyway,' I muttered. 'That's yesterday's business; and it was never my top priority. D'you get that stuff from Susie?'

He nodded and opened his briefcase. 'Has my pal from forensics been?' he asked, as he took out a sheaf of A4 documents.

'Has he just. I've only just finished cleaning the powder off the desk and the kitchen units. He lifted a few prints and I gave him mine for elimination – I want them destroyed, by the way, Mr Dylan, once this thing's over – plus as many as he could get from Jan's hairbrush.

'Not having a full set of Jan's prints is going to be a problem for him, if he finds one that looks odd.'

Mike shook his head. 'Not really, Oz. The prints will only come into play once we've caught someone, as part of the chain of evidence. One dab won't point us at a suspect – that sort of thing doesn't happen.'

He dropped Susie's photocopies on to the desk, and spread them out. As I had recalled, there were up to a hundred of them.

'These,' he said, 'are the purchase ledgers for the health

care division of The Gantry Group, stretching back ten years. They're the files that Jan took away with her.'

'What are these places anyway? Nursing homes?'

Dylan frowned. 'Not exactly, though I suppose most people would call them that. These aren't the sort of places where you park your granny. Because of the nature of the care they provide, they're actually classed as private hospitals. They look after geriatrics sure, but also people with pre-senile dementia and the terminally ill: they take in a lot of cancer patients.'

I picked up one of the sheets. 'Are there separate purchase records for each place?'

'No. Susie says that because of the size and the nature of the business they've operated on a group basis for the last ten years. All their major purchasing is done centrally.'

'I see.' I looked at the sprawl of records on the desk. 'Let's split them. You take the first five years, I'll take the second. You ready to enjoy your day off, Inspector?'

He scowled at me. 'Sure; digging for dirt in my girlfriend's company . . . without a bloody clue where to start looking.'

We sat down facing each other across the desk; he was on what had been my side, and I was in Jan's place. Until I saw the truth of it before me, I had no idea how much was involved in running a chain of small private hospitals.

There were stationery purchases, office equipment, office telephone costs, office furniture, office cleaning, office heat and light, newspapers and periodicals, hospital cleaning materials, bedding, towels, soap, miscellaneous sanitary items, hospital furnishings, hospital heat and light, hospital telephone costs, nurses' uniforms, nurses' footwear, pharmaceutical supplies listed by drug purchased, other medical supplies listed by quantity, ambulance costs, petrol costs, hospital indemnity insurance costs, hospital fabric insurance costs, staff recruitment costs, miscellaneous costs and sundry expenses. I'm sure there were others too, but that's all my mind could cope with at the time.

For hours we sat there, working as methodically as we could, taking each annual total and checking it against items listed under that heading during the year, making sure that everything added up, looking for anomalies. Everything did; there weren't any.

Occasionally, the phone would ring, but I left the answering service to pick up messages. Occasionally, one of us would go through to the kitchen for a coffee refill. But mostly we just worked away in silence, reconciling the records, proving to ourselves that while Mr Joseph Donn may have been inadequate as a Finance Director, the book-keeping staff he oversaw had at least been meticulous.

It was well into the evening before Dylan finally cracked. 'Oz, this is bloody useless,' he moaned, leaning back in his chair. 'Your wife was a chartered accountant, and a bloody good one there's no doubt. You and I are a couple of number-blind idiots with calculators. Without a hint from Jan, which we haven't got since her notes have vanished, we're never going to crack this. And if we did we'd probably find that the office junior was into the tea-money, that's all.'

I knew that wasn't true, since I could remember how excited Jan had been; but he was right in pointing out that without her guidance we were stumbling about in the dark.

'Come on, Mike,' I said. 'We're both knackered. Let's take a break, go for a pint and a curry, and see if that gives us inspiration.'

'You're on for that,' he replied rolling back the chair and standing up. 'I'm going for a slash first though.'

As he left the room I sagged down in my seat and let my head fall back, allowing my tiredness to close my eyes. I sat there, looking at gathering blackness as my mind cleared. Then, gradually, the picture in my imagination took on light and shade and colour and out of it, Jan's face appeared. She was sitting where I sat now, and her head was turned sideways looking at me. Her laptop was switched on, and the screen was bright.

'This is what I do,' she said, 'when I want to keep something important, so I can refer back without digging out my notes.' She turned to the laptop. I watched her as she pulled down a list of menu items, and selected 'Note Pad', then began to type. I couldn't see what she was writing, but I knew that didn't matter.

It was only when my eyes snapped open and I found myself staring at the ceiling that I realised I had been asleep for a few moments, and dreaming. I shook my head, trying to remember that scene, the moment when Jan had shown me that computer short-cut, but I couldn't. I was certain . . . and I still am . . . that it had never happened in life.

Nevertheless, I took the laptop out of its drawer and switched it on. Fortunately the battery was still on full charge. I felt a thrill of excitement as it booted up, as I pulled down the Menu Items and selected Note Pad.

The first small page was a list of birthdays. Mine, Mary's, Jan's dad's, my dad's, Jan's Uncle Bob's, Jan's Aunt Betty, Jan's Aunt Mima, Noosh Turkel, Ellie, Jonathan, Colin. I hit the icon in the corner to move on.

I shuddered as I looked at the page. For an instant I was frightened, very frightened, until in my mind's eye, its waking eye this time, I saw Jan smiling. My fear vanished, replaced by a pure, adrenalin-pumping, rush of excitement.

There was a note on the page. 'Pharmaceutical supplies anomaly. Temazepam and diamorphine. First five years; second five years.'

I was still staring at it when Dylan came back into the room. 'Sorry I was so long,' he said, casually. 'I decided a

Turkish Delight was called for. You ready to go, Oz? I could murder that curry now.'

'Forget the curry, Mike,' I murmured. 'Look at this.'

He did as I told him, peering at the screen over my shoulder. Dylan's eyesight was slightly on the blink but he was too vain to wear glasses.

'Oh my Christ,' he gasped.

'Never mind the detail for now,' I said. 'Let's check the pharmaceutical totals for those years.' Each yearly total ran to two pages. I scrambled among the pile of papers to find the twenty sheets for which I was looking.

On the annualised purchase totals, pharmaceuticals showed as a single category. For the first five years of the period we had been scrutinising, the totals showed very modest annual variations, slightly up in three of the years, almost unchanged on one, and down in another. During the most recent five years, the figures were also consistent – but six times higher.

'Jesus Christ, Mike,' I muttered. 'This is it. "Temazepam and diamorphine", the note said. I know what Temazepam is, a sedative; but what sort of medication is diamorphine?'

'On the street,' he answered grimly, sounding far more serious than I'd ever heard him before, 'you'd call it heroin.'

'Let's get into the detailed records,' I suggested. 'Let's start with year five and year six for comparison. Tick off each of the purchases then see how many of each we have.'

Dylan nodded and picked up the year five records; I went to work on the other.

He was finished first. 'What have you got?' he asked, when I was through my check. 'I've got four purchases of Temazepam and four of diamorphine.'

'I've got twelve of each. Five years ago The Gantry Group health division started to buy these drugs on a monthly basis, rather than quarterly.'

As we stared at each other, I could see desperation in Dylan's eyes. 'If this is what I think it is, what's it going to do to Susie and Jack?' His voice was almost a groan.

'Don't jump at this, Mike,' I said, trying to reassure him. 'Maybe the patient profile changed five years ago.'

'It didn't. Susie told me that the division has traded unaltered in size and sector for the last ten years.

'We need to look at detailed purchase records, Oz. These drugs have been bought through pharmaceutical wholesalers. Someone signed the order forms; there'll be copies in existence. Let's go and see Susie. Right now.'

'Mike, is that wise? This is her company we're investigating, after all.'

'We've been through this, Oz. She gave us these records, didn't she? We can trust her.'

'Believe it or not, mate, I wasn't thinking about that; I was thinking about your job. This is freelance activity, remember.'

'Stuff my job. Anyway, what we have isn't conclusive. I can take it one step further at least.'

I was unconvinced, but I nodded nonetheless. 'Okay. We might as well crack this tonight if we can. Before we go, though, I'd better check the day's phone messages. These days I have to remind myself that I still have a business to run.'

I picked up the phone on my desk and dialled the retrieve code for the answer service. I was told that I had seven messages; I pulled my pad across and picked up a pen to note the details of each.

The first five were from clients, but the sixth wasn't for me at all: it was for Detective Inspector Dylan, from his friend in the Strathclyde Police scientific department.

'Hello Mike,' said the voice of the man I had met earlier. 'I thought I should let you know about this right away. I lifted two odd prints, first two fingers, left hand, in the classic place, the underside of his desk, where I dusted. Then I found the same two prints on the underside of the kitchen work surface, just where the washing machine housing is.

'They don't belong to your pal, and from the size I knew they couldn't have been his wife's. So I ran a quick comparison check on them and I got an answer. It's a bit naughty. We shouldn't have these dabs, because the guy was never prosecuted, but you know how it is; sometimes we just forget to destroy them.

'The bloke's name's O'Rourke. Gary O'Rourke.'

57

I don't know why, but I didn't tell Dylan about the message; not then at least. I suppose I reckoned he had enough on his plate, and that if I overloaded his brain a few circuits might blow.

All the way out to Susie's I wrestled with it, trying to get my head round it, trying to imagine what motive Gary O'Rourke might have had for breaking into my flat that could be connected with the GWA business. Maybe he had rumbled me and wanted to find out a bit about me. After all, he hadn't been in Barcelona. He'd been back home in Glasgow when Jan died.

Maybe he hadn't taken the papers. Maybe that was another burglar. Maybe they had passed each other in the hallway and said hello. Maybe another special forces trained explosives expert had booby-trapped my washing machine. Or maybe Gary had done it in the hope that I'd do my own washing when I got back from Spain.

So many maybes, only one certainty: Gary O'Rourke had been in our flat, searching our desk, pulling our washing machine out of its housing.

Dylan didn't notice my silence as I drove the pair of us to Clarkston, because he was wrapped up in his own. I hoped that he was genuinely concerned about the effect of the business on his girlfriend, rather than beginning to fret after all about the impact on his own career if it blew up in our faces.

It was just after eight when we arrived at Susie Gantry's semi-detached house. Fortunately she was in; we ace detectives hadn't thought to call to find that out before we left.

There was none of her sparkly, nervy bonhomie as she opened the door. I guess the expressions on our faces must have ruled that out; that and the fact that she noticed Mike was carrying his briefcase.

'Hello boys,' she greeted us, as she showed us into her sitting room. 'You look completely puggled. I take it you haven't just dropped in for a drink.'

'Not just that, love,' said Dylan, 'although I won't say no. We've picked up the trail that Jan was on. We need your help to take it further.'

'I'll do anything I can. What do you want?'

Mike was about to tell her, when I interrupted. 'Before that, Susie,' I asked her, 'does the name Gary O'Rourke mean anything to you?'

She stared at me, frowning, puzzled. 'Of course it does. He used to work for the group, as our supplies manager. He's my cousin.'

Dylan's head turned towards me as if it was on a swivel, then swung back to his girlfriend. 'He's what?'

'My cousin. He's my Auntie Norah's son; she's my father's sister. I haven't seen him in months though; not since he said he was fed up and went off to take a job with Everett Davis.'

'Have you got a photograph of him?' I asked her.

'I should have.' She crossed to a cabinet set against the wall and took out a thick album, then leafed through its pages. 'There you are. That was taken at last year's May Ball in the City Chambers.' She held the volume up, pointing to a photograph. I recognised all three people in it at once. Susie was in the centre, flanked by the bulky figures of her father on her right, complete with chain, and a blond man, whom I had last seen only twenty-four hours earlier.

'What made you ask that?' she queried.

'He's the guy who took those papers from my flat.'

'I don't believe you,' she gasped.

'I'm afraid it's true. One of Mike's SOCO buddies lifted his prints from my desk.'

Glancing at Dylan, I said, 'Sorry mate, that was one of the messages on the message service tonight. I should have told you earlier, but I had to get my own head round it first.'

I turned back to Susie. 'Can I ask you something else as well? Is there any way he'd have been able to get hold of a key to the flat? You see, there couldn't have been any sign of a break-in, otherwise Jan would have noticed it when she came in. If she had done, she wouldn't have done the washing. She'd have called the police.'

She frowned again, and chewed her lip. 'Well,' she began. 'We did have a bit of a problem with the woman who bought your flat first. We didn't get full payment for a while, so we decided to keep a set of keys on the Q.T., just in case we needed to take drastic action. I thought they'd been handed over, though.'

Her face was drawn and pale as she stood with her back to the fireplace, the album hanging limply in her hand. 'Look, leaving Gary out of this for a minute, what is it you need?'

'We need order forms for drugs,' said Dylan. 'How does the health care division order its pharmaceutical supplies, love? Do you know?'

'Course I do,' she snapped at him. 'We have a fully qualified group pharmacist. Her signature has to be on all the purchase orders which we give to the wholesalers, and she has to countersign every delivery slip. She's responsible for distributing drugs and other supplies to each of the hospitals. The Chief Nursing Officer in each place is responsible for their security after that.'

'Do you file the copy order forms and delivery slips separately or are they in with all the purchase receipts?'

'They're kept separately. Joe Donn keeps them in his safe.'

'In that case,' said Dylan, 'we need to get in there. Do you have keys?'

Susie had recovered her temper, but not her complexion. She was still chalk-white. 'Yes, I have keys to everything. Take me to the office and I'll open it for you.'

'Better if you take your car,' I suggested. 'We might have to go somewhere fairly quickly afterwards. We'll follow you.'

She looked puzzled, as, once again, did Dylan, but neither of them argued.

The evening traffic had largely died away, and so the drive to the headquarters of The Gantry group didn't take long – fortunately, for I still didn't want to get into any discussion with Mike about Gary O'Rourke. I had never been to the office before, so I was surprised by the modesty of the building, compared to the size of the business which was controlled beneath its red-tiled roof. It was set behind a low wall, with head-high railings and a privet hedge behind, anonymous save for a painted, blue-on-white sign on the gateway reading simply, 'Gantry', and for a brass plate at the door, listing the companies which were registered there.

'Doesn't look as if the book-keeper's working late tonight,' I said, as we climbed out of my Frontera in the otherwise empty car park, and followed Susie inside.

'Fuck him if he is,' Dylan muttered. 'I'm not in a mood to fanny about with him.' There was no need for concern. The building was in darkness as we stepped inside, and Joseph Donn's first-floor office was empty.

The safe which Susie had mentioned turned out to be one of a series of fire-proof, bomb-proof, concrete-filled filing cabinets on the wall facing Donn's varnished desk. She opened it with a key, pulled out a drawer and turned to us. 'Which years do you want?'

'Six years ago,' I answered, 'the year after that, and the last full year. That'll let us see what's going on. How long's your head chemist been with you?'

'Eight years. Her signature should be on them all. Her name's Kerry Guild.'

I took the three folders from her, and opened the most recent. 'I don't know why, but something tells me that it won't be.'

The big bold signature, 'K. Guild', was on the first form I looked at, and on the corresponding delivery slip which was stapled to it. It was for a consignment of paracetamol. It was on the second set of forms too, for Ranitidine tablets. The third form was an order for diamorphine. It was signed 'Gary O'Rourke'.

I showed it to Susie. Her hand went to her mouth as she gasped, 'Oh my God!'

'That's what Jan found out,' I told her. 'For the last five years, your health care division has been buying, quite legitimately, large quantities of Temazepam and diamorphine. Now we know who's been doing it.

'Our guess is that those drugs weren't here long, only they didn't go to the hospitals. They went to the streets, for Christ knows how many times their nominal value.'

'But how could Gary sign those orders?' she asked.

'He did vocational training in the RAMC, didn't he? What's the betting he could prove to the wholesalers that he's a qualified pharmacist?'

Susie sat on the edge of Joseph Donn's desk. She looked crushed.

'Listen love,' I said, as gently as I could make myself sound, 'I have to ask you this. You must have told someone about the work that Jan was doing for you, and where she had reached with it. You said you haven't seen Gary for months. So who was it?'

She sat there, blank-eyed, and shook her head. 'No. I didn't.'

'Susie, you must have told someone. I know it. Was it your father?'

We looked at her for a while, until finally, she nodded her head: not very vigorously, but she nodded it. 'Yes,' she said. 'I told my dad, and the silly old bugger must have let it slip to Gary.'

'Are they close, then?'

Susie nodded again. 'I wouldn't say Dad treats him like a son, but yes, they're close. Gary worships him, that's for sure.'

As I gazed down at her, I almost heard a click as the last piece of the jigsaw slipped into place.

'Susie, I think you should give all those records to Mike, the last five years at least. Then I want you to go home, and not to talk to anyone at all, until you hear from us again. Is that okay?'

She pushed herself off the edge of the desk. 'Anything you say, Oz.' She pulled the rest of the records from the drawer and handed them to Dylan. 'But Michael, don't make it too soon before your next visit. I like my men to bring me good news, not disaster.'

We watched her as she locked the safe, then followed her downstairs, and outside. We watched her as she drove off, into what had become the night.

'Jesus,' said Dylan at last. 'Gary bloody O'Rourke. The boy gets around, doesn't he. I'll bet he punts the drugs out through that so-called security firm he worked for. Bastard.'

I let him swear on for a bit longer before I tapped him on the shoulder.

'Mike,' I said, quietly and evenly. 'Remember you and Susie were supposed to be coming to the GWA show in Newcastle, only the Lord Provost had the tickets off you?'

'Yes: I wanted to go too, but he just commandeered them.'

'Well that night, I stood beside Gary O'Rourke while he held the door open for his idol, his Uncle Jack. Not a single flicker of recognition passed between them. Not a "Hello, son," not a "Hello, Uncle Jack". Not a smile, not a twitch, not as much as a "Thank you".

'Yet the same Jack Gantry made a point of telling O'Rourke what Jan was working on. Why d'you think that was?'

Dylan stared back at me. I think that he could have been a bit scared by the sound of my voice. I think I was too.

'It's time you and I paid a visit to the Lord Provost, Detective Inspector,' I said.

'I don't think that's a good idea, Oz,' Mike protested, weakly. 'This is Jack Gantry we're dealing with, after all.'

I laughed. 'I don't care if it's the Devil himself. Come to think of it, maybe it is.'

58

I know, I should have given some consideration to Mike
Dylan's position as he directed me through the streets which
led to Jack Gantry's house. After all, I had been concerned
earlier about the potential effect of our extra-curricular
investigation on his CID career. But that was then.

As I drove through Pollokshields, the only thing in my
mind was my wife: Jan carrying our embryonic child, Jan
excited by her forensic examination of the Gantry accounts,
Jan touching that washing machine, Jan in the time it took
the electricity to course through her body, her awareness of
what was happening before the current blew all the circuits
in her brain and stopped her heart for ever.

I could have exploded, gone over the edge, but I didn't.
Instead, I did as I had before; I built that trusty shell of ice-
cold anger around myself, feeding from it as we drew closer
to the man who, I was sure, held the answers to all my
questions of the weeks gone by. I had no clear idea of what
I would do when I came face-to-face with him. All I had was
determination that when I had finished, his life would be in
as many pieces as mine.

'This is it,' said Dylan, hauling me back from my dark
thoughts to the present. 'His house is at the end of this cul-
de-sac.' I turned right, as he indicated.

It was a short street, nothing much to it at all really, half
a dozen houses down either side and one at the end: Jack

Gantry's home. An opening to the driveway gaped at us, but I couldn't see the house from the roadway, since the view was blocked by mature trees down either side of the carriageway and by a high hedge beyond.

What I could see was the dark shape of a Range Rover, parked under the trees, and inside it, almost filling it, an even darker form. Switching off my lights as we cruised up behind it, I drew the Frontera to a halt. Without a word to each other, Dylan and I climbed out and walked up to the driver's door. Gently I tapped at the window.

Everett Davis started in his seat, banging his head on the roof. He had to turn on the car's electrics to lower his window, but when he had he looked at us angrily.

'What you guys doing here?' he demanded.

'Naw,' I said. 'We saw you first. What the hell are you doing here?'

'I'm thinking, man,' he growled. The sound made me imagine unlucky souls lost in the veldt, hearing a noise like that just before they found themselves added to the local menu. 'I'm thinking about kicking that man's door down and strangling the mother with his own chain.'

His eyes glistened as he looked at me. 'Diane's in there, man.' The growl had become a moan.

'Not again, Ev,' I protested as I leaned against the car. 'First Liam, now Gantry.'

'It's true this time, Oz,' he muttered. 'This morning I didn't get up till later; we'd decided we weren't going into the office. When I come downstairs she was just finishing a call . . . on her mobile, so I didn't pick up any extension and hear her.' He glanced at me. 'You gimme another reason why she wouldn't use the house phone.

'So I set a trap. I told her I'd decided to go to London this afternoon, to look at a venue. I packed an overnight bag and I left. But instead of going to the airport, I just drove back up the street and I waited, parked behind a skip someone had hired and left out there.

'I waited for hours, man. I was just about to admit to myself that you were right and I was an idiot, when she drove out. I just stayed a few cars behind her and followed her; followed her right here. She drove in there and parked right in the garage. I could just see over the hedge when she walked to the door, and I could see who opened it.' He paused.

'I waited ten minutes, then I saw a light go on upstairs.'

He looked at me plaintively. 'Oz, I know you don't do matrimonial stuff, but would you come in there with me, just as my friend?'

I think I must have looked like Dracula when I smiled at him in the dark, to judge by his expression. 'Of course I will, Everett. Mike and I are going in there ourselves anyway. Tag along with us. If you're lucky you might get to kick the door right enough.'

He nodded and climbed out of his car, closing the door as quietly as he could.

Jack Gantry's house was impressive enough for a Lord Provost, but not overly large for a multi-millionaire; a red sandstone villa on two floors, with a grey slate roof. The driveway was all monoblock paving rather than gravel, so we were silent as we walked up to the front door.

There was a double garage at the side, with a single wide door, which was open. As we approached, Dylan stepped across and looked inside, then motioned me to join him.

There was a motor-cycle inside, a big powerful Kawasaki job. 'That's O'Rourke's bike,' said the detective. 'I recognise the number. Let's just be a bit careful in there.'

I looked over my shoulder and out of the garage at Everett, and felt myself gleaming inside with anticipation. 'With him as back-up, pal, it isn't us who have to be careful.'

We stepped up to the front door; I felt totally in command, but I let Dylan ring the bell for form's sake. All the ground floor was in darkness, but as Everett had said, one big bay window on the first floor showed light behind its drawn curtains. I told the giant to stand to one side, in the darkness beyond the door, so that he was out of sight.

We waited for a full minute, then Dylan rang the bell again. Finally, the curtains moved and a face peered out. I reckoned it was the first time I had seen Jack Gantry without his gold chain. We gazed up at the window, until it swung open.

'What the hell is this, Mike?' the Lord Provost exclaimed as he leaned out. His hair was messed up and he was wearing a heavy tweed dressing gown.

'We have to talk to you, Jack. Open up.'

'Indeed I will not, Inspector. Now get the hell off my doorstep. You too, Oz.'

'I don't think so, Mr Gantry,' I called up to him. 'Either you let us in or my big friend here . . .' Unbidden, but dead on cue, Everett stepped out of the shadows '. . . will take your house apart, stone by stone, just to get to you. You're nailed, Lord Provost, you and your murderous bastard of a nephew.'

I smiled at him. 'You do have an alternative, though. In a place like this you're bound to have a library and a pearl-handled revolver.'

In an instant, Gantry regained his equanimity, goaded, I guessed by my challenge. He beamed down at me, at his most avuncular. 'I don't think so, young man. That's not my style. Just hold on for a minute or two, and I'll be down.'

'You better tell Diane to get her ass down too,' Everett barked. The Lord Provost had no quick comeback for him. He closed the window.

When he let us in a few minutes later, he was fully dressed, in grey slacks, an open-necked shirt and, of all things, a smoking jacket. As we stepped into the big hallway of the villa, we saw Diane, in a leisure suit, standing half-way up the stairs.

'Honey,' said Everett, far more calmly than I had expected, 'you get in your car and go home. I'll be back later.'

She shook her head.

'Honey, I promise you I will not lay one finger on this son of a bitch.'

She stared at him, still scared speechless. 'He won't, Diane,' I told her. 'I'll see to that.' She didn't understand me . . . no one did at the time, probably not even me . . . but eventually she grabbed her handbag, which was hanging on a Victorian hat stand at the foot of the stairs, and ran out of the door.

'How gallant of you, Everett,' said Gantry as we followed him through into a small panelled room, which appeared to be a study. 'Is it a duel you'll be wanting?'

'You heard what I promised her. If I was going to touch you, your back would be broke by now. I just want to hear what you got to say.'

'About Diane? Nothing. I like beautiful women, and every so often I find that they respond to me. Not to my money, or my office, you understand; that's not what I like. They have to respond to me, as a man. Diane does; or did, I suppose I should say now.'

'Do you want her?' Everett barked.

Gantry looked at him, almost down his nose. 'Good God no!' he said. 'She was drawn to me, she had a need, I fulfilled it. That's it.

'Don't blame her, Everett. Blame yourself if anyone. You assume that she's as wrapped up in your appalling business as you are. She isn't, man. She'd like some of your time for herself, every now and again. She even wears those ridiculous costumes in your shows to provoke you, but she never manages to . . . or so she tells me.' He sneered at the huge wrestler.

'Your business is a pantomime, Everett, full of role-play, and so is your life. But in life there has to be real action, man, not make-believe. That's what she's been missing.'

Gantry seemed to have switched into full campaigning mode. The way he was going I was afraid Everett would wind up thanking him for shagging his wife, so I decided to put a stop to it.

'Let's leave Diane out of this, Lord Provost,' I said. 'There are lots of things I want to ask you. First off, why did you set your nephew Gary O'Rourke up to sabotage the GWA?'

Everett's eyes bulged as he stared at me. 'He what!?' he roared.

Dylan took him by the arm. 'Quiet just now, big fella,' he said, as if he was soothing an elephant.

Jack Gantry ignored them both and stared at me. 'You have to ask me that?' he retorted. There was no show; his anger was as quick and genuine as that of Everett. 'You really have to ask me that? Don't you understand me at all? Don't you appreciate what I stand for?

'Man, I loathe and detest everything his tawdry, paltry organisation stands for. I am the First Citizen of a great European cultural capital, yet I have to put up with these freaks, with their human circus, cheapening its very name, and making it a laughing stock all over Europe.

'They're worse than the footballers; at least there's some spurious cultural heritage there. Mr Davis's stuff has no substance. It's a disgrace to my city.'

'So why did you allow it to happen in the first place?' I asked.

He scowled at me. 'It was forced upon me,' he said. 'By the national level of my Party. Some fool of a Scottish Office

Minister decided that it would be a Good Thing For Glasgow to have a European organisation based here. I had personally negotiated that the Turin Symphony Orchestra would relocate to Glasgow. I had personally arranged the deal through Locate In Scotland. Then Everett appeared with his prancing pantomime Sports Entertainment nonsense.' His voice rose, then fell back to its normal level.

'I tried to tell the Secretary of State that it was totally unsuitable, but he's from an Edinburgh constituency. He laughed in my face and said that it was a money-maker, and that no one ever made a profit from a symphony orchestra, so the GWA deal would go ahead.

'Those people ignored my wishes, Everett, but I determined that I would not tolerate your presence in the city for one minute longer than was necessary. So I made enquiries, and I worked out how you could be driven out. Like any other businessman, you are reliant entirely on the goodwill of your customers. I reasoned that if I could destroy that, I would destroy the Global Wrestling Alliance.' He laced the words with contempt.

'So, as soon as I heard that there was a vacancy in your ranks, I sent my nephew Gary along to apply for it. I never had any doubt that he would get it. I didn't even have to give him a personal recommendation, although I would have, if it had come to that.

'Best that I didn't though. No connection between Gary and me; no case to answer, see.'

'And Diane,' muttered Everett, slowly, 'was she in on it?'

'Good God no. She might betray you between the sheets, my friend, but she couldn't stand it if anything happened to you. If she'd known what I was up to, she'd have told you right away.'

'O'Rourke,' I asked suddenly. 'Where is he now? We saw his bike in your garage.'

'Ahh,' said Gantry. 'Yes. Gary. Yes. I might as well tell you. He's in a freezer in the basement, as a matter of fact.'

Cold as my anger was I still felt a chill run through me.

'Greedy boy,' the Lord Provost exclaimed. 'He turned up last night wanting two hundred thousand for his trouble, so that he could get out of the country for a while. I told him that he'd blown it, so he was getting nothing. He became difficult, aggressive, so I stabbed him in the chest with a Kitchen Devil. Bloody sharp, those things are, you know.

'I know I should have called your chaps in there and then, Mike, but I just panicked. I was in shock, couldn't think straight; so I stuck him in my old freezer while I gathered myself together.'

Something went out of me then. I was taking immense, if perverse, satisfaction out of confronting Gantry, but beyond him there had lain O'Rourke. My game plan had been to have him lead me to O'Rourke, so that I could do for him myself. Now this man – this madman, as we could all now see he was – who had robbed Everett and me of our wives in different ways, had stolen that prospect from me too.

But I regrouped, repaired the crack in my cold armour and pressed on.

'And Jan,' I asked him, quietly. 'What about Jan?'

He looked at me with his first show of regret. Not remorse, that's different; this was only regret.

'Aye son,' he said. 'I'm sorry about that, but it was necessary. Thanks to my hot-headed daughter, and to her own skill as an accountant, your lass was about to find out about Gary's wee sideline, and to tell Susie. I had to stop her from doing that, at all costs, I'm afraid.'

'Gary's wee sideline,' I repeated. 'So you did know about it.'

'Oh yes. Almost from the start. I was still running the

business when he dreamed it up, so I spotted it within the first two months.'

'So why didn't you turn him in?' asked Dylan, incredulity written all over his face. 'Why did you cover it up?'

Gantry laughed at him, and shook his head. 'Michael, Michael, Michael, I am a politician, first and last. The job of the politician is to give the people what they want; not to *tell* them what they want – that's the real, patronising, Old Labour way – but to *give* it to them.

'And what you and those like you must know but are afraid to admit is that the poor, ordinary underprivileged folk in all big inner city areas want Temazepam and the like, and they want heroin. For good or evil those things have become part of their culture and they want them: more than that, they will have them, come what may.

'So, as a good politician, what's my responsibility? That's right, it's to give it to them.'

He looked at the policeman, blandly, as if lecturing a child. 'Which would you rather see happen, Michael? You know my views on the danger of criminalising drugs.

'I ask you what's more desirable; to see the housing schemes bled dry to pay for all sorts of uncontrolled poisons – all to make some local criminals, and ultimately some Colombian, or some Burmese, even richer – or to turn a blind eye, as I did, while my nephew gave them a quality supply at prices that let them feed their kids?'

'For fuck's sake, man,' Dylan screamed at him. 'In these schemes, it's the kids who are on smack!'

The Lord Provost stared at him, genuinely astonished by his reaction. 'In every walk of life, Michael, there are good parents and bad.'

He gathered his jacket around him. 'Listen, I've really had enough of this now. Call your people, Inspector, and have Gary taken out of my freezer. I'll give you a full statement. My nephew came to my house and asked for money to get out of the country. I turned him down and he attacked me. It was self-defence.

'As for everything else we've discussed, you must realise that was off the record. I will never repeat it, either informally, or under caution. You three may allege that I said it all, of course, but it'll be your word against mine.' He paused and beamed at us.

'And remember, I'm Jack Gantry.'

That was it for me. He stood there, and I knew that it had been him I'd really wanted to kill all along, even more than I had wanted O'Rourke. All of a sudden that became the most important thing in my life. I went for him with nothing but my bare hands, to finish him if I could. My first punch, a right hander, staggered him, but the second, a shorter blow, stunned him and knocked him down. I was on top of him then, my left hand tight round his throat squeezing the life out of him, my right fist punching, punching, punching; trying to smash that bland, benign, calm, unspeakably awful face.

All the time, Dylan stood transfixed above me, watching me killing the Lord Provost. It was Everett, eventually, who prised my hand from his throat, and very gently, his great arm wound round my waist, lifted me up and off him.

'That's enough, buddy,' he said. 'You mustn't let the man ruin your life any more than he has already.'

He sat me down in an armchair, and everything left me; my strength, my anger, and the last of the restraints which my mind had placed upon my grief. I was back on top of that old Greek wall once more, but this time, there was nothing held back.

59

I woke, and sat bolt upright in bed. Someone had drawn my curtains, but the sun was full on them so my room was light. I swung my feet on to the floor, noticing as I did that I was still wearing my boxer shorts, walked to each window and threw them open.

It was a bright spring day outside, the kind that gives you energy by the very sight of it, the kind on which Jan and I, when we were kids, used to jump on our bikes and cycle to St Andrews. Not today though; I felt exhausted.

I went into the bathroom, stepped out of my boxers, and into the shower. Normally I'd have shaved first, but somehow I couldn't be bothered.

When I trotted downstairs, barefoot, in my jeans and a check shirt, Dylan was there. So was Everett, standing in the doorway of the living room, carrying four large pizza boxes. I counted heads and guessed that two were for him. I was surprised to find that I didn't have to piece together memories of the night before. They were all there, crystal clear, right up to the point at which the police surgeon had given me a sedative.

'So,' I asked the world in general, 'what's the news today?'

'Well, for a start,' said Mike, as Everett disappeared into the kitchen, ducking below the door, 'the gold chain will be round another neck very soon. Gantry's been sectioned. He was examined by two psychiatrists during the night and they agreed that he's clinically insane, and probably has been for a long time.

'He's a hypnotic personality, but under it a total megalomaniac with his own idea of the difference between right and wrong. In another age he could have been Hitler.'

I laughed. 'In this one he was Lord Provost of Glasgow. The principle's the same.' I dropped onto one of the sofas.

'Okay, guys,' called Everett, emerging from the kitchen. 'Lunchtime for you two, snacktime for me. Git outside these.' He handed pizzas to Mike and I, each cut into eighths, then returned with two plates, as I had assumed, for himself.

'So how have things wound up at your workplace?' I asked Dylan. His face fell.

'I am deep in the shit,' he said. 'Going to arrest the Lord Provost on my own was a step too far. My promotion's jiggered; Christ, I'll be lucky to stay a DI.'

'Hell with that, man,' said Everett, abruptly. 'That ain't going to happen. I'll write a personal letter of thanks to the Chief Constable for what you did to catch O'Rourke and Gantry. I'll even tell him that if anything bad happens to your career, my next letter will be to the Editor of the *Herald*.'

He grinned. 'That ought to see you all right. They tell me I am a big man around here.'

'What about Susie?' I asked.

Mike's face fell once more as quickly as it had brightened up. 'I went to see her as soon as they'd taken her dad away. It was a difficult conversation, as you'd guess. Naturally, she's broken up by what's happened to him. But worse than that, Oz, she's completely racked with guilt that what she let slip to him led to Jan's death.'

I smiled at him weakly. 'Well, you tell her not to be. I go further back than that with the guilt thing. If we'd never met you that night in Babbity's she'd still be alive. If I hadn't come back from Spain and married her, she'd still be alive. Susie's no right to blame herself; I reserve that for myself. She's got a big enough burden to bear.

'You and she going to be all right, d'you think?' I asked him, with a sideways look.

'Bastard,' he grinned. 'You mean, am I moving out of your place and back in with her? I am as it happens, for now. We'll see how it goes. It'll be difficult at first, I know, but I love the girl. Someone has to help her through the tough times, and I'm first in the queue.'

We concentrated on our pizzas for a while. When Dylan was finished, he wiped his mouth and stood up. 'I've got to get back to work, mate,' he said. 'Your keys are on the sideboard. I'll call you.'

I watched him, as he headed for the door. Suddenly, like me, he had become an older, more sensible, and maybe more likeable, character.

And that left Everett, in the act of killing off his second pizza, to the last anchovy. 'I gotta go too, man,' he said. 'I just dropped by to see you were okay, and to tie up tomorrow.'

'Tomorrow?'

'Sure. The GWA is safe, the pay-per-view was a sensation, and on the back of that, I just had a very informal approach from HomeView, the US cable network that shows CWI. Things are heading our way.

'You got a job as a ring announcer for as long as you like. How about it?'

I reached another of my instant decisions. 'You know what?' I told him. 'I think I'll do it. The money's good, it'll get me out of the house; and anyway, I like you guys.

'Mind you, Ev. I'll want a few weeks off soon though. I want to go back to Spain for a holiday. I think I need one.'

'That'll be no problem. See you at the airport tomorrow,

ten am. It's Frankfurt this week; guest commentator Jerry Gradi. I'm not on the card so I'm flying over late. You can come with me, and catch up on the fight bill on the plane.'

He rose, like a time-lapse film of a skyscraper being built. I had to ask him. 'How about Diane?'

He looked down at me. 'Hell, Oz, maybe I'm as crazy as Gantry, but I love her. She just got captured by the man. Shit, a whole city did. I can't kick her out of my life. You, of all people, gotta know that.

'See you tomorrow.'

'Yes. I'll look forward to it.' I showed him to the door. Somehow, he felt like family.

So there I was, left alone, but not for long. I had just finished clearing up after Dylan . . . as usual . . . dusting, shaking down my duvet, and putting a load into my new washing machine, when the video-buzzer from the street door sounded.

I went to answer it, and saw Prim's face on the screen. She wore her rarely seen contrite expression. 'Sorry I got precious on Wednesday,' she said, through the speaker. 'Can I come in?'

'Okay, but you'll have to find the flat for yourself.'

I timed her. It took her four minutes.

'Hi,' she said, as I let her in. 'I thought I'd have a day in Glasgow before I went back. You know me, the parents exasperate me after a while.'

She stepped into the living room, but unlike anyone else who had ever seen it for the first time, made no comment at all. 'So how are you?' she asked.

'I'm fine. I had a busy night last night though, so I'm a bit tired today. I'll need to rest up, for I'm off to Frankfurt tomorrow.'

I led her through to the kitchen and made her a coffee. I

couldn't help but notice that she didn't look at the washing machine, at all.

Back in the sitting area, she looked out of the window, across Glasgow, as she sipped from her mug. At last she looked across at me.

'Oz,' she began, 'the truth is I'm not sure about going back to St Marti.'

'Why not?' I asked her, cautiously.

'Well, I've been thinking. I'm too young to vegetate out there. Also I just can't cut myself off from the people I love. My mum and my dad, that is, even though they drive me loopy at times.' She hesitated.

'And yes, you too; even if I understand that you can only ever have one soulmate.'

We looked at each other for a long time. Nothing showed in my expression; I had nothing to show.

'Anyway,' she continued, 'I've been to see a nursing agency and there's the possibility of a casualty job in the Royal. I was thinking I'd get myself a flat in Glasgow. I've had it with Edinburgh, like you.

'What do you think? I mean, would it upset you in any way, to have me around, even if we're only in the same city? Or would it be better if I just went back?'

I stared at her, and at the future. 'You get yourself a flat,' I told her. 'There's some nice stuff for rent down in the Merchant City.' She looked at me, almost gratefully.

'But you don't really want to be a nurse again, do you?' I said. 'You told me when we met that you were finished with that career.'

'That's true, but it's what I do. It's what I'm trained for.'

I shook my head. 'No, there's something else you've done. Listen, I've agreed to carry on this GWA stuff for a while. If I do that, and I will, I'm going to need a partner in my main business.'

She stared at me, wide-eyed with surprise. 'What, back to being Phillips and Blackstone?'

'Stuff that for a game,' I told her, straight away. 'Blackstone and Phillips, and no nonsense.'

I could see her head about to nod. 'I want you to think about this before you agree,' I said. 'We're friends, and we work well together, but it's a business arrangement. We work from an office, not here.

'Outside that, I've got to get a life, and so have you. I'll be back from Frankfurt on Sunday night. Call me then. Unless you've gone back to Spain, that is.' I stood her up and marched her to the door.

'You've changed indeed,' she said. 'I like the new bloke though; as much as the old. I'll call you.'

I stood in the doorway and watched her until she reached the end of the corridor. She knew it, and waved to me as she turned the corner.

I went back inside and sat in my captain's chair. I tried to look out of the window at the afternoon city, but my eyes grew heavy, and gradually my head fell back.

As it had done on the afternoon before, a vision of Jan formed itself in my mind. She was sitting in a field – one of our places, hers and mine, just outside Anstruther. She was wearing a purple dress, and she was smiling.

Now you can buy any of these other bestselling books by **Quintin Jardine** from your bookshop or *direct from his publisher*.

FREE P&P AND UK DELIVERY
(Overseas and Ireland £3.50 per book)

Oz Blackstone series

Blackstone's Pursuits	£6.99
A Coffin for Two	£6.99
Wearing Purple	£5.99
Screen Savers	£6.99
On Honeymoon with Death	£6.99
Poisoned Cherries	£6.99

TO ORDER SIMPLY CALL THIS NUMBER

01235 400 414

or visit our website: www.madaboutbooks.com

Prices and availability subject to change without notice.